WAVES OF YOU

L. RENÉE RICHARD

Copyright © 2024 by L. Renee Richard

All rights reserved.

ISBN: 979-8-9920441-0-2
Hardback ISBN: 979-8-9920441-6-4

No part of this book my be reproduced in any form or by any electronic or mechanical means, including information storage and retrieval systems, without written permission from the author, except for the use of brief quotations in a book review.

No generative artificial intelligence (AI) was used in the writing of this work. The author expressly prohibits any entity from using this publication to train AI technologies to generate text, including, without limitation, technologies capable of generating works in the same style or genre as this publication. The author reserves all rights to license uses of this work for generative AI training and development of machine learning language models. No generative artificial intelligence (AI) was used in the creation of the cover art, or interior. The artist and author expressly prohibits any entity from using this art to train AI technologies.

Cover Design by: Designs By Charly
https://www.designsbycharlyy.com/

Interior Formatting by: Designs By Charly
https://www.designsbycharlyy.com/

Initial Editing by: My Brother's Editor
https://mybrotherseditor.net/

Editing by: Editing Done Write
https://www.editingdonewrite.com/

CONTENT WARNING

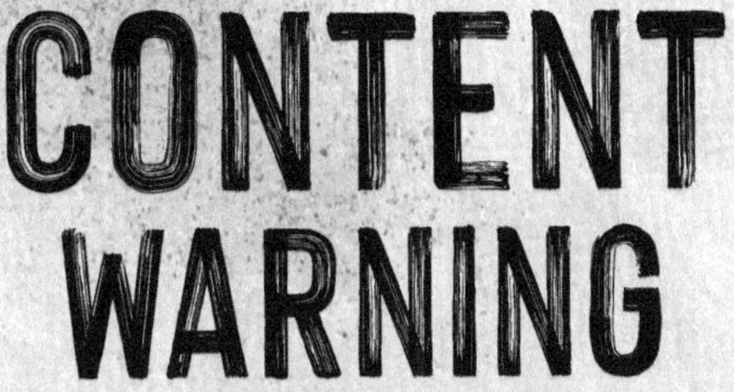

This story contains explicit sexual content and is intended for readers over eighteen. Other topics may be triggering to sensitive readers.

Please check my website, L. Renée Richard, for more details and a complete list of trigger warnings, further information, or updates if there are any concerns about your mental health. Your well-being is my utmost concern, so please proceed with caution.

WAVES OF YOU

Liv is tired of the uncertainty of their relationship.
She has a plan.
Meet Brodie at the beach.
Clarify their relationship.
What she doesn't plan on doing while working her shift in the ER is meeting Dax, her swoon-worthy patient. They plan to meet up the next day, celebrating the last days of spring break on Padre Island.
There's just one problem—Brodie, her childhood best friend and recent ex-boyfriend. When she receives a video of him with another girl, she knows that they are not getting back together.
One last day at the beach is the most memorable of her life—the sparks between Liv and Dax are undeniable. The future held so many possibilities. That is until they witness Brodie's traumatic accident.
Pulled in two directions, Liv must choose between her new feelings for Dax, and Brodie, someone who had always been there for her.
She makes a choice, but is it the right one?

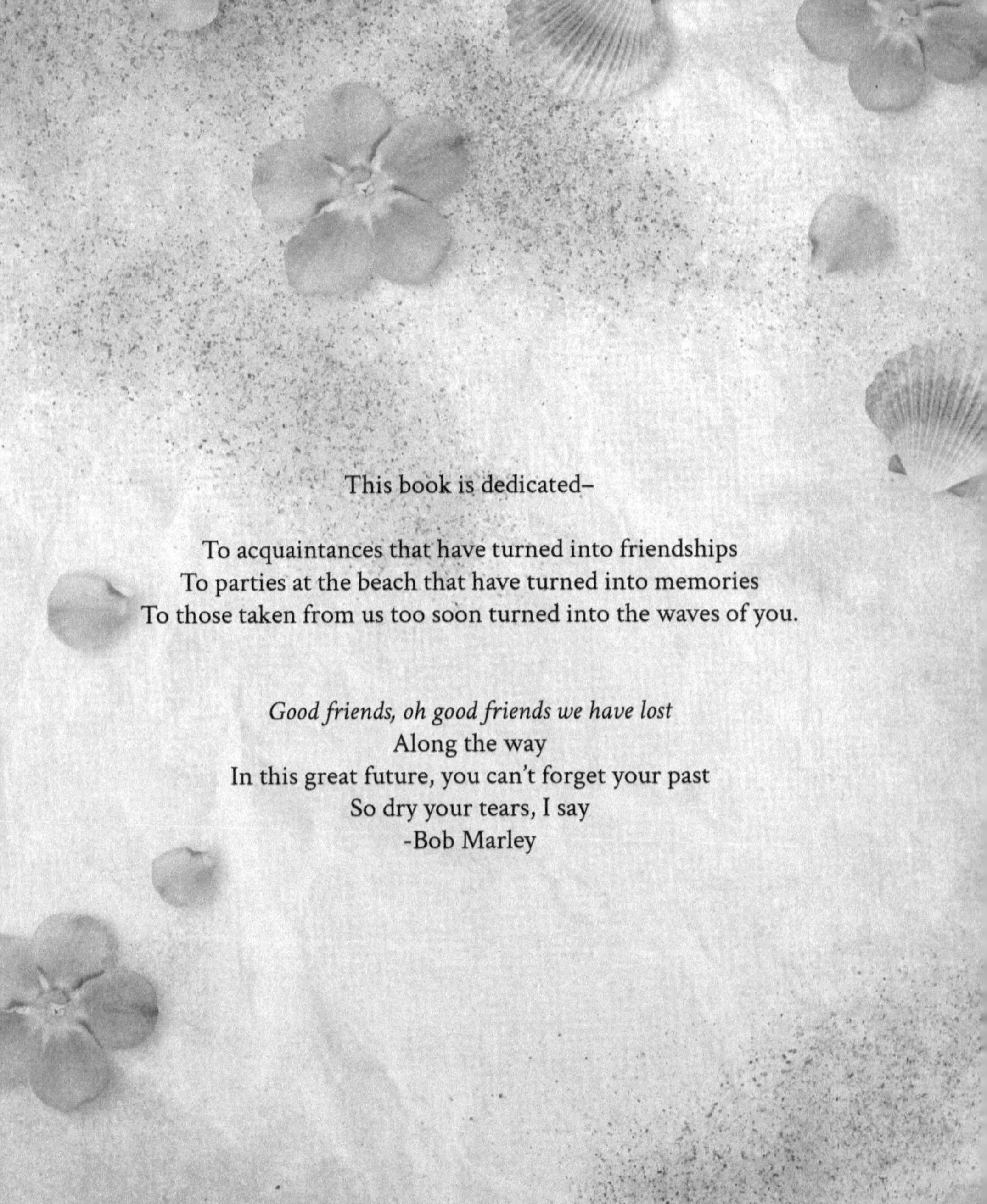

This book is dedicated–

To acquaintances that have turned into friendships
To parties at the beach that have turned into memories
To those taken from us too soon turned into the waves of you.

Good friends, oh good friends we have lost
Along the way
In this great future, you can't forget your past
So dry your tears, I say
-Bob Marley

PROLOGUE

I sit in the waiting room surrounded by my friends and Brodie's family, watching the hospital staff going in and out through the operating room doors, hoping for an update on what happened after Brodie was rushed into the OR.

Another patient is being moved down the hall on a hospital bed, an IV bag of fluids dripping in sync with the beeping monitor as he passes by. Every sound is intensified, every smell more potent.

Dax is by my side. His thumb rubs circles in a continuous soothing manner on the top of my hand. The rhythmic motion settles me as the weight of his calloused fingers offers me the stability my hand needs not to shake. The fact that he hasn't left my side speaks volumes about his character. The way he handled the situation at the beach. The authoritarian personality and calm with which he controlled the situation—the accident. If I weren't so shell-shocked, I would have been turned on. If it had not been Brodie there on the wet sand, limp and unconscious. If a million things were different.

Brodie's parents are here. It's a stressful time for all of us without dealing with the awkwardness of his parents' divorce and the bitterness between the two parties. His dad must have flown down the interstate to get here in record time.

Everyone sits in silence, waiting to hear the outcome of Brodie's surgery. Finally, after what seems like an eternity, a man wearing blue scrubs accompanied by a female in similar attire exits the operating room doors and asks for his family. His parents walk down the hall and stand within view to receive the much-awaited results. It's as if time stands still, and it's so silent you can hear a pin drop. Except for the steps on the freshly waxed, tiled floor, no other sound exists.

The surgeon speaks, and then Brodie's mom raises her hands to her mouth and a sob escapes, relinquishing a terrible cry of pain. Brodie's dad just shakes his hands around, asking spitfire questions, not allowing a moment's pause for an answer. The surgeon just shakes his head in acknowledgment. His dad puts his hands up to his eyes and lowers his head. The surgeon touches his shoulder and says something to them before walking back to our group. I rise from my chair as though I am being pulled toward this invisible force.

As I stand, the surgeon stops at our group and says, "Is there a Liv here?"

I stare, stunned and unable to speak. I feel a nudge from my side.

The surgeon begins to speak, and I don't hear what he says. He repeats, "Brodie is awake and was asking for you specifically. He wants to see you."

I gasp. A breath let out that I didn't realize I was holding as it rushes out. I feel Dax bring my hand to his lips and gently kiss it. The heat of his mouth makes me shudder. He releases my hand without saying a word, telling me to go. I follow the doctor without looking back. I know he won't be there when I return to the waiting room. This is goodbye.

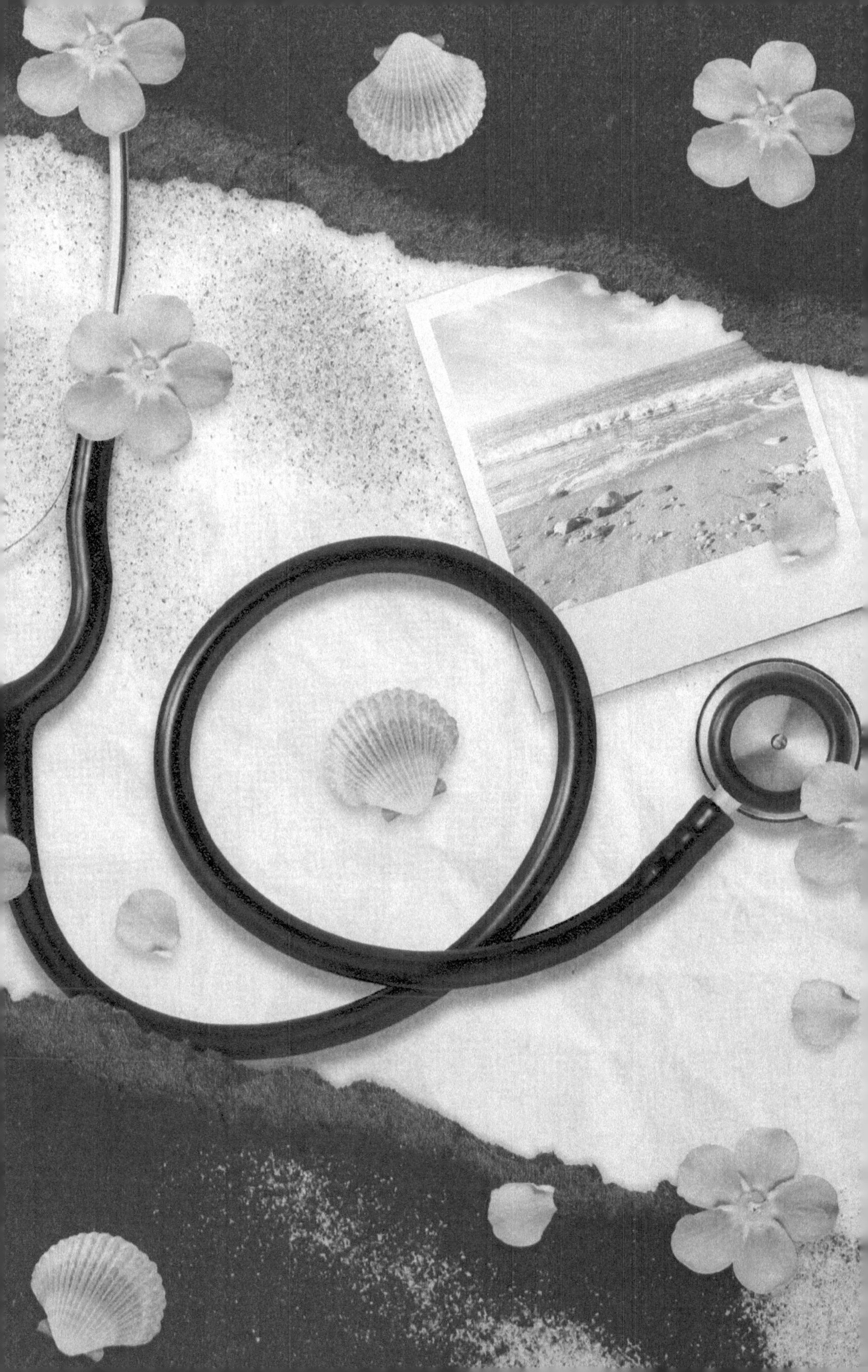

CHAPTER ONE

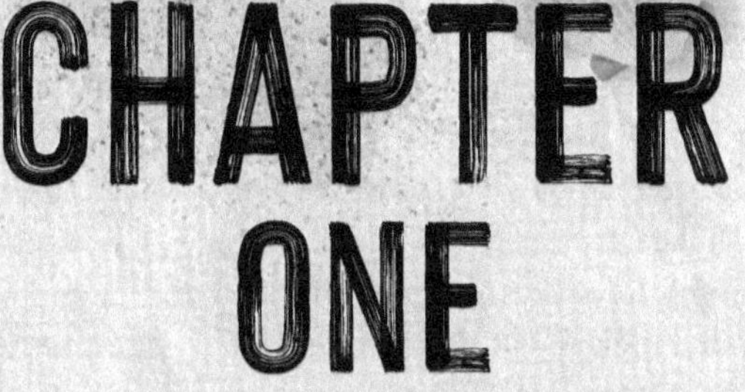

LIV

Something about driving with the windows down while cruising over the causeway makes me smile. The second I lower the window, the familiar scent of saltwater washes through the car. The beach has always been my happy place, and I was damn lucky to find an apartment and job so close to it.

While I make my way down the highway toward work, I steal glances at the view. The waves, the people sunning themselves on the beach, the surfers in the water, and even the seagulls squawking overhead make me smile. I drink it all in for a moment... that is until the hot-as-fuck blast of steam assaults my face and I'm ripped back to reality.

God, it's hot as Hades today. I pull at my shirt as the sweat trickles down into my cleavage. I turn off on the next exit ramp and pull into the employee parking lot of the Bayside Hospital Emergency Department.

"Great," I mutter to myself. Quickly looking around, I see multiple ambulances parked in the designated bays. It's going to be a busy night. "What else is new?" I breathe out on a long, exaggerated sigh.

This is the norm for the start of any weekend, but this isn't just any weekend. It's spring break on Padre Island—guaranteed to supply an endless amount of ER visits from sun-induced dehydration to broken bones to college kids who have one (or five) too many beers. Lucky me.

With my work bag slung over my shoulder and iced coffee in hand, I make my way to the front doors. I say a silent prayer and hope that if I hide my badge and don't make eye contact, then no one will stop and ask me anything. This is my reasoning, at least, to not be bothered with a million questions before I start my shift.

I walk past the triage desk in the emergency room and subtly scan the packed waiting room. It's already filled with patients. I head to my locker, throw my bag in and make a spot for my lunch in the fridge, gently squishing it into a packed space.

Geez, I hope my leftovers from dinner last night don't fall out because that would royally suck. I had blackened catfish the previous night, and I plan on reheating it later. Nothing worse than stinky fish in the lunchroom, I chuckle to myself. Besides, there are worse smells in this place.

I keep a firm hold on my iced coffee as I leave the break room. I wish I could shoot this stuff straight into my circulatory system to get one immediate, gratifying caffeine rush. Lord knows I need it this evening. Working the night shift can be challenging, but not even the white noise produced by my oscillating fan could put me in my usual death-like sleep. I blame the grounds crew mowing at my apartment complex for four hours straight for my lack of energy today.

Although I'd like to blame it all on that, it isn't the real reason I had shity sleep. I've had a ton of crap on my mind lately, namely the unpleasant subject of my current boyfriend, Brodie. Being in a perpetual state of limbo with this guy is just dragging me down. Our relationship status is something we decided to chat about this weekend. It shouldn't be this hard. We've known each other practically our whole lives.

Before I go too far down that rabbit hole, I shove these thoughts to the back of my mind.

First things first, I just have to get through this shift. I walk to the nurses' station, take one last swig of my highly caffeinated drink, and reluctantly place it in the cubby. It sits among countless other beverages, condensation pooling all around the surface.

The assignment board is already updated. I scan it quickly and begin my hunt for Emma. I need to get a report on her patients so she can get out of this place. At least one person will be having fun tonight. Why did I sign up for this shift? Oh yeah, I need the money.

I shift my gaze down one of the corridors and spot who I'm looking for. Blond hair piled on top of her head in a messy bun, Emma is not only a nurse that I happen to be relieving at shift change but also one of my best friends. As high energy as ever, I can hear her excitedly babbling to one of our attendings. Her hand gestures raised above her head are so fast that I think she may accidentally smack him in the face. There's a reason people refer to her as the Energizer Bunny.

We both took the sign-on bonus offered at the hospital after our nursing school graduation a couple of years ago. She took a job on the twelve-hour day shift, while I decided to take the opposite twelve-hour night shift. My decision to take the less-desirable shift allowed me to enroll in classes for my bachelor's degree. Classes during the day, work at night. Grueling schedule for sure, but it's getting me where I want to be, so I'm sucking it up and embracing the chaos. My social life has taken a hit between school and work, but I'll graduate with my BSN in a couple of months and then continue to Houston, where I've been accepted into nurse practitioner school. Soon I'll be leaving this town and moving on to bigger and better things.

Emma catches my eye, and I nod to let her know I'm here.

As I walk toward her, she flashes me a huge smile. "Thank God you're here. It's been hell today."

I can't help but stifle a laugh. "You say that every shift."

She carefully counts the remaining narcotics in the bin and enters the correct count before closing it. "I only say it because it's true." She giggles. "I hope your night is better, but looking at the stack of pending charts…" she trails off and gives me a sympathetic frown.

Ready to brave the shift, I chuckle and head toward the nurse's station. "Judging by the waiting room, I think I'm forever and eternally fucked tonight. Let's hope nothing memorable happens."

Emma gently squeezes my shoulder before shoving some charts into my hands. "Come on, Liv, I'll give you a report on my patients. Room ten has some pain meds ordered, and I'll give her those before I leave. Can you reassess her pain in a bit?"

Thank goodness for Emma. The woman looked extremely uncomfortable when I peeked in as we passed her room. I do not want her to wait for her pain medication until after our shift change.

"I'll be back in a few minutes to give you a report on the rest of my patients. The sooner I do, the sooner I can get my drink on tonight." With that, she turns on her heels and prances down the hall.

Ten minutes later, Emma pops back up by my elbow. I'm only half-listening as she gives me the sign-out on her patients.

"The labs on the patient in room eight just came back, and room two is…" She can tell by the look on my face that I'm in no mood for work. "You know we're all going to miss you tonight, right? It's the first time in a long while that we've all been able to get together."

I don't need the reminder. The fact that I am missing out on tonight is a bit of a sore spot. Our mutual high school friends are returning again for the continuous spring break beach party. The days at the beach, sea sculptures, and live entertainment are just some things that happen on the island during this carnivalesque time.

"You have no idea how jealous I am right now, Em."

She makes a melodramatic pouty face while holding both arms out for a hug.

I give her a quick squeeze, feeling utterly deflated. For a second, I consider telling my manager I'm not feeling well so I can go home. But my stupid conscience won't allow it. I will only call out from my shift if I'm dead or dealing with some other near-death experience. I'm not sure if even that wouldn't require a call-out. As tired (and jealous) as I am, missing work is not an option. I need every penny for graduate school; the move to Houston won't be cheap.

"I'll see them tomorrow, Em. Actually, in less than twenty-four hours, you know that." As positive as I try to sound on the outside, I'm internally cursing this shift. "Well, I want lots of pics tonight to make me feel like I am there with you guys."

"Of course," Emma quickly replies. "You know we will. I expect to meet up with the whole gang later tonight, and I will send pics of that. You better go straight to bed after your shift and get the best four hours of sleep because I am picking your ass up by noon, got it?"

I laugh. "I expect a large iced coffee and preferably a greasy breakfast burrito."

She laughs as she grabs her bags and heads toward the door. "Naturally, only the breakfast of champions for my bestie," she says over her shoulder. "I'll see you tomorrow!" And with that, she grabs her purse and giant water bottle and heads for the door.

I shuffle my feet in dramatic flair. Yup, I am definitely not ready for this shift.

As soon as she leaves, I spot Dr. Hall, the handsome thirty-eight-year-old ER physician with a reputation for flirting with the staff.

"Hi, Dr. Hall."

"Hey, Liv. Glad you're on tonight." He throws me a wink.

Typically, that little gesture would have perked me up, but even that doesn't help my mood. "Thanks," I reply. "I've got some updates. The labs are back on the patient in room eight, and the completed chart for review is queued first in line when you get a chance."

I am met with kind but tired eyes, almost reflecting my own. "Great," he mutters as he quickly goes to retrieve the chart.

I check on my other patients and quickly chart and update vital signs. Dr. Hall comes over and informs me that he printed out the discharge instructions for bay eight, and they can go. At least someone is getting out of here quickly tonight.

I gather all the instructions and check to see if she needs anything else before making my way over there. The drape is still closed, so I call out her name before I peek in.

Mrs. Shea replies, "Just a minute, dear. I am just pulling on my shirt."

I wait patiently for her to finish and help her to the waiting room. As I pass the discharge instructions to her, we see her husband pulling up in front of the entrance. As I watch her drive away, I can't help but think about what the next patient will bring.

I let the ED tech know that the bay is empty so they can clean up the room and prepare it for the next patient. Our department is certainly busy, but thank goodness it's efficient. I grab the following chart in the queue and look at the chief complaint—ankle pain, related to a surfing injury.

"Well, that's a total surprise," I mutter as I make my way to the waiting room and open the door. "Dax Johnson?" I call out.

No reply. I see two guys sitting in the chairs wearing board shorts, T-shirts, and flip-flops, chatting animatedly with each other. When they get up, I bet there will be sand all over the seats too.

A quick scan of them shows one has a bruised and swollen ankle. That has to be him. But as my eyes wander up from the ankle in question, I notice the rest of him. I feel myself start to zone out a bit as they continue their conversation, and my eyes drift from his ankle up to his legs and over his lean body. He must be the most attractive man I have ever seen. Around six foot four inches, toned, tan, and totally delicious. His long, muscular legs are streaked with blond hair. His T-shirt is tight against his chest and shows off his narrow waist. His shorts sit low on his hips, just low enough that I catch the shadow of a V pointing straight to where I'm trying *not* to look.

I realize both are still oblivious to my announcement and the fact that I've been so blatantly staring at them. I look away as my cheeks begin to heat. I notice a couple of patients smirking at my lack of subtlety. I give myself a mental slap and call the name again.

"Dax Johnson?" My voice comes out an octave too high, and I pray they overlooked that too.

I see the pair halt their conversation, and one raises his arm. "That's me, coming."

His deep voice pierces right through me and sends a wave of butterflies straight into my stomach. He tries to get up but stumbles almost immediately, trying to avoid putting weight on his ankle.

I go to grab a wheelchair just in case he needs it. When I return, I see he's made his way across the waiting room—holding on to his friend's arm for support. It's then I notice his arms. Thick, muscular arms with every nurse's dream of pipe veins running up his forearms. If a forearm porn show were a thing, he would be the star. I lift my vision to his face and catch him staring at me with amusement.

Was I that obvious? My face immediately flushes with embarrassment, and it becomes about a hundred degrees too hot in the room. My blood seems to have been rerouted and is collecting in my now scorching face.

Taking a deep breath, I try to regain an ounce of professionalism and look up. I'm instantly met with the most exquisite pair of penetrating blue eyes. Wow, is there anything wrong with him? Oh yeah, his ankle.

He stares at me with such intensity that I feel he can almost read my thoughts as his gaze also shoots to his ankle. I immediately look away in embarrassment because he knows what I was thinking.

"Do you need a wheelchair?" I ask in the most squeaky-sounding voice I have ever heard myself make to further my humiliation.

He looks at the wheelchair and then back at me, smiling. As if he couldn't make me feel any giddier, a dimple appears on his left cheek, and I feel a slight warmth spread between my legs.

I try to move forward but feel my feet locked in place. It's as if my shoes are cemented to the waiting room floor. Damn, can I be any more pathetic?

I clear my throat and try again. "Do you need a wheelchair?"

He shakes his head, and I feel his unwavering stare, but I avoid eye contact this time. "No thanks, I can walk," he says while grabbing on to his friend's arm for support.

I go to put the wheelchair back and hit the button for the automatic door.

He begins to walk, and I hear him say, "This might take me a minute."

I reply over my shoulder, "That's fine. You can take your time with me. I mean, umm, no need to rush." I immediately rush around the corner and smack my forehead. Someone just shoot me now and end my word vomit. "We don't have far to go," I add. "Just around the corner."

We make it to the empty bay, and I notice that his friend hasn't come with him. I grab a hospital gown from the cabinet and hand it to him. As he reaches out for the gown, his fingers brush my palm. The touch is soft but electric. The zap immediately shoots through my hand into my body, making me tingle all over. Jerking my hand away and wondering if he felt that too, I take a step back to close the curtain and give him privacy. But let's be honest, I just need some space to pull myself together.

"I'll let you change and be back in a bit to check on you."

Before I can leave, I hear that deep voice say, "Miss?"

I pop my head back through the curtain.

He glances at the hospital attire with a questioning look on his face. "Do I really need to put this on? I mean, it's just my ankle, and I am wearing shorts. I'll probably just need an x-ray, right? Quick wet read by the radiologist, and I'll be on my way." He flashes me that dimple again.

I stare at him dumbfounded. He's right, and I realize I've been on autopilot, distracted by his unyielding gaze and that damn dimple. "Um, yeah. You can stay in your clothes." I manage, fighting the urge to see more of his body.

His use of medical terminology and willingness to question instructions intrigue me. Most patients comply without a word. Is he in the medical field? I want to ask, but I'm too flustered, desperate to escape before my blushing face betrays me.

"Have a seat on the stretcher, and I'll get you a pillow to elevate your leg and an ice pack while you wait. My name is Liv, and I'll be your nurse this evening. You're right about the x-ray. I'll go throw the order in now, so you won't have to be here any longer than necessary. How is your pain right now?"

I'm surprised I could get out a couple of coherent sentences in a row. Autopilot phrases I commonly use seem to be taking over my thinking. He looks at me with those smoking blue eyes, and I then notice lusciously thick lashes surrounding them.

Staring fixedly at me, he says, "Not too bad."

Why do guys have such thick eyelashes while women have to pay for that stuff?

He slumps back onto the stretcher and brushes his hand through his hair, still not looking away. It makes my breath hitch, and I look down at his leg to hopefully break the tension in the room.

"Good, then I'll have one of the techs bring you that pillow and an ice pack."

As I begin turning away for the second time, he stops me by saying, "Liv, I thought *you* were going to bring me those items."

I glance up and see the amusement on his face. He knows that I find him attractive. Now he is just fucking with me. Cocky much? I need to get it together.

With as much disinterest as I can muster, I turn back around and say, "I'll try, but otherwise, someone will be back shortly. If I cannot make it back sooner, that is." Before I close the curtain, I add more sway to my ass. I might as well play this up.

I head straight for the nurse's station to grab a tech and ask them to bring the items over. I'd like to avoid further embarrassment if possible.

I pick up my iced coffee and take a few large gulps. My mouth is dry, and my heart is hammering in my chest. I wonder if he feels the same way. Maybe it's all in my head? Either way, it's going to be a long night.

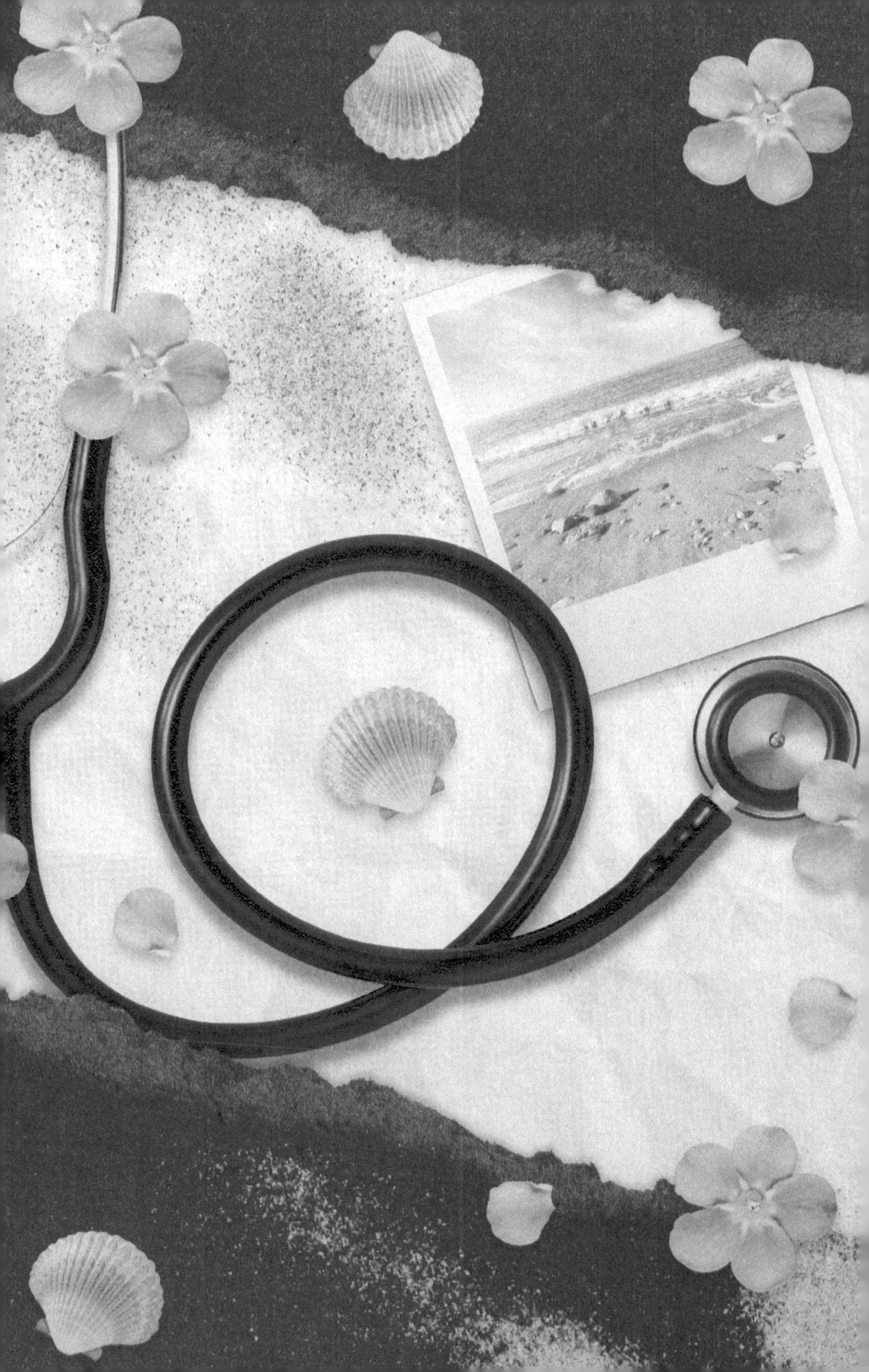

CHAPTER TWO

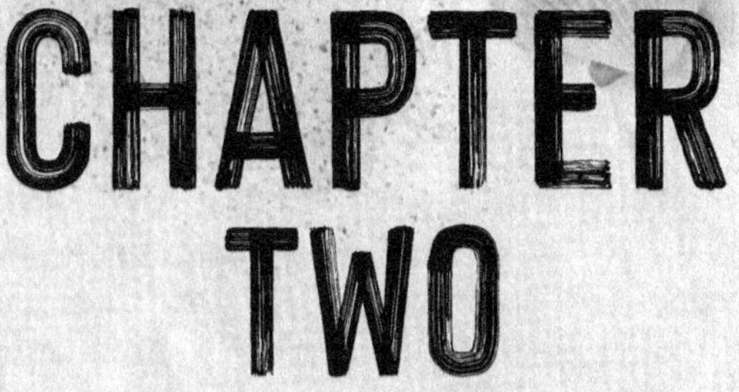

DAX

How did I end up in this god-forsaken emergency department on a Friday night? I should be out partying. I should be getting laid. I *should* be doing anything else someone my age would be doing other than sitting in here. But my father, the orthopedic doctor extraordinaire, insisted I come to be evaluated. I finally get some time to cut loose when I end up in a hospital while on a short vacation. All work and no play make Dax a grumpy man.

I rein in my self-loathing and decide to make the best of my remaining time, despite this minor inconvenience.

I knew a FaceTime call to get his opinion was a bad idea. I mean, it's only *slightly* busted. Likely just a sprain. But he insisted on x-rays, and since his cocky ass has no trust in the radiologist or my medical opinion, he wanted a copy of them for his review. He recommended I go to this facility since one of his buddies practices here. He seems to know people everywhere, but he is one of Houston's best sports medicine docs. I guess this isn't a surprise.

I should be thankful he's my dad. His success was what made me want to go to med school. He wanted me to follow him into sports medicine, but my interest has always been in ortho trauma. Yep, just another year, and I'll be done.

The stress of my fellowship is relentless. Long clinic days, late nights in the OR, and on-call shifts leave little time for myself. In my rare off hours, I find solace in surfing the Gulf of Mexico's Texas coast. Most people dismiss it for choppy, inconsistent waves, but I know better. With strong winds or post-storm conditions, the jetties offer surprisingly good breaks. Hurricane season? That's surfing nirvana. Despite the exhausting schedule, I cling to my goal of someday living near the water, chasing the perfect wave.

Which is how I ended up in my current predicament.

I rarely have time for vacation, but an unexpected break in my schedule allowed me to come to Padre Island with a few buddies down the coast. I figured we'd check out the surf scene and let loose a little, and that's exactly what we've been doing–surfing during the day and beach parties at night. A much-needed mini-vacation. Not going to lie, the beautiful women scattered all over the place aren't terrible, either.

This surfing accident was a stupid mishap that threw a wrench into our plans. It was a gorgeous day, and the waves were epic. My friends and I had been surfing since nine a.m., but I wanted to go out one more time before we headed back in to get ready for the night.

I felt the wave roll up behind me as I pushed off the board and rose to ride the wave in. The moment I stood, one leg slipped off the board while the other, unfortunately, remained fully planted. A sharp stab of pain shot through my ankle, and I knew something bad had happened.

Tumbling not so gracefully into the water, I managed to make my way back to my board and paddled back to shore. I looked down at my ankle and saw the swelling setting in, not to mention the lovely shades of blue and purple already streaked across my skin. After a quick call to my father, my friend Jameson helped me limp back to the Jeep and drove us to the ER.

I don't want to be in a hospital on my vacation. If anyone looked my way when I arrived, they would have seen me pouting like a five-year-old who had just dropped their ice cream cone on the ground. It is, by far, the last place I want to be.

When I caught sight of my nurse, I was immediately struck by her beauty. Liv, as her name tag revealed, was tall with striking honey-colored eyes and long brown hair cascading over her shoulders. Her natural tan suggested she enjoyed the outdoors, a refreshing change from the city girls I'm used to. Despite the pain in my ankle, I found myself wanting to know more about her.

The brief moment our hands touch as she offers me a hospital gown sends a jolt through me. I notice her cheeks flush, and I can't help but wonder if she feels the same inexplicable pull. As she turns to leave the room, the faint scent of coconut and vanilla lingers, leaving me with a strange mix of attraction and curiosity I haven't experienced in a long time.

She quickly informs me that she will get me a pillow to elevate my leg and a fresh ice pack for my ankle. But she just as quickly takes back her offer. She tries to delegate this to a tech that is passing by. *Oh no, you don't, my little nurse.* She's not getting out of my sight for long.

I make a playful pass at her reminding her that she said she would bring the items to me. "Ah, ah, ah. You said you'd bring them to me."

I see the briefest upturn of her lip, but she's trying her best not to be affected by my words. "I'll try, but someone will be down soon to take you to x-ray." She gives me a quizzical look.

I don't elaborate. I don't want to tell her that I'm a doctor, at least not yet. People always get weird when I mention it. Besides, today I am not Dr. Johnson. I'm just a guy enjoying his spring break who just happened to fuck up his ankle.

Well, I was enjoying it up until this happened. Although, I can't say that. Luckily, she doesn't ask, though. She just nods and walks out. I notice she has a bit of sway to her hips, and I let out a small, appreciative growl. I want to take ownership of those hips.

Not now, though. I'll have to wait for my chance.

And boy, do I wait. I'm left on my own for at least another hour before I hear someone behind the drape call my name.

"Yeah, that's me," I respond quickly.

A middle-aged woman gets a wheelchair and checks my armband to confirm that it matches her order on a slip of paper. "Ankle slash foot x-ray?"

I look at the wheelchair. "Yeah, surfing injury today. I can walk though."

She looks back at my ankle and then at me. Laugh lines crease the corners of her eyes, and she replies, "I am sure you can, but this will be faster if I take you in a wheelchair. We have to go to the x-ray department, which is all the way down the hall. If it is broken, then the ED doctor won't be happy that I let you walk on it without crutches."

Not wanting to be a pain in the ass, I agree and sit in the fucking chair.

As we're rounding the corner, I see Liv, my nurse. Great, she'll love this. She has a massive smile on her face, displaying her perfect white teeth and the most adorable glint in her eyes. It's the kind of smile that makes me think of a kid throwing confetti in the air at a birthday party.

"See you in a bit, Mr. Johnson."

I see her biting her lip to stifle a laugh, all paid at my expense. Oh, dear Lord. The only thing better would be if she called me Dr. Johnson while wearing that outfit. That's a fantasy I would like to role-play. She can call me Dr. Johnson when I'm balls deep inside her later.

I smile back and give her a raise of my hand, allowing her this small laugh at my expense. *For now, anyway, my little nurse.* I'll give her that satisfaction. *Game fucking on, Liv.*

I hear my phone ding in my pocket, and I check the new message while I am being wheeled down the hall for my x-ray. Jameson sent me a GIF image of a hot nurse bending over. Cleavage is spilling over as she attempts to auscultate nothing but the air. Underneath the image is a question about getting her number. Something tells me that even if she knew I was a doctor, it wouldn't impress her. To her, I am just a guy in my twenties. Little does she know this guy wants to ask her out.

I start to wonder if this happens to her often. Do guys at work ask her out? Has a patient asked her out before? The possessiveness I feel makes my heart rate escalate. The thought of someone else hitting on her elicits a primal response involving me ripping someone's head off. I mean, I don't know this woman or if she is involved with someone else. I already don't care if she is because I know she will be mine–it's only a question of when. There was no ring on her finger, and as tanned as she is, I know there never was.

I need to find out more about her.

We get to the radiology department, and I'm placed on the x-ray table where I lie flat. The freezing-cold plates are held against my foot to get pictures from different angles. When they're done, I ask the radiology tech if I can have copies and let her know that my dad is an orthopedic sports medicine physician in Houston, and she promises to have them for me and a radiology report per my request before I leave.

"You're lucky you have a doctor in the family, Mr...."—she looks down at my chart—"Mr. Johnson. You seem to know a lot about what's going on here. Do you work in medicine too?"

I hesitate but figure I may as well tell the truth. "Yeah, I'm also an orthopedic surgeon specializing in trauma surgery. I'm almost done with my fellowship training and will start as a partner in my father's group soon. You know, the whole father-son thing."

It's a long shot, but since we're being chatty, I could try and get more info on that attractive nurse of mine. "Hey, I was wondering about the nurse, Liv, that's taking care of me."

She looks at me with one eyebrow raised. "Oh? What about Liv?"

I try to be nonchalant, but I can't figure out a way to ask about her without being blatantly obvious. "I mean, do you know her? Has she worked here long?" I take a quick breath. "Is she involved with someone?"

She smiles and replies, "I've worked with Liv for a few years here. She started as a new graduate but worked as an ED tech while working through school. I don't think she has a steady boyfriend but was seeing someone off and on."

She pauses to think for a second, drumming her fingers on the counter. "I think he's in an architecture school in Houston. I've heard her mention him a time or two. You're not the first patient to ask about her." She raises her eyebrows and motions for me to get back in the wheelchair.

Pushing me out the door, she continues, "Unfortunately, she won't be here long. She leaves in a couple of months after graduation. She is finishing up her four-year degree in nursing. She works nights and takes classes during the day. She's been busy, but the girl is extremely driven."

I didn't expect that much info, but I am grateful for the little window into her life. "So she's leaving here, huh?" I say more to myself than anyone. Disappointment rushes through me. I don't live here, so it would never work anyway, I think, trying to reason with my unreasonable brain. "Do you know where she's going?"

She looks at me with the slyest of smiles. "Yeah, I do, actually. She's going to NP school in Houston. Isn't that where you live?"

I turn my head back quickly and smile my biggest smile at this clever woman. "Why yes, it is."

"I know. That's why I gave you the extended version of an answer to your question."

With the information the radiology tech gave me, I can't help but feel this was part of another plan. Like I was supposed to meet this woman. I am more determined than ever to make her mine.

CHAPTER THREE

LIV

After an onslaught of patients, I'm finally catching up on my charts. I glance up at the clock and see it's almost eleven now. I quickly make a mental list of what needs to get done:

1- Call transport to get Mrs. Herr in bay ten up to her room.

2- Check the labs on the patient in bay five.

3 - Check in on Dax in bay eight.

I refresh my computer screen and see that his x-rays are back. Since ETA on the transport for Mrs. Herr is thirty minutes, I'll bump a handsome surfer guy with a beautiful body up on my list.

I make my way over to his bay, thinking about his broad swimmer's shoulders and deliciously tanned skin. Not that I noticed. Okay, of course, I saw. How could I *not* have noticed? Gosh, even his name is hot. I tell myself it's all part of my job—observing the patient from head to toe is one of the first steps in assessing a patient. Although, I don't think drooling over a patient was covered in nursing school. Not to mention my on-again-off-again boyfriend wouldn't exactly appreciate the ogling I've been doing.

Before I can get to his room, the x-ray tech makes her way to me with a little grin on her face. "Well, Liv, that handsome young man was asking about you. Wanted to know if you were single."

I stare at her with surprise as she hands me some papers and continues. "He asked for copies of his x-rays to give to his dad, an orthopedic surgeon in Houston. He *also* informed me that he's a doctor there as well."

Did he ask about me? My stomach does a little flip as the information runs through my brain. But the way he looked at me... I thought he might have found me attractive, but I didn't know he would be so bold as to ask if I am single. And a doctor? I guess it isn't that surprising, given he seemed to have medical knowledge. He's not too much older than me. He didn't even mention it.

I take a deep breath to calm down my racing brain. All of a sudden, I find myself not wanting him to leave.

I hear his voice behind the curtain, mumbling something I can't make out. "Mr. Johnson?" I call out hesitantly before slowly pulling back the curtain. "I have your discharge paperwork ready."

He's lying on the stretcher with his ankle on a pillow. One hand is behind his head, and the other is struggling with the TV remote. That's right. I may have placed him in a better room, even if it was the overflow room we frequently use when there are too many patients in the ER.

Before I take another step, my breath hitches in my throat. His shirt has risen up his stomach showing his rock-hard abs peeking out from the bottom. The V-cut pointing to the apparent bulge inside his board shorts is so flawless I can't help but stare. Yep, the aponeurosis of the external oblique muscles that women since the dawn of time have swooned over.

Then I swear I see his cock twitch, making me rip my eyes away as my face heats with embarrassment.

"Liv?" he says, clearly enjoying my moment of temporary insanity.

I jerk my head upward and see him swing his legs over the stretcher while his eyes remain locked on mine. How can one look make me feel devoured and consumed without a single touch?

"Am I ready to go?"

My face remains flushed as I bring my eyes to his paperwork, trying to stay professional. My brain says focus, but my body is ready to jump up and leave with him.

Particularly when I realize he's still freaking staring at me.

My heart is going at least a hundred and fifty beats per minute, and my breathing quickens. I think he's noticing and liking that he has this effect on me because when I glance up, I see a brilliant smile plastered across his face.

A heartbeat passes, and my mind is flooded with images of naked bodies, crumbled sheets, and waking up to that smile in the morning.

What is wrong with me? These thoughts are not appropriate. But I'm unsure how to handle it as this has never happened before with a patient. And all of a sudden, it's way too hot in here. I must be reading way too many romance novels—my guilty pleasure when I am not studying or working.

I regain some semblance of normalcy and hand over the x-rays and wet-read report he requested from the radiologist.

"The preliminary reading report shows no fracture. The injury is likely just a sprain. But it can be quite uncomfortable and take weeks to return to a baseline level of functioning." The following words roll off my tongue, since I give every patient instructions when they leave the ED. "Mr. Johnson, if your symptoms worsen, you experience increased pain or swelling, or if you develop a fever, please return, and we will see you again."

He nods in understanding. I see a glint of humor in his eye.

I can't hold back, even though I know the answer to this question. "Are you in the medical field? You seem to know much of what's going on." I know I put him on the spot, but I'm curious to see if he's honest.

He gives me a conflicted look. "My father is a sports medicine physician. He insisted I get a copy of the report for him to look at."

I wait for him to tell me that he is also a doctor, but that information never comes. He just continues to stare at me as if he wants to ask me something but doesn't know how to go about it.

I hear his phone ding. He apologizes as he types out a quick text reply. I start to walk away, but the curtain moves before I can pull it back. The same guy who was with him in the waiting room earlier steps through and extends his hand to me.

"Hi, Liv, I'm Jameson, Dax's friend. Is he ready to go?"

I shake his hand and look back at Dax in question. How the hell does his friend know my name...unless they had been texting about me? What the fuck is happening here? I look down at my nametag, and it is flipped backward. Yep, without a doubt, they were talking about me.

Jameson continues, not waiting for a reply. "So... are you planning to go to the beach tomorrow? We were wondering, since you live here, what the best mile marker is to go to? I mean, a local person would be the best one to ask."

My brain short-circuits once again, and before I can answer, he boldly asks, "Where do *you* plan on being tomorrow when you go?"

I look between the two men and see the glimmer in Jameson's eye after the onslaught of multiple questions. Dax just continues to stare at me, waiting for me to speak.

"Um, we usually go to the mile marker by the pier, number 228. You can't miss it, and yeah, I plan on being there tomorrow. I have friends back from college. They won't take no for an answer. I need to finish this shift so I can get home and crash. I hope I can get enough sleep. They're picking me up around noon. I don't think I have a choice. I do need the relaxation, to be honest." Why am I rambling? Please, God, please make this verbal diarrhea just stop. I am such a basket case.

I hand Dax his paperwork, careful that our hands don't touch again, and look down to notice the splint is already placed around his ankle. I didn't even see him put it on. Maybe he didn't think I was capable, and honestly, I didn't want him to see the reaction he had on me with my trembling fingers. Pathetic, I know.

I hold the curtain open for them and hear Jameson behind me say, "Hopefully, we will see you tomorrow, Liv."

I turn back to reply, but I am met with a wall of a rock-hard body. It takes a second to realize that my body is embarrassingly splayed flush against his and only a second longer to register how much of him I can physically feel.

His hand quickly comes to the small of my back to steady me. Unable to move, I stay there, paralyzed. Neither of us moves. His chest presses into mine, and I can feel his breath next to my cheek.

"I hope to see you tomorrow, Liv," he whispers.

Goose bumps spread across my neck and down my arms. His grip on my back tightens for an instant before releasing me. He steps around me and strolls out with his friend, only limping slightly now that the splint is on.

I stay frozen in place. I would have thought the whole thing was a dream if the faint blond hair on my arms were not still standing at attention.

I look at the nurses' station and see Megan's mouth hanging open. She mouths, "What the fuck." A smile spreads across her face.

Okay, I guess it's safe to assume that I didn't imagine the incident. Wow, that was intense. I walk over to Megan, and she looks at me with wide eyes.

"What was that about?" She laughs.

I shake a little because I don't know what to say. "I think I'm going to take my fifteen-minute break now. Do you mind covering my patients for a minute?"

She quickly agrees as I give her a brief report on pending labs. I retreat to the lounge with my iced coffee in hand, hoping to cool myself off. Condensation is dripping off the cup onto my hand. Unfortunately, it's been sitting out there for a while, and it isn't exactly cold anymore. Not that it would have helped anyway. I wish I could go home, get my old faithful pocket-sized shegasm out and release some of this sexual tension.

Note to self, purchase a new toy with two-day shipping.

The rest of the night passes by with the regular events for a night shift in the ED. I glance up at the clock. It's three a.m., and I decided I better eat my dinner now while it's slow. Things have died down a bit, but the ER is so unpredictable. Never say the word *quiet* for fear of eliciting some kind of massive influx of patients. It's the unspoken rule.

The break room is empty, and I sigh in relief to have thirty minutes of uninterrupted time. I grab my food, make some tea, and sit at the farthest table in the staff lounge.

Pulling my phone out, I wonder if those bitches have remembered to update me on all the great times I am missing out on tonight. Several message alerts come across the screen. A few texts and videos were sent from Emma and our other bestie, Ainsley. I scroll back and start at the beginning of the messages.

A few pictures come through first. Emma has her arm draped around a hot-looking guy kissing her cheek as she takes the selfie. What a nut. That girl has fun no matter what. It's like she lives every day as if it were her last. She was also the best study partner anyone could ask for in nursing school. After we studied, we always had a beer at the local dive bar down the road.

I click on the text message and see a pic of my friends, each tossing a shot back. The caption says, "Friday night shots." I notice the fourth shot on the bar with my name written with a Sharpie on a napkin. "Wish you were here" comes through next—another couple of selfies with mutual friends from school. I see Brodie in the background with our other friends, Chrispin and Zach. They are all on the dance floor, and I can't help but feel sad that I'm not there.

I've missed Brodie. He's been my on-and-off boyfriend since high school. Before that, he was my childhood friend. I've known this guy since I was like five years old. I was crying on my first day of school, sitting inside a tire that was positioned upright on the playground mulch. The perfect hiding place. He talked to me and held my hand to help me out. We quickly became inseparable. It was always his hand that reached out to me. Whether it was to get out of a car we were packed into on our way to a party or help me onto the back of his jet ski. We were there for each other into our teenage years when we took things further than friendship.

His dad is a neurosurgeon in Houston. He left his mom when Brodie was in high school. He divorced her and remarried his office nurse. Talk about a cliché. He tossed away the woman who had stuck by his side through a grueling medical degree and raised his kids. Then he replaced her with a newer and much younger model. What a slap in the face.

Brodie took it hard, and I was there for him through it all. I held his hand after he put a fist to the wall and again when he walked down the aisle with his dad's new and improved wife. And he was there for me when my father died of a tragic hit-and-run accident. The driver left the scene, and my dad was brought in with life-threatening injuries.

My mom, an operating room nurse, received a trauma alert call that night on her scheduled work shift. She got the biggest shock of her life when she realized that the trauma-alert victim was her husband. My dad.

I'll never forget that night. I rushed over to the hospital when I found out, and Brodie was the one to drive me when I called him. He never left my side, still holding my hand even at the funeral and in the following weeks during my stages of grief.

We should make it through the four years of separation. Brodie is away in Houston for college. That is the reason I am going to Houston for graduate school. This will give us a chance; we need to be with each other. More committed. Let's see where our relationship goes. I even have dinners with his mother on my days off. I have no reason to believe otherwise that we won't end up together. He is finishing up school and starting the graduate architect program. I will be starting a graduate program too. Those plans come to a screeching halt when I see a video message come through from Ainsley. I open it and almost choke on my reheated catfish.

Ainsley: Oh, Liv. We're so sorry. We needed you to know. Call us when you can.

My heart pounds against my chest as I open the video. What. The. Actual. Fuck. It's of a scene at the same bar. The dance floor is packed, and empty glasses are scattered on the high-top tables. The level of drunkenness has increased.

The video zooms in on Brodie off in the corner by the bathroom. He has a girl with long black hair pushed up against the wall. One of his hands is on her upper thigh as he holds her leg around his waist. She's wearing a short black skirt with a purple halter top, and her breasts mashed against his chest. They are grinding against each other to the music, and his face devours her neck. Her head is thrown back in ecstasy, and his other hand is locked onto her fake boob. The video ends. I can only imagine what happened next. Who is she? Did he take her home? Or did they just screw right at the bar?

I sit there completely shocked, my heart hammering in my chest. The video was clear. That was Brodie, my boyfriend, sucking face with another girl.

My fingers hover over my phone. The urge to call him and scream through the phone that I saw everything burns through me. But I am at work, and I can't break down here. I also won't give him the satisfaction of lying to me. I'm guessing he will try to deny it all. But I don't need any proof. I saw it with my own eyes. Is she with him now? Is she lying in his bed? The thought sickens me. The deception is too great to be undone.

With trembling fingers, I type out a quick reply to Ainsley and Emma.

Liv: Who is that with Brodie?!

Ainsley: We don't know. One minute we were all dancing, and the next, he was against the wall making out with that girl. Then they disappeared.

Emma: We're so sorry, Liv. Are you ok?

Liv: Honestly? I'm not sure. I have to finish my shift. I'll talk to you guys tomorrow.

Ainsley: Call us if you need us. We'll see you tomorrow. Get some rest. We love you.

Yeah, sure, I think to myself. *Will sleep come quickly?*

My appetite is gone, and I throw my food in the trash. No tears come. I feel shocked and hollow. The discarded fish will fill the room with an unholy stench, just like the video fills my mind.

I leave the break room and head out to finish my shift until, finally, at six forty-five, my relief arrives. I need to get the hell out of here. I only have two patients to report on, and there isn't much to say—a complaint of dental pain and a person with a migraine seeking pain meds. I get my things from the lounge and leave feeling completely empty. A tear falls down my cheek as I pull out of the parking lot and drive back to my apartment while the sound of Dua Lipa's *"We're Good"* fills my Jeep's speakers. I must have left the radio on when I left for work last night.

When I get to the apartment, I throw my stuff on the counter and go into the bathroom. I strip my clothes off, leave them in a pile on the floor, and step into the shower. I let the steam hit my face and try to wash off the memories of the video.

As I replay the day in my head, I see Dax's face and let out a libidinous exhale. I feel a throbbing in my clit, but I don't have the energy to fulfill that need right now. My emotions are like a roller coaster–the highest high and the lowest low.

I get out of the shower and throw on a tank top and pajama bottoms. Grabbing a Benadryl, I poured myself a shot of whiskey. Hoping to numb the pain, I toss the pill and the strong liquor back. I'm off for the next couple of days. My friends should be here in a few hours.

I hit the pillow and curl into my bed. I thought replays of Brodie and the bimbo would wreak havoc on my brain, but instead, images of Dax fill my thoughts as I drift off into a complete slumber.

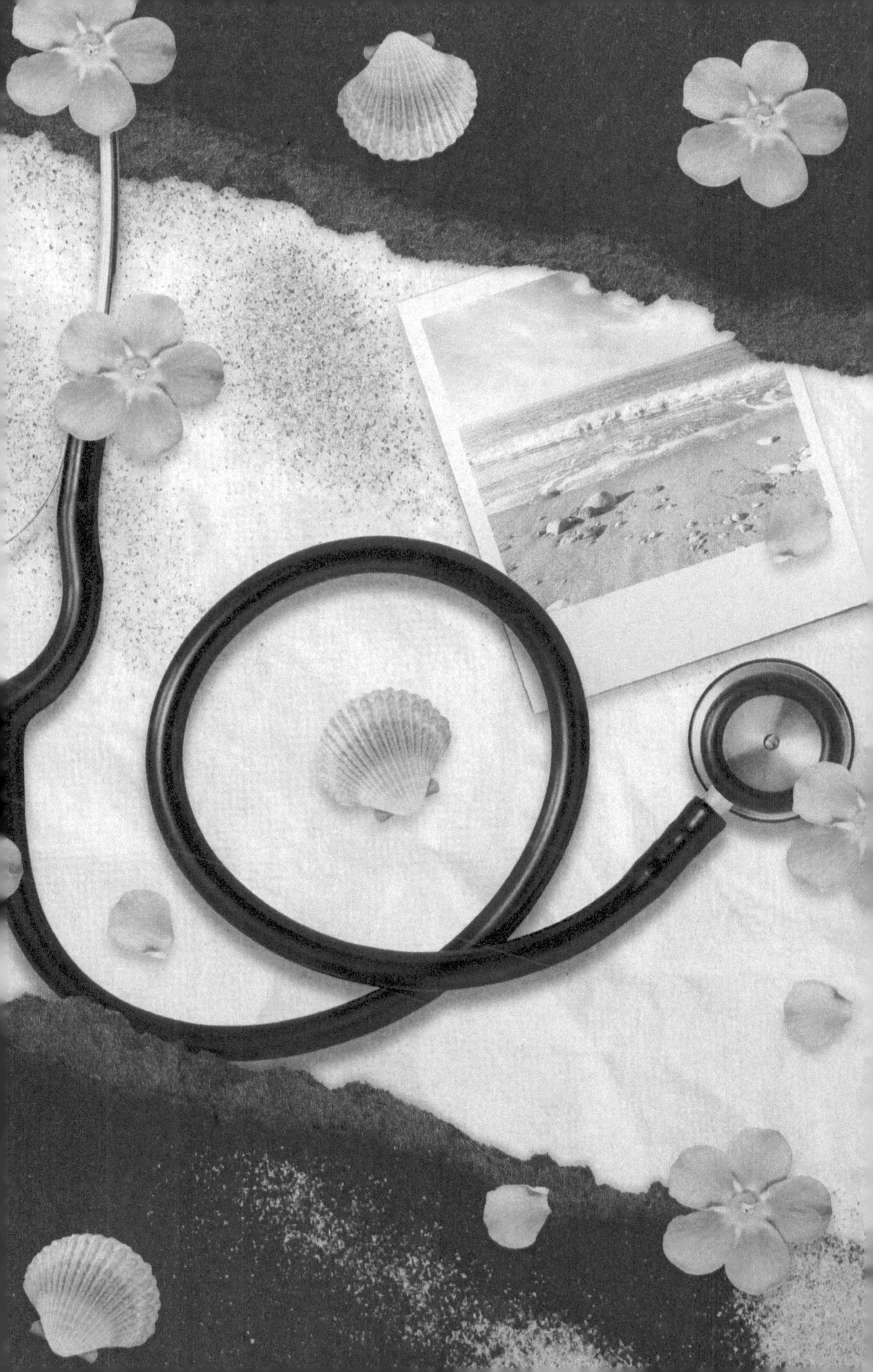

CHAPTER FOUR

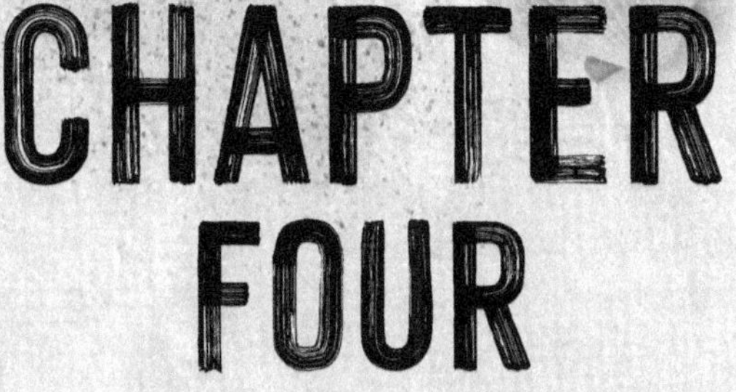

DAX

The sound of waves crashing against the shore wakes me up. The monotonous rhythm lulls me in and out of a dreamy haze as I blink my eyes, adjusting to the light. But I find myself hoping to drift back to sleep. The dream about a particular hot nurse is too good not to continue.

Reaching my arms above my head, I stretch fully on the crisp white linen, pushing my head back into the down pillow. Only then do I realize the painful erection that's tenting the sheets. It's no wonder. Liv invaded my dreams with her full lips and sexy body.

Reaching down, I wrap my hand around my shaft to take care of this aching desire and pump toward a much-needed release. Thankfully, I have a room by myself, so no one hears the sleepy moans that escape my lips.

Liv is by far one of the most gorgeous women I've ever met. She's naturally beautiful, and her confidence just adds to her attractiveness. The attention I gave her seemed to crack her confidence a bit, and I love thinking that I have that effect on her. I want to know how someone so stunning could be so unsure of herself despite her best attempt at appearing so. Perhaps there is a reason, an ex, that made her that way? All I can do is reminisce about her. The way she fit perfectly pressed against me.

I need to see her today. See if the chemistry was, in fact, my imagination or perhaps a deeper connection. My lust-filled brain keeps my hand pumping, and an orgasm rips through me just as my alarm goes off.

Anxious to start the day, I pull up the surf report on my phone, and the announcement blares through my Bluetooth speakers. The information broadcast describes the wave height and the high temperature today, reaching ninety degrees–a scorcher.

Big waves and sunshine equal the perfect beach day.

I swing my legs over the side of the bed. My feet hit the cool tiled floor, and my mood immediately plummets.

The dull pain immediately reminded me that I won't be surfing today. "This fucking ankle," I grumble.

I throw my air splint back on and head out to the balcony. The salty air hits me in the face, and I hear the sound of seagulls in the distance, each one cajoling in a playful banter sweeping down toward the water.

The day is early, but I can already feel the humidity building in the air. As the day continues, it will roll in and settle like a thick blanket, mostly offering no reprieve. But for now, the view and the feel of the ocean air are perfect. I sigh in contentment and take in the peaceful scenery before me. Thankfully, I can enjoy such a tranquil paradise.

I go downstairs, craving my morning coffee and find James, Eric, and Theo sitting at the breakfast nook, eating breakfast tacos and scrolling on their phones. "Thanks for waking me, fuckers. Did you at least save me anything to eat?"

Eric throws a bag my way. "Yeah, asshole. I got you two breakfast tacos from the Taquería Maria restaurant down the road. You're welcome, by the way."

Mouth watering, I immediately grab the tacos and dig in. "Thanks," I say around a mouthful of food. *The greasy goodness is perfect*, I think to myself as I make haste opening the foil wrap on the second one. I search the cabinet, grab a couple of Advil, and swallow them down with my food. My ankle may keep me from surfing, but I refuse to limp around all day.

"How's the ankle?" James asks.

Rolling my eyes, I start to walk away. He chuckles and doesn't even look up as I flip him off and head for the bathroom, shoving the rest of the last taco into my mouth.

I finish my shower and let the cold spray run over my body for a few minutes before I get out. After hearing the weather forecast for today, a cold shower seemed like an excellent way to start the day.

I dry off quickly and run the towel through my hair before throwing on some board shorts and a T-shirt. I need to leave soon to avoid traffic on the causeway heading toward the beach. We had made tentative plans with Liv to get together at the beach. At least, that's what I remember of that conversation.

I'm anxious to get to the spot she told us about last night. Spring break means that there will be tons of people along the coastline. Mostly college students, girls in skimpy bikinis, and guys trying to impress them, but every age and walk of life will be there too, eager to enjoy the weather.

But I only want to see one woman today.

Thoughts of Liv and the dirty things we did in my dream come back to me. I reach into my shorts and moan as I take my cock in my hand. Thinking of Liv, I chase my release for the second time this morning.

We leave the house around ten and stop at the local convenience store. It's packed with people all with the same idea. Everyone stocked up on beer, water, and snacks for the day. Thankfully, we thought ahead and only needed more water.

I push my way toward the back and grab a case. I manage to pay quickly and load the water into the cooler. The last thing I need is heatstroke on top of the bum ankle. Which I realize is feeling much better after the Advil. We pull out of the parking lot and begin the sandy drive to the beach.

I want to get a prime location near the sea sculpture art displays. This event is popular. It attracts many people who not only admire, but judge sand art for monetary prizes and prestige.

As suspected, many cars are on the road leading to the sandy shoreline. We pass many drivers and see even more cars parked along the side of the road. We have four-wheel drive, and even though the sand is packed down, we wouldn't chance it in a front-wheel-drive car or, worse, rear-wheel drive. Getting your vehicle stuck in the sand is a royal pain in the ass. Most islanders have had this happen to them once in their life. Luckily, southern hospitality is a common trait when a volunteer asks if you need help getting unstuck.

Our beach sticker permit is on the windshield corner and fully displayed. Our super-duty truck moves glacially through the line of cars when I spot the pier. I let the guys know to park somewhere in close proximity to it. I see Jameson's smirk in the rearview mirror.

"Got something to say?" I comment with a half-laugh.

He shakes his head. "Nah, man, but do you think you'll find her? I mean, this place is starting to get packed."

It's ridiculously crowded. I know as the afternoon approaches, it will only get worse. If she isn't here already, I doubt she'll be getting a spot on this side of the pier. I remember her saying her friends would pick her up around noon, and with the traffic, it might be later when she finally gets here. I try to suppress my disappointment.

The memory of her face and the scent of her hair floods my senses. I remember leaning in and whispering into her ear while her coconut-smelling hair brushed against my cheek. I'll find her today. I *need* to find her today.

We pull into a spot that gives us a good view of the pier and the surrounding beach. Hopefully, it will make it easier to spot her. One o'clock hits, and I'll make my first stroll up and down the beach.

I leave my splint in the truck. The soft sand isn't great on my ankle, but it seems to be okay down by the water, where the sand is more packed down. I let the cold water rush over my feet as I walk. Each wave that washes up is like a little cold pack to the lingering swelling at the joint. Maybe it just feels cold compared to the heat and humidity in full effect. My eyes scan the crowd, but I don't see her.

I see a row of Jeeps and trucks parked in a circle as if they slept here last night. A neatly dug pit is in the center, filled with firewood. A big tent with a grill and endless coolers sits off to the side. Bathing suit-clad bodies are scattered around. Some play drinking games, others dance, and some simply lounge in the sun. They have a sweet setup going on. Everyone seems to be laughing and having a good time. Clearly, they are old friends. They appear to be in their twenties, maybe a few years younger than us.

Bob Marley, "*No Woman, No Cry,*" is playing on the speakers. I see people from the crowd go up, making their way into the circle of friends. Some go and hug each other or just wave when walking by. Whatever it is, this group seems to know a lot of people. Locals maybe? I see a couple of them continuing to look up as if they are looking around for someone but, not finding their target, they return to their conversations. Each time a car comes close, they look up, shake their heads, and then quickly fall back into their conversation.

Our truck is parked with enough space to set up a few things beside it. The cooler is brought out, the chairs set up, and we settle in for the day. Theo and Eric were in charge of getting the food together, and being the resourceful, lazy people they are, they called up a local deli and had them prepare the food for the day. Since James and I were stuck in the ED last night, we got the easy out and needed to get the drinks.

Sandwiches, wraps, potato chips, brownies, and cookies are pulled out. I chuckle under my breath but secretly applaud their resourcefulness. They know their domestic limitations enough to delegate this task to the experts.

Jameson picked up local craft beer and Coronas, complete with salt and limes. He also grabbed a couple of bottles of wine. I pick up the bottles of wine and give Jameson a quizzical look. He just shrugs his shoulders and smiles.

"For the ladies," he says as if it's the most obvious thing in the world. "The lady at the liquor store told me these wines were good choices."

I dunk the wine bottles into the cooler ice and face him. "I'm pretty sure I saw these same bottles at your house. A Pinot Grigio and Rosé, huh?"

His eyes shoot up to meet mine in mock anger. "I have a sister, asshole. I also like wine on hand if I bring a girl back to my house to entertain. It's hospitable."

I shake my head, nodding in agreement. "Sure, buddy, whatever you say."

The chairs are laid out, and I gently plop myself into one, throwing my leg up on a cooler to elevate it. The Advil helped immensely, but I know it won't last all day. Settling in, I grab my iced coffee and phone to snap a few pics of my surroundings.

As I bring up my messages, I notice that I missed a call from Tatiana. Funny, I think, I haven't thought about her since my accident. Tatiana and I are, hmm... What are we? Not "together" and not "exclusive." Although, at times, she seemed to want it to go in that direction. I held firmly to the fact that we were not in any label and continued to keep my options open. I hope she is doing the same. But, not my problem if she isn't. I was upfront with her.

Finishing my career is my priority, not putting a Mrs. before any woman's name. Tatiana didn't seem to be looking for that either, which is one of the things that interested me about her. Friends, colleagues with benefits suited us just fine. She's a physician, too, and has her career. On paper, she seems like the logical choice for me, but I can't get to that point of any commitment with her. My parents are deeply in love and have a happy marriage. I know what I want. It's the same.

I quickly shoot her a text apologizing for missing her call and letting her know I'll see her at work. Maybe it's time I close the door on whatever it is between us.

I put the thought in the back of my mind and drop my phone back into my pocket. Throwing my sunglasses on, I look up, finding my friends relaxed in their chairs. Eric and Theo have iced coffee in their hands, but Jameson cracks a beer.

"What's on the agenda for today, guys?" No one wants to go to the club tonight, so we have the whole day to relax on the beach.

Jameson shifts toward me. "I'm up for whatever. Just gonna hang today and enjoy our last day here before we head back tomorrow morning."

Eric and Theo both speak up in agreement.

"Do you think Liv will have any other hot nurse friends with her today?" Eric pipes up.

"Maybe not another nurse, but I'm sure she isn't coming alone," I say.

Eric and Theo look up at me over their sunglasses. "Man, the girls have been plentiful in this place," Eric replies. "Theo has already hooked up with two different girls in the past few days."

"Can't help it that I'm irresistible," Theo gloats.

"And awfully cocky," I add, throwing an empty water bottle at him.

Theo looks over my shoulder to the group of women chatting by the circle of Jeeps and trucks, and I see something catch his eye. Glancing back, I can tell some of them are looking over here. With my sunglasses on, I can tell no one can see what I am looking at, so I take my time searching their group, hoping Liv may be there. I only have one day and one shot at meeting this girl here, and I don't want to screw it up.

A blond-haired guy walks up to the girls, and they're clearly angry with him. I hear their shrill voices from here, and one even throws a punch right into his chest. He doesn't seem to react. He just keeps looking out to the line of cars, obviously looking for someone. One of the girls waves at him to return to his friends, and he shakes his head at her but leaves without an argument.

Wonder what that's all about. The idiot definitely fucked something up.

The temperature and humidity continue to climb as predicted. Thankfully, we have enough sunscreen to last the day, which is precisely what I need, considering I don't plan to leave until I find Liv. I want to get to know her. I want to learn more about the spunky little nurse who has invaded my mind and occupied my thoughts since last night. I have yet to think of anything else, and I won't until I find her.

CHAPTER FIVE

LIV

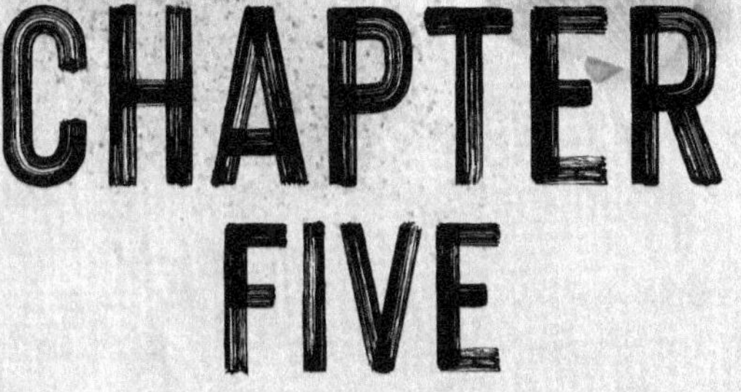

My dreams torment me. Punish me without abatement. Visions of two tangled bodies pushed up against the wall. The lust dripping in a veil of sweat from his forehead. The scent of salty ocean water mixed with unrelenting male arousal. The sound of clashing teeth hitting together in a frantic kiss. I can feel club-style music bass vibrating throughout my body.

I pull away quickly from the embrace to see Dax's face looking back at me. The possessive nature of his intense stare. He leans into my ear, sucking my earlobe with one word whispered, echoing in my mind. *Mine.*

I try to pull Dax back to me in an embrace, desperate for that connection I need, but instead I reach only air. There is nothing but emptiness. My rapid heart rate feels as though it's echoing in my ears. I wake, startled from my sleep. Was it real?

I take in the scenery around me—my dresser, the sound of a fan across the room that provides a routine white noise after my night shift ends. I'm awake before the call from Val comes through; she is letting me know they are on their way over. I throw the covers off dramatically, befitting my mood—unrested and unsettled. My bed looks like I was at war with it—sheets are haphazardly strewn across the floor, the mattress slung slightly askew from the box frame. I tossed and turned all night, trying to erase the video from my memories. Alas, it was futile. Instead, Dax, my patient, and I replaced the actors in the slightly pornographic video. That was all kinds of fucked-up.

Once in the bathroom, I clear my mind and hastily get ready. I don't want to make the girls wait on me. I quickly wash my face and brush my teeth. I grab my bikini off the bathroom door hook and put it on. I apply a minimal amount of makeup. Tinted moisturizer and rouge gently spread over my cheeks, lips, and eyelids, finished with waterproof mascara complete my repertoire.

There isn't much eye redness or swelling this morning. I didn't cry as much as I thought I would last night after hearing about Brodie's betrayal. I guess the Benadryl and shot of whiskey helped to ensure that wasn't the case. I am not too surprised by this. I honestly thought he might not have been faithful, but to do it so blatantly, throwing it in my face. In front of my friends, where the news would get back to me. In a town where many people we know could have seen this. It's a slap in the face, and I'm angry. Yet I can't deny what's right in front of me. The truth is, our connection has been somewhat lacking lately and some of the passion has fizzled out of our relationship, but we had a good foundation. Why wasn't that enough? I would have preferred the comfort of the friend zone over the pain his betrayal has caused. It makes me want to throw up. I deserve better than this.

The nausea attempts to return as my mind replays the video again. I have to turn off my thoughts if I'm going to make it through the day. I have to get it together. My friends will be here any minute.

I take a quick drink of water, chasing back the bitter taste of bile and betrayal, and continue attempting to enhance my curls and smoothe any residual frizz. The humidity will be unbearable, and I will do everything I can to tame these locks in place. Beach hair it is. It gives me at least a sense of some control, as stupid as it may sound. The hair product smells terrific too.

I hope to have a repeat of last night—Dax whispering in my ear. The feel of his lips buzzing about my neck made every hair on my body stand on end with excitement. I haven't had this sort of response from a guy, one that makes me feel that electrical spark people talk about or read in books. I didn't think it existed. I wonder if I imagined it. I need to know more than ever if what I felt last night was real. Maybe the dream made me believe or play it up more than what I thought I felt just a few hours ago.

I proceed to grab a couple of hair ties for my wrist in case it's windy at the beach then add an extra set of clothes, a swimsuit, and Toms shoes for later into my beach bag, just in case I need them. I get dressed quickly, putting on a pair of shorts, a tank top, and my favorite pair of flip-flops. Before leaving my room, I get a couple of towels and sunscreen.

"Now, I have everything for a day at the beach," I mumble to myself as I shut the light off in my room.

I go to the fridge, pack my cooler bag with a couple of cold packs, and add some drinks. I also make sure to grab a couple of bottles of Pedialyte. I usually have one of these before I do any drinking, especially if it is outdoors, with the heat and salt compounding the effects of dehydration. I am a nurse, after all. This method seems to be tried and true for drinking alcohol in any setting, and I will avoid sickness at all costs today.

When I see Brodie at the beach, I want to be in my right mind. Will he come up to me? To apologize or, worse, deny the video. The proof. I don't want him to manipulate me into thinking what I saw on the video could be construed as anything more than what it was—him enjoying another woman's body.

I hope Dax is there. I don't want to miss the chance of getting to know him, even though that is a remote possibility, since I doubt I will even see him again after today.

As I am loading up some snacks, the doorbell rings. I look through the peephole to see Emma, Ainsley, and Val.

I answer the door to let the girls in. They immediately all stare at me. I look down, and Emma reaches out for my hand.

"Oh, sweetie, I am so sorry. Are you okay?"

I shake my head but look up and attempt a smile that doesn't quite reach my eyes. "No, but I think I will be. I have you all, and I want to go out today and spend time with my friends."

Ainsley moves in to hug me. "Are you going to confront him today? If you are, I think you should do it sooner than later."

I also notice Anisley's tightly pursed lips. Hopefully, it isn't more bad news. I couldn't take any more; frankly, I didn't think I cared.

"Sooner than later, before everyone is drinking, so they have some wits about them."

I nod in agreement. Val goes to hug me too. "I think you should ignore him. Let him come up to you. You are too classy to make a scene, Liv."

I raise my hand. "Guys, there is no way I am causing a scene. I have to clear the air, but I'll have to see how he is too."

They all look at me. They feel sorry for me, and I hate that feeling. I got the same pity at my dad's funeral service–apologies. Well, I refuse to feel that or accept that look today.

"Come on, guys. Let's go have some fun. I sure do need it." I close the door to my apartment, and we start our drive out to the mile marker, where our friends are waiting for us.

After about an hour in traffic, we finally make it to the line leading to our spot. People are stuck in this line either cruising the beach r looking for a sliver of sand to park their vehicle. If you don't get here early, you are unlikely to get a prime location.

It's close to three o'clock when I spot our little click of friends with the entire setup in action. Crispin is waving in the air like air traffic control. I hear him call out to Rhett. He and Zach spring up from their chairs and run over to the tent. They start maneuvering things around, then stand in the spot, holding it open when I am the next in line.

I quickly pull my Jeep into my spot with ease. I hear Sublime pumping from the speakers and jump out. I go over to my friends and grab a quick hug. Emma, Ainsley, and Val jump out of the Jeep. Emma sticks two fingers into her mouth and whistles over to the guys. They drop what they are doing and quickly grab our stuff from the back for us. Now that's southern hospitality.

They place all the stuff on the sand and lay it out. I go to grab my iced coffee, finish that up, and readily pour a jug of Pedialyte in its place. I can feel the heat and know I need to stay on top of my fluid intake today. Someone offers me a beer, but I decline.

I hug a few more friends, and as I am pulling away, I spot Brodie. When he sees me, we just hold each other's stare. We connect, and unspoken words travel in waves through the breeze—*I know what you did.*

Emma notices this interaction and elbows Ainsley for an intervention. Ainsley walks right up to me and grabs my arm. I see her shake her head to Brodie as she leads me away.

What did I expect him to do or say? I saw the look in his eyes. It was riddled with guilt. He knows that what he did was wrong. Good. Perhaps it was that he was caught. Does he regret it?

I honestly don't expect to feel this way now. Even though I know I should feel angry, I do not. Either way, I'll have to talk to him today. We need to clear the air soon. Spring break will be over, and everyone will return to finish school. Except, I won't leave. I'll stay here, but I will finish up too. Where will we go from here?

I go to my girlfriends and stand around catching up with my old buddies from high school. I'm staring out into the ocean and go over to the water to dunk my feet in. It's cool compared to the heat of the sand. Despite the music and laughter from all around, I remain focused on the hypnotic sound of the waves that help to clear my mind and feel centered again.

As I am heading back to the Jeep, I feel like someone is watching me. I look around and don't notice anyone, so I grab my towel and start walking to my chair. When I look up, I spot a guy with sunglasses sitting in a chair across from our row of parked cars. His leg is elevated on an ice chest with an air splint on it. He smiles at me, displaying perfectly white teeth. He takes his sunglasses off and waves. I tilt my head and smile at him.

Dax.

I also give him a little wave, but then he gets up and says something to his friend. I recognize him as the friend who was with him last night in the ED–Jameson. I think he said that was his name. He starts to walk my way, and I just stand there watching him. He walks over to me, and I see Emma looking back and forth between us.

She comes up to me. "Who is that?"

"That's the guy," I say.

"Who?"

"His name is Dax, and he is 'the' guy."

She touches my shoulder. "Girl, you have some explaining to do."

I laugh. "He's the patient I told you about from last night. I told him I would be here."

Dax approaches me as I'm recounting last night and stands only inches away.

I look at him and say, "You found me."

He grabs my hand lightly and looks me in the eye, igniting same sparks I felt yesterday. I know now that I didn't imagine them. He brings my hand up to his chest, looks at me hard, and says, "Now that I've found you, what am I supposed to do with you?"

I pull a loose strand of my hair and place it behind my ear. "I guess we'll find out," I tell him as I lead him to a chair under the shade.

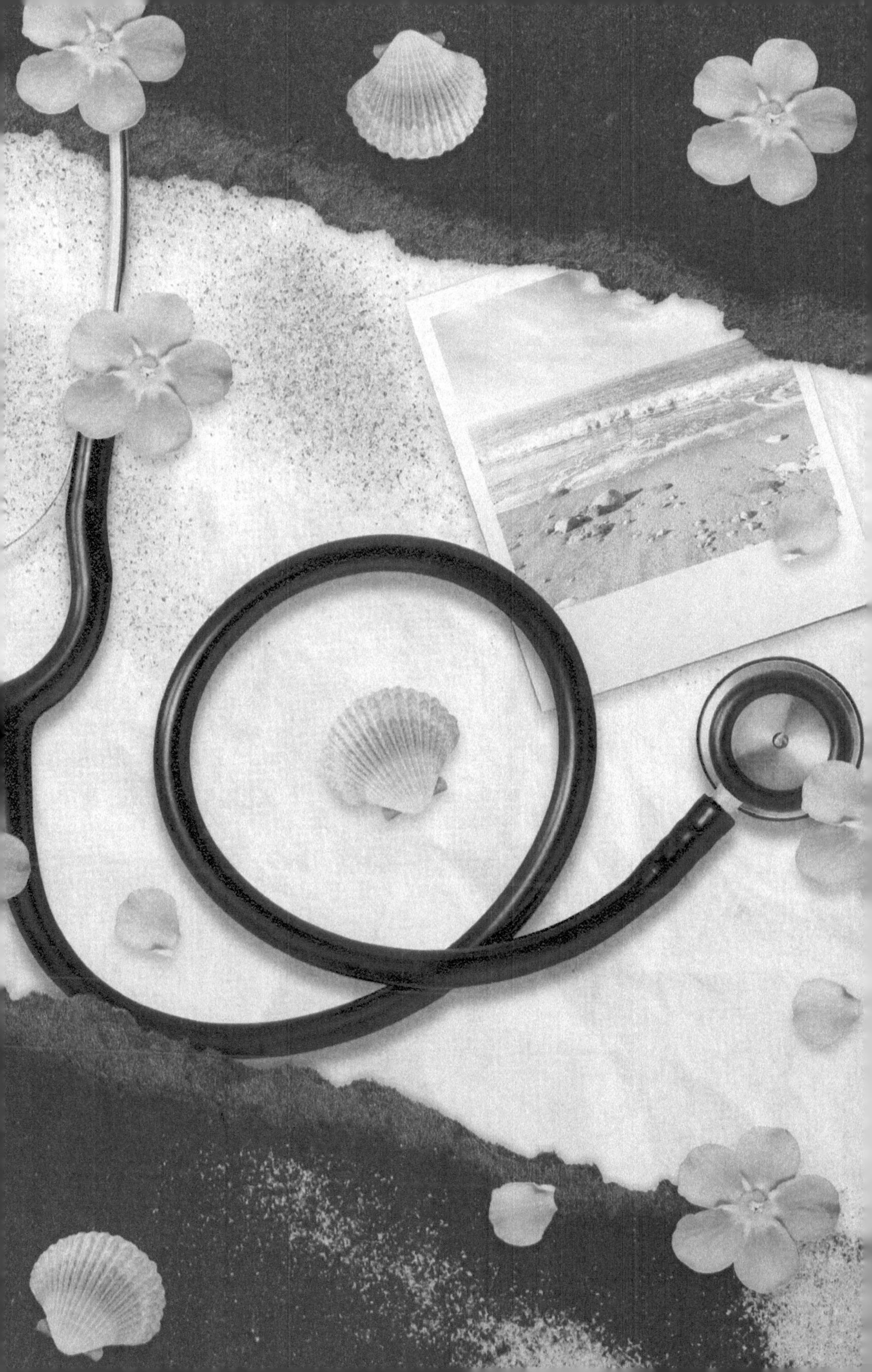

CHAPTER SIX

LIV

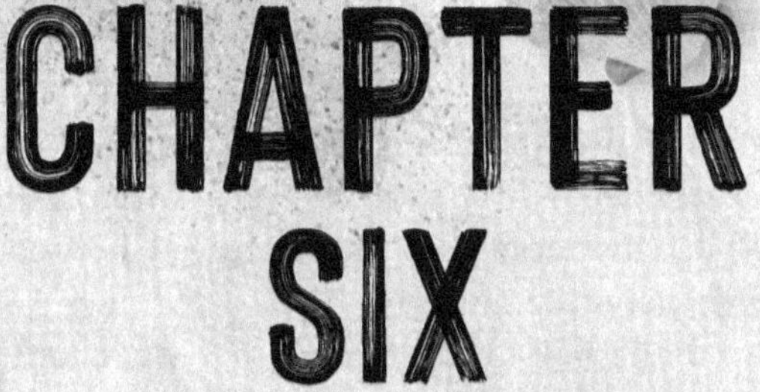

We sit and chat like old friends. The conversation flows easily, and I laugh at his witty sense of humor. His friends come over, and he introduces me to the other guys, Eric and Theo. I remember Jameson from the ED.

"So Dax was a good patient last night?" I ask.

"No, but then again, I'm not the nurse he wanted," he says with a wink.

A blush immediately rushes to my face. Thankfully, Dax takes pity and pretends not to notice my embarrassment. He just shrugs in agreement.

"That's true," he agrees.

My other girlfriends hang around with us, and the guys all talk to them. Even my guy friends from high school are friendly toward them and engage in usual topics of conversation like sports and work. Brodie is the only one avoiding the group. That's more than okay with me. My anger is still running high. I'll chat with him in a bit.

Some of our group goes to play volleyball, and I get up too. I spot Brodie, his back to me, talking with a couple of girls, and decide it's better to get this over with. It's better to chat with him before the drinking happens.

"I'll catch up with you in a bit," I tell Dax.

"Cool, I'm going to go freshen up my drink." He goes off to join the group of friends.

As I get closer to Brodie , I begin to overhear their conversation.

"I don't want to talk, Alexis," he says curtly.

She reaches out to grab his hand, but Brodie pulls back. "Well, that sure didn't stop you last night. But then again, there wasn't much conversation going on." She lifts one eyebrow at Brodie, almost willing him to deny this in front of her friend.

My brain catches up to the scene, and I realize the girl in front of him is the one from the video. My body freezes, feet immobile in the sand. She shifts slightly when she doesn't get the attention she was hoping for and continues trying to persuade him.

"I suppose we didn't talk much, though, did we, baby? I'm totally okay with that." Her hands reach up to touch his shoulders before gliding down his arms.

Brodie flinches at her touch but just shakes his head. "Last night was a mistake, Alexis, and I'm sorry I led you on."

"A mistake?" she counters, sounding confused and slightly agitated.

I attempt to unfreeze my stupid feet and head back before they spot me, but my movement catches Alexis's eye. Recognition crosses her face. She seems to know this type of behavior–the only kind that comes from a guy caught cheating.

Holding my eye, she steps closer to him and purrs into his ear, "Well, I guess we gave each other multiple mistakes last night, huh, Brodie." With that, she winks at me.

Brodie follows her line of vision to see me watching the exchange. He goes to reach for me, motioning for me to stay, but I start to run away.

"Liv, wait!" he yells and begins to run after me.

For some reason, I stop. Anger flows through me. This isn't how I imagined this conversation going, but it's unavoidable now.

Alexis looks at me and snickers. "Enjoy my sloppy seconds…and thirds." She flicks her long black hair over her shoulder and saunters off. She looks like a tan, cosmetically enhanced Barbie doll–very plastic and artificial with about as much personality.

"I know, Brodie. I heard and saw everything." The words flow out of me in a rush.

His head tilts slightly in confusion. "What do you mean saw?" Brodie questions. hesitating on his words, not realizing it's obvious he's trying to hide the truth.

At one point, I would have thought this adorable as his eyebrows pulled together and his lips thin. Such amazing lips that I could never get enough of at one point. Now all I see is deceit, waiting to spew out the next lie.

I pull out my phone and show him the video. His face fills with rage.

"Someone fucking sent that to you?" he screams, not bothering to hide his anger.

"I'm assuming that is a rhetorical question, Brodie." I'm beyond annoyed. Why is he even mad? "So, I guess you weren't in a committed relationship with me after all, huh? This between us was just killing time for you? Gave you something to do when you were in town?"

He looks shocked by my outburst, as if my words are a physical slap to the face. "No, Liv!" You were always it for me. I have been faithful. That"—he points at my phone—"was a horrible drunken mistake."

I hold up my hand to stop him as he attempts to come closer. "No, Brodie. You can't use the excuse of being drunk. We worked through all that, remember? All the NA meetings. Will you use that as an excuse the next time it happens? Who knows if this is even the first time that this has happened? I would *never* have done this to you. Maybe I cared more about you than you did about me." The words pour out before I can stop them. "How could I ever trust you now?"

He looks down at his feet like a toddler who was just scolded. "I'm so sorry, Liv. I never meant to hurt you. I would give anything to erase that mistake. You're my best friend, and I feel like I'm dying inside right now." His eyes fill with tears, and I turn to walk away, not wanting to see his tears fall. He grabs my hand, yanking me back. "Please, give me another chance Liv, to prove to you that I'm sorry."

I shake my head. "No, Brodie, it's over." This time, when I turn to walk away, he lets me.

The walk back to where my friends are standing is painful. Emma immediately notices my somber mood and takes my hand.

"I take it you talked to Brodie about last night?" she asks.

I tell her what happened to explain that I came face-to-face with the girl from the video.

"No!" she gasps, covering her mouth in shock.

"Oh yes." I sniff, barely holding back tears. "Brodie told her it was a mistake. I overheard their conversation. She also told me to enjoy her leftovers or something to that effect. I don't remember the exact words because I was trying to make my brain keep up with what was happening."

"Whoa," is all that manages to come out of Emma's mouth. "That's crazy, girl. What happened next?" she replies eagerly awaiting the next juicy detail.

"He told me it was a mistake and was drunk-impaired." I make air quotes for emphasis.

Emma knows Brodie's history, and I can tell by her expression that she isn't buying that story either. "Oh, using *that* excuse, is he?" she mutters.

"Like drinking and bad choices are a medical condition of his. He also doesn't want us to be over. He wanted me to give him another chance which, of course, I denied him. I mean, I could never do that, right?"

She looks resigned but agrees. "Do you think you can trust him again?"

I look at her, and with absolute certainty, I say, "No, I told him it was over."

"Well, all hell." Emma shakes her head. "What about this Dax guy? A spring break fling, then?"

"I'm not sure," I tell her. But as my heart picks up a little, I know I want to find out.

It is starting to get late as the evening approaches. The sky is streaked with beautiful shades of blue and pink hues. I go to search for Dax, hoping to spot him. I *need* to find him. His friends are still around, so I know he is here somewhere. I look over to where they are parked and see him sitting in the same chair he was in when I first pulled up to the beach. "Wicked Game" by Chris Isaak, fills the speakers.

I go over to talk to him. He's all alone and seems to be deep in thought. He sees me approach, and a hint of a smile crosses his lips. I walk up to him and sit in the chair he motions to.

"I was wondering where you went." He lifts one eyebrow, places his sunglasses over his head, and looks at me. "I went looking for you but saw you were talking to a guy. You looked pretty upset. I came back over here to give you some privacy."

I nod in acknowledgment. "How much did you hear?"

He sits up, linking his hands over his legs, bringing him closer to me. "Enough that I could tell you without reservation that there isn't enough alcohol in the world to make me see anyone else but you."

The way that he looks at me makes me want to believe him. Is it possible to feel love at first sight for someone? All that fairy tale shit that little girls grow up to dismiss because it is just too good to be true.

"Can I have your number, Liv?"

I stare at him, briefly glancing down before lifting my chin to meet his gaze again.

"I would like a chance to get to know you. I don't think I will be able to stop thinking about you after just a couple of days."

He must see the hesitation in my eyes because he adds, "Not all guys are like that."

I just nod in concession. Before my better judgment can argue against it, I tell him my cell phone number.

He calls it and says, "There, now you have my number too. I was told that you are moving to Houston soon, and that's where I live, you know."

"I think I might have heard that," I say as a smirk spreads across my face. "When are you heading back to Houston, Dax?"

He remains focused on me, saying nothing. After a few seconds go by, and I don't think he will answer, he replies with a sigh, "In the morning." His hand gently passes through his hair as he looks out at the ocean and the tide coming in. "This is the end of our short vacation, and we leave tomorrow morning."

"Oh," is all I can say at this point.

He grabs my hand and intertwines our fingers together. With that action, I can feel all the unspoken words between us. I just wish he didn't have to leave in the morning, taking the possibilities of more with him.

CHAPTER SEVEN

LIV

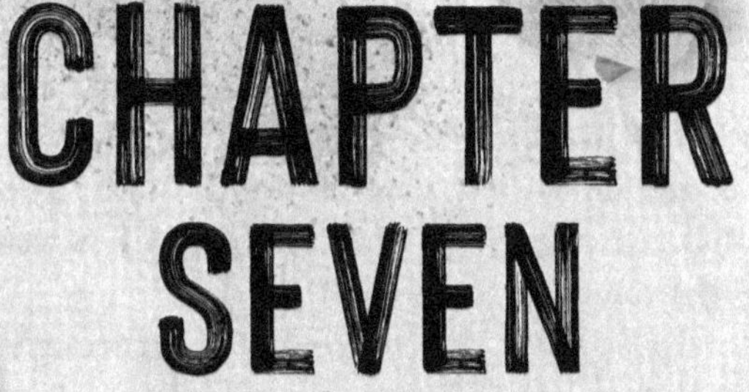

As the day wears on, the people on the beach begin to thin out. Parents take their kids home, and older couples head back for dinner, leaving the remnants behind, indicating a good time was had by all.

We surfed, played music, and enjoyed the company of good friends all day. And we have no intention of going home yet. Sandcastles still line the sand, and more intricate pieces are roped off from where the sea sculptures were judged. The guys managed to gather enough wood to make for an epic bonfire, and we'll be lighting it up soon. Although the day was a scorcher, the temperature began to drop slightly, taking most of the oppressive humidity with it. The breeze off the water feels good against our sun-kissed and sandy skin.

This will end sooner than we would like, and then everyone will return to their lives–school to finish up, work to return to, and time to reminisce about another spring break in the books. With the memories we made today, I know it'll be a year to remember.

Thankfully, after my altercation with Brodie, the day progressed with ease. As I make my way toward the grill, I can smell the food cooking, and my mouth waters, suddenly realizing how hungry I am. And it's not just me. I see my friends slowly making their way toward the tables we have set up like moths to a flame.

The guys are grilling up the fajitas, and the tortillas are on the portable burner being reheated to place into a warming pouch. The scents of bell peppers and onions fill the air, as well as the mouth-watering scents of beef and chicken marinated fajitas on the grill. Our favorite V & V sausage, a staple at any south Texas bar-b-que, is being placed into foil trays and covered to prevent sand from being scattered throughout our food. Sand gets everywhere, and unless you want a mouth full of it, you need to take extra precautions and cover that shit up. You learn that quickly when having a cookout at the beach.

We gather in a procession and make our way through the buffet-style spread. I load my plate up, since I haven't had much food today–my appetite was poor, and my stomach was in knots. I sit with my friends, and Dax slides into the chair next to me. His thigh brushes mine, and just like every other time we touch, little sparks fly at the contact. I can feel the heat from the day emanating from his skin. I want to lean into him but hold myself back.

I sense someone staring at me and look around but see no one. We chat away while we eat, and it's only when Emma calls my name that I look over to her and notice Brodie. His brows are furrowed, and his eyes bore into mine with a dejection. Boy, if looks could kill.

I keep my face impassive and maintain eye contact as long as I can, not wanting to be the one to look away first. When I think that I can't stand to look at him anymore, he shakes his head and looks over at the waves. He heads in the direction of the water, but not before I notice that he picks up a bottle of Jack off one of the tables.

My stomach clenches for a moment, knowing that if he starts drinking straight alcohol, it's a recipe for disaster. I try to shake the feeling in my gut and cross my fingers that he had some food to soak up the alcohol. I didn't see him in line to get something to eat, but I can't let this concern me any longer. He is *not* my problem anymore.

We have been off and on over the past few months, and if there was any doubt, his actions last night made things very clear on where we stand. When things get tough, he seems to find one vice or another to placate whatever is bothering him instead of handling things like an adult.

I've had enough.

I realized I haven't been in love with Brodie for a while. Our longtime friendship kept things going. I love him, but I haven't been in love with him in a long time.

I fist my hands at my side and release them a couple of times, trying to clear my head. Dax immediately looks down as if he can read my mind, and then his eyes meet mine. He holds my gaze and lifts his hand to my face stroking his thumb gently over my skin. His touch is magnetic, and I let myself lean into him.

"He'll be okay," he says. "He just needs time to come to terms with it. Don't think this is your fault for any reason, Liv."

I grab his hand and hold on to it and look into his eyes. "I've already spent too much time thinking about this today. I just want to spend the rest of the time we have here together. If that's okay."

His gaze drifts down to my lips for a moment, then he flashes me his perfect orthodontic smile and nods. "That's more than okay with me. Are you done eating?"

I look down at my remaining taco and bite the last bite.

He just laughs. "Want anything else?"

I give him my most pensive face and shake my head. "Nope, all done. Now let's have some drinks."

He stands up and grabs both our plates before I can react. I trail behind him as he takes them over to the trash.

"I could have done that, Dax."

"No, I want you to relax. I can take care of this, and I want to take care of you."

He tosses the plates in the bin, meanders over to me, and suddenly pulls me into his arms. It catches me a bit off guard, and I fall forward into him. Every nerve is instantly on high alert. I can feel my breasts press against his chest, my nipples pebbled against my bikini top. His hands dip under my top, and I can feel his warm palm on the small of my back. My arms come up to wrap around his neck, pulling us closer together.

"And here I thought I was taking care of you. You're the one with the busted ankle," I tease. "I believe you needed a nurse yesterday, and you had to settle for Jameson's subpar skills, but I'm here now."

He brings his head down and nuzzles his face into my neck, breathing deeply. God, he feels good in my arms. Heat flashes through my body, and a pulse begins between my legs. These feelings seem too intense to have in such a short time, and I feel the need to try to downplay this as much as possible.

"Let's see where everyone has gotten off to."

We make our way over to the fire. The scent of wood burning and the bonfire's heat permeates the air. Our fingers stay intertwined as we walk as if it's the most natural thing in the world. I can see Emma up ahead, and I lead him toward her. All our friends are getting together closer to the fire. I feel a wave of nostalgia, bringing me back to the time when things were different—simpler, when we were all younger and had our entire future ahead of us. There were frequent parties and friends to keep us busy. It all seems like a lifetime ago. We were all happy and together. I love these guys. We have been friends for a long time. Most of my life, really.

I see Zach and the rest of our friends gather around, and he takes out his guitar. He starts to play and belts out a Guns and Roses song. "Used to Love Her" starts playing, and everyone joins in singing. This is what we do—we hang out, play music, drink, and just enjoy being with each other alongside a roaring fire.

Everyone is drinking and enjoying themselves. I catch Brodie off by the water, chatting animatedly with his buddies. He seems okay, and that takes a huge weight off my shoulders. A weight I didn't know that I was carrying.

The night progresses, and the music and drinks continue to flow. Dax has been by my side all night, and I do not hate it. I'm having a perfect time with him. I look off in the distance toward the sand dunes and see two figures emerging.

"Is that E-emma?" I stutter, totally confused. "What the fuck? And is that Jameson?" I stand and point in their direction.

"Well, isn't that interesting." Dax smirks over at his friend. "They're coming this way and trying to be discreet." He chuckles.

I grab onto Dax, pushing his face in their direction. Little do they know that I spotted them, and there will be many questions later. They finally make their way back to the group, and the party continues. I feel free for the first time all day and enjoy the company, knowing that this might be the last time we all get together.

With all the festivities going on, my thoughts continue to go back to Dax and how it's so easy and natural to be with him. I suddenly realize that I haven't had this much fun in a very long time.

Brodie returns to the group, swaying as he walks, clearly drunk. I can't say that I feel sorry for him. He needs to take responsibility for his actions and grow the fuck up.

Brodie grabs a bodyboard lying on the ground and runs sloppily toward the water. He is very athletic and has been in tip-top shape throughout high school. He does a front flip and lands on the board, and our group of friends hoots and whistles. I shake my head and laugh. He is always the center of attention.

He sees me watching, and his laughter stops. His eyes search mine for a moment, and I think he might come over, but then he thinks better of it.

Dax sees the interaction and pulls me in. I don't hesitate and lean in to absorb the warmth that he offers. He feels my body relax next to his and draws me in farther. I couldn't resist the pull if I tried. He leads me over to the side, and we discuss plans for the near future. He tells me about his fellowship, and I tell him about my plan to move this summer.

"Emma and Jameson looked pretty close, don't you think?" He laughs, and his eyes spark with mischief.

"Why do you say that?" I shake my head and look up.

"Well, if you saw how they looked after returning from the sand dunes..." He trails off and shrugs. "Maybe he was just escorting her back from the Porta Potty. You never know," Dax quickly interjects.

"Nope, I saw the guilty walk of shame from the sand dunes while trying to maintain that look of innocence plastered all over her face."

Dax gives me one of his panty-dropping smiles. "Well, I'll be damned. I guess he couldn't resist. That seems to be the theme, doesn't it, Liv?"

I place my hand on his chest and look into his eyes while playfully batting my eyelashes. "Why, whatever do you mean, Dax?"

"Oh, nothing, babe. it's just that you ladies seem to be ruining us for every other female," he says jokingly. But I can see the truth in his eyes.

His mouth is inches from mine, and I can feel his breath on my lips. He leans in to close the gap between us. His lips ghost over mine, causing a tingling feeling over my lips. His tongue swipes over my lower lip, and I allow him entry. He deepens the kiss, and my whole body is lit on fire.

I go to grab onto his neck but find myself threading my hands through his hair. His hands are spread across my lower back, pushing me against his hard-toned body. He breaks away quickly, and his eyes widen. That's when I hear it—a scream that makes us freeze. Broken from our trance, we turn toward the bonfire where the noise seems to be coming from.

"Help! Someone help!" a person shrieks.

We both take off for the shore, sprinting toward our friends. As we get closer, my heart hammers as I take in the scene before me. What we find makes us want to go back in time at least a few minutes to when our kiss held the possibility of everything.

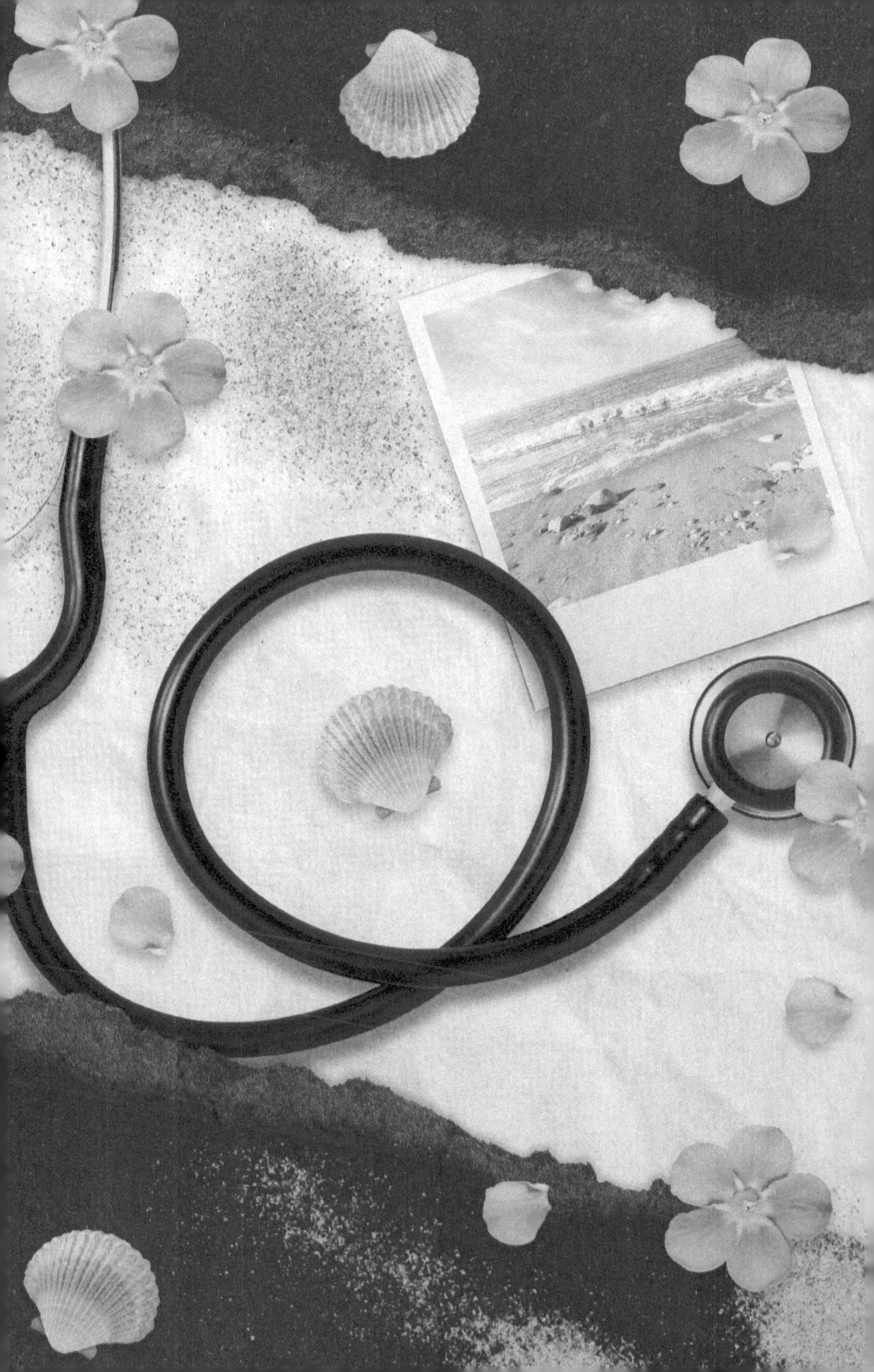

CHAPTER EIGHT

DAX

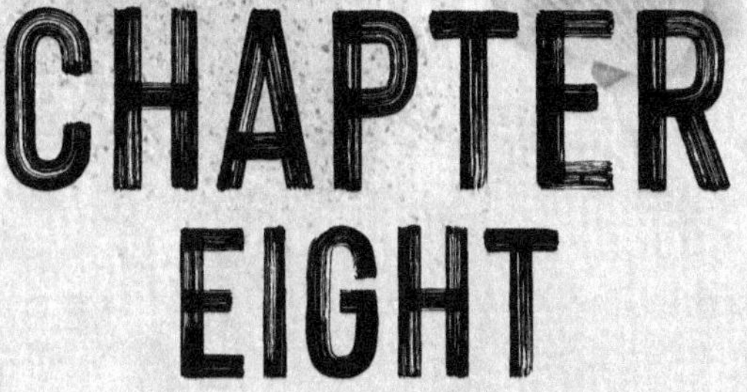

Liv's hand tenses in mine as we run to the scream's source. My heart hammers in my chest, and I can hear Liv's breath coming in frantic gasps. Skidding to a stop, a horrific scene awaits us.

I first notice Brodie lying in the wet sand. My eyes dart around the scene, instinct from medical training taking over. I look for signs of obvious trauma, but the one thing that stands out above all others is that Brodie is entirely still, his body sprawled out on the wet sand, limp and unconscious.

A small cry leaves Liv's lips, and she slaps a hand over her mouth. The look of shock and disbelief is written all over her face. I drop her hand and run over to Brodie, placing my fingers on his neck to check for a pulse. A tiny bit of tension leaves my body when I feel a steady, thrumming pulse under my fingers and I see his chest rise to let me know he's breathing.

"Brodie, can you hear me," I shout. "Did anyone call 9-1-1?" I keep my eyes trained on Brodie while Liv, Emma, and Jameson come over to help.

"Do you need help moving him?" Jameson asks as he crouches down beside me.

"N-no!" I stammer out a little too forcefully. "No one moves him. He could have a neck injury. We need to know what happened."

"I saw the whole thing," I hear a voice from the crowd. "Brodie was doing front flips on the bodyboard. He went to do another, but he slipped on the board. Bro, he landed on his neck and then just went limp." He stutters, "I-it didn't look good, man."

My body has gone on autopilot, my training taking over like a well-oiled machine. I shift myself over Brodie's head and place my hands on either side of his neck to hold it steady. A small groan escapes Brodie's lips, and I wonder if he's in pain.

"What's the ETA of the ambulance?" I bark out.

Ainsley says, "I called as soon as it happened, I don't know, like ten minutes ago."

Just as she says it, I hear the faint sound of sirens in the background. As I look up, I see the flashing lights heading down to the sand.

Thankfully, with all the traffic today on the beach, the sand is packed down pretty well. The less trouble the ambulance has to get here, the better. I try to wake Brodie again, but he still doesn't respond. The ambulance comes into view, accompanied by the police.

Paramedics jump out and race toward us with the backboard. They swing into action, placing a neck collar on and then gently moving him to the board and onto the stretcher. As they make their way to the ambulance, the police ask the crowd if they witnessed the accident, but everything starts to fade away as I look at Liv.

Her face is pale, and silent tears stream down her cheeks. Her arms are crossed over her chest as if to keep herself warm, but I can see her body visibly shaking from shock. Within two strides, I'm by her side.

"Liv, are you okay?'"

She doesn't answer. Her eyes are fixed on the sand where Brodie's body was lying just seconds ago.

I step in front of her and grab her shoulders to try again. "Liv, talk to me."

Still, I get nothing. I gently raise my hand to her chin and tilt her face up so I can look into her eyes.

"Liv, are you okay, baby?" I repeat.

The anguish in her eyes is there, but also something else. She goes to open her mouth to say something, but words escape her.

"Talk to me, Liv."

Her eyes meet mine, and the pain I see in them almost brings me to my knees. "It is all my fault," she whispers in a breath, dropping her gaze down to her feet.

I wrap my arms around her, holding her tight against my chest. "What? No, Liv. This is not your fault. You had nothing to do with this."

Her body trembles in my arms, and I realize she's crying. "Didn't I, though?" she mumbles into my chest. "He was upset because I called things off, and he started drinking. I know he has poor coping skills and uses substances to cope." The words come out garbled as she sobs, burying her face into my shirt. "I should have stopped him. I should have been a better friend to him, despite what he did. Now it all seems stupid in comparison."

"Look, Liv, this isn't your fault, he made a bad choice, and it was a terrible accident. Maybe we should go to the hospital."

My words seem to snap her out of it because she takes a quick step away from me, eyes now wild with concern. "Yes. I need to call my mom to see if she heard anything about Brodie coming in."

She starts to jog back up to where our stuff was, and I do my best to keep up with her.

"Okay, let me find the guys, and we'll take you."

I split from her to gather my friends and, thankfully, find them all at the truck. Everything is packed up and ready to go.

"Hey, guys, we need to give Liv a ride to the hospital."

"Of course," Jameson replies, jumping into the driver's seat and turning on the truck. "We'll wait here for you."

My brain is spinning as I head back to get Liv. As an orthopedic trauma surgeon in training, I've seen unfortunate injuries like this all too often. My brain is anticipating the worst, but I'm hoping I'm wrong for Liv's sake. I find Liv frantically stuffing her things into her bag.

"Ready when you are, Liv." She gives me a quick nod as she throws her bag over her shoulder and walks to her friends. I hear her tell them she's heading to the hospital and they can meet her there.

"Don't worry about the stuff," I hear Emma say, "the guys will get it loaded up, and they will meet us there too." The girls exchange a few hugs, and I can see tears brimming on all of their eyes.

"Ready?" I say tentatively behind Liv.

She turns and says nothing but grabs my hand tightly, and our fingers link together. Her grip on my hand doesn't falter as we walk toward the truck.

I sit Liv in the back seat of the truck and slide right next to her. Theo and Eric are already in the front, and Jameson gets in last on the other side of Liv.

"Liv, what hospital would they be taking him to? I need to plug in my GPS to get there," Theo asks as he searches for the closest hospitals.

"Bayside Hospital," she says quickly. She stares straight ahead, but her hand stays locked in mine, knuckles white from how hard she's holding on to me. I rub my thumb along the back of her hand, hoping it will calm her nerves even a little bit.

I put my other hand on her thigh and give it a slight squeeze. She shivers.

"Are you cold? I have a long-sleeve T-shirt in my bag."

"I'm not cold," she replies.

Although it was only three words, I'm glad she finally said something. She looks at me and leans closer. I can see little bumps start to form on her arm.

"You have goose bumps all over."

"Yeah, but I don't feel cold."

Another shiver seems to run through her, and I just continue to hold on to her.

"Don't worry. We are almost there." Jameson looks at the GPS. "We should be there in less than ten minutes, Liv."

"Thank you," she says so softly I almost don't hear it.

Liv's phone pings with a text message, and she grabs it from her bag to look at it. "It's my mom. She said that there was a trauma activation called, and they're ready in the OR should he be taken in for surgery." A pause. "She didn't realize it was Brodie," she chokes out.

"In most traumas, they don't immediately know names, just the condition of the patient," I say, even though, as an ER nurse, she likely already knows this. I grab her tighter. "Hang on, Liv. We are almost there."

Theo turns, and we're heading toward the ER parking lot. He swings into a parking spot, and we jump out.

Liv starts running, and we follow behind.

"I'll meet you guys inside," I call after them.

Although my ankle improved earlier, the adrenaline rush from the last hour is running out, and my ankle begins to throb. I get to the doors slowly and walk inside. Liv is by the nurse's station, talking to someone she seems familiar with. I walk up, and she turns to me. Her eyes are still blank but filled with tears as before.

"They're evaluating him in one of the trauma rooms. He'll head down to get a CT scan soon. They can't give us any more than that because of patient confidentiality."

I kind of figured that out, but I just nod. "Let's find a place to sit and wait. Are his parents on their way?"

"I...I have no idea." She gets a little frantic and grabs her phone to call them just as a woman in her early fifties runs to the desk asking about Brodie.

Liv gets up quickly and runs over to her. I see them embrace, and she looks toward the waiting area straight at me. She turns straight back to Liv, and they continue talking.

My friends make it over to me and find seats as the waiting room quickly starts to fill up with family and friends waiting on any news about Brodie.

Liv walks back over to me and is joined by Ainsley, Val, and Emma. The girls embrace as they walk, doing their best to offer support. Brodie's friends are here too. Everyone looks grim and anxious to get an update.

The time ticks by, and after what feels like forever, the ER doctor and surgeon come out to speak with Brodie's mother. Liv tenses next to me. She doesn't stand to go with them but sits frozen, eyes locked on the conversation. I struggle to listen to the chit-chat around me. I don't know Brodie and don't want to eavesdrop, but for Liv's sake, I want to know what's going on.

I hear them explain the emergency surgery he needs and its risks. Brodie's mother sobs, her body shaking with each breath she takes. A family member guides her from the room. A nurse soon returns, advising us to go to the second-floor surgical waiting area.

Part of me feels like I should leave. I barely know Liv, and I certainly don't know Brodie. But it's physically painful to think of leaving her. I couldn't walk away right now if I tried.

The next couple of hours pass in a haze. Everyone is emotionally and physically exhausted. Every once in a while, I hear a hushed murmur or someone stands to stretch, but otherwise, the room is quiet.

The silence is broken when a tall man about the same age as Brodie's mom runs over agitatedly. He wants to know exactly what's happening and who is taking care of his son. He causes quite a commotion as we all sit there watching this transpire.

Liv looks at me and whispers, "His dad is remarried and lives in Houston. He's a neurosurgeon and quite full of himself."

I nod in response, thinking, hopefully, this is the change we need to hear some news soon.

After another painfully long hour, a man wearing blue scrubs accompanied by a female in similar attire exits the operating room doors and asks for the family of Brodie. It's as if time stands still. You could hear a pin drop as Brodie's parents stand and walk toward them. Their hushed voices are too faint to make out. But everyone's gaze is laser-focused on the conversation happening in the room.

The surgeon speaks, and almost immediately, his mom raises her hands to her mouth, and a sob escapes before she cries out, almost crumbling to the floor. His dad shakes his head as if he didn't hear something right, and then he begins asking spitfire questions, not allowing a moment's pause for an answer.

The surgeon listens patiently and offers a few answers. His dad puts his hands up to his eyes and lowers his head. The surgeon touches his shoulder and says something to them before walking toward our group. As he gets closer, Liv pulls her hand from me and stands.

The surgeon stops at our group and says, "Is there a Liv here?"

I look at Liv as she stares at him, stunned and unable to speak. I give her a gentle nudge from the side.

The surgeon begins to speak, "Brodie is awake and is asking for you specifically. He wants to see you."

Liv gasps, and I let a breath out that I didn't realize I was holding in. I bring Liv's hand to my lips and place a gentle kiss on it. She squeezes my hand quickly and looks down at me. Her eyes are red, and tears are about to fall.

"I have to go," she breathes.

I release her hand, and she steps away from me. Without saying the words, we both know this is goodbye. I see her slowly walk away, following the doctor. She falters when she gets to the door, and I almost think she's going to stop. But she just straightens her shoulders and continues.

I guess this truly is goodbye, at least for now.

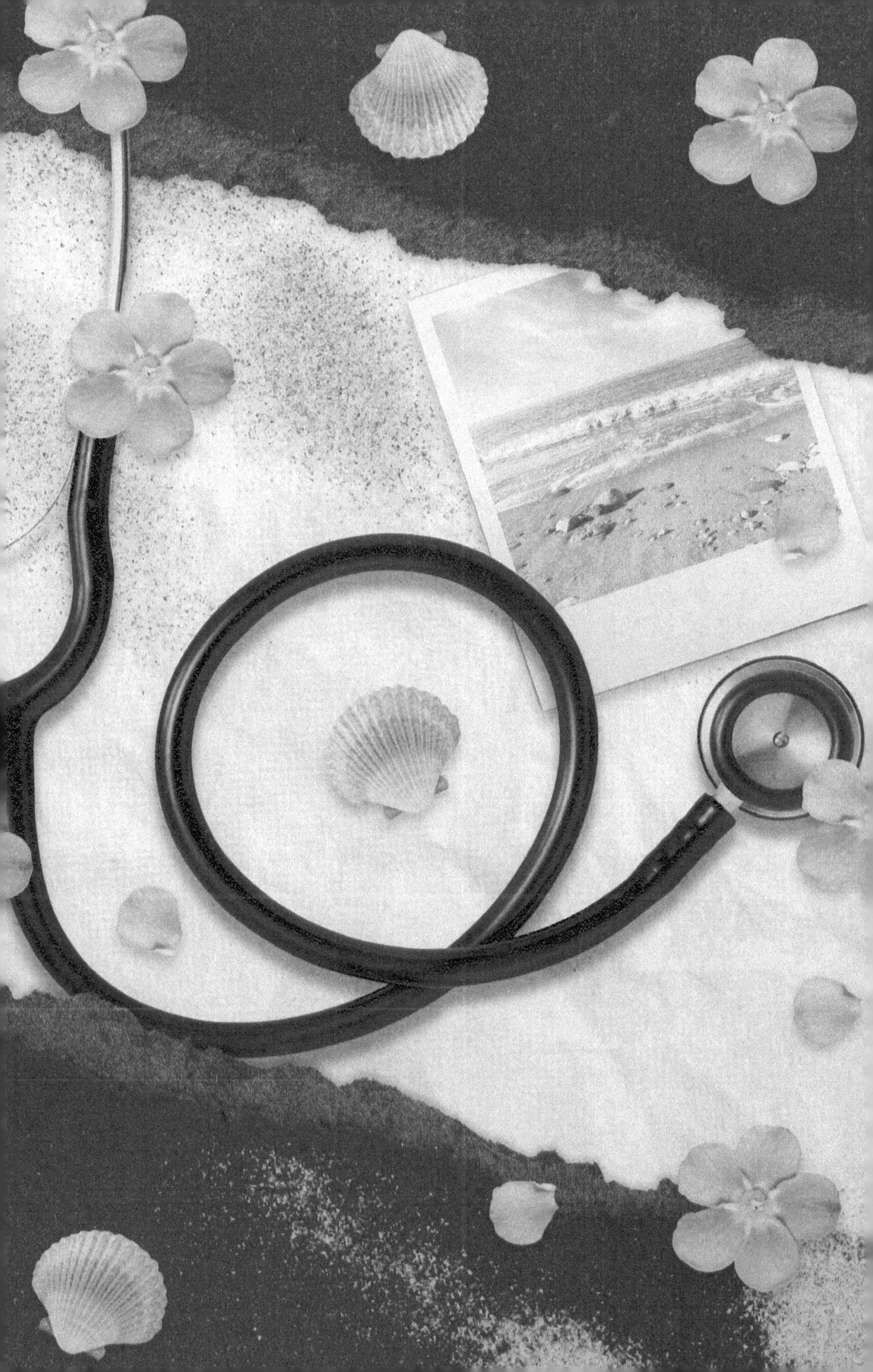

CHAPTER NINE

LIV

They say that if you love something, you should set it free. As I stand to follow the surgeon that leads me away from Dax, this is the phrase that runs through my mind. I think about all the possibilities that could have been. Is what I'm feeling for him love? It's only been a couple of days. How could that be possible? But I know I haven't felt this way before about anyone. The feelings we shared in that short time were electric.

A wave of shame washes over me as I realize I have never had feelings like this with Brodie.

We were friends for so long that our romantic relationship fell into place. More out of convenience than because of love. As I amble behind the doctor, our relationship flashes before me, and the truth of it all stares me in the face. He was a good friend, but the spark was missing—the ovary-flipping, skin-tingling, panty-twisting lust that I naturally have with Dax. The man I apparently just set free.

When did I become Brodie's crutch? His enabler. Someone who was there for him when he fell into self-destructive behaviors. Like now. But how can I walk away? The guilt would wreck me. It's wrecking me now.

I follow the doctor down a long hallway, and he pauses in front of the door.

"He asked for you as soon as he woke up from surgery. I'm not sure how much he remembers from what we told him. It's going to take a while for him to come to terms with the fact that he is now paralyzed."

Paralyzed. The word shocks me to my core. The world seems to stop as the meaning of what he just said sinks in.

"He's paralyzed?" I hear my trembling voice say.

"Yes, I'm so sorry. We can talk more about what this means for him tomorrow. I know he just wants to see you. I'll give you both a minute."

He turns and walks off to the nurse's station, leaving me alone in the hallway. I close my eyes and take a deep breath before putting my hand on the cold door and pushing it slowly open.

The dim overhead lights glow from behind his bed, casting a little light over his still body. Endless wires and tubes run from under his sheets, and the only sound I hear is a steady "beep" from the machine next to him. His skin is pale, and his eyes are closed.

My heart beats faster as I stare at my past lying motionless in front of me. The door clicks shut behind me, and I flinch, scared I'll wake him, but he doesn't move. Slowly, I walk into the room and pause at the side of his bed.

I watch his chest rise and fall, unsure of what to do or say. Tentatively, I reach out and thread my hand through his. The moment I touch him, his eyes fly open and meet mine. But the rest of his body remains still.

"Liv," he whispers. "You're here."

"I'm here, Brodie. I'm here."

Tears begin to fall down my cheeks as his eyes close again and he falls back asleep. He is in and out of sleep for the rest of the night, and I stay by his side. When he wakes up and they tell him again of his paralysis, he yells while simultaneously crying. I hold his hand through it all, praying I can do something to take his pain away. We did this for each other during every other hardship in our lives. I can't leave him now.

The weeks that follow are a blur. I force Dax out of my mind and continue to work at the hospital, relying on routine tasks to get me through each day. And I manage to finish school, although each class, each homework assignment, and each test feel like I was in a haze.

Throughout it all, if I wasn't at work or school, I was at the hospital helping with Brodie's rehabilitation. While everyone else returned to their everyday life, mine has been thrown entirely upside down. The visits from friends to see Brodie decreased, and phone calls and care packages stopped coming. But I stayed. As always, I remain the only constant in his life.

At the end of most days, I lay in bed and cry. How did we get here? Why did this happen? My thoughts are plagued with "what ifs." Our spring break was supposed to be about clarifying our relationship or breaking up. Not ending as me being a caregiver for my now paralyzed, cheating, sort-of boyfriend. Everything changed in the blink of an eye.

Most nights, I dream of Dax. Of his brilliant smile. Of the way his hand felt in mine and the way his skin smelled. And how my name sounded coming from his lips. But I wake in the morning plagued with guilt. How can I be thinking of Dax when Brodie is going through so much? So I continue pushing Dax out of my mind and robotically moving throughout the day.

It's been eight weeks since the accident. The surgery helped to alleviate the spinal cord compression, but the damage is done. Brodie's injury cannot be helped any further. *He's paralyzed.* The surgeon's words still haunt me.

In the days following his surgery, we learned he had suffered an incomplete spinal cord injury, leaving him with limited use of his arms and no use of his legs. Rehab has helped him with some arm movement, but simple things like feeding himself are still a struggle.

I was there every day as he tried again and again to do simple tasks. Some days he seems like he's making progress and others, he doesn't even want to try. Now that inpatient rehab is ending, he is being transferred to his father's house today in Houston for more recovery and in-home care with a private provider.

Graduation was last week. I didn't go. It came and went without much excitement. My family and friends tried their best to get me to participate, but I couldn't even bring myself to care. I'd rather just start the move to Houston and prepare for a temporary travel assignment in the downtown area before I start my future graduate school.

A knock jolts me from my thoughts. "Coming," I blurt out as I head for the door.

I quickly check the peephole and notice it is dark outside. Where did the time go? I see Emma standing there with her phone in one hand and a coffee in the other. I undo the chain at the top of the door and the deadbolt lock to let her in.

"Hey you."

She rushes in and attacks me with a hug. "Hey, girl. How are you?" Breaking the hug, she walks into my apartment without turning around. "Just thought I'd come to check on you after I got out of work," she says over her shoulder.

"Thanks for thinking of me," I reply, following along after her. She pulls my hand and sits down with me at the kitchen table. "Did Brodie make it to Houston okay?"

I go to the breakfast nook and retrieve the glass of wine I had been drinking before she stopped by.

"Not sure. I assume he is all settled in. Do you want a glass?" I lift my glass up, drain the rest, and pour myself another.

Emma looks at me with concern. "Have you heard from Dax?"

I stop mid-pour at hearing his name–a name I have tried to forget so the thoughts of him lessen in my mind. I finish pouring her a glass and hand it to her, not caring that she never said yes when I asked or that she's currently drinking coffee.

"Not since the last text message he sent me about a month ago."

Dax had sent me a text message the week after the accident. ***I am thinking about you.*** Only a few words, but I read and reread them a thousand times. And a thousand more times, I attempted to write back. I tried to formulate the words to express everything I was going through but came up blank. When I didn't respond, days turned into weeks, and I just couldn't answer him back. Despite what I feel about Dax, I keep replaying the weekend in my mind and can't seem to shake the idea that if Dax hadn't been there, then Brodie wouldn't have been drinking so much, and the accident wouldn't have happened.

Is it displacing the blame? Yes. Do I still long to feel Dax's body against mine again? Hell yes. But I block it out because the guilt is all-consuming. I close my eyes and again see Brodie's body in the wet sand, unconscious, and I ache. I go to lift my hand and begin to rub my chest. The ache is so intense that I can't make it stop.

Emma notices this, looks at me with sympathetic eyes, and shakes her head in understanding. "Liv, you know this isn't yours or Dax's fault, right? He made those choices—to cheat on you, to get drunk, and to flip drunk when he knew he shouldn't. You can't blame yourself for another person's bad choices. I won't let you."

Emma says everything I already know, but why does it hurt so bad? We move to the living room and chat for a while.

"How's the packing going?" she asks.

"Slow," I say as I move to get up and get another box to continue the monotonous process.

Before I can ask her to help, she blurts out, "How would you like a roommate in Houston?"

My eyes widen in shock, and my mouth drops open. "What?" I stammer.

"You heard me. I was thinking about taking a travel assignment. I figured now would be as good a time as any. And then we could stay together."

I can feel my face light up with excitement as tears brim my eyes. "I would love that."

"Good," she says as she brings me in for another hug. "I called the recruiter for the travel agency in Houston and gave my two-week notice at the hospital today."

I look at my friend, dumbfounded. "Are you sure, Emma?" I have to ask because I don't want her to uproot her life because of me.

She hesitates momentarily. "I have overstayed my welcome here anyway." She laughs. "I was getting too comfortable." She waves her hand dismissively and purses her lips.

I don't really understand her remark and wait for her to explain further, but it doesn't come. Maybe it's selfish, but at this moment, I finally feel some happiness come back into my life. Her support means everything to me, more than she will ever know. I won't be braving the city alone and will have someone to share the rent with. My mind starts to spin with possibilities.

"I'll call my job placement and make sure they can secure a place with two bedrooms. It shouldn't be a problem, and it will allow us to look for a place we can both like living in once we get there."

We say our goodbyes and promise to chat later.

I pack up more things and come across an old photo album. I pick up Emma's wine glass and pour what's left into my glass. I grab the album and plop down on the couch, abandoning my packing. I look at the cover but already know what I will find when I open it up.

Brodie made me a scrapbook a couple of years ago with memories of all of us together through the years. Being a phenomenal artist, the scrapbook is a work of art. Each page is decorated and filled with graffiti, along with pictures. The title of the book, *Waves of you,* is brilliantly painted across the front with a tumbling wave at the bottom. My fingers trace the outline of the words before I open them up.

The memories come flooding back as soon as I see the first picture. Us as kids, times we played in the sand, field trips where I was feeding a seagull part of my sandwich, and a picture of Brodie super pissed off because the seagulls fighting for morsels of said sandwich flew above us and pooped on his jacket.

I laugh to myself as I remember that day. He threw his coat off and wouldn't talk to me for the rest of the trip. As pissed as he was, I couldn't help laughing the entire ride home. By the time we returned to my house, he was laughing too. Our giggles became infectious to each other.

My hand automatically comes up to my chest. I am rubbing at the same spot over my heart where I've had so much pain over the past couple of months. I continue to flip through the pages and am flooded with memories that led us both here.

I get up from the floor and go to wash my face, needing to wash away the tears I didn't realize were falling as I leave the bathroom. A text message alert pings through my phone. I grab my phone off the kitchen counter and almost drop it when I see Dax's name on the screen. With shaking hands, I place it up to my face to unlock the screen and prepare myself for what he could say to me. A million thoughts barrel through my mind. I haven't heard from him in over a month, but I still think about him daily.

I click on the message, and it's a link to Chris Isaak's "Wicked Game" song we were listening to on the beach before the accident. When the possibility of there being an "us" was still there. The link underneath the music is the same message he texted me the first time. ***Thinking about you.***

I'm speechless. My legs go weak, and I drop onto the couch, staring at the screen. What should I say? How can I explain what these past couple of months have been like for me?

Coming up blank and needing to calm down, I head to the bathroom to shower. Turning on the water, I undress and look at myself in the mirror. Staring back at me is a face I barely recognize—the hollowness in my cheeks, dark circles under my eyes, and a frown on my mouth. The reflection of guilt disappears as the mirror fogs and the billowing steam rises from the shower jets.

I hit play on the surround speaker, and the bathroom fills with the voice singing about lost love. I place my head in my hands and cry. I cry for the guilt I am overcome with. I cry for a love lost. And I cry for how the waves of you have now ceased to exist.

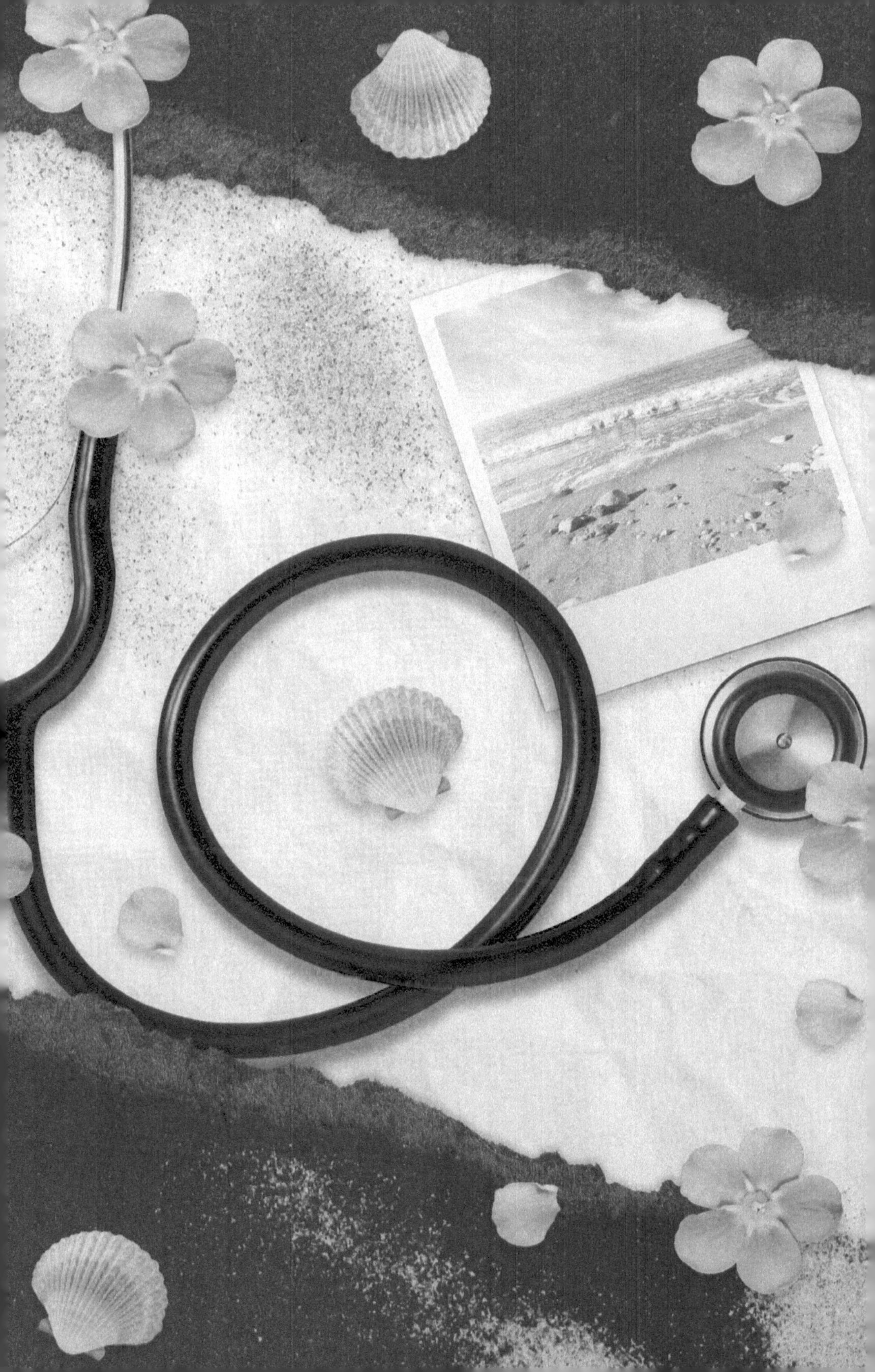

CHAPTER TEN

DAX

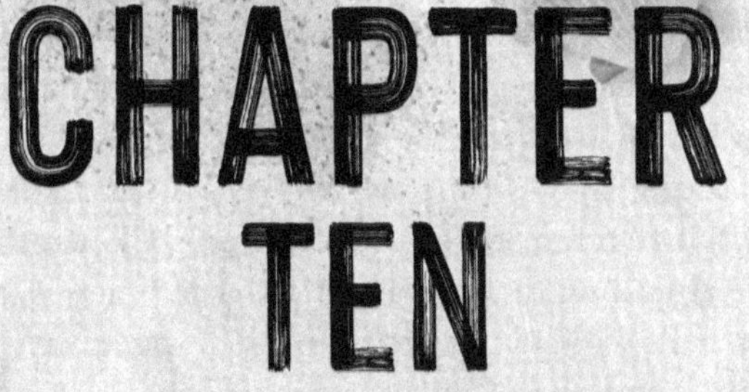

I look down at my phone and instantly frown. The messages I sent to Liv have gone through, but I'm still waiting for a response.

"Great," I mutter to myself.

I toss the phone on my desk and slump back into my chair. At some point, I will have to accept that she isn't going to answer me back. Maybe I was wrong and she didn't feel the same way I did. It must have been all one-sided. But I can't help remembering the exaggerated way our bodies instinctively pulled toward each other.

Sighing again, I slink farther into my chair and feel the sting of rejection and defeat wash over my tired body. A ping from my phone stops my rambling thoughts. A glimmer of hope crosses my mind for a split second. *Please, let that be her,* I pray silently.

Instead, I see a text from Tatiana. I exhale gruffly in irritation and begrudgingly open the message. ***Are you coming over later?***

I take a minute to think of a response. Do I want to go over? Or would I rather sit here in self-pity? I take a deep breath and decide I need to move on. I need to get Liv out of my mind.

Sure, I respond. I see the three dots appear and then disappear.

Another message comes up. ***Looking forward to it.***

I drag myself to the kitchen, grab a beer, and crack it open while I start to get ready for the night and what's ahead.

Tatiana Belov is as true to her name as possible. She is a Russian beauty with ultra-blond hair and signature red lipstick that matches the red-sole shoes she often wears. She is sex personified. She carries herself on a lean, toned frame with long legs that are sinful to anyone who watches her glide through the hospital halls. For some reason, I caught her eye, and she often seeks me out in the halls during the day or at work functions.

We met at the hospital while we were both in residency. She chose anesthesiology, so we often worked together in the operating room. She is now a full-time attending in a private anesthesia practice, and I decided to do a fellowship. Following in my dad's footsteps was always the plan for me. I idolized the man, and one of my most significant life accomplishments is that I will soon be done and become a partner in his practice.

As I drive to her ultra-modern townhome in the uptown Houston area, my brain ping-pongs back and forth between Liv and Tatiana. The hold Liv had on me after only a few days still feels surreal. I can still feel her hand in mine and remember how her hair smelled when she was near. I memorized the curves of her body, and on more nights than I can count, I've thought of her as I found release alone in my bed.

A car pulls out in front of me, cutting me off and returning me to reality. Three thoughts come to me clearly: Liv is gone. Probably moved on. I need to as well.

I repeat this new mantra to convince me further as I pull up to Tatiana's residence. I grab the bottle of wine I bought before getting out of my ride and heading to the door. Before I even get there, she opens the door casually but oh so seductively leans on the doorframe. She looks me up and down as I walk up the stairs toward her.

"Hey, handsome," she purrs, pulling me in by my collar and kissing me.

Her kiss is soft at first. Her lips graze mine before she pulls me closer and separates my lips with her tongue. I try to drop my keys and phone on the table inside the door but miss miserably, and I vaguely hear the clatter as they hit the tile floor.

My arms circle her waist, and I lift her up, pressing her breasts against my chest. Her long legs instinctively wrap around my waist, and I kick the door closed with my foot. *This is what I need,* I find myself thinking. A distraction. A physical, lust-filled distraction.

My hands drop from her waist to her perfectly round ass, and I move like a man on a mission toward the couch. I stalk through the living room until my knees hit the couch and throw her down roughly.

A breath of air leaves her mouth as she lands on her back before seductively biting her lower lip and opening her legs. Her tongue darts out to swipe over her bottom lip while devouring me with her eyes.

I take a step back to catch my breath and focus. Images of Liv pop into my mind, and I fight them back, despite wishing more than anything that it is her writhing in front of me, not Tatiana.

"Come here," she drawls in her sexy Russian accent, and my mind reverts to the present.

It's only then that I really look at her. Thin red straps run over her shoulders, and as my eyes move down, I see the lacy red fabric of the teddy that barely covers the rest of her body. It's thin over her round tits, allowing the pale-pink nipples underneath to show through.

As her legs part, I notice the material parts right over her pelvis, the lace gone from over her most private area, revealing exposed, pink, glistening skin. My hands move of their own accord, unbuckling my pants quickly as a primal hunger takes over. My pants drop, and the belt buckle echoes loudly through the room as it bounces off the travertine tile. I stand above her in my underwear with my aching cock tenting the cotton barrier. She notices and licks her lips quickly, sitting up and crawling toward me.

"You want me to help with that?" she says, barely above a whisper.

I reach for my cock and take it out. "Yes," is all I can grunt out as she reaches out and takes me in her hand.

I hiss when her skin meets my engorged flesh, and my breathing picks up. I look down as her head moves closer to me; all I can see is the back of her blond hair. As soon as her soft wet lips meet the head of my cock, I gasp, the moist heat of her mouth making my thoughts scatter.

"Take it all," I growl, curling my fingers into her hair and pushing myself deeper into her throat.

She murmurs something around my cock, but all I feel is the vibration in her throat that sends me close to my undoing. I thrust in and out, fucking her mouth and relishing how it feels around me. I hear her gag and can see saliva dripping out of the corner of her mouth, but that doesn't deter me from the easy, forceful way she allows me to pump in and out.

I close my eyes and let my head fall back. Liv's face is there as soon as blackness falls across my eyelids. Liv's mouth is on my cock. It's her that's circling my head with her tongue. When I feel the tightening of my balls and the tingling at the base of my spine, letting me know that I am starting to come, I hear a ping of my cell phone. I ignore it, fist her hair tighter, and continue.

"I'm coming," I moan, giving her no time to pull back, and shoot my load down the back of her throat, forcing her to swallow.

I watch her as she cleans me, licking up every drop of my release. I reach over her, take the drop running down her chin, and coat her lips with it. She licks her lips afterward as if savoring the taste of my cum.

She returns to the couch, and I turn away to get my phone. My body is relaxed, and as I look over my shoulder, I see an over-eager Tatiana waiting to be fucked in her crotchless teddy.

I grab my phone from the floor and flip to my messages. The breath leaves my lungs in a whoosh as I see a name I didn't plan to see—Liv. I quickly pull up my boxers and fumble with shaky fingers to click the message open.

"Come back, Dax. I need you," I hear Tatiana beg, but her voice is barely audible over the beating of my heart in my ears.

I open the message and read her response. ***I am always thinking of you.***

I freeze. A million thoughts cross my brain. *Is she thinking of me? Should I respond? What should I say?* A whimper behind me makes me turn my head, and I stumble back and look at Tatiana. She must see the shock on my face because she stands up and walks over.

"Is something wrong?" she asks, but I put my hand up to stop her.

"No. Nothing is wrong. It's nothing," I say as I walk to get my pants and begin pulling them back on.

"You look like you've seen a ghost. I can take your mind off it," she says while trailing a finger up my arm. I shake her off and tuck in my shirt.

Her lust-filled eyes immediately darken, and suspicion crosses her face. She looks confused and hurt but isn't sure what to make of the situation. If she only knew how I felt about hearing back from Liv. Liv, the ghost of my not-too-distant past, present, and hopefully future. I button up my jeans and look at her.

"I should…I should probably get going," I manage to get out.

She takes a step toward me now with apparent anger on her face, quickly replacing her concern. "You have got to be fucking kidding me right now."

I can't even look at her. "No, I have to go."

"Does this have anything to do with the text you just got?" She throws her shoulders back and crosses her arms over her chest, clearly annoyed. Her head tilts as she sees the guilt in my eyes. I have no idea how to respond, and my brain can't think of a reasonable thing to say.

Ultimately, I go for honesty and just reply, "Yes." A one-word answer without further explanations.

"That's it?! That's all you have to say?" Her voice rises in octaves. "You aren't even going to explain?"

I go to the door and grab my wallet and keys from the floor. "I'm sorry. Maybe we can talk later, but I have to go now."

I feel the door slam at my back before I even make it to the first step. I know that was a total dick move to make, but my head isn't in the right place right now. What the hell did Liv mean by that? I have been given the biggest head fuck of my life. No response from her at all, and then, BAM, she hits me with that.

My head wants to be frustrated, but I feel like my heart is dangling on a string, and Liv is holding the other end. My history with women is by no means a secret. I'm a good-looking guy and a surgeon at that. I get fucked on the regular, but I've never had a connection with any woman as I did with Liv. She has a hold on me I just can't explain.

I get into my car and pull away, throwing music on the radio to help calm my thoughts. I need to get home and take a cold shower. I'll also need to apologize to Tatiana at some point, but not tonight. I'll let her cool off. We have to work together; unfortunately, that is one of the hassles of shitting where you eat. It was unavoidable. I'll have to see her tomorrow at some point. Tatiana is by no means exclusive with me. I've dated other girls, and she knows that.

Does she date other guys? I wonder. Throwing that hypothetical situation in my mind, I think of how I would feel if another guy put his dick in Tatiana. My immediate reaction: I wouldn't care. I wouldn't be jealous at all. I never staked a claim to her or said we were exclusive. We had never even discussed a relationship before. I always figured it was just casual sex between two consenting adults. She must feel that way, too, right? A nagging feeling in my gut tells me she probably doesn't.

"What the hell did I get myself into?" I mutter as I pull onto the highway and head for home.

My mind drifts back to Liv, and I think of her being with someone else, and my blood boils. Immediate fury and panic set in, and I clench and unclench my fists on the steering wheel as I drive. I try to get that thought out of my head. I feel like throwing up when I think of her sucking another guy off, and a murderous rage rushes through me. What the actual fuck is this about? Why has this girl got me in such a head spin? I have a gorgeous woman throwing herself at me who gives a decent blow job, and I leave a guaranteed fuck because of a few words responded back from a text message. I hit the steering wheel with a pounding smack.

"Dammit." I need to go home and clear my head of this girl.

I finally reach my apartment, throw the car in park in the garage parking, and head inside. Throwing my keys on the foyer table, I head to the decanter and pour myself two fingers of whiskey. I swallow them back in one go and set the glass back on the table.

I head to my bedroom and begin to undress as I head to the bathroom. I can smell Tatiana's perfume lingering on my clothes, and I need to get rid of that fast. It's nauseatingly floral, and I need to rid myself of it before it makes me sick. I would generally like the smell of my conquests on me for the night, but now the scent is suffocating. I toss the clothes in the hamper and throw the water on in the shower. The steam and mist settle around me as I stare at myself in the mirror.

"Get a hold of yourself," I say to the somber person looking back at me.

Stepping into the water, I let it hit me in the face and rain down over my body. The pulsing spray is soothing, and I begin to feel more awake and a little more like myself. I adjust the showerhead to a different massage setting and let it hit my body.

Thoughts of Liv go through my mind, and I remember sitting next to her on the beach. Her hair flowed in the breeze, and we talked for hours. We held hands like teenagers, and I soaked up every minute we were close to each other. I looked at her as if I just couldn't get enough.

Those images go through my mind as I start to stroke my cock. I soap up, allowing my hands to rub smoothly from base to head. It's slippery and warm, and I imagine I'm between Liv's legs and not alone in my shower. This isn't the first time I have jacked off to thoughts of Liv, and it certainly won't be the last. Even though I shot a load in Tatiana's mouth just an hour ago, I start to feel the tingling in my spine and the familiar tightening of my orgasm beginning.

I continue to pump harder, and my breathing becomes more ragged. I lean against the tiled shower to steady myself as the most intense orgasm rips through me, and I continue to pump through it until the last of the waves stops.

I feel shredded.

I stand under the spray, trying to figure out what I should do about Liv. I just can't seem to let her go.

CHAPTER ELEVEN

LIV

ONE YEAR LATER

I lie back on my bed, look at my phone for the thousandth time, and see the message Dax sent me months ago. I can't bring myself to erase it, despite how miserable it makes me to read it.

I moved in with Emma, and our two-bedroom apartment is the perfect space for two mid-twenty-year-olds trying to figure out their lives. School is grueling, but I'm getting it done. Couple that with work and being there for Brodie, my life has become insanely busy.

My travel assignment went well and I saved some much-needed cash. At the end of my contract, I was pleasantly surprised when the emergency department director offered me a job. They were even willing to give me a per diem status that would allow me to make some money with a shift differential and schedule flexibility so that I could focus on school. And with my full-time student status, I was able to take a health plan that the school offered—one less thing to worry about.

Emma and I sometimes work the same shift, which means we catch up while carpooling there and back. It seems just like old times. Our most recent discussions have been around Ainsley and Piper, since they will be coming to visit us soon. It'll be nice to have them here so we can let loose for a bit.

I get up and throw my phone in my bag. My life runs on a tight schedule lately, and I'm currently late for a group study session. "Here we go again," I mutter as I gather my stuff and make my way to the door.

A few hours later, I return home to an empty apartment. Emma must still be at work. I grab my workout stuff and decide to get a quick run in before I make my way to Brodie's dad's house for our frequent visits. I need this time to clear my head before I head over there.

It is so surreal to be sitting with your friend and former boyfriend, knowing that things will never be the same. We will no longer dance together, walk to the movies, ride bikes along the shore, or be intimate with each other ever again. The events that happened that night had lasting repercussions. They run on a haunted loop inside my head.

I decide that I need some rage music to fill my mind and try to erase the negative thoughts that are a constant background in my life. I pull up Godsmack, and the song "Mistakes" starts its intro.

I take off through the complex and onto the sidewalk. The lyrics fill my head, and the anger and guilt wash through me with every word and every step. I increase my speed as feelings attempt to purge out through my pores as the sweat drips from my body. My feet pound the pavement, and my lungs burn.

After the song finishes, I begin to slow down, knowing that I won't be able to keep up that pace. I click through my music, scrolling for the next song. I see a '90s hip-hop station and flip to that. Some motivating Eminen, perhaps. Yep, that'll work, I think to myself.

I get lost in my thoughts, and my watch alerts me to my target running goal and time. Not too shabby, three miles in twenty-seven minutes. I wipe the excess sweat off my forehead as I slow down to a walk. My breathing returns to normal, and I realize I'm just around the corner from a Starbucks I go to often.

An unsweetened passion fruit iced tea will do just the trick allowing me to cool off and rest for a bit. I need to check my school emails before going to Brodie's house anyway. Once I get there, we usually fall into a routine of small talk before I crack open my books. It's a convenient place to get my homework done. I get to spend time with him, and it's quiet, so I can focus on what I'm doing. A win-win on all accounts.

Sometimes, his night nurse will even cook us something while I visit. And as a student with a limited income, I'll take all the free meals I can get.

I turn my air pods off and attempt to tame my hair down after the run by pulling it into a messy bun. I'm sweaty, but a quick glance at my reflection in the glass shows me that I'm relatively presentable, so I push the door open and head in.

The place is packed. Great. So much for checking my email. I guess I'll just order to go then. I'd like to take a cold shower before going to Brodie's anyway. I place my order and stand off to the side, shooting a text to Emma.

Where the hell are you, girlie? I just went for a run and am getting a quick drink at Starbucks. Do you want anything?

I pocket my phone again and look to see if my drink is ready, and that's when I hear it.

"Venti Americano for Dax!" the barista yells out.

"Dax." I mouth the word before I realize I'm doing it.

Adrenaline pumps through me, and my hands begin to shake. My eyes dart around the room and land on the one person I never thought I would see again. It's Dax. *My* Dax stands up from a table to get his drink.

I stand there mesmerized by his stature. He's here, across from me. I take him in, the slim fit of his jeans and the perfect-fitting plain tee that hugs his tight body. It looks expensive, all of it. I see the chunky watch on his manly wrist as he reaches out and grabs his coffee. Just his proximity makes all of my senses come alive, and suddenly, it's hard to breathe.

As if he can feel my eyes on him, he turns to look in my direction, and our eyes meet.

Dax looks at me with a shocked expression, his mouth slightly open. He closes it slowly, and I can see Adam's apple bob as he swallows and steps toward me. His eyes never leave mine, and the intensity of his stare penetrates through me as he continues walking my way. His jaw tics, and I can see confusion, passion, and relief cross his face in rapid succession.

He sees my slow perusal of his body, and I see his eyes narrow. His eyes are homed in on mine like a predator stalking its prey, trying to calculate if he has to chase it down so he can take what is his.

Like an apparition that might disappear again in a flash, I guess I can feel his reluctance to look away with the way I vanished. The barista calls my name, and I just stare at him.

He tilts his head toward her while maintaining his sights on me. "Are you going to get that?" he asks with a slight upturn of his lip.

He lets his gaze drop down to my lips, and I nod, unable to speak, and go to get my drink. As I walk to the counter and closer to him, I can feel the weight of his stare on me. Why is he looking at me like that? Is he upset? Is he happy to see me? I'm tempted to turn around to see if he is staring at my ass.

Instantly, I'm so glad I wore the tight running shorts that show off my long legs. But then I remember I'm also a sweaty mess from my run. An embarrassed blush flushes my cheeks. I shake the thought from my head, thank the barista for my drink, and brace myself as I turn back around. A million scenarios play out in my mind, but what I see is not at all what I expect.

His eyes capture mine again, but then he looks away to someone else. That's when I see a tall, well-dressed woman walking toward Dax. She goes to place her arm around his waist, and I see him move away slightly, but not out of her hold.

We look at each other again, and I take a step away. I can see when he realizes I'm moving toward the door, not him. I push through the crowd of people, desperate to get outside and into the fresh air. I stumble outside and begin to half walk, half jog away.

"Wait! Liv!" I hear him call behind me.

There's a desperation in his voice that I can't ignore, but I'm too scared to stop. I don't know what makes me speed up, but I do. Is it the sophisticated woman that held his embrace but not his attention?

I don't allow him time to follow as I slip through the crowded sidewalk across the street. I make the mistake of turning back and see him looking for me as the tall blond also looks in my direction with a blank look on her flawless face. She sees me but doesn't offer any help for him to locate me.

My heart continues to pound, and tears begin to well up in my eyes. Dax is with someone else. He's moved on. The realization stabs through me. My phone pings again, and I automatically reach for it, secretly hoping it will be a message from Dax. But it's a text from Emma.

I'm picking up some things for the girls' upcoming visit. Do you want to come?

I read and reread it a couple of times before it sinks in. My brain is simply not working quite right. The blond bombshell pops back into my mind, and unexpected jealousy tears through me. Immediately, I reply.

YES.

I see a laughing emoji, and she replies: ***Well, that was easy. I thought I was going to have to bribe you. I know how much you hate shopping for clothes.***

I might not have the look of class like that woman, but an updated wardrobe will help me feel better. And maybe some new running clothes.

I'm already wondering if I'll bump into Dax again, and I'd like to look a bit better next time I see him. I manage to text her back to let her know that I'm going to shower and visit Brodie for a bit, and then I'll be home. A thumbs-up and heart emoji come up, and I throw her a kissing emoji face so she won't think anything is suspicious. I see another text message, and my stomach tumbles.

It's Dax.

Where are you? I want to talk to you. Then another text message comes up immediately. ***Please, Liv, I need to see you.***

I turn my AirPods back on, trying to drown out the memory of his voice in my head. Did he move on from us? Was there always a girl?

"Move on from us," I repeat back to myself.

What am I thinking? We were never an "us." Right?

I can't do this. I can't get close to him again with what I know now. Besides, I can't compete with that woman.

I look at the text message again, playing over today's events at Starbucks. He was never really mine. And I walked away from him that day in the hospital. With a sinking feeling in my stomach. I set him free, and he's gone.

I make my way back to the apartment. As I stand under the shower, I wash the cold sweat off my body and the soon-to-be cold, distant memories of a man that I can't seem to have.

CHAPTER TWELVE

DAX

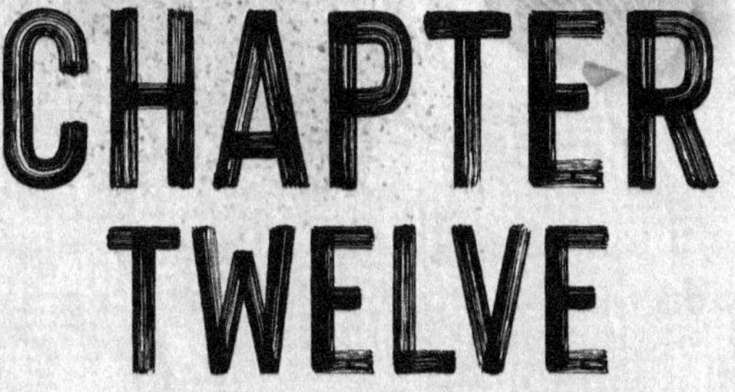

I run out the door and hold my breath as my eyes dart around, frantically looking for her. My eyes scan the people mingling on the sidewalk, and then I see her. She's jogging away from me, her messy bun bouncing on top of her head and her AirPods in place.

I call her name as I race in her direction. No response. I shout louder. Her pace slows for a moment, and I think she may turn around, but before I can even grasp that bright idea, she picks her speed back up again.

I step off the curb to cross the street but a truck whizzes in front of me, making me jump back. By the time it passes, I manage to catch a glimpse of her just before she turns the corner and is out of sight.

No. No. No. I lost her again. And for some reason, it hurts just as much as the first time. Is fate keeping us apart? Well, fuck that. It makes me even more determined to piss off the fates, go after her, and make her mine. It must be some primal caveman mindset, but nothing makes me want this woman more than seeing her repeatedly walk away from me.

With no other option, I begrudgingly head back into Starbucks. Tatiana returned inside after I told her I'd be right there. By the look on her face, I know she saw everything—my surprise from seeing Liv and then my desperate attempt to chase her down.

I've been avoiding this conversation with her. Although we've never claimed to be exclusive, I know she feels more for me than I do for her. She's been a warm body to fuck and companion to pass the time. But she's also a colleague, which makes circumstances slightly more complicated. But I have no future with Tatiana. I know my future. And I just watched it run away from me.

Tatiana has my coffee in her hand, and I look down at it as she tries to hand it to me. When did I give her that to hold on to? After I saw Liv, everything became a blur.

I take the drink from her hand, and she holds my stare.

"You want to tell me who that is?" She takes a sip from her skinny vanilla latte and patiently waits for my response.

I can hear the *tap tap tap* of her toe on the ground as her impatience builds. Not knowing what to say, I go for the truth.

"Her name is Liv. We met during spring break and when I went down to Padre Island with the guys," I blurt out and then stop, hoping it'll be enough for her but knowing she'll want more.

"O-k-a-y," she draws out. "Why were you chasing her?" She looks at me as if she is trying to figure out a complex puzzle.

"I, um, have some unfinished business with her."

Not a lie. But that is not exactly the entire truth, either. However, I'm not giving her any more.

She seems to sense the end of the conversation and turns to walk away. Not knowing what else to do, I follow her out.

We walk another block in silence to where our cars are parked, and she leans in for a kiss. I turn my head at the last second, and her lips land on my cheek. Her eyes find mine, and a mixture of confusion and irritation crosses her features. Without another word, she gets in her car, and I close the door, waving goodbye as she drives off. As I walk to my car, I pull my phone out, hoping with everything in me that I'll see a response from Liv.

"Goddammit!" I hit my car roof as I try to regain my composure.

I don't know why this girl has gotten under my skin, but I need her as

I've never needed anything before. I want to know how she is and how school is going. I wonder how things are at work and if she's settled in Houston. And most of all, I want to know why she never responds to my texts. Other than the confusing as fuck response that she is "always thinking of me." What the fuck does that mean, and why does it have me completely pussy whipped.

I get in my car and decide to go home. I need to see the guys tonight and have enough beers that I forget the confusing situation I'm currently in. We're meeting up at our favorite sports bar, where the food is decent and the music is loud. I actually have a day off, and I'm not on call until Sunday. I might as well at least try and have some fun.

I go home and get into the shower. I wash quickly, not letting my mind drift to Liv. Although my cock doesn't get the memo, and it's standing at attention before I even know it's happening.

I blast the cold water and shiver my way through the rest of my shower. I shave quickly and throw on jeans and a T-shirt. I called an Uber, so I don't have to worry about driving home since I plan to do minor liver damage tonight.

I look at my text messages, and my heart jumps as I see a response from Liv. One word, *Ok.*

Okay? Okay, what? What does that even mean?

I close the message, not knowing how to respond, and I text Jameson instead to let him know I will be there soon.

His response comes quickly. **Sounds good, dude. Everyone's here. We just ordered wings.**

I step out of the Uber and make my way into the bar. The guys are all there sitting in our usual spot with beers and wings already being consumed quickly.

"Hey, man! Thought you'd never get here," Jameson barks out over the loud noise of voices and music playing.

"Yeah, I got a little headfucked this afternoon right before getting home, so sorry I was late." I call the waitress over and ordered a beer.

As soon as she leaves, Jameson picks the conversation right back up. "What? What head fuck? Is that code for Tatiana deep-throating your cock again?" Jameson laughs as he high-fives Theo, who is sitting next to him.

"No, not exactly," I say as the waitress hands me my drink.

She winks at me and walks away, swaying her ass as she goes. I stare after her, thinking of that night in the ER when Liv walked away from me that same way.

James catches me looking and snaps his fingers in front of my face. "Ha," Jameson comments as he tilts his head at the waitress. "Simone is her name, and I do like me a redhead. Anyway, what happened? What were you saying about this headfuck?" He slams the rest of his beer down before settling back into his seat, waiting for my reply.

"Remember that girl, Liv, from the beach at Padre Island?"

Jameson's eyes go wide at the mention of her name. "Wait a minute! Tell me you did not see her today?"

I just nod my head. "Oh yeah, I did. She literally ran away from me, and I didn't get a chance to talk to her. Tatiana was there, and it was awkward as fuck."

"Fuck me," Jameson says.

"We were in Starbucks, and I saw her there. She just came out of nowhere. One minute I was waiting for my coffee, and the next, I had a staredown with Liv. We were so close that I wanted to reach out and touch her, but Tatiana came over and put her hand on my waist. It spooked Liv, and she grabbed her drink and ran out the door. I had barely said a few words to her before she was gone again."

Jameson snorts. "Well, Liv keeps slipping away from you, doesn't she?"

We sit at the table, and the guys start talking about the work week, the usual events in our life, and plans for the weekend. I am only half-listening, and Jameson seems to notice.

"You still have your head wrapped around that girl, don't you?"

I take another swig of my beer and shake my head. "Yup, still thinking about the girl that got away."

"Well, she didn't get away, did she? You saw her again, and she's now in Houston, right?"

"She did say that we could talk but didn't allude to when or where. She was busy and just sent a quick reply, but I may just be reading too much into it."

"Well, at least you know what coffee shop she goes to. Maybe you can stalk her there." Jameson winks, and then I see something catch his eye.

He gets up quickly and makes his way to the door. That's when I notice the short little blonde girl who just entered through the door. Her eyes light up when she sees Jameson, and shock runs through me when I remember who she is.

Well, today is just full of coincidences isn't it?

I see Jameson pull her into a hug, and the girl beams up at him like they are old friends. It isn't until Jameson points my way and she looks at me that

I remember her name–Emma.

"Holy shit," I mutter under my breath.

He has her by the arm and is leading her to our table. "Dax, you remember Emma, don't you, Liv's friend?"

I go to pull her in for a hug, and she laughs. "Well, gentlemen, what a warm reception I'm getting this evening."

Theo and Eric wave at her, and she gives a little royal wave like the Queen of England.

"Well, I guess the whole gang's here tonight." She turns back to Jameson, and they quickly begin to catch up.

I almost have to wait my turn to ask her the most important question: Where is Liv? Is she coming here? Will I see her tonight?

After an eternity, I finally attempt to break into their conversation. "Hey, Emma, can we get you a drink?"

She turns her attention to me with a smile. "Sure, I'll take a gimlet."

Jameson laughs. "A what? Isn't that what old people drink?"

She flashes him a megawatt smile and replies, "Well, I guess I am an old soul, Jameson. It also helps when it's later on in the night, and I just end up getting soda water with a lime, and everyone thinks I have the fastest elimination process of alcohol consumption."

I snort.

"All right, one gimlet is coming up. I love it when you talk nerdy to me," he whispers loudly in her ear so everyone hears it anyway.

Jameson goes to the bar that is now beginning to become crowded. Emma looks right at me and huffs. "Just ask me already."

I look at her and tilt my head to get a good read of her. Before I know what I'm doing, the words spill out of my mouth. "Have you talked to Liv? How is she doing? Is she coming here tonight?"

She smiles widely, clearly loving that I want all this information on her friend. She then proceeds to catch me up on all that is Liv. "Well, she was torn up after the accident. She feels so guilty, like it is somehow her fault that he ended up like this." She talks fast as her fingers play with a wisp of her hair, but I don't miss a single word.

Jameson comes back with her drink, and she takes a big swig and continues speaking.

"I moved to Houston for her, you know. She was a wreck. I was so worried about her and told her I was ready to make a new life for myself. Start a new adventure. Honestly, I couldn't let her come here by herself. She didn't even walk the stage after graduation."

I just stare at her, dumbfounded. "I tried to reach out to her," I manage to say, but my brain is still trying to catch up with the new information.

"Yeah, she told me. She seems to have put all her focus into school and this per diem job we have at the hospital."

This piques my interest. I sit up straighter. "Where does she work?"

She thinks before she speaks. "I don't want to tell you anything more because I think you both need to talk first."

"I saw her today," I say, almost like I am speaking to no one in particular, like it's just a statement.

She nods, encouraging me to continue.

"I was with some woman from work. We work together."

She eyes me skeptically. "Is that all? Just work together?"

Well, not entirely, but it's nothing serious.

She looks at me with sympathy in her eyes. "If you want to make a go with our girl, you will have to try harder. She fell for you that weekend. And it scares her. And she is living with so much guilt that it is suffocating her. If you care about her, then don't stop trying." She says goodbye to us and embraces Jameson.

We watch her head off to a table where there are some people she clearly knows as they stand to grab her a chair. We hear her laugh, and Jameson moans. I look at him and can relate to the somber mood that has taken over our table. Eric and Theo look at us and laugh.

"Man, you guys are pathetic."

Jameson stands and shouts, "Shots?"

"Let's do it!" Theo says, and Eric and I shake our heads in unison.

As we down our whiskey, I think about another lonely night with my thoughts consumed by a long-legged girl with honey-colored eyes.

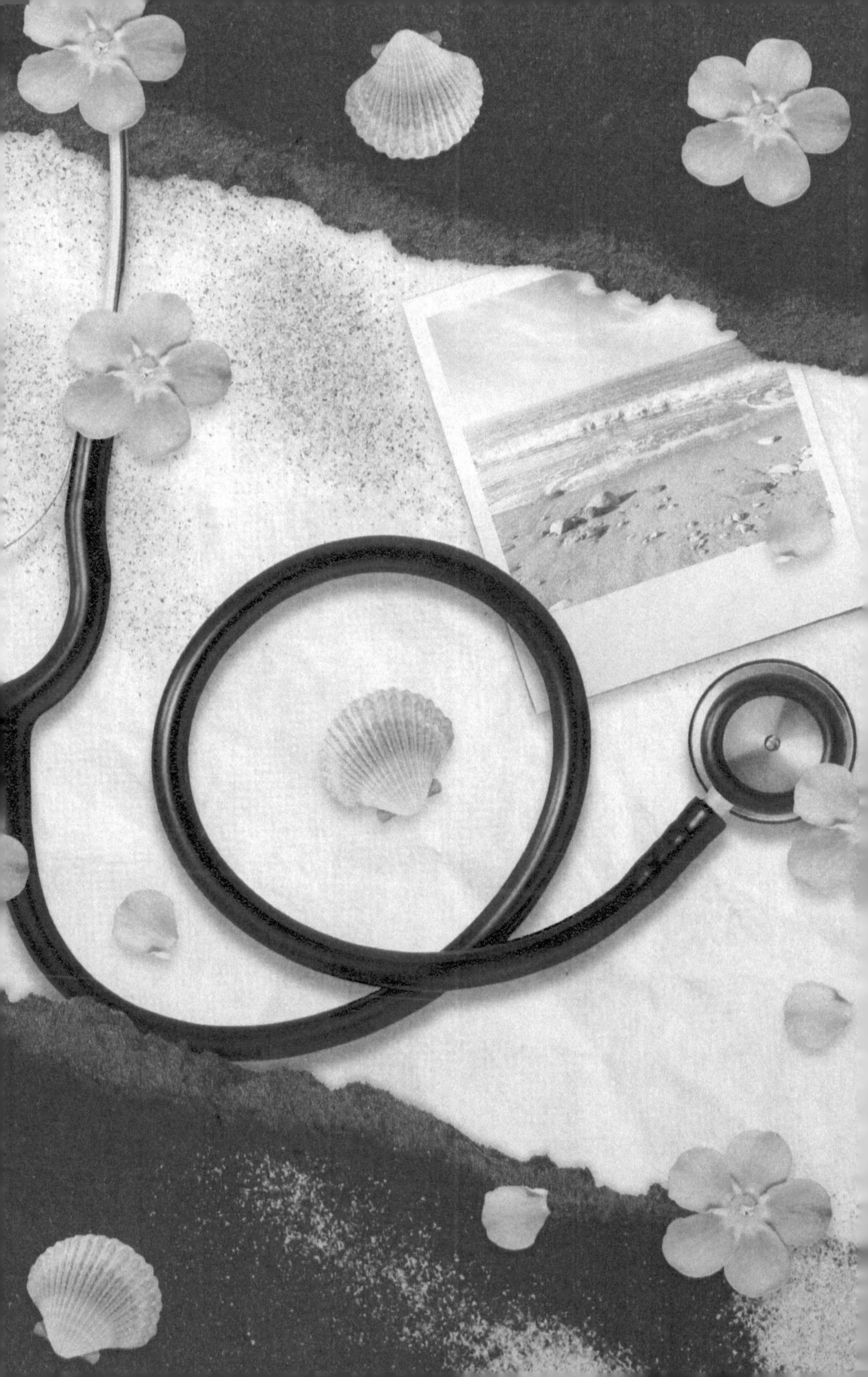

CHAPTER THIRTEEN

LIV

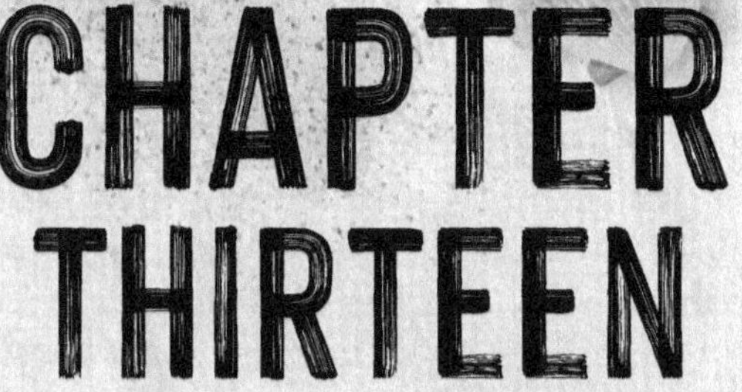

I return to the apartment and throw my phone and AirPods on the table. I am immediately hit with the most fragrant smell. I see a large bouquet of red roses on the kitchen table. I go to read the card and see they are for Emma. I mean, of course, they are for Emma. Who would send me flowers here?

I see the signature of the name Eduardo. Hmm, who is this guy? I definitely would have remembered that name. Oh, well, that's a topic for conversation when I next see that girl.

I proceed to strip out my running gear. I've lost a little weight, but running helps as an escape to clear my head and is a great form of de-stressing. And today, I really needed to clear my head. Seeing Dax made me feel all sorts of things. Desire, confusion, longing, did I mention desire?

I shake my head and move into the kitchen. I need to eat something post-run, so I grab a quick pre-made energy drink from the cabinet and add a couple of ice cubes to the blender to make it cold. I grab my shake bottle, load it up with the product, and dump a scoop of powdered peanut butter to finish it off. I drop the little metal whisking ball into the cup, screw on the top, and shake it up.

"Ah, much better," I murmur as I take my first sip.

I stroll half-naked to the shower and look at myself in the mirror. I turn from side to side and think about the girl with Dax today at the coffee shop. She's a beauty and very different from me. She was classy and elegant in an Eastern European way, and I look…well…I look not that. I see nothing exotic or enticing about myself. She looks like she fits with Dax.

But I want to "fit with Dax," I think to myself.

My mind wanders back to the coffee shop. He looked nothing like the guy I met at the beach, and I reminded myself that we didn't know each other at all. Not that I expected to know everything about him after one weekend, but the connection we shared was impossible to deny.

He said he wanted to talk. And I want to talk to him too. I want to know if he is seeing anyone, if he still thinks of me, and if he felt what I felt that weekend at the beach. But as my heart starts to pick up at the idea of talking to him, Brodie flashes in my mind, and the guilt returns.

I place my shake on the bathroom counter and jump in the shower. It is cold and helps to wake me up and clear my head. I feel so sleep-deprived these days.

I towel off, quickly throw on one of my favorite Athleta dresses, and don a pair of Vans to complete the ensemble. I run my fingers deftly through my semi-dry hair and plait a long braid thrown over my shoulder. I apply a little tinted moisturizer, a blush stick that coats my lips in a matte rose finish, and toss on some mascara.

Definitely plain.

Tonight is a study night at Brodie's, so I collect my books and place them in my messenger bag. I grab my key and phone and head to the door. I sent Dax a response earlier today with one word: *Okay.* I didn't know what else to say. Should I have blurted out that I can't stop thinking about him and, *of course,* want to talk to him? I couldn't do that. So, okay, I had to do it. At least it opens the conversation to hear what he has to say. But he never responded, and I don't know what to make of that. I don't have time to think about it as I jump into the Jeep and head out to Brodie's father's house.

I pull up to the gated community and am quickly let in. My information is stored in the residence list, and the attendant knows me well since I often come by. I pull into the circular driveway and grab my stuff. I walk up to the door and let myself in. Brodie's stepmom walks up through the living room as I walk in. This woman he had an affair with also worked in his office. I am cordial to her but have zero respect for that homewrecker.

My thoughts must be displayed on my face because she sees me and says, "You know where to find him," as she walks straight past me without a second glance.

"Thanks," I mumble as I run up the stairs two at a time to where Brodie's suite is located.

I knock and hear Brodie's voice from his chair reply, "Come in."

I dramatically open the door and pretend to sashay through the hardwood floor onto the rug in front of the gas fireplace. There's not much I can do for him, but I can still make him laugh. A chuckle permeates Brodie's chest, followed by a deep, productive cough. I throw my stuff down on his chaise lounge and quickly make my way over to him.

"You need some water?" I go to the pitcher that sits by his table, promptly fill it up, and hold the straw to his mouth.

He takes a drink, and it seems to settle him. I look away, and once again, the guilt rears its ugly head. Brodie can read me like a book, and he sees the pain in my face.

"What are you studying today?" he asks, clearly trying to keep me from overthinking.

Glad for this change of subject, I fetch my bag and crisscross my legs on the floor to retrieve my stuff.

"Well, I am getting ready to start my clinical and get to be at the hospital now. I even get to see patients and write orders." I waggle my eyebrows like I'm super impressed. But all joking aside, I am totally prepared for this rotation and am super excited about it.

"That's cool," he says.

"Is it okay if I turn on the gas fireplace?" I ask. "I like the ambiance while I study."

He pulls a smile that is so Brodie and says, "Sure, make yourself at home."

He uses the remote feature on his wheelchair and comes in my direction. He places himself by me, turning on some music through voice recognition. "Any music you want to listen to?" he asks.

"Yes, I want to listen to waves crashing on the beach."

He looks at me in a haunted way, and I quickly take it back.

"Or we could listen to NSYNC?" I try to make light of the situation.

He would constantly make fun of me for my love of all things NSYNC or Backstreet Boys. I even had the dance down to "Bye, Bye Bye." This seems to do the trick, and the light returns to his eyes.

"You gotta do that dance." He laughs.

I stand up from the floor and toe off my shoes. I roll my neck around, and he lets out a laugh. "All right," I say, making a little room to fist pump the air.

He moves his chair around to get the full view.

"Ready?"

He now looks thoroughly amused. "Hit it."

I snap in the air.

The music of the '90s boy band infiltrates the air, and I step into action. We are almost back in time with the music as our thoughts filter along as the passing beats. When the song ends, we start laughing. I fall to the floor with nostalgic happiness.

Brodie is smiling too, and I grab his cup from the table and down the drink.

"Here, I'll get you some more water."

He watches me get up and refill his glass. When I return, he is still staring at me.

"What?" I ask, not wanting to know the answer to that question.

"I just really miss you, Liv. I wish things were so different."

Not wanting to dive into this deep conversation because I cannot deal with this heavy talk right now or anytime soon, I change the subject.

"Well, I'm wasting time getting this assignment done. Are you still going to help me? I need all the help I can get."

He answers quickly with, "Let's get started."

With that, we are shifted into the world of medical assessment and comorbidities. Not the most fascinating stuff for the weekend, but at least I am getting my work done and spending time with Brodie.

The hours go by, and I'm mostly done with my assignment. I start to yawn, and Brodie offers to see if I want tea or anything to drink.

"Do you think I can get it to go?"

"Of course. I'll have Melissa get it for you."

Melissa, his care provider, is a godsend. She helps out Brodie so much and makes it possible for an attempt at a good quality of life.

"I am going to finish this up, and I need to head on out. Do you want me to get anything for you at the library for my next visit?"

"Yeah, some more audiobooks if you can?"

"Sure thing! Anything in particular you want?"

He thinks about it for a minute and says, "Maybe something historical, like early America or the Mayflower?"

"Wow, really trying to entertain yourself, huh?"

He snorts and says, "Well, surprise me then."

I think about this for a second and voice my thoughts. "What about *The Outlander* series? Time travel, romance, and some history all thrown in. The perfect combination."

"Sure, why not."

"Great, I'll grab the first in the series. It's lengthy, so be prepared."

He looks around the room and then back at me. "Well, there's not much I can do these days, so it's fine."

I feel that guilt resurface, and I swallow hard. The lump that resides in my thoughts always seems to be there. I turn around and start putting my stuff away. I grab my cardigan that had fallen off the chair during my dance routine and put it back on. Melissa knocks on the door we left partially open and hands me my drink.

"Here you go, Liv. Lady Gray, with one pump of vanilla and frothed almond milk."

I look at her adapted version of a London fog latte with a genuine smile. "Thank you so much; it's perfect."

"Well, I know it is your favorite, so enjoy."

"Do you need anything, Brodie, before I settle in?"

He just shakes his head.

"Well, I'll walk you out, Liv, if you want."

I run over to Brodie and give him a quick hug. I hear him take in a big whiff of my hair before I pull away. Every time I leave, he does the same thing. I've worn the same product in my hair for years–a distinctive earthy floral by Aveda–and he always loved the way I smelled. All it does now is make me sad to the point of tears.

Melissa and I leave the room and close the door behind us as we walk down the stairs to the front door. I use this time to ask her how Brodie is doing. She looks at me and places her hand on my shoulder with a light touch.

"He's okay, Liv. He realizes that he is responsible for his mistakes, and he owns that. I suspect that you should realize this too. Have you talked to anyone about this? A professional?"

I shake my head and look down.

"Don't be so hard on yourself. This was a terrible accident and not your fault."

"I know," I reply, still avoiding looking at her. "I better get going."

She opens the door and watches me walk to my car. "Be safe," she says before I close the door to my Jeep.

I retrieve my phone from my messenger bag and plug it into the charger to listen to my music on the drive home. I see a message from Emma.

You will never believe who I ran into at our after-work sports bar! Jameson from spring break, and he wasn't alone.

Oh boy, I think to myself. I bet I know who he was with. I better meet up with Dax before he finds out where I live and I don't have the willpower to turn him away.

Would I turn him away?

I go to my playlist and hit the song "Summertime Sadness" by Lana Del Rey. The music infiltrates the Jeep, and I hit the button to put the windows down. I drive through the dark residential area listening to the beats as I drive the long way home, lost in my thoughts.

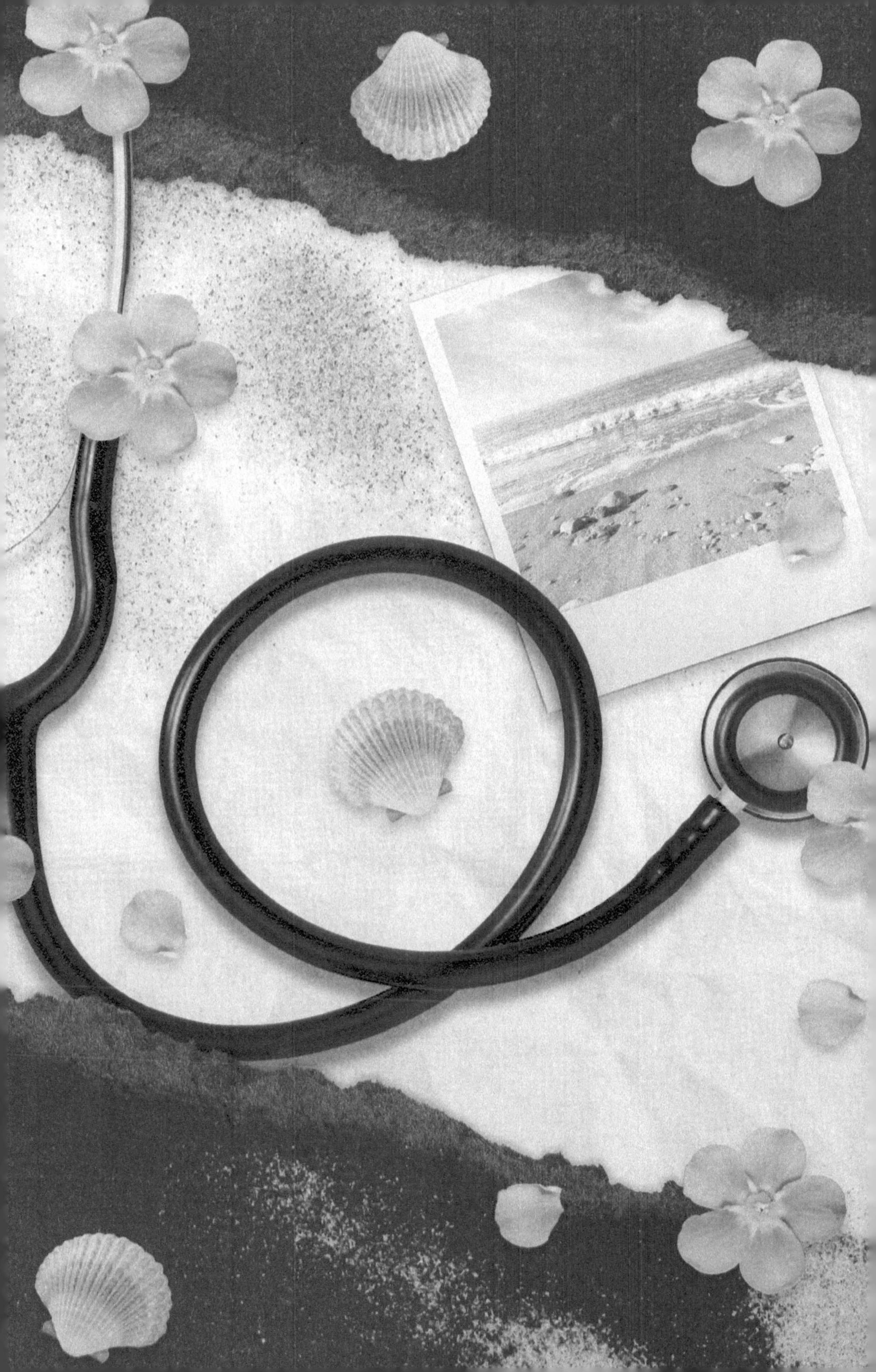

CHAPTER FOURTEEN

DAX

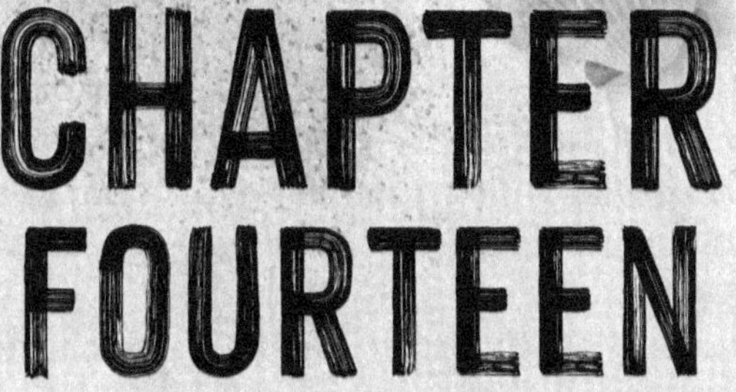

The crowd increases as more people make their way into the club. The heavy bass of the music drums in my ears as I shoulder through sweaty bodies, making my way to the bar.

I get the bartender's attention and order a couple of shots of tequila. Making quick work of those, I order a third for good measure. My thoughts start to get a little fuzzy, and a smile plays on my lips.

Perfect, I think, pushing off the bar and heading toward the bathroom.

A buzz to take the edge off is precisely what I need. As usual, there's a long wait for the women's room, and my eyes scan the line as I get closer. I appreciate all the various beauties from afar but purposely don't make eye contact or acknowledge anyone. I walk past them all, eyes locked on the men's room door. Thankfully, there's no one in line, so I am in and out quickly.

Walking back to the table, I pull out my phone and consider sending Liv a message. I usually avoid drunk texting anyone, but she seems to be the exception to all my rules these days.

A warm body bumps against my chest as I type out a text. It's the red-haired waitress, Simone.

Simone pushes her breasts up against my chest and holds on to my arm to raise her lips up to my ear. "I get off at one if you are still here. I'll make it worth your wait." She steps back, winks, and then walks away.

I watch her walk away, unsure what to make of that offer. For a split second, my brain screams, "Go for it." Even in my drunken state, I know I'm still yearning for Liv.

I smile as she walks away. My eyes are on her, but I'm thinking about someone else. However, when I turn around, I'm met with a disapproving stare from Emma. Although she is conversing with Jameson, she witnessed what just happened with Simone, and she's clearly not happy about it. Her expression makes my stomach bottom out, and I can't have another strike against me with Liv.

I know it's wrong, but I whisper-shout to Jameson and place my hand on his shoulder to steer his attention and Emma's. "Simone stopped me to say she gets off at one, if you are interested, and she'll make it worth your wait."

It is what she said, just not to him. He gives me a shake of his head and snarls, which immediately lets me know that he fully understands how I displaced the facts in front of Emma.

Emma rises off the chair and grabs her purse. "And with that, I'm out. See you later, guys!" she shouts at us over the music to no one in particular as she makes her way through the crowd straight out the bar's door.

Jameson watches her leave and then rounds on me in a fury. "What the fuck, Dax?"

I look at him apologetically and say, "I'm sorry, but I panicked. She saw Simone come up to me, and I couldn't have her tell Liv that I'm a piece of shit that can't keep my dick in my pants."

He picks up his drink. "Well, if the shoe fits…" he trails off as he takes a large gulp of his drink.

"What was I supposed to do, Jameson? I meet this girl I like, and then everything in the universe tries to prevent us from getting together."

Jameson just shakes his head and downs the rest of his drink. "So what is she then?"

I look at him and can't seem to explain what it is about Liv because I hardly know myself. "I don't know what it is. But there's something about her. We connected at Padre Island, and I want to see if it's real, you know?" I slump back into my chair, grab a beer, and throw back half of it.

"I hope you know what you're doing, dude. She seems like she went through a terrible ordeal, from what we saw that night and what Emma told me so far."

I look at him quizzically. "What has Emma told you so far?" I ask, mimicking his words.

He shakes his head. "Look, you just need to talk to Liv."

That pisses me off, and words are flying out of my mouth before I can stop them. "I know, dick, that's what I've been trying to do."

He shakes his head at me. "Let's get one last drink here then."

We order another round of drinks and decide to make a night of it. Might as well, since I don't feel like being alone with my thoughts.

Jameson downs the rest of his drink and signals to the guys that we are heading out. "Come on, Dax, let's get out of here. Maybe you'll get lucky."

I go to pick up the tab. It's the least I can do after ruining Jameson's chances with Emma tonight. I don't know what is happening with those two, but I know they must have hooked up during spring break. Liv and I saw them returning from the sand dunes with their clothes half off. He never admitted to it, but I have a pretty good hunch.

Not wanting to leave cash on the table, I see Simone walking by and wave at her. She smiles seductively at me and puts her tray down at the bar.

"Hey, what's up."

I hand her my tab and a couple hundred bucks. "We are leaving, and I didn't want to leave cash at the table."

She arches an eyebrow.

"Thanks for the offer, but I'm not interested in meeting up later."

She shakes her head in disbelief. "Your loss," she says as she retrieves her serving tray and moves with ease through the crowd.

I make my way out and push through the doors. The cool breeze immediately hits me and sobers me up a bit. Jameson eyes me suspiciously.

"I told her I wasn't interested," I say flatly.

He smiles at me and laughs. "Where to now?"

"Want to hit up a club?" Theo asks.

Eric agrees, and I can't disagree because I still need a distraction, even if it's just more booze and loud music. Jameson pulls out his phone to Uber us a ride to a club. "My frat brother from college owns this club downtown, not far from here. We can VIP there if you want."

VIP treatment sounds precisely like what we all need. Five minutes later, we get into the Uber and start the quick drive to the club. Pulling up, we see a massive line at the door, but Jameson tugs us through the line and goes straight up to the bouncer.

"Hey, we are on the VIP list for Jameson Havelka."

The bouncer looks at his papers and nods. He pulls the rope out for us to pass through. "Go on, straight in, and up the stairs. I'll let them know you are on your way, Mr. Havelka."

Someone opens the doors for us, and we are immediately engulfed in people. The music is loud, and we can barely hear each other. I see Jameson motion with his hand, and we head to a bar.

"Stay here. I'll grab shots, and then we can make our way up."

After what seems like forever, Jameson returns with four drinks and a sour face.

"What's up with you?" I ask as he passes out the drinks. We take our tequila shots and place them on a table we managed to grab.

"I just saw Emma." He pauses and then continues looking directly at me. "She was with Liv."

At those words, my heart skips a beat–more like I was punched in the chest, and my breath blows out in a whoosh.

"Where?" I ask but don't wait for the answer as I make my way to where Jameson ordered the shots.

I scan the crowd but don't see Emma or Liv. I turn back and mouth "where" to Jameson. He points to a spot near the bar, but they are nowhere to be seen. I make my way back to the table, eyes still darting around.

"They're not there?" Jameson asks while scanning the crowd himself. "Weird. Let's go up to the VIP lounge. We can get a better look from above. I doubt they left yet."

The VIP section is a different world. We take our seats, and a waitress comes over immediately, and we are offered bottle service with our favorite tequila—Don Julio 1942. The waitress sets us up with drinks when a tall guy in a custom-tailored suit makes his way toward us. Jameson looks his way and goes over.

"Hey, Eduardo, thanks for the hospitality, man. We appreciate it. Nice club, too."

"Good to see you, brother. Glad you could make it."

Introductions are made all around. He has a few guys who fall behind him as he speaks but doesn't introduce them to us. It is a bit odd, but I figure they must make up the security personnel in this place.

"Enjoy yourselves," he says as he walks away. "I have to get back to work, but maybe I'll get a chance to drop back by later."

We say our goodbyes, and I quickly scan the area again for Liv.

"Chill out, dude," Jameson says while looking over at the dance floor. "Let's see if we can find that nurse of yours."

And I can't help but smile when he says "Yours."

Jameson hits me on the shoulder and points over to the side of the dance floor.

"Where!" I ask frantically. Not able to make heads or tails of the throng of dancing bodies below.

Jameson looks at me like I'm crazy. "She's right there. Are you blind?" He points at some ethereal-looking creature in a metallic dress dancing with her back to me.

Her hair is plaited in a braid and turned into a bun. I notice some strands have gotten loose and are sticking to the sweat on her neck. My eyes follow her every movement, and my heartbeat picks up. My trance is broken. A guy moves toward her and rests his hands on her hips. Before she can turn to see who it is, he pushes himself close and starts to grind up on her. Staring at his hands on her, anger rips through me, and I immediately see red.

"Let's go." I hit Jameson on the shoulder and motion to the dance floor.

He tells Eric and Theo that we will be right back. Theo has a girl on his lap, and Eric is talking to the waitress. I make my way through the crowd, eyes locked on my girl.

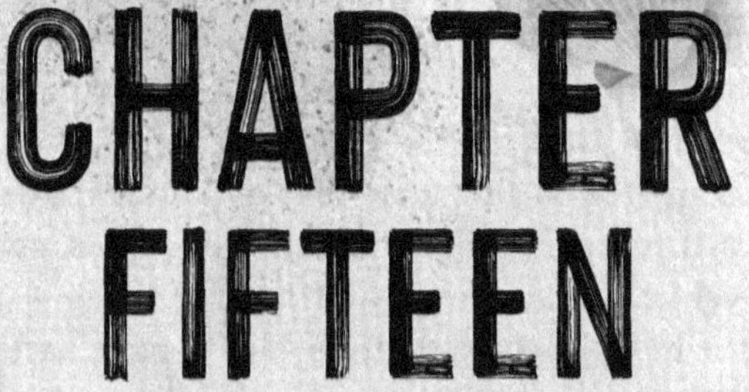

CHAPTER FIFTEEN

LIV

I had just got home from Brodie's house, and I felt like utter shit. I'm probably the only young person spending this weekend night alone at home. *How pathetic am I?*

I'm debating whether to take a nice bath after taking a big swig of my wine when I hear my phone start to ring. Who the fuck actually calls anyway? Only my mother would be calling, making me wonder if that's her and if something terrible has happened.

I run to retrieve my phone that I just placed on the charger at my bedside table. I see Emma's name flashing with the call. I answer it before it is sent to the land of unanswered voicemails.

"Hey, girlie! What's up?"

I pick my wine up to take another drink when I hear Emma yell through the phone. "Get dressed and meet me out. I need to dance, and you're coming now."

I start laughing. My plans for a relaxing bath are squashed because I know she won't take no for an answer. The last time I said no to her, she showed up at my door and practically dragged me out with her.

"Yeah, okay, I guess I could. Where are we meeting?" I jot down the name of the club as she rambles on. I break the conversation to ask her what the dress code is for tonight.

"Wear something sexy, like that cute backless jumpsuit or sparkly gold dress with long sleeves and plunging neckline."

I burst out laughing. "Okay, so something low cut and short, am I right?"

"Yes!" she practically screams through the phone.

"I'm on it, boss. I'll be ready in thirty minutes. I'll meet you there."

"Call me when you pull up, it's a big club, and I'll come to get you," Emma shouts before ending the call.

I plug my curling iron in and hurry to take a quick shower. I jump in and use some fragrant bath gel with my loofah, run a quick swipe of the razor because you never know, and jump out from the relaxing spray.

I decide on the metallic-looking dress with the low back and deep-cut V at the neckline. A quick braided updo will show that off nicely. I curl a few strands that have come undone from the bobby pins and give a quick spray to lock the style in.

I laugh as Emma's words sound off in my head. That girl is always the life of the party, and I have to admit that I am looking forward to this impromptu dancing at the mystery club.

Being new to Houston is fantastic. There is always so much to do, and I haven't even begun to enjoy myself here. There seems to be endless studying and work. Most of all, I'd like to get my mind off Dax. As much as I try, he is always there, invading my every thought.

I do a smokey eye with nude lip gloss and apply tons of mascara. I put some gold hoops in my ears and a couple of matching simple gold bangles to tie it all together. I grab my wristlet and sit to strap my high-heeled sandals. Then just as I stand up, the Uber update says it's minutes away. Perfect timing.

I get in the car and see that a girl is driving. "Hey," I casually say as I get into the back seat of the vehicle.

She looks at me in the rearview mirror and smiles. I also plug in the coordinates to the club and share the ETA with Emma so she knows where I am. I pull out my phone and pull up the limited conversations I have had with Dax. I replied *okay* in my last text message with him and never heard back. I decide to be brave and send another text to follow up. After several attempts at a reply, shoot off a quick text and hit send before I can change my mind.

Let me know when it is a good time for you, and I'll see what my schedule looks like. I think it would be good to talk.

It's a long text compared to what I've been sending, but I think we need to clear the air. I text Emma and let her know I am a block away in case she may not be checking her phone, and then put my phone away.

The Uber driver pulls off on the side of the road. "That's the place right there." She points to a large building with what appears to be a long line out front. "Good luck," she says. "I hope you know someone to get you in."

I had no intention of going out tonight, but here I am, staring at his very busy-looking club.

I reluctantly get out and start walking up to the club door, looking to see if I can find Emma. I decided to get in line and hope to at least get a couple of songs. At this rate, it will be closing time.

As I go to move away, I hear a guy shout my name. This big burly guy at the door waves me up. I look back to see if he is talking to me, since I have never seen this guy before. When I look to his left, I see a little blonde girl half his size–Emma. She's waving to me, screaming my name, and laughing. I make my way up to the front of the line and ignore the rude comments and ugly death stares I am getting right about now. He lifts the rope, and I walk through.

Emma immediately grabs my hands and pulls me in, wrapping me in a hug. "Let's go, girl."

"Oh my god!" I shout out. "How did you get us inside? The line is crazy!"

She laughs but doesn't answer and continues pulling me through the crowd. After we are halfway through, she stops and points to the bar.

"Come on, let's get a drink." We pull up to the bar and place our order for a couple of tequila shots each. "You look hot, Liv. That dress is amazing."

I'm weirdly flattered. Emma compliments me all the time, but tonight feels different. I needed an escape from the craziness of my life, and I wanted to look good tonight. No, not good. Freakin' sexy as hell.

"Thanks, girl. Let me get this shot for us."

The bartender goes to give us our shots, and when I go to pay, he says, "All set. They're paid for."

Emma just looks around, and the bartender points down the end of the bar. Emma's eyes narrow, but I don't see who she is looking at. I figure it doesn't matter. I'm happy with my free drink, so I stop searching for the mystery buyer.

"So, how did you get us in here?" I ask again, throwing back my shot and immediately turning back to the bar to get another. Maybe mystery drink buyers will help us out again.

"Funny story," she starts to tell me as she takes her shot. Sucking on a lime, she discards it in the now-empty glass and grabs my shoulder. "I took care of the guy that owns this place in the ED this week. Well, not exactly him, but his security person that we hurt. I can't go into details because of patient confidentiality, but he said that if I came here, he would put my name on a list to show his appreciation."

"Well, look at you! That's amazing. Was he the one who comped our drinks too?"

The bartender has already refilled our shots. We toast to lasting friendships and down our second one.

"No, it wasn't the owner, it was someone else."

I look at her and can immediately tell she is hiding something.

"Do I know the guy who bought the drinks, Emma?"

She looks down at the bar. Emma looks relieved. "Yes," she says as she turns back to me. "It was Jameson."

My eyes widen, and I look at her in disbelief, thinking I must have heard wrong. "Ummm, excuse me, who?" Heat blooms in my cheeks, making me want to fan myself. I'm too young for a hot flash, but this must be what one feels like because my whole head feels beet red. I think I can hear the pulse of my heart in my ears.

"Guilty," Emma says. "I ran into Jameson this evening with Dax."

At this, I physically pale.

"Liv, are you okay?"

"Yep." I immediately look around but don't see anyone.

"He's not here now. I don't know where Jameson went off to, and I didn't see Dax with him anymore. He was at the sports bar earlier with him. Maybe he stayed at the other bar."

Without further questions, I point to the dance floor. Needing to move, walk, dance, or do something other than just stand here panicking. "Well, you made me come out, and I'm ready to dance."

She smiles in relief and grabs my arm, leading me toward the dance floor. "I thought you'd never ask."

We push into the crowded dance floor and let the beat take over. The two shots start taking effect, and my nerves ease the slightest bit. As we dance, I can't help but scan the crowd. As my eyes wander, I finally look around and see the enormous club.

The luxurious interior and state-of-the-art sound systems blare EDM, pop, and other dance music galore. The lower level is a vast sea of bodies dancing and grinding under the strobe lighting. Upstairs, people are overlooking the dance floor, and there is seating up there as well, and it's roped off.

I grab Emma's arm and point to it. "What's that?" I lean in and yell into her ear.

"Oh, that's the VIP section of the club. I didn't ask about that entry. I was just happy to get us in without a wait."

"It's okay. I was just curious. I don't plan on getting off this dance floor until we're ready to leave."

"That's my girl," Emma praises with her hands up in the air.

"Clarity" by Zedd begins to play, and I grab Emma's arm and pull her to dance with me. Giggling like teenagers, we throw ourselves to the mercy of the music.

The music pumps, and we get lost in the crowd of bodies on the dance floor. I throw myself into the feeling and vibrations of the music enhanced by the tequila flowing through my system.

All of a sudden, I feel someone different dancing with me. I continue this through the song. When I push back into them and let my body glide with theirs to the pulse of the beat, this person feels taller. An arm goes to wrap around my waist, and the strong hands feel good. The large fingers splayed across my abdomen don't bother me one bit. It feels so good to be touched, and I enjoy the tingles creeping into my core.

A piece of my hair falls out of the braid. A hand goes to push the hair out of my face, and I still as he tucks it behind my ear. The fingers touching my face give me shivers.

My heart nearly stops when I look up at Emma and see the look on her face. She's surprised, but there's mischief in her eyes.

I know that touch. I know that feeling. I stop dancing and slowly turn around. Suddenly, I'm met by a large muscled frame and green eyes that bore into mine. I suck in a breath as I look into the face of Dax.

CHAPTER SIXTEEN

DAX

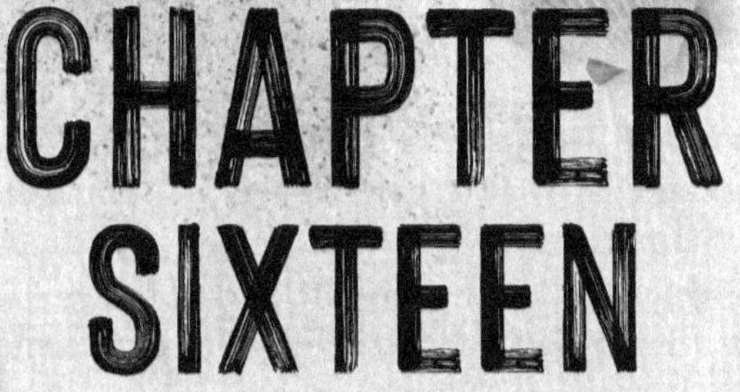

I see her dancing like sin and salvation made just for me. I carefully approach her from behind as I make my way through the crowd of sweaty bodies grinding to the techno beats.

I move closer to her and begin to move and sway along with her ethereal movements. I reach out to touch her, and my fingers graze her hip before I gently push my palm around to rest on her stomach. My heartbeat picks up, and I hold my breath for a moment, afraid she may pull away. I'm already thinking of what I'll do if she runs away from me again, but at that exact moment, she leans into my touch.

As the music changes to another song, she starts to grind against me. She pushes her ass back into me as I pull her closer, my fingers splaying across her toned abdomen. I bury my face into her hair, closing my eyes and breathing her in as we sway to the beat. I glance up to see Jameson dancing with Emma.

I can't believe I'm here, with her in my arms.

My hand moves up automatically to push a loose strand away from her face and gently tuck it behind her ear. She shudders at my touch as if it's a familiar sensation and drops her head back to my shoulder. A moan escapes her lips as she looks out over the crowd and catches Emma's eye. Emma's mouth falls open in shock, and Liv freezes in my arms at that exact moment.

She suddenly turns in my arms, and our eyes meet. Her body is pressed to mine, and I can feel the thrum of her heart against my chest. The song continues, but any noise ceases to exist around us.

We stare at each other, faces inches apart, unable to speak, but her feelings are written across her angelic features: shock, desire, confusion, lust.

"Dax," she breathes, mainly talking to herself, as if she's wondering if it's me standing there in front of her. "I guess we should talk," she says but makes no move to pull away.

She is again seemingly talking more to herself than to me. I lift my hand to her cheek, my thumb slowly caressing her bottom lip and onto the curve of her jaw.

"Later," I say against her lips a second before my mouth crashes onto hers.

I swipe my tongue over her lips, and after a second, she relaxes and allows me entry to deepen the kiss. Her lips are unbelievably soft, and she tastes like vanilla and tequila. She moans quietly against my mouth as I gently bite her lower lip. We're lost to each other, to the kiss and the way our bodies are pressed into each other.

I hear someone clear their throat next to me, and a hand lands on my shoulder, instantly bringing me back to reality and the fact that we're still in the middle of a dance floor, making out like teenagers.

We break the kiss, and I pull Liv even tighter, instinctually wanting to keep her with me, protecting her from whoever interrupted us.

Jameson gently squeezes my shoulder and yells into my ear so I can hear him over the music. "Hey, dude, why don't you guys head upstairs." He points up to the VIP section where we were sitting with Theo and Eric. I'm still in a daze, but I intertwine her fingers with mine. There's no way I'm letting her out of my sight now.

"Follow me," I mouth to her, and she nods and smiles.

With our hands locked tight, I lead her off the dance floor to our table upstairs.

We melt into the crowd of inebriated clubbers, taking the stairs to the VIP lounge. Emma and Jameson are close behind us. We get to our table, and Eric and Theo stand up to greet the girls. A couple more girls showed up there after we left our table to hunt down Liv and Emma.

I pull Liv onto my lap in one fluid motion, still not believing she's here. Emma slides in, and Jameson is next to her. A tall brunette comes and sidles up next to Jameson and throws her arm around him. She says something in his ear that is meant for a private conversation. Emma snorts unceremoniously and looks away, clearly annoyed. Theo and Eric laugh but their eyes dart from Emma to Jameson to the brunette. Jameson keeps a straight face and, without a word, simply removes her arm from his shoulder and looks away, ignoring her completely.

The music is loud, drowning out her angry response to his lack of interest in her. After she yells at him about being a terrible lay, adding yet another moment of awkwardness, she gets up and leaves.

"Do you want a drink?" Jameson asks her, not even acknowledging that there was another girl there a moment ago that he had obviously hooked up with.

She nods, and he waves the waiter over. I watch this all transpire and realize that maybe I am not alone in this situation of pining for a girl from Padre Island.

A minute later, Eduardo comes back to the table and has a big smile on his face. I realize it's not directed at Jameson but at the girl beside him— Emma.

"Emma," Eduardo practically purrs her name as if he is completely unfazed by the daggers Jameson is currently shooting at him with his eyes.

"Hey there, Eduardo," Emma says in her ever-pleasant manner.

Whatever I was telling Liv is cut off mid-sentence as she sweeps her attention away from me to Eduardo. What the fuck.

"Thanks so much for letting us into the club and setting us up tonight. That was so hospitable of you," Emma continues.

Liv looks between them both and agrees by shaking her head in acknowledgment.

"Liv and I are having such a great time."

I see Jameson now visibly tense. Eduardo notices this movement and curls his head to his friend's side, studying him. What am I witnessing here? He turns his attention back to Emma.

"I'll be in touch. I have to go tend to some business, but please enjoy yourself and let me know if you need anything." With that, Eduardo leaves, and we all look at Emma, who is blushing.

Liv leans over to Emma and loudly whispers something about flowers. Emma shakes her head and whispers something back in Liv's ear, which I cannot hear since the music seems to have gotten louder, if that is at all possible.

Jameson tries to act nonchalant, but I know him well enough to know that that's total bullshit. He's pissed. Does he know something about Eduardo? There is a story between Jameson and Emma that I will have to ask him about later.

Liv fidgets slightly in my lap, and our eyes meet again. My mind is blank. All this time wanting her. Dreaming about her. Lusting for her. Now she's in my arms, and I don't know what to say.

I feel the heat radiating off Liv's body, and she settles back into my lap. Her skirt has ridden up, and my hand rests on her bare thigh. My thumb draws circles on her warm skin, and I focus on the satin-like feeling of her leg. I look into her eyes and see the lust transfixed on me that causes the pulse to rise in my chest. It feels hard to breathe with her so close. I shift her in my lap as my erection starts to press against her. I know she can feel it because she starts to squirm. I pull her tighter to me and whisper in her ear.

"This is what you do to me, baby. I can't help it with you sitting on my lap."

She melts into me further, and I move my hand a bit higher up her thigh. This is so different from that first-time meeting months ago. If the night had played out differently, had Brodie not been injured, would I have had her that night? Would I have made her mine months ago? I know the answer would have been an irrevocable yes. Now, I cannot deny the feelings I have for this woman, and I don't want to pretend that I don't want her. The question is, does she want me as much?

The night continues with this play between Liv and me. Eduardo, ever the gracious host, sends complimentary shots our way, and we are all pretty drunk as the night progresses. Liv and I dance a bit more as we grind against each other on the dance floor.

The last song is playing, and lights are going up. Liv tells me that she has to run to the bathroom, and I go to close out my tab.

"I'll be waiting for you."

She turns, still walking backward. "Don't make promises you can't keep, Dax."

Smiling like the cat that ate the canary, I likewise mutter, "Game on,

Liv."

Emma takes this opportunity to come over and chat as her friend saunters away. "Treat my friend well," she screams in my ear.

I look at her and see that she's smashed. "She's been through a lot, and I don't want to see her hurt." She pokes me in the shoulder, meaning to drive her point home, but I think it's more to steady herself than anything.

I don't see Jameson around, so I stay with her while she sways back and forth. I doubt Liv will be happy with me if I let her best friend pass out on the dance floor.

I motion to Theo and tell him to grab her water. Jameson returns with her water that Theo hands him on his way over. They exchange a few sentences, and Theo slaps him on the shoulder, laughing. I ease her over to the chair, and she smiles.

"Thanks, Dax. I may have had too much to drink." She hiccups and laughs as she raises her hand to cover her mouth.

"Drink up, babe," Jameson says as he pushes the cup to her mouth.

She drinks it all and hands it back. I grab my phone and call an Uber before I search for Liv in the crowd. I see her making her way back over, catching my eye and smiling. Before she gets back to me, Eduardo stops her, and they chat for a few minutes. She walks back to us as I am about to make my way over there.

"What did he say to you?" I immediately ask, not bothering to hide my jealousy.

She just looks at me and turns to Emma. "Eduardo wanted to ensure you were okay and called a car to take you home." I don't know if she realizes she didn't say take "us" home. Her hand squeezes mine, and my heart pounds in my chest as I pull her closer.

"How are you getting home? Are you going with Emma?" I ask.

"Can I stay with you tonight?" she says almost at the same time I ask her about her going home.

"You are definitely coming home with me tonight, Liv," I say as I place my mouth against hers and kiss her hard.

"Okay, guys." Theo hits my back, and I grab onto Liv.

"Let's go," I say as I walk toward the entrance with Liv tucked into my side.

I look back to see Eric and Theo laughing at my expense. Jameson is helping Emma to step out of the club. Just as Eduardo promised, a car is waiting to take Emma home. Jameson helps Emma in the car and tells the driver to wait. He comes over to us.

"I can get her home if you want to stay out longer. You're more than welcome to come with us, but I am staying. I just want to ensure she is okay, you know?"

As Liv is about to answer, I pull her into me and answer for her. "Tell Emma she will see her tomorrow when I drop her off." With that, I turn to walk toward my Uber waiting for us a few cars down.

As we walk away, I hear Jameson yell, "It's about time," right before he slides into the back seat with Emma and shuts the door.

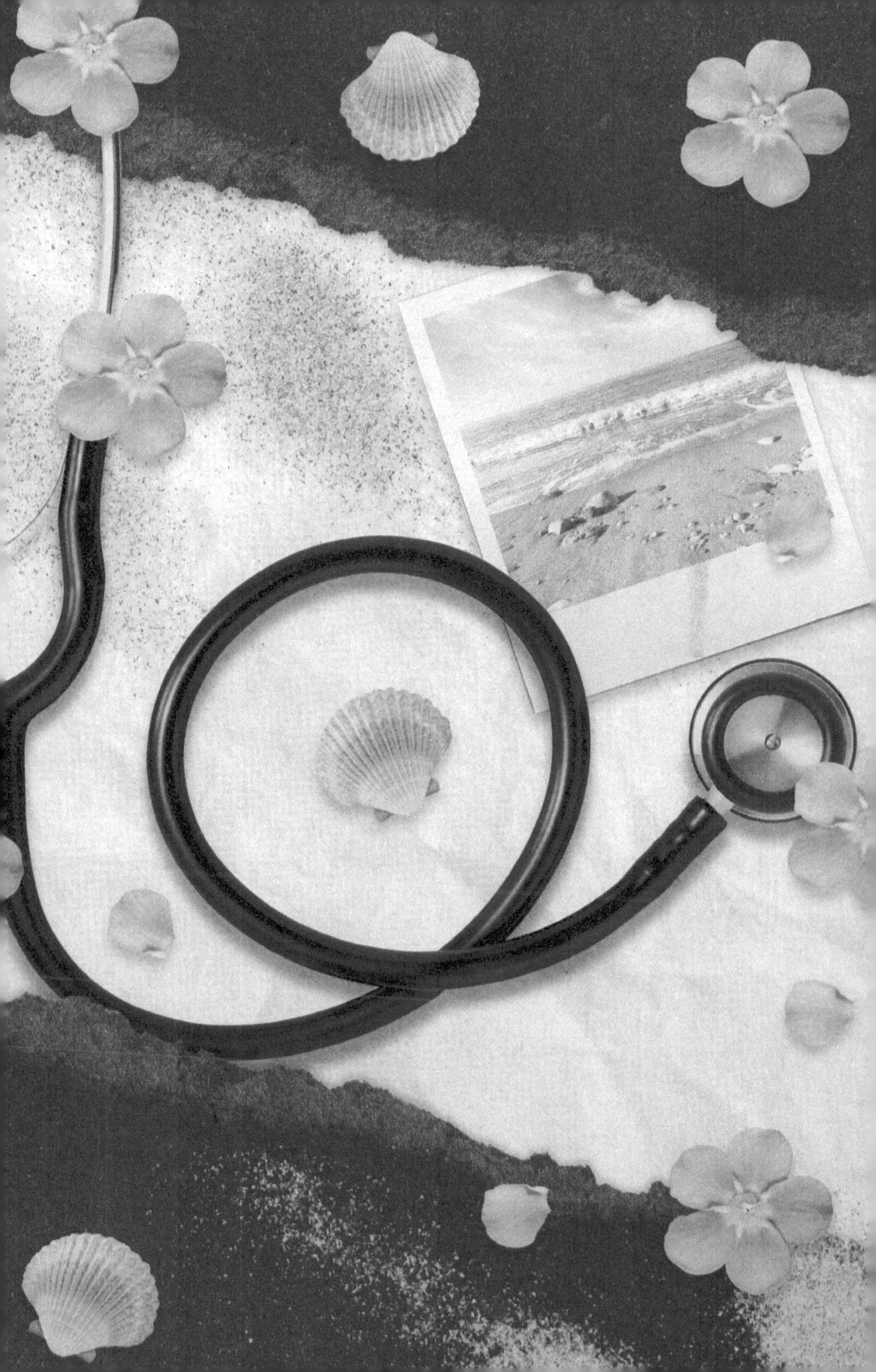

CHAPTER SEVENTEEN

LIV

I get into the Uber car with Dax, and a million thoughts go through my mind. It's hard to think with him in such close proximity. My senses are on overdrive.

He drapes an arm across the back of my shoulder and pulls me into his side. I can feel the warmth of his body, his hard-muscled thigh pressing against my own. My heart is beating out of my chest, and I'm sure he can sense that too.

He turns his head and gently kisses my hair, and I melt a little inside. This moment, being with him, heading back to his place, is something I've been thinking about and wishing for months to happen.

I take a deep breath and struggle to get my nerves in check. He was with that beautiful woman not too long ago… Is anything more going on between them? Did he break it off? I say a little prayer, hoping that's the case because I don't feel I can compete with that woman. She was extraordinary, and I'm, well, I'm pretty ordinary.

We drive in silence, both of us trying to figure out what is happening. Downtown Houston passes by in a whirl through the windows. The city looks calm and pretty; the streets are practically empty this morning—such contrasts to how it feels during the day with the constant chaos and traffic congesting the city. We turn into Dax's apartment complex and pull up in front of a high-rise building.

"This is it," he whispers in my ear.

I know he means we've reached his place, but I can't help the feeling that he is saying something more. I look up at the towering building, wondering what floor he's on. Could we live here together? Would I like it here? I wonder if we would raise kids in the suburbs?

I shake my head at the rapid-fire questions that go through my mind in quick succession: thoughts about a future with a guy I barely know.

I look over and see Dax looking at me with a tilt of his head as if he is trying to read my thoughts. I am glad he can't because he would be fleeing from the crazy ideas I have about us.

"Where did you just go, Liv? I swear, I wish I could see into your head and reassure you."

I give him a small smile, and he tucks a loose strand of hair from my braids behind my ear. He grazes my cheek with his hand. He drops it down to take my hand in his.

"Come on, let's go inside."

My heart practically beats out of my chest as he pulls me out of the car and leads me into his building. We take the elevator up, and I lose track of what floor we're on. The space is so tiny that I swear I can hear his breathing match the beating of my heart. A rhythm in sync as we wait an infinite amount of time, and the doors finally open.

We walk down the hall, and he stops to unlock and open the door without letting go of my hand. I assume he thinks I am still a flight risk after what he witnessed of my past behavior. I can't blame him either because the feeling of bolting back through the elevator doors isn't out of the question.

I'm scared of this man and the emotion that has become so intense in a short time. I can't stop the way my heart rate picks up when he is near or my skin buzzes with electricity when he brushes against me. The way he holds me makes me feel safe in his arms.

I walk through his front door, and he pulls me into his body. My head tips back, and my eyes flutter closed, expecting him to ravage me. But instead, he asks if I want something to drink.

"Um…sure, just some water, please," I manage to stutter out, feeling like a fool for thinking he would kiss me. "Your place is beautiful."

And it is. I look around and take in the modern furniture and neutral tones. He has it tastefully but simply decorated. It's masculine, sexy, and suits him perfectly.

He sees me looking around, and a brilliant smile spreads across his face as if it's just hit him that I'm here. He walks over to his kitchen, and that need to escape rushes over me again.

"Where is your bathroom, Dax?" I say, immediately feeling like I need a moment to myself.

"Just through the hall, first door on the right."

I turn around and head to the bathroom.

"Liv," he calls after me.

I turn around before I get to the door.

"I'm so happy you're here."

The honesty in his voice and the longing in his eyes are palpable. I close the door quickly, place my hands on the bathroom counter, and hang my head. What is this man doing to me? I look up in the mirror at my reflection and see a woman with flushed cheeks and smudged mascara.

I quickly use the bathroom and make myself presentable. I hear music playing and quickly recognize the song "Infinity" by Jaymes Young playing on his surround sound speakers.

I open the door and spot him with his arm on the island with my drink in his hand. I realize that he isn't going to come over to me, so I make my way over to where he is standing in all his magnificence. He is the perfect male specimen. His shirt is untucked, and his sleeves are rolled up, exposing those impressive corded forearms displaying muscular arms. I can't help but be drawn to him.

He never takes his eyes off me as I walk toward him, his eyes drinking me in. He hands me my water.

"Thirsty?" he asks.

I grab the water and take a drink. "You have no idea."

I feel beads of water falling on my lips and I lick them. His eyes smolder as he grabs the glass from me and puts it behind him on the counter. He reaches up to rub his thumb over my lip, and I move closer. His other hands wrap around my waist, and he pulls my body flush with his. He stares right into my eyes.

"You have no idea how long I've wanted this," he practically growls before his gaze drops to my mouth.

He leans in, and his lips graze mine in the gentlest of ways. His tongue darts out to lick my lip. Tasting. Teasing. My mouth parts and my breath catches in my chest as I feel his breath exhale over my lips. A sigh escapes me when he deepens the kiss, crushing his lips to mine like a starved man.

I swear I might pass out with the onslaught of heated emotions. Any chance I had of acting indifferent is gone. My protective shield around my heart crashes as I let him take me. Somewhere in my mind, there's a little voice telling me to be careful, but my traitorous body can't deny the magnetism I feel for him.

Heat builds between my legs. My panties become slick. The feeling of his hands on me is overwhelming as they slowly travel down my back to my ass, pulling me even closer as I push my hips forward, trying to get the friction I desperately need. One of his legs slides between mine, making them open, and I gasp as he grinds his thigh onto my center. All my blood seems to have rushed to my groin, and my clit swells with its own heartbeat.

I can feel his erection growing, pushing into my hip as he continues to take my mouth, tongue darting in and out, giving me an idea of what else he wants to do.

I can no longer deny what will happen tonight.

I break the kiss and look up at Dax. He looks at me with lust-filled eyes, and I can see he is afraid I will stop this.

"I need you, Dax."

Relief instantly washes across his face. His strong hands circle my waist as he lifts me, and I wrap my legs around him. His mouth retakes mine, and he blindly walks us down the hall, not stopping until we reach his bedroom.

He throws me on the bed and immediately starts unbuttoning his shirt. "You have no idea how long I have waited for this, Liv."

He drops his shirt to the floor and leans over to slip my dress over my hips. The light from the hall spills in and washes over his muscled chest and abs. A little trail of hair begins at his belly button, coursing down below the waistband of his pants. I trace the V along his lower abdomen, curling my fingers into the top of his pants and pulling him closer. He shivers, and goose bumps rise on his skin. He looks down at my body and fixes his eyes on my black lace underwear.

"God, you're beautiful," he says under his breath as he gently grabs my thong and pulls it down my leg, removing my shoes with it. He drops to his knees and wraps his arms on either side of my hips, pulling me down to the edge of the bed. "So fucking beautiful" is the last thing I hear before he buries his face in my pussy.

He slowly licks a line straight through my center and stops at the top, sucking gently on my clit. My back bows off his bed, and I can't hold back the moan as he eats me like I'm his favorite dessert.

His tongue flattens and pushes onto my clit before he starts making slow circles around it. My brain short-circuits as flashes of light blink behind my closed eyes. He increases his speed, alternating between sucking and licking and fucking me with his tongue.

I move shamelessly, getting the angle I need to get the desired effect. I push my fingers into his hair, pull him even closer, and grind on his face. His attention returns to my clit as he slowly pushes two fingers inside me.

"You taste so good," he mumbles into my pussy.

And that's all I need. He sucks once more, and I shatter. I am moaning his name and rolling my hips in his mouth. The orgasm is so intense that it washes through me like a tsunami, and he licks me through every second.

The sensations from the aftershocks are almost as fierce, and I whimper when he continues to lap me post-orgasm. He crawls up my body, his face wet with my arousal.

"I need you," he growls, repeating my own words.

He lifts me from the bed and spins me around, pulling the zipper down and guiding my dress over my hips. His fingers unhook my bra, pushing it down over my shoulders before throwing it to the floor. I stay still, gazing at his bed, feeling his warmth behind me. I don't want to move for fear I'll wake up from this heavenly dream.

His soft, warm lips land on my shoulder as I hear his zipper pull down and his pants hit the floor. It's exactly what I need to snap out of my haze, and I turn to take him in. I've dreamed of Dax's cock before and want to see if my dreams did it justice. He pulls his boxers down, and his stiff, thick cock springs free. My mouth salivates, wanting to taste him. I want him in my mouth. I need him in my mouth.

Tentatively, I reach out, rubbing my thumb across his broad head, spreading a drop of precum that leaks from the tip. I see his ab muscles clench, and he tightens his grip on my hips. I circle my hand around his shaft and bring it down, stroking him in one long movement. He shudders and pulls my hand away.

"Later, Liv. Right now, I need to be inside you. I can't wait any longer."

His mouth crashes into mine as he pushes me back into the bed and brings his body over mine. I can taste my arousal on him, but can't be concerned about it in the least bit. His knees move my thighs wide, spreading me open for him. He holds the base of his cock as he rubs himself through the wetness that has collected between my legs. He drags his thick length up and down through my slick center. His gentle movements pressing into my already sensitive clit is almost enough to send me over the edge again. He angles down the tip of his shaft right at my entrance.

"Look at me, Liv."

I do as he says and looks up at him.

"I want to see you as I fuck you for the first time."

With that, he enters me in one quick thrust, and my head falls back on the bed. I am filled to the hilt with his thick cock. Unlike the gentleness he showed me before, he thrusts in and out hard. He must realize his animalistic reaction as he slows a moment to lean over and take one of my breasts in his mouth. His tongue circles my nipple and bites down gently. The mixture of pleasure and pain making me moan his name.

"Liv, you have no idea how badly I've needed to hear that."

He pulls back and returns to fucking me with punishing thrusts. His eyes are fixed on my breasts, bouncing up and down from the force of his impaling cock. The sensation is so deep that I feel on the verge of another orgasm. I pull my legs apart even farther, needing more of him.

"Deeper, please, Dax, deeper."

My breath starts to quicken. I can feel Dax fuck me harder as sounds of the bed hitting the wall echo through the room. I am almost on the verge of release. He moves his hand between us to pinch my clit, which sends me into an intense climax. His thrusts become erratic; a moment later, his body tenses as he empties himself inside me.

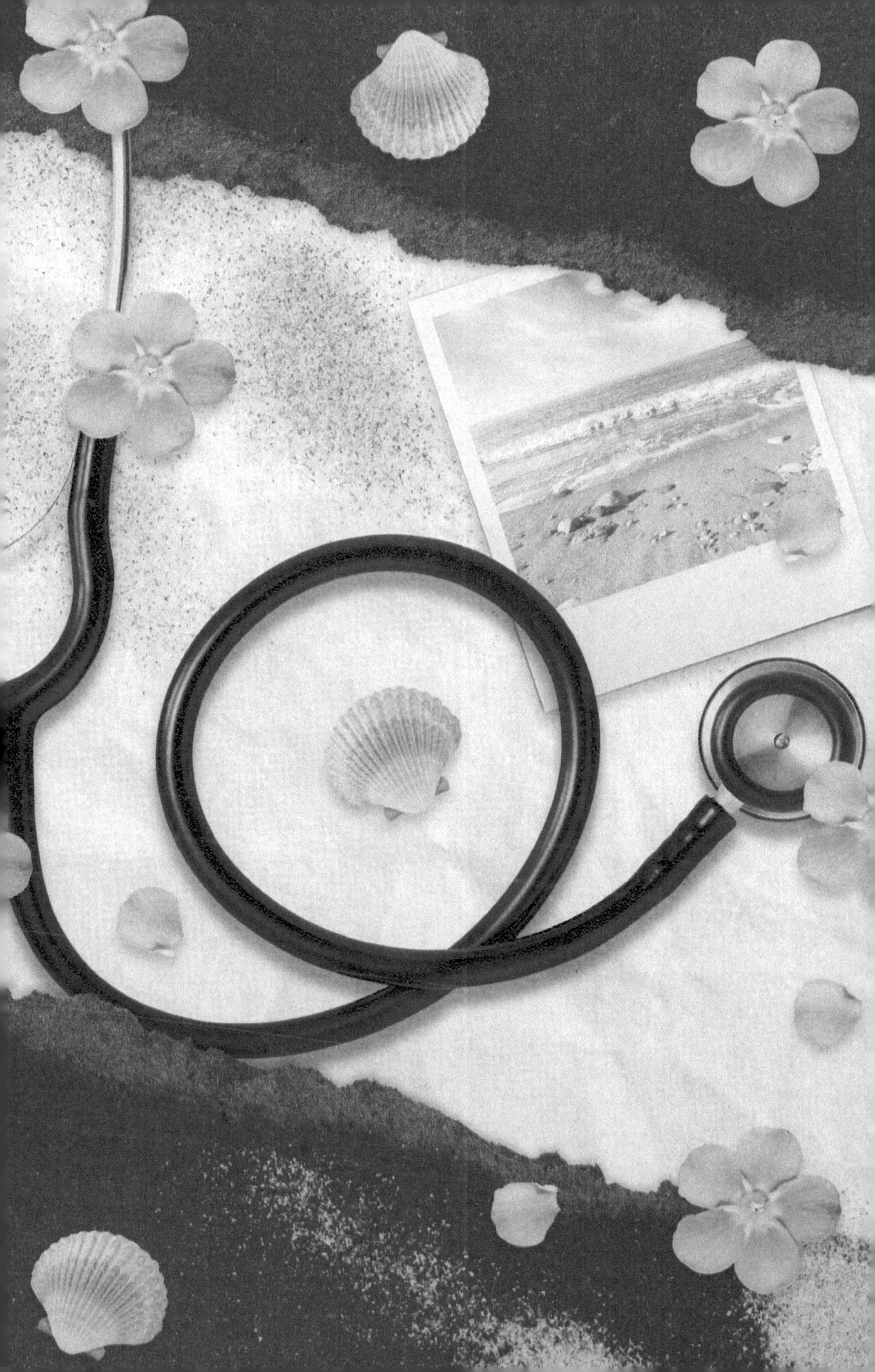

CHAPTER EIGHTEEN

DAX

I feel myself let go as I empty my cum inside her. The hot liquid inside feels warm against my already sensitive skin. I stay there briefly before pulling out. I release her and see my semen dripping down her leg. This makes me realize two things. One, that looks hot as fuck on her. I could get used to seeing this. Liv, with my cum dripping down from her pussy for a lifetime or more. Two, that immediately makes me realize that my semen is dripping down her leg. Meaning that for once in my life, I forgot the condom.

Holy shit. I am now freaking out. I stare, looking at Liv, and she must sense my feelings. "I have never come inside a woman without protection," I stammer. "I mean, ever."

I grab at my hair while tugging it. I can't believe I forgot to wrap it this time. I must have been thinking with my dick to let this happen. Instead, I rephrase my thoughts into a better question.

"Liv, um, are you on the pill? I guess we should have had this discussion sooner, huh?"

She just stands there looking at me, and I can already guess what her answer will be. "My last boyfriend was Brodie, and we haven't been together in a while, but I have been on the pill to regulate my periods, mostly because they are so inconsistent."

I look up at her and rub the back of my neck in concentration. I move to stroke her cheek next. "Great, I should have asked first."

At least she is on birth control, ending that discussion of a possible pregnancy scare. How many people have gone through this same scenario— questioning the use of contraceptives after the fact? Then find out they are going to be a parent. I think hard about it. I do want kids with Liv, which should freak me out more, but it doesn't.

"I enjoyed going bareback with you, and now I can't wait to do that again."

I move to press her into me and grab her tight around the waist. She pulls away, laughing. I then walk off in search of a towel. I haven't known this woman for that long, but I do know that I want her in my life. It is just the timing of an unexpected pregnancy is not the best with us both beginning our careers and not being married. My parents will definitely not approve of that.

It also makes me realize that I don't know much about Liv's parents. I have heard a little from what she said about her mom working at the hospital and her dad passing away. What would they have thought of an unplanned pregnancy? I need to make a point of meeting her mom. Perhaps after the gala my mom is co-chairing, we can plan to get together during the holidays to spend time with each other's families. That will help to solve that dilemma.

I'm not an old-fashioned type of guy or religious by any means, but I want Liv to have it all. The big wedding and house if she wants. She deserves that. And of course, as long as it is with me.

I lay there spent. I lean over to kiss her and leave for the bathroom. I return quickly and go to my bureau to retrieve a shirt for Liv. "Lift your arms, Liv."

She does as I say, appearing unable to form words. I cover her with the shirt. I catch her sniffing it.

"What are you doing?" I chuckle as I see the most adorable expression on her face.

"It's just so soft and smells like you."

"Me?" I look at her questioningly.

"Yeah, like sandalwood and clean laundry. I swear I could smell it sometimes when I was thinking about you."

I pull my underwear back on and flop back into bed. "You thought about me often, beautiful?"

I pull her on top of me, and I lay there underneath, wondering if she's gonna try to leave. It's clear I want her here, but I need to reassure her.

Right on cue, she asks, "Should I call an Uber?"

I look at her, confused, and then kiss her again. "No, you're staying here."

I hope that clarifies enough for her as I place her head on my chest, kissing her forehead. Her breathing slows, and the rise and fall of her chest against mine soothes me into a wave of peaceful sleep.

CHAPTER NINETEEN

DAX

My alarm goes off in the morning, and I silence it. Thankfully, it's within reach because I'm unable to move. A warm, soft body is pressed against mine, Liv's head is on my chest, legs entwined with mine. I watch her sleep. The way her mouth is slightly open. Her eyelids fluttering, as if she is in the last state of REM sleep, dreaming before she wakes.

I reach for my phone on the nightstand and snap a few pictures of her sleeping. I want to remember her this way—in my bed with this blissed-out look on her face after I thoroughly fucked her last night.

I close my eyes and drift back to last night, remembering how she moved when I touched her. The little whimpering sounds she made when I rubbed at her clit and when I found the right angle; she wasn't shy about what she wanted. She hung tight as I fucked her hard and she came around my cock, panting out my name as she climaxed.

Click. I snapped a mental picture. The memories of that night are now seared in my brain.

I touch a piece of her silky hair that fell out of her braided bun from last night and twirl it gently between my fingers. I push it behind her ear, my calloused hands brushing against her smooth cheek. Even though it's only been a few hours, I want her again.

My cock swells at the thought. What would it be like to wake up to her every day? More blood pools low in my groin. A future with Liv? Is that possible? Will she want the same thing? I push the thoughts aside and focus on the angelic woman in my bed. I pull back the cover and slowly drink up her lithe body.

I unlink her body from mine. My eyes take in her breasts, flat stomach, and cleanly shaved pussy. I crawl over her and push her legs apart with my knees. She stirs and moans quietly, wiggling a little underneath me. I lower myself to my belly and drop my face to her entrance. I spread her lips wide with my fingers, give her a swift lick, and gently suck on her clit. Her hips move, and a louder moan escapes her.

I look up to see her looking at me with hooded lids, cheeks flushed. I lick her at a slow pace while holding her eyes. God, she is beautiful. And she tastes like heaven.

She grasps my hair and pulls me closer. I give her small, measured strokes and lap at her clit. She moves around, trying to add friction, starting to grind against my tongue. I can't hold back any longer and attack her with unexpected savagery. I lap her as a man starved would. And I am. I have been denied months from her and this physical closeness.

She grabs harder onto my hair, but I couldn't give a fuck. Her panting increases and I suck harder. She starts to pulse around my tongue, coming on my face. I continue to lick as the last of her orgasm abates. She exhales and pushes me away when I try to draw out more of her release.

"Too sensitive." She attempts to cross her legs to move out.

I laugh as I pull her into me and kiss her. She kisses me back fully, and I am sure she can taste herself on my tongue. If she does, she doesn't comment on it. Much like last night. I trail little kisses down her jaw to her neck.

"Good morning," I murmur into her neck.

"Good morning, Dax."

My name on her lips is the sweetest sound.

"That may have been the best wake-up I've ever had," she says, still blinking sleep from her eyes.

"Get used to it," I say, hoping she understands the unsaid promise of more nights and mornings together in our near future.

I get up, pulling her with me and ignoring my rock-hard cock pushing against my boxers. "Get dressed, and I'll make us some coffee," I say, drawing on a pair of gray sweatpants.

She gives me a wicked smile.

"That's my second favorite thing to do in the morning from now on."

She blushes and turns to find her clothes.

I leave the room, hoping my hard-on will abate for a moment, and make my way to the kitchen. We both needed coffee after the night we had. I have a slight hangover, but it's not too bad, considering the number of shots we drank last night.

I grab a few Motrin from the kitchen drawer and down it with a glass of water. I lay a couple out for Liv, in case she wants some too. I can only imagine she will have a headache today after the tequila shots with Emma and the guys last night, not to mention our nearly sleepless night.

My thoughts are interrupted as I see Liv walking toward me, wearing one of my shirts and nothing else, and damn if she doesn't look hotter than her killer dress from last night.

A possessiveness comes over me as I see her yawn and lift her arms to fix her hair. The shirt rides high on her thigh but stops just before it bares herself to me completely. I pull her into an embrace and kiss her neck.

"How do you feel this morning, baby? Do you need some Motrin? I left you some on the counter. Here, take this." I step away to grab her some water and move the Motrin in her direction.

She smiles. "Thanks. Yes, I need to drink some more water, too. I have a dull headache that would suck if it turned into a migraine. I need to refill my medication since I have more migraine attacks in the fall for some reason. I slept well, even though we didn't sleep much." She pushes her face into my chest as if she's shy, then looks up at me. "The wake-up was also award-winning."

I almost spit out my coffee as I see her smirking.

"Got any more of that coffee?"

She turns away from me to look into a cabinet, lifting onto her toes and pushing her butt back as she reaches for a mug. I shift my body behind her and hold on to her hips as I grind my cock against her ass, my hard-on coming back fast.

"Keep that up, and you might not walk for the rest of the week," I growl into her ear as I tug her lobe between my teeth.

She laughs and leans her face around to kiss me quickly as she steps aside to grab her coffee.

"It's wise not to get in the way of my morning cup of joe." She takes a sip and relaxes. "Rain check?" she teases.

I can't hide the smile as I enjoy the playful banter between us. It seems so natural and effortless.

"What are your plans for today?" I ask as I resume drinking my coffee.

We are both standing in the kitchen as if this is a normal thing for us.

"I'm going to visit Brodie today. I usually spend some time with him on Sundays."

It's as if she splashed cold water on my face. I judge her facial expression, which has gone somber. I am about to ask about that situation when her phone rings. She goes to look at who's calling and sends it to voicemail. She places her coffee cup down and walks over to me. She gives me a hug and a quick kiss on the cheek.

"I need to go. I have a ton of things to do today."

"I'll take you," I quickly add, not wanting to be away from her just yet.

She looks at me and smiles. "Okay, I'll get changed."

She leaves to go back to my bedroom. I grab my coffee and pull on a shirt, waiting for her as I stare out the window that overlooks the city.

She makes her way back into the kitchen, dressed in last night's clothes and her hair piled on top of her head.

"Ready?" I ask.

Although, as the word leaves my mouth, I have an unsettling feeling and fear that I may not see her again after this. I can't let that happen. I need to make sure I see her again.

We walk out in silence, both of us unsure of what to say. I open the door for her, and she gets into my car. I slip into my seat and reluctantly start the engine.

"Where to?'"

She gives me her address, and I pull away slowly. The continued silence that fills the car is deafening. I hit my playlist and "Texas Sun" comes on by Leon Bridges. I think back to that day on the beach. How the sun shone, and Liv was hot as sin in that bikini.

I put the windows down since it feels good and it's breezy today. The wind is blowing her hair, and I don't think I can ever tire of looking at her. The constant desire threatens to rip me apart if I can't be near her.

Unfortunately, the ride is short.

Five minutes later, driving to her place becomes tense. She continues to look out the window as we drive, and I don't know what to say.

When can I see you again? Call me later. What is going on with Brodie? None of them feel right. And a moment later, we're pulling up to her place.

"Want me to walk you in?"

She looks my way and smiles sadly. "No, I need to go."

I feel her slipping away, so I grab her arm and pull her toward me. I hug her tightly and smell the sweet scent that seems to bathe her skin as I reluctantly let go. I pull her face into mine and kiss her. I continue to kiss her as she moans into my mouth. She places her hand on mine and pulls away. I search her eyes, trying to figure out what she's feeling.

"I'll text you later?" I say in a pleading voice.

She just nods as she steps out of my car without looking back. I watch her walk up the stairs into her apartment, where she unlocks the door and walks in. I sit there for a couple of minutes, wanting to run after her. That seems to be what I've been doing since she walked back into my life at Starbucks that afternoon.

I pull away from the driveway and start to head back home. Instead, I decided to hit the gym before I have to do some prep work for my day of surgery tomorrow in the operating room. We have a gym in the building where I live, but it lacks a lot of the equipment I like to use. That's why I also have a gym bag in the back ready, in case the opportunity presents itself and I get out of work early or a case is canceled. It's the surgeon in me–always prepared.

I will be there early tomorrow as I have a long day ahead, continuing into the evening. I decide to work myself to the bone, exercising to get this pent-up frustration out of my mind and deal with the current situation I find myself in.

I have to tell Tatiana that whatever we had is officially over. I don't want to screw up my progress with Liv thus far.

I run for what seems like forever on the treadmill, until my legs want to give out. I hit the stop button and feel a sense of accomplishment. I wipe the sweat off my neck and face as I reach for my water bottle. I shoot off a text to Liv that says, **thinking of you.** I gather my things and make my way to my car, heading home. As I get into the car, my phone alerts me of a text message.

A reply of, **always thinking of you**, is sent back.

I exhale a breath I didn't realize I was holding as I reread her text message, a smile spreading over my face. I once again wonder if things had gone differently that night at the beach, if Liv and I would be in a relationship now instead of the uncertainty of limbo between us. I am willing to wager a yes to that without reservation.

I will have to gain her trust and make her realize that I am the person she needs. The person she looks to for comfort. The person she looks to for her future.

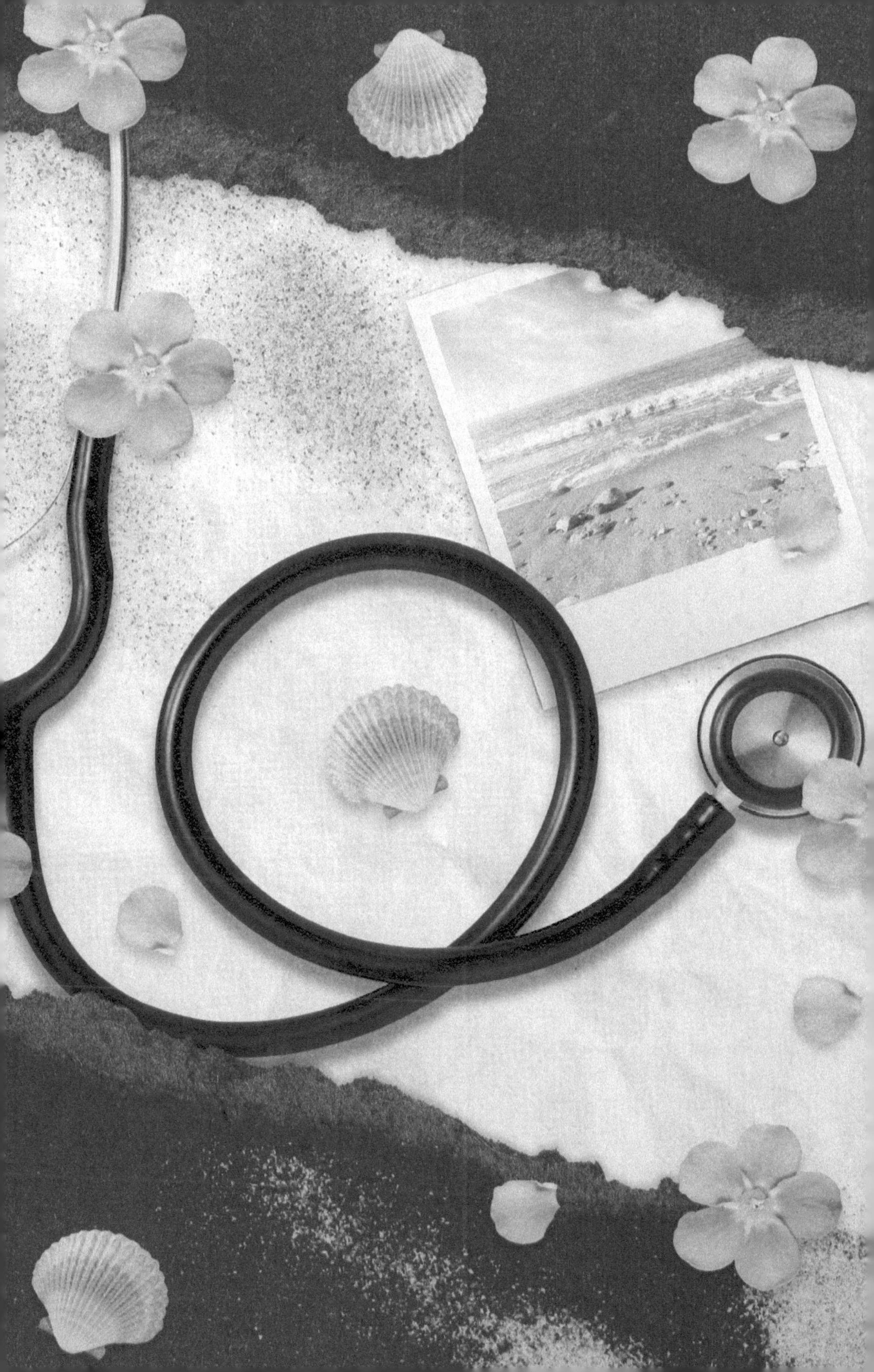

CHAPTER TWENTY

LIV

I miss Dax as soon as I step out of his car. I get my keys and push open the door. I didn't look back as I walked in; if I did, I knew I'd just end up running back into his arms. He is addictive. His scent overtakes my senses and makes me crave more of him.

He is most definitely all man—the way he took possession of my body. He took it freely, yielding it to his every whim. I melted under his embrace and yearned for more. I don't think I can ever get enough of Dax. From the moment I met him, something drew me to him, a magnetic field that tethered his soul to mine. I don't believe in twin flames, but I totally get the whole Machine Gun Kelly and Megan Fox thing they keep referring to about each other. That must be what a soulmate feels like. Like I was made for him and vice versa.

I reluctantly make my way into the apartment and put my things down on the chair in the foyer.

As I move into the living room, I see clothes thrown haphazardly around—a shirt, a pair of pants, panties, bra, oh my. Emma had an eventful night as well. I wonder if Jameson had a good night too.

I go to get a glass of water and see the door open to Emma's room. I am about to say hello to Jameson when I look at another face—Eduardo. He pushes his hand through his hair and greets me in a bashful way that I know is complete bullshit. There is nothing timid about this man.

His white tank undershirt allows for a full display of his tattoos. I must not have noticed them last night because he hid them well. They go all the way up his arms to his neck. He grabs his shirt and pants unabashedly, strolling in his boxers in front of me. I am mouth open, full-on staring at the complete specimen of this man in front of me. He displays power and wealth that radiates off him in aces.

I also noticed a vibe I didn't sense before, and it's dangerous. I attempt to make eye contact and say, "Hi?" It comes out more of a question.

He laughs. "Hi, Liv. I'll be out of your hair in a second." He throws his arms out. "Just need to get dressed." He puts his clothes on in front of me and grabs his keys off the coffee table in the living room. "I'll see you later. Have a good day." He winks and walks out, disappearing as quickly as he appears.

I am getting the full story when that hooker wakes up. That will have to wait until later. I need a shower badly.

I shower, dress quickly, throw my hair in a messy bun, and head out to see Brodie. As much as I want to talk to Emma, I know she probably has a massive hangover, and anyway, I'll get the scoop from her when I have more time. I usually visit Brodie on Sunday afternoons. It's been our thing for months. I load up my Jeep and speed away to his house. The song "Boyfriend" by Dove Cameron comes on, and I think about my dilemma with Dax.

I still have many questions for him, such as who was that girl he was with and what I am to him. It's best not to ask this stuff now and just let it play out. I thought I had lost him after I set him free. He somehow returned to my life. *If they return, they're yours.*

I ponder all these things as I pull up to the gated community where Brodie's house is located. I'm let in by security and drive down the street until I approach his house. I turn off the engine and get out of the Jeep. Once again, I'm greeted by Brodie's nurse.

"Hi, Liv. How are you today?"

I return the smile and greeting. "Hi, Melissa. I'm good. How's Brodie today?"

"You seem happy today. To what do we owe this spring in your step? Good night's sleep, I take it? Or not enough sleep?" she asks with a knowing gleam in her eye.

I snort and try not to meet her gaze. How she can see through me is a mystery. Melissa isn't much older than I am, but she is much wiser than her years. She is married with kids, and I find her very perceptive about things. My cheeks immediately blush.

"Um, a little bit of both, I guess. Emma and I went out last night and danced a lot."

She looks at me, smirking. "Well, that's good, Liv. You need a little fun in your life. Brodie is good. Although I think he's a little depressed, rightfully so."

I look down at my shoes and kick at nothing on the floor. "Yeah, he has every right, I suppose."

She grabs my arm. "Come on, let's get you your favorite latte."

I give her my biggest genuine smile of gratitude as we walk into the kitchen.

I never see Brodie's dad or his stepmom when I come over. It makes me sad to think that he is here all alone. His dad works a lot, and I assume his stepmom stays out of the way, considering how she broke up his mom and dad's marriage. He hasn't had many visitors since the accident and his move back to Houston. All the friends he once considered to be close, have moved on with their lives. The sad realization that he is alone is starting to become apparent. I want him to know that despite all that happened to him and what happened between us, he can count on me for friendship. That will never change us.

I knock on the door and push it open. "Hey, Brodie, what are you up to?"

I see him in his wheelchair looking up at the TV where there are pictures of all of us scrolling along, displaying various times of our high school years. I look up at them and move toward the TV.

"Oh my goodness. Look at that." I start to laugh and see him throwing me into the water, and I come running after him with this look of fury. "I remember that. You lost my sunglasses when you threw me in. I was so mad at you because they were new and expensive."

He looks over at me with a small tilt of his lip, letting me know he remembers too. "We certainly had some fun times, didn't we, Liv?"

I go over to him and sit on his lap. I pull him into a hug and kiss his cheek. "Yes, Brodie, we did." I get up from his lap and go over to retrieve my bag. I start pulling out my books.

"So, what is on the agenda for today?" He moves his wheelchair over to me, and we sit by the window to get comfortable.

"Oh, the usual schoolwork, but tomorrow, I get to go to the hospital and meet the nurse practitioner from the general surgery group where I will be doing my rotation. I am looking forward to it. It allows me to see other practice areas besides the emergency department role. Who knows, maybe I'll like it there and change my mind about where I want to work."

I start to lay out my books, and Melissa comes in to see if I need anything besides my latte. I thank her, but I just want to spend time with Brodie, and then I need to get a good night's sleep to feel my best for tomorrow.

I explain things to Brodie about what is expected of me, and he laughs. It's nice to hear him laugh.

"Are you going to ask tons of questions like you always do?" he replies with a playful expression on his face.

I look at him. "What do you mean?"

He just shakes his head. "You were always the one in class that asked the most questions. I laughed because you had to know exactly how something worked down to the molecule."

I hit him playfully on the arm. "Well, I'm curious. There's nothing wrong with that."

We both continue to enjoy each other's company. It starts to get late, and I begin to pack up my books. When I stand, I see a sad look on his face. He quickly changes it over to a small smile.

"Good luck tomorrow, Liv. I hope you have a good day. I want to hear all about it when you visit me next time."

I embrace him and stay for a bit longer in the hug. "I will give you all the updates. I promise." I give him a quick kiss on the cheek, and his lips turn to meet mine. I pull back, momentarily shocked, and see the same expression on his face. He looks remorseful.

"I'm sorry, Liv, I forgot. It used to be just a normal motion between us that I just reacted without thinking."

I give him another quick kiss on the cheek to let him know that it's okay. This time his lips do not meet mine, and I walk toward the door.

"I'll see you soon, Brodie." I leave the room with a slight wave as I walk through the door feeling in my gut that many more changes are coming for both of us.

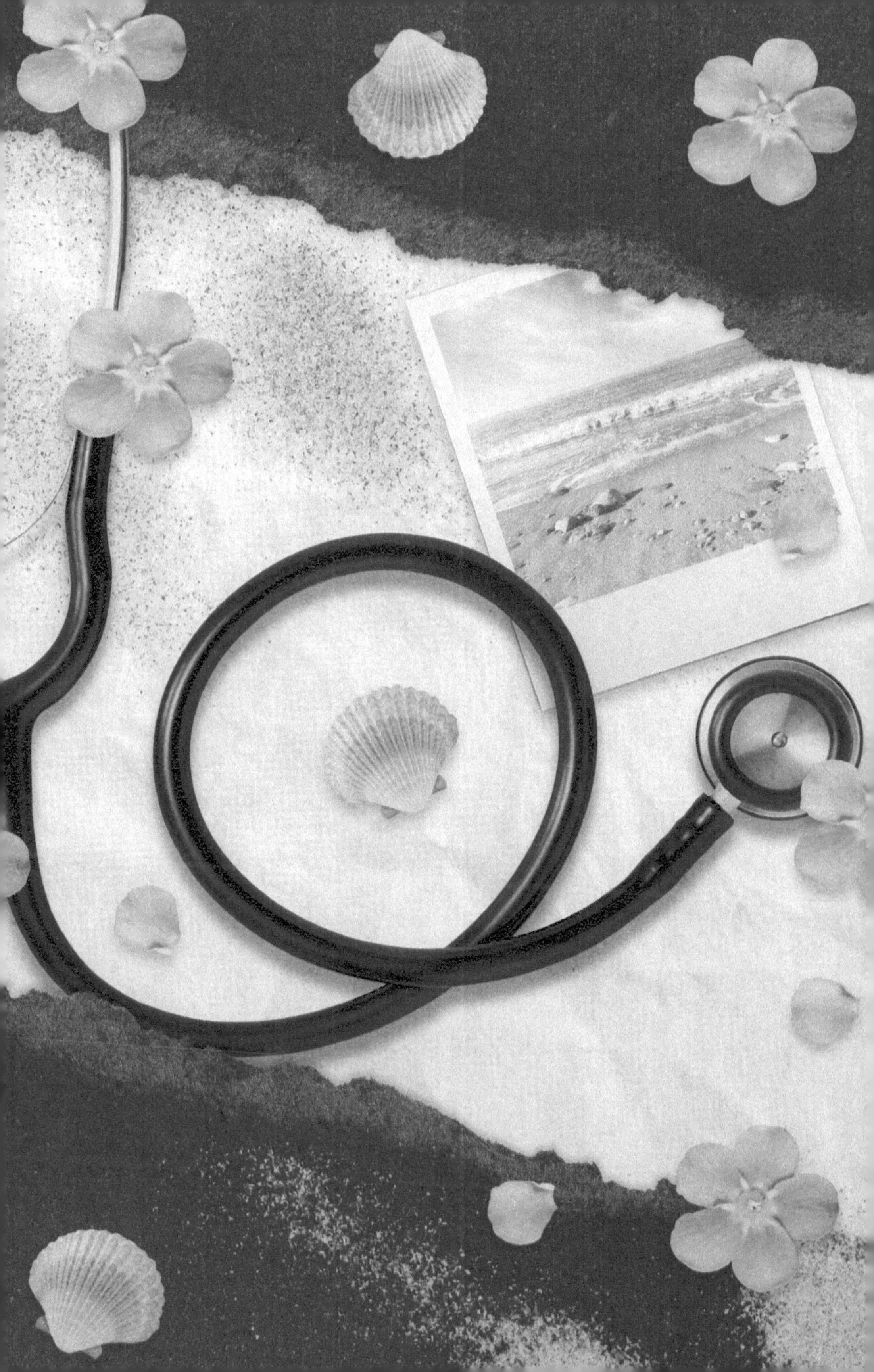

CHAPTER TWENTY-ONE

DAX

After I dropped Liv off at her apartment yesterday morning, I headed to the hospital. I have a long case scheduled in the OR, so I try my best to focus on the day ahead. But my mind continues to drift back to Liv and how she felt in my arms and her warm body against mine, waking to her beautiful face.

Strangely, I woke up feeling rested, despite not sleeping much. But it's not just my body that feels calm; my brain seems at ease too. Maybe it's because she was always on my mind, and now that I, hopefully, have her back, I can finally relax. I was worried I'd never see her again, and the thought downright scared me.

Although, I still don't know where we stand exactly. What if she doesn't feel the same? I shake my head, trying to rip that thought from my brain.

I know that she is mine, especially after last night. There's no denying our chemistry—this pull toward each other. I thought it was all in my head, but now I know for sure that it's real. Now that I had a taste of her, I'm craving more.

My thoughts never stray from Liv as I make my way to work with a smile on my face. I wonder what she's doing this morning and if she's thinking of me too.

She mentioned starting a new clinical rotation for her NP program, so I send her a quick text. **Good luck today. I'm sure you're going to do great.**

The hospital is busy with the morning shift change, and I make my way to the OR, passing friendly faces as I go.

"Good morning, Dr. Johnson," I hear one of the OR nurses say. "You're looking happy today."

"Morning, Sue," I say over my shoulder as I head to the locker room to change. I strip down and pull on my scrubs, glancing at my phone before dropping it into my pocket. There's a text from Liv.

Thank you, chat later, followed by a kissing emoji.

I can't help but smile as I make my way out toward the pre-op area. I look down at my watch and realize I have time for a coffee before things get started, so I head to the café to get an Americano before I start my day.

I walk up to the counter and look at the menu. Although I already know what I'm getting; it's the same every day.

"Morning, Doctor," the cashier, Melanie, croons. She's a shameless flirt. Rumor has it she has slept with half the OR staff. "The usual?" She goes to twirl her hair subconsciously as she says this, and my lip turns up in a smirk.

"Yes, thank you."

She turns around slowly and begins to get my coffee. I am checking my phone for emails when I hear a voice behind me.

"Hey, Liv, want to meet up later to study? We can go to my place or maybe the library?" Melanie hands me my coffee. "Have a good day, Dr. Johnson." My face must display the shock I feel because she then says, "Are you okay?"

"Yeah, fine. Thanks."

Drink in hand, I slowly turn around, and there she is. My Liv. She is standing right behind me. My eyes roam her face, which shows a suppressed laugh, and her eyes are alight with humor.

She looks at me and, in a playful tone, says, "Well, good morning, Dr. Johnson."

My cock twitches in my pants as I try to play it cool. I see the guy she is with shift uncomfortably at her side. I look at him and extend my hand.

"Dax Johnson. I don't think we've met." He moves to shake my hand and then I add, "I'm Liv's boyfriend."

I quickly look over to Liv to gauge her reaction, and I see her lips part for a second as if taken by surprise, and she quickly introduces her fellow student.

"Dax, this is Adam. He's in my class."

"Hey, man, nice to meet you," Adam replies uncomfortably.

I shake his hand and squeeze slightly more than necessary. My possessive side is coming through. Liv and I are still looking at each other as I hear him say, "I'll catch you later, Liv," and he hurriedly steps away from us to order his coffee.

Her entire presence draws me in like a magnet. I step closer purely out of instinct. "Hey, baby, I didn't know you would be at this hospital today." Really stressing the word *this*. I gently caress her cheek, and she leans into my hand.

"Well, you didn't ask. We didn't exactly talk much last night," she whispers.

The most adorable pink blush rushes up her neck into her cheeks, and it takes all my self-control not to pull her into my arms and lock my mouth with hers. But she was right; our night was filled with more moaning than talking, as well as other animalistic sounds. We reconnected through multiple orgasms, not conversation. And we barely had time to talk this morning.

But that needs to change. I want to know everything about her. Not just about school, but her goals and her future. I feel the need to know her completely, and it can't happen soon enough.

"What time do you get out of here today?"

She looks at her watch. "I'm not sure, but I better get going. I don't want to be late to meet my instructor on my first day here."

"Okay, I'll call you later then."

I lean in to give her a quick kiss on the cheek and make my way out the door. I turn back to see that guy waiting for her with a fucking coffee in his hand and extending one to her. He sees me and smiles like the cat that got the canary as he hands it to her. I've got too much going on today to worry about him, and I feel slightly better now that he knows I'm her boyfriend.

Boyfriend. I'm Liv's boyfriend. She didn't deny it or get spooked when I said it. Happy jitters roll through me as I go up the stairs to the second floor that leads to the operating room.

I don't know what possessed me to claim Liv as my girlfriend, but suddenly, I just did, and it felt as natural as breathing. She may not believe me now, but I intend to prove to her that she is, in fact, mine and only mine.

I have a smile on my face as I hit the button to go into the OR. The door slides open, and as I turn the corner toward the back room, I see Tatiana. She waves at me and heads over in my direction.

"Hey, Dax. How are you?" she practically purrs at me as her hand runs down my arm. "I was hoping you could be my date this weekend. I have this work party I need to go to, and I need a plus one."

Stepping back to distance us, I look at her and hesitate. She picks up on my demeanor quickly and squints at me in suspicion.

"What's going on, Dax? You usually love this kind of thing. Especially the after-party at my house." She winks and tries to step closer to me again. I am about to reply, but her pager goes off, dismissing me as she walks quickly down the corridor. "We'll talk later, Dax," I hear her say as she turns the corner, her white coat swishing behind her.

Well, this gives me some time to chat with her about Liv later, and at least I have time to decide how I will let her know I have a girlfriend now. I laugh, thinking I didn't give her a choice. *Damn straight,* I think to myself. *Lost her once; I will not lose her again.*

With that, I look at the scheduling board and see that my patient is ready for me in the OR. I push thoughts of Tatiana and Liv aside, make my way in, and get to work.

The rest of the day goes by without incident. The cases went as smoothly as I had hoped, and the patients all did well. I make my way up to the inpatient floor to do rounds on a few post-op patients and hopefully discharge them home.

I stop by the nurses' station to see which rooms my patients are in and pass by a few nurses charting on their computers. A familiar smile catches my eye as I see a nurse that I hooked up with before. Annoyance flows through me as I try to figure out how to avoid her. She looks up at me, and I awkwardly wave and continue about my business heading to the charts.

I'm not a total dick, but I don't want to encourage her. She's a stage-five clinger, and I don't want to risk screwing up anything with Liv.

As I reach for the chart, I feel her hand come up to stroke my forearm.

"Hey, Dax, I haven't seen you in a while. Maybe we could go out for a drink sometime after work?"

I wince at the thought and her touch. I see something move in my peripheral vision, and I look at Liv at the desk, trying her best not to look at me and hide that she is listening to this exchange. I gently remove the girl's hand from my arm.

"Sorry, Jasmine, but I'm seeing someone."

Surprise flashes across her face. "Oh. Okay. No problem," she stammers and turns away, hurrying down the hall.

I let out a deep breath and make my way to where Liv is still pretending to look at a chart.

I lean over and whisper into her ear, "Twice in one day I get to see my girlfriend's pretty face."

She quirks her lip up with a hint of a smile.

"I could get used to this, baby." I give her a quick kiss on her forehead and walk away.

I look back and see her staring at me. I turn and notice Jasmine looking at her as well. Well, that takes care of that. I'm sure that in about another hour, the gossip mouth of the south, Jasmine, will let everyone know about my interaction with Liv up on the floor. That's not such a bad thing. While staking my claim to Liv, I've also hopefully sidestepped any women who may have been hoping I'd ask them out again.

Before Liv, my track record included one-night stands with a few women at the hospital. But I'm happy to give that up. Liv is everything to me now. I wonder if the gossip will make its way to Tatiana. I need to deal with that sooner than later.

I head back to the office and ponder when I'll see Liv again. I can only hope it will be tonight.

CHAPTER TWENTY-TWO

LIV

I watch Dax walk away and am at a loss for words. That is two times in one day that he claimed me to be his girlfriend. But that nurse on the surgical floor… She has a history with him. And what about the bombshell I saw him with at the coffee shop?

Nerves bubble up in my belly, and my thoughts start to race. Should I get tested for STDs? How many women has he slept with around here? My insecurities flare. I've been cheated on before. I don't think my heart could take it again. Brodie gave me quite the complex.

"No," I whisper to myself, trying to stop the downward spiral of my thoughts. "Dax is not Brodie. Dax is different."

Great, now I sound like a crazy person talking to myself. I've known that this is different since the moment I met him. Never have I felt this strong attraction to anyone before. My phone vibrates, and it's a text from Emma.

Hey! The girls are coming to visit. It's gonna be hella fun.

I silently thank Emma for the happy distraction and reply quickly.

When? I can't wait!

It has been too long since I have seen my besties, and I look forward to them visiting us. I desperately need a night out. The only other time I went out, I ran into Dax. That encounter had ended on a good note. I will have to see how this plays out, but I must guard my fragile heart.

I push the door to our apartment open and drag myself in. It was a long day at the hospital. My brain and body are exhausted. I hear music coming from Emma's room and wander down the hall toward it.

I still haven't asked her what was up with Eduardo being in our apartment when I got home. I need to know so much about that story, but Emma is usually a closed book. She is the happiest person I know. Always full of energy and lively. She is the best friend I could ever ask for, but she never talks about herself or her past. I always feel like there's something about her she holds back from me.

As close as we are, I don't know much about her childhood; she never talks about her parents. In fact, I sometimes feel that I don't know her at all, even though she is always there for me. I mean, she even moved here with me to Houston to make sure I didn't fall apart after the accident with Brodie and being low on funds for grad school.

Also different from me, Emma never has a money problem. She's a saver and rarely spends anything but still manages to afford the finer things. It must be all her savings from her job.

I hear the shower turn off, and she makes her way out of the room in a towel. She opens the door and jumps back. "Oh dear god, I didn't hear you come in."

I laugh and look at her. "Did you just get home from work?"

She makes her way over to the kitchen and grabs a wine glass. She lifts a glass at me in question, and I nod earnestly. She honestly looks a little rattled, and I feel bad about startling her. She shakily pours us both a glass of chardonnay and then proceeds to plug the bottle with some fancy Houdini device.

"Here, you look like you need this." She hands me my glass as she gets a bit more comfortable. "How was your first day?" She takes a long pull from her glass and waits for my reply.

"Good." I eye her up and down, noticing her avoiding my scrutiny by asking me pointed questions. "I saw Dax there," I say quickly, bringing my glass to my lips to hide my smirk.

She raises her hands. "No way!" All her tremors are now gone.

I shake my head, nodding in confirmation. "I saw him twice, actually. Once in the café, and once on the floor when I was reading a patient's chart."

I think back to seeing Dax and how shamelessly all those women were flirting with him in the vicinity of the nurses' stations. He brings so much attention to himself with all that manly hotness. I am glad that he is so attractive and into me, and I worry at the same time that I won't be able to hold his attention. My expression sours at that thought.

Emma pulls me away from these negative thoughts and asks, "Where did you go, Liv?"

"Huh?"

"You are so into that head of yours that you get lost."

I remember Dax saying something similar to me. I get out of my negative thoughts and shake them all away.

"You seemed deep in thought and then made this unhappy face." Emma stares at me, waiting for an explanation that won't come.

Two can play that game, Emma.

I take a swig from my wine and look at it with worry. Then the verbal diarrhea commences. "I just saw girls throwing themselves at him. But he introduced himself to Adam as my boyfriend and then called me his girlfriend when I saw him on the floor. It was a shock initially, but it felt right, so I went along with it. But..." I hesitate. "But I just hope I am enough. What if I am not enough? Look what Brodie ended up doing."

Emma comes close to me and rubs my arm. "Hey, where is this coming from, Liv? You are smart, beautiful, and one of my best friends."

This makes me laugh. "You think I'm beautiful?" Mimicking Cher, my favorite character from the movie *Clueless.*

Emma snorts, acknowledging the reference and choosing not to be distracted by it in her line of questioning.

"Is that all you got out of that little pep talk? Yes, I do think you are beautiful. I know this because I don't have ugly friends."

I fist pump the air at this comment with a "Damn straight," as it gets the desired reaction Emma was hoping for.

Emma is now beaming at me. My thoughts turn somber as I look her in the eye.

"I guess Brodie just did a number on me. The cheating made me feel like I wasn't good enough, and I feared Dax would lose interest. I don't think I can take that kind of rejection twice."

Emma seems to ponder my response, then shoots up from her seat. "I'll be right back. I'm going to throw on some clothes and put my hair up."

I go to refill my wineglass and throw on some music. Halsey's "Bad at Love" starts playing, and I immediately begin dancing. Emma enters her room and laughs at me, singing into my wine glass.

"That's my girl."

She also starts singing the lyrics with me, and we dance around in the apartment, not spilling a drop of alcohol from our goblets of wine. She refills her wine glass, and I quickly down mine, asking for another refill.

She questions me with a finger pointing out in a scolding manner. "Don't you have school tomorrow, missy?"

I nod, not missing a beat of the songs that continue to play through Spotify. We laugh and throw ourselves onto the couch. Another song ends, and I watch her sip her wine.

"So, will you tell me why I came home and saw Eduardo practically naked in his boxers, pulling up his pants?"

She winces at first.

"I saw him coming out of your room as I was getting home. Imagine my shock when I saw him and not Jameson. What's going on, Emma?"

I don't think she will say anything, but then she surprises me and starts to speak.

"I sent Jameson home, and Eduardo came over after Jameson left. I didn't plan on anything happening between us, but it did, and that's all there is to it."

I ask anyway, despite her apprehension in answering my questions. "How did you meet him?"

"Long story short, an employee of his was injured at the club, and I guess that was what brought him in. I took him into the trauma bay to get him placed on the monitors and called the doctor.

"Trauma bay?" I ask with wide eyes, contemplating what injury it could have been to necessitate a trauma bay.

She looks at me and bites her lip before she answers. "Stab wound to the hand."

"What?" I practically scream.

"Oh, it was nothing, really. Needed some stitches and didn't hit anything important in the way of vessels. Weirdly, it looked more bloody than the wound was. Lucky, actually." She stops to think about that for a minute before proceeding. "Eduardo showed up, said something to his employee, and sat in a chair, staring at me while I worked."

Sensing that she doesn't want to get into it, I let it slide for now, but I plan on revisiting this subject later. I mean, what is up with that situation? *Stabbed?* I thought Jameson mentioned that night that he and Eduardo were frat brothers.

I get up from the couch and place my wineglass in the sink. Grabbing a glass of water, I return to the couch with Emma.

"So when are the girls coming?"

Emma perks up and shouts excitedly, "In a few weeks!" She is practically vibrating with excited energy.

Just like nothing happened, she is back to the same fun-loving Emma.

"Well, we will have to plan a great outing for them and show them the town."

Emma nods her head in agreement and adds in, "We also have to go shopping for outfits to go out in. I want to take them to Eduardo's club and hang out in the VIP section with them. I think that they will enjoy that, don't you?"

I nod in agreement. "Sounds like a good time, Emma, but I don't have much money to go shopping. I am on a pretty strict budget right now."

She puts her hand out, nudging me to take it. "Don't even worry about it, Liv. I got you covered, girl."

I think about Emma's money and do not understand how she does it, making her money stretch so far. She has such exceptional clothes. I wish that we were the same size so we could share outfits.

I get up from the couch and tell Emma I have a couple of things to do before heading to bed. I grab a Pop-Tart from the pantry and enter the bedroom. I love Pop-Tarts—my one guilty pleasure.

I am looking forward to the girls coming to visit. I answer their comments on the group chat and express my eagerness to see them all. It gives me something to look forward to. I need that now. Things are improving with Dax, and I see Brodie once, sometimes twice, weekly.

I think back to Brodie and feel that he looks sadder every time I visit him. I know he must be depressed about his situation. Who wouldn't? I just can't help thinking he looks exhausted. Exhausted from his life now, maybe? I'll need to bring this up slowly with him the next time I go over this week to ensure that he isn't having darker thoughts. Since I have known him so long, I can tell his moods, and right now, they are somber.

I lay out some clothes for school tomorrow and prepare my work bag, looking over a few notes on my patient's medical history for tomorrow's clinicals. I can't wait until I graduate and this is behind me. It is so much work, and with everything else on my plate, I wish it were this year.

I see Dax has called when I go to brush my teeth, and I return his phone call. He picks up almost on the first ring.

"Hey, baby, what are you doing?" His deep voice makes me sigh, but I quickly cover it up with a cough.

"Just getting ready for bed. You?"

I hear the fridge opening and closing very quickly. "Making a quick snack before I go to bed. I just wanted to hear your voice before I crashed."

I get into bed and pull up the covers. "Well, I'm already getting in bed, and as soon as my head hits the pillow, I'm out. We don't exactly sleep much when we are in each other's company."

He chuckles. "No, we definitely do not sleep. And I can't wait to not sleep with you again. Good night, angel. I hope I get to see you tomorrow."

"Me too," I say. "Night, Dax."

I snuggle into my pillow and think of Dax claiming me like he did last night. The thought pulls my lips into a smile as I drift off to sleep.

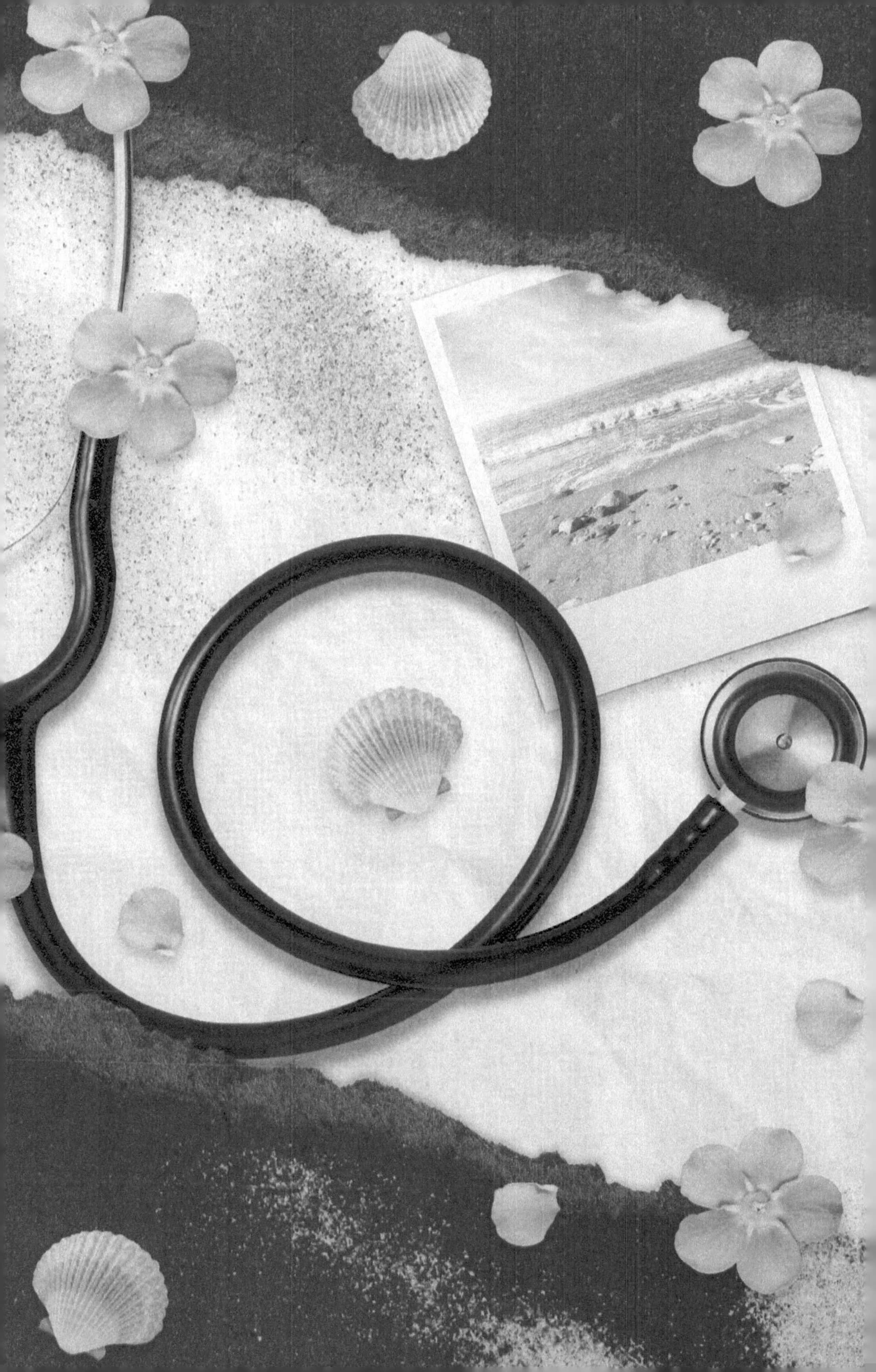

CHAPTER TWENTY-THREE

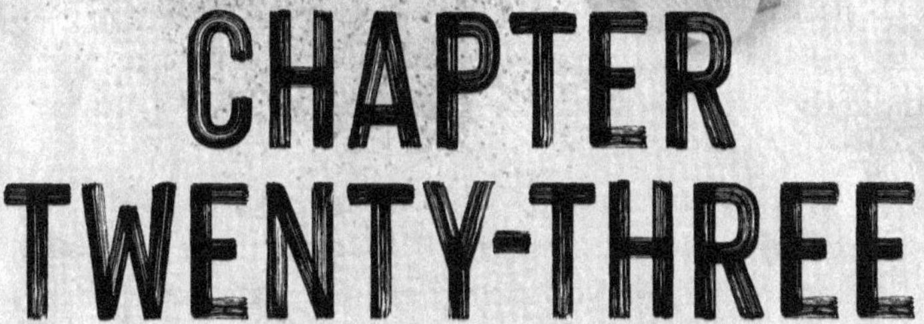

DAX

Last night was an endless stream of phone calls. A few admissions came through the ED, ensuring that my day was going to be busy. Thankfully, my travel mug was filled with strong coffee, and I slowly gulped it down as I drove to the hospital, the comforting bitter taste driving the sleep from my brain.

The hospital is busy with shift change, and I make my way to the surgical floor, hoping to bump into Liv before my day gets underway. My eyes scan the hall, but she's not there.

"That would be too convenient," I mutter and turn to make my way to the operating rooms.

As I push through the door, I see her. It's her gorgeous brown hair I notice first, and my dick twitches in my pants as I see her start to laugh. The hard-on I was about to sport deflates quickly as I notice she's walking with that same asshat from yesterday. He has his hand on the small of her back as he guides her down the hall.

My heart rate speeds up, and red clouds my vision. I start walking over to them as they open a doorway to the stairwell. He ushers her inside, and I hurry, clenching and unclenching my fists in a fury. I promise myself that if he has his hands to himself by the time I get there, I'll act gentlemanly, but if he's touching her, all bets are off.

I open the door and step through, not believing what I see.

I hear hushed tones, and Liv's voice sounds shaky when I hear her say, "Adam, what are you doing?"

I let the door slam shut, making my presence known. Adam's head snaps up, and his eyes meet mine. In the same breath, he takes a step away from Liv, trying to feign innocence. Liv turns toward me, her eyes wide, her bag clutched tightly to her chest. She breathes my name like a prayer.

"Dax."

I slowly walk toward the guy who had his hands on her, trying–and failing–to control my anger. *Was his name Adam?* I think to myself.

"Hey, Adam, What are you doing?" I punctuate the words with spit flying out of my mouth.

Adam, who is about the same height as Liv, looks up at me as I stop next to him.

I have my hands in my pockets, so I don't immediately punch him and get my privileges suspended or, worse, my privileges revoked. When it comes to this woman, I just don't make the best decisions.

When I get close enough to touch her, I take my hands out of my pocket, grab Liv's bag, and fling it on my shoulder as I take her hand in mine. Trying to ignore the jerk in front of me, I turn to look at her,

"Are you okay?"

Her eyes are wide when she looks at me but then immediately soften at my question. She says nothing and just shakes her head, nodding yes. The move is barely perceptible, but I see it.

I turn to Adam, my rage lowering just slightly now that I have her hand in mine. "I must be crazy because it looked an awful lot like you were hitting on my girlfriend."

He doesn't back down, and I must admit that he shows some balls, considering he is about six inches shorter than me.

"I didn't realize Liv had a boyfriend." Adam looks at me and then at Liv. He must see the murderous look on my face because it's only then that his face pales.

"Oh, you forgot me from yesterday, huh?"

Adam looks anywhere but at us and quickly grabs for the door handle leading out of the stairwell. "Bye, Liv. Sorry, if I misread the signals." The words leave him in a rush. "I'll see you in class."

The door slams shut, and the sounds of my exhale fill the stairwell.

Liv looks at me with her big doe eyes. "Signals?" She shakes her head back and forth. "No way."

I bring my hand up and run the pad of my thumb over her lips as I step closer. "Was he trying to kiss you?"

She answers my question with a question. "What if he was?"

I move closer to her. My lips ghost over her neck, inching toward her ear. "That would not be a good idea."

I hear the uptake of her breath as the hair on her neck rises beneath my lips, grazing up and down her neck. I make my way to her mouth, kiss her gently, and step away. "I have a problem with guys hitting on my girlfriend."

She raises her hand to my cheek. "I have a problem with girls hitting on my boyfriend," she counters.

"You don't have to worry about me wanting another woman, Liv. I only want you. Since that day at the beach, you are the only thing I have wanted. Come on, I have surgery to get to, and I think you have clinicals, right?"

She nods. I open the door to the stairwell, and we walk hand-in-hand down the hall, eliciting a stare or two from hospital staff, wondering who this woman I have on my arm is.

We get to the elevators, and I hand her bag back to her and place a chaste kiss on her lips.

"I'll call you later."

I walk away and turn before heading toward the operating room as she steps into the elevator. I throw her a wink, and she rolls her eyes and smiles as she hits the button for her floor.

The days are long. The traumas never cease, but I get through my surgeries and walk across the parking lot to our office suites. It makes it convenient to have our offices next to the hospital. In a few months, we will open our own surgery center to do elective cases, instead of going to the main OR. This won't affect me much because I do mostly trauma, and those are more acute care patients needing a hospital stay.

My fellowship in trauma is going great, and I love my job. I'm glad I branched out and decided not to follow in my father's footsteps with sports medicine. This field is much more exciting than repairing ACL injuries on athletes and the not-so-athletic.

I enter the building and am greeted by the receptionist as I make my way through the employee door.

As I'm making my way to my soon-to-be office, I pass my father's door, and he calls out to me. "Hey, Dax. Can you come into my office for a minute? I need to talk to you."

I head in, and he closes the door after me, extending his arm toward a seat. "What's up, Dad? I just got out of surgery and have a few things I need to catch up on."

He sits and steeples his hands together. "Your mom and I wanted to remind you about her fundraiser for the hospital. As you know, she works very hard with her committee to make the Ride the Waves fundraiser a success for our hospital. Being the committee chair, she wants to ensure you are in attendance..." he trails off.

My mom does this every fall. She considers it her baby. Raising money for various hospital departments to ensure they get something they need that isn't in the capital budget. Last year it went to the labor and delivery unit to provide new ultrasound machines for the gynecologists and fetal heart tone monitors at the bedside.

"As you also know, the money will be going to our department this year."

He moves toward the back of his office, staring out the window—no doubt contemplating all the things he'd like to get with that money. I am sure it is some million-dollar piece of equipment.

He turns abruptly back to me, pinning me in my seat with his stare. "Your mom wants you to bring a suitable date. I thought I would give you ample time."

I laugh. "Suitable date? What does that even mean?"

He quirks his lip and says, "Yeah, you know, someone that isn't going to embarrass your mom."

I sit up straighter and level my dad for the shock of his lifetime. "Well, I thought I might bring my girlfriend to it this year."

His jaw practically hits the floor. He blinks a few times and shakes his head as if he misheard me. "You have a girlfriend?"

I can understand his shock. I've really never had a girlfriend. I've played the field since high school and fucked a lot of women. With a singular goal of my career at the forefront, I was only afforded the potential for random hookups and one-night stands. That was my go-to, and he knows it. Although I try to keep it from getting around, the rumor mill here is something else, always making it far worse than it is. I never saw myself in a relationship, but I have also never met the right person.

"Her name is Liv."

With that introduction, I begin to tell my dad when and how I met Liv. He listens with interest, but I can tell from his eyes he isn't sure how serious I am. Like he's waiting for me to say, "gotcha!" and come clean that it was a joke. That, of course, doesn't happen.

He looks pleased when I finish and stands as he walks me out the door. "I can't wait to tell your mom."

"She will love her," I say instantly.

My dad can't help but smile. "Anything that makes your mom happy makes me happy."

I shake my head in agreement. "I think I'm beginning to understand that sentiment now, Dad."

He clasps his hand over my shoulder and squeezes. "When can we meet this woman of yours?"

I stride through the door and offer, "Next weekend? That will give Liv time to process meeting my parents when I spring it on her."

He laughs. "Good plan," he says as he retreats into his office.

Now I just have to tell Liv.

I go back to my office and get caught up on my work. I pull up my text messages and see Jameson texted me, wanting to grab a quick beer after work. Sure, why not.

I type out a quick response and ask where we're meeting. My phone chimes right back, and I glance at the text "**the sports bar.**" Predictable.

The hours fly by, and before I know it, it's late afternoon. I leave the building and call Liv. She picks up on the first ring.

"Hey, Dax."

Dear God, I love the sound of her voice. "Hey, baby. How was your day?"

"Good, although I think you have successfully scared Adam off. He won't even look at me, and I needed those notes from him about our assignment."

I chuckle, feeling pleased with myself. "I can't say that I am sorry about that. Hey, I wanted to ask you a question."

There is a pause. "Okaaaay?" she asks tentatively, dragging out the word. "What is it?"

I'm unsure how to go about this, so I just blurt it out. "I want you to be my date for my mom's fundraiser. It's called Ride the Wave Gala. Most importantly, I want you to come over to meet my parents next weekend, if that's a good time for you. I'm not on call and wanted to ensure you are available." The words rush out in one long breath.

"Wow. Umm, that's a lot to take in," she says.

I reply, "Which part? Wanting to be seen with you or introduce you to my parents?"

"Both," she quickly states. "But, I would love to. I just wasn't sure of your intentions. You just surprised me, I guess."

"Great, I told them we will be there next week. Also, I think you know my intentions, Liv. If you are confused, I'd be more than happy to clarify it for you again later." I chuckle. "Anyway, I'll let you go. I'm meeting Jameson at the sports bar tonight for happy hour. He wants to talk, and I can only imagine what it's about this time."

Liv is silent for a minute and then begins to speak. "I wonder if it's about Emma?"

"Why would you say that? Is there something that happened?"

I hear her tapping something. Maybe her fingernail on the phone.

"I'm not sure yet."

"Well, that's a bit evasive."

"Sorry," she quickly rescinds her prior comment. "It's probably nothing. You have a good time, and I'll chat with you tomorrow."

I don't want to miss her again in the morning, so I tell her to meet me at the café in the morning. She agrees and quickly hangs up. I stare at the phone, wondering what the situation she wants to avoid discussing with Jameson and Emma is about. I guess I'll find out soon. I'm slightly worried about him but can't help my excitement for my girl with long legs and honey-colored eyes.

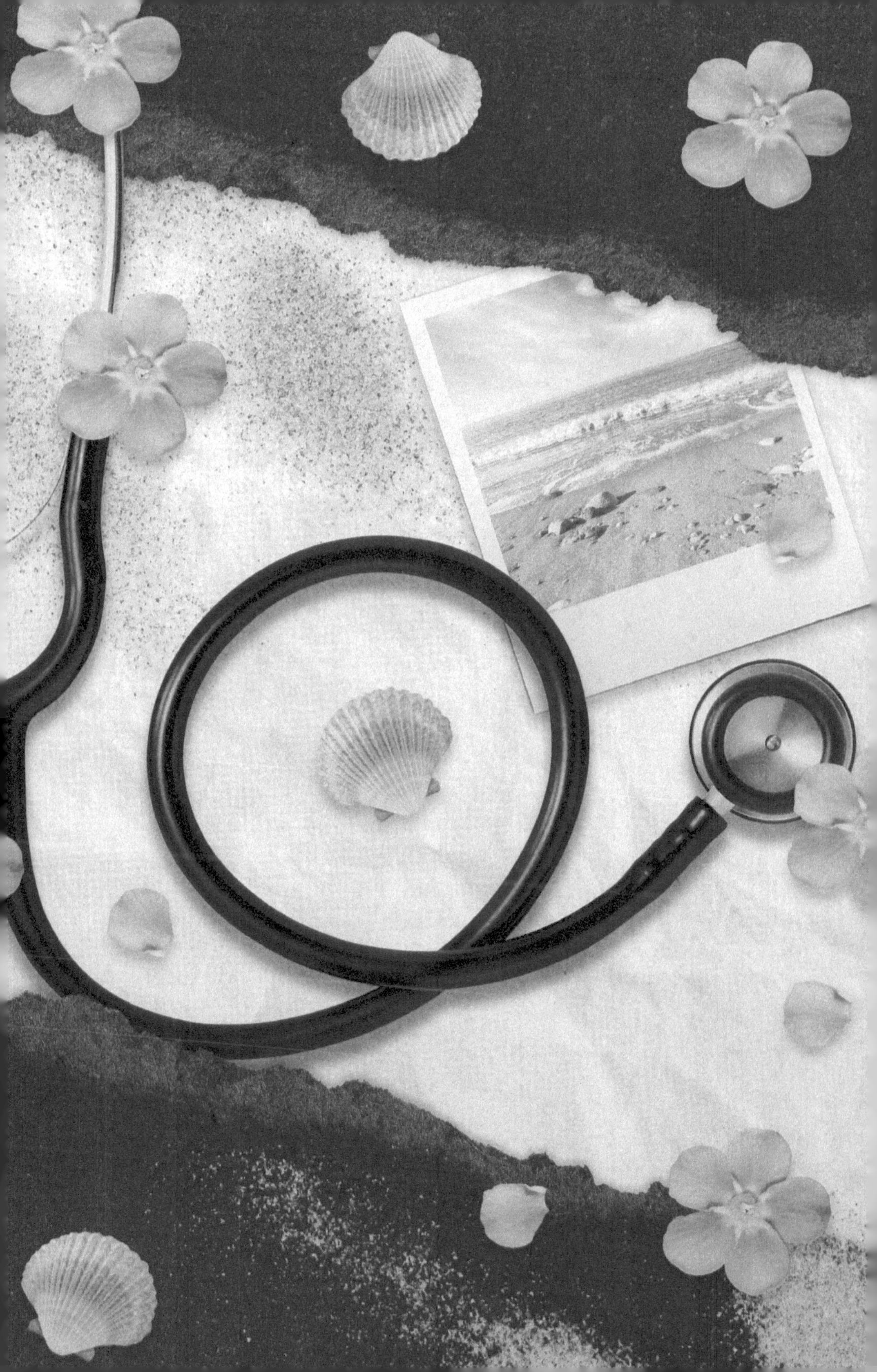

CHAPTER TWENTY-FOUR

DAX

I push the door to the bar open and make my way through the crowd. People eye me, their gaze traveling over my clothes as I walk by. Judging by their looks, they don't think I belong here.

I had back-to-back meetings to end the day and didn't have time to change out of my suit before I left. At least I left the jacket in the car.

I clasp Jameson around the shoulder in greeting as I finally make it to our table. He looks up at me and seems to be deep in thought.

"Why does it look like your fuckin' dog died, brother."

I drop into the seat next to him and lift my finger to flag down a server. Of course fucking Simone is already sauntering over to us. Geez, can't I get a break in this place?

"Hey, handsome. What can I get you to wet your lips?"

I moan in aggravation. She cocks an eyebrow upward in an attempt to be sexy, but it has the opposite effect on me. To be honest, she looks like the Joker from *Batman* with her painted eyebrows, heavy eyeshadow, and red lipstick.

"I'll take a Stella. Jameson, you ready for another?"

Without taking his eyes off the table, he lifts his nearly empty beer bottle and nods. "Yeah, I'll take another one. Why not?"

Simone saunters off, and I let a few seconds pass, hoping he'll spit out whatever is bothering him. Minutes pass, and he says nothing.

"You okay, dude?"

Before he can answer, Simone is back with our drinks. She pours mine into a frosted glass, hands Jameson his draft beer in a mug, and then leaves us. I wonder if he was waiting for her to deliver them so we would be uninterrupted. Just as I am about to ask again, he starts talking.

"I think Emma is fucking around with that guy, Eduardo," he blurts out in a breath. Well, that wasn't what I was expecting.

"Your frat brother?" I ask.

He nods.

"What makes you think so?"

"His story is similar to how you met Liv. He was in the ED, probably from some shady shit, and saw her. She's on his radar now, and I don't think I can compete with him. I don't know *if* I want to compete with him."

I try to play devil's advocate and ask, "You don't know for sure, right? I mean, this could just be a wrong assumption."

He shakes his head and says, "No, he is fucking her."

I take a swig of my beer, trying to process this. Eduardo is a slimy fucker, and I don't want him near Liv if that's the case. I have heard stories from Jameson about Eduardo. I don't know the guy personally, but I trust Jameson's judgment. That dude is bad news and involved in some shady-as-fuck shit. I'm sure that he uses his club to hide illegal activity. Then again, I could just be watching too many mafia movies.

I reiterate my question to Jameson. "How do you know, or are you just suspicious with no proof?"

He hasn't drunk his new beer yet. He is just holding it like a lifeline, staring at the amber liquid as if it contains the secrets to the universe or, more importantly, Emma.

"I took her home that night we left the club. The car Eduardo set us up with dropped us off, and I walked her in. I assumed I would stay the night with her. She had a lot to drink, and I wasn't expecting to sleep with her. I wanted to take care of her. Instead, she decided that she wanted me to go. I mean, what am I supposed to say? I used her bathroom really quickly and then bailed. I'm just glad that the car hadn't left yet. It's almost like it waited for me, knowing that I'd be back—"

I interrupt to see if there is anything I am missing in his story. "So, you walked her in, ensured she was okay, and then made the trek back to your side of town?"

He nods. "Yeah, I kissed her good night and told her to call if she needed anything, you know?"

I look at him, waiting for him to continue his story. He grabs his beer while taking a large drink. Waiting for the rest of the story, he explains what I need to know.

"I left in the car, but then I thought, I think I left my wallet back at her place. Maybe it fell out when I went to her bathroom? I told the driver to go back to Emma's apartment.

"When we drove up, I spotted a familiar car parked in front–Eduardo's black Porsche 911 Turbo. But I didn't get to investigate any further because when I opened the door, my wallet fell out of the door. I must have dropped it in between the car door and the seat. That solved the case of the missing wallet. Now I just need to understand what the actual fuck Eduardo was doing there at Emma's apartment. She didn't want me to stay there. Was she planning on Eduardo to stop there later all along? Was that the plan... to shack up with Eduardo?"

I stay silent and let him get it all off his chest. He starts to stay something else, but I cut him off. "Is Liv in any danger? I can't have her around Emma if Eduardo could pose a threat to her safety."

Jameson seems to think about this and tilts his head as if the answer to the question will pop into his mind if he seeks it out harder.

"I don't know, honestly. When we were in school, I thought maybe his family was involved in the Mafia, but I knew that that was a bit crazy. Some illegal dealings, for sure."

"Is Emma involved in that too? Like Eduardo?"

He finishes off the rest of his beer and wipes his mouth with the back of his hand. "Nah, I doubt it. Look at her. She's harmless."

"I just wanted to let you know. You've made your intentions clear about Liv. I know that you wouldn't want her around this shit. I thought maybe Emma was interested in me, but now there is some competition."

As if on cue, Simone returns and motions with her fingers to our drinks. "Refill, guys?"

We both shake our heads. "Can you bring a couple of shots of tequila instead? Don Julio 1942, if you have it?"

She nods and walks off. At least she isn't trying to hit on me again. I have zero patience for that tonight.

"I appreciate you telling me. I want to protect that girl with all I have. Today, I saw some guy corner her in the stairwell. He was trying to touch what was mine, and I swear I could have punched him. He was such a pussy too."

Jameson laughs. "I feel sorry for all the guys that look at Liv with a possessive fuck like you."

"You mean a boyfriend like me?" I quirk my eyebrows up and down.

"Shut the fuck up!" Jameson looks at me in disbelief.

"I shit you not, my friend."

"Well, damn it to hell. I didn't think I'd see the day Dax claimed someone as his girlfriend."

I ponder, letting him know the rest. The conversation I had with my dad in his office is still fresh in my mind.

"I guess you should know that I told my dad about her today. My mom was talking to him about me bringing a presentable date to her fundraiser this year."

Jameson laughs. "Well, can you blame her? You brought that girl with a subzero IQ and looked like a high-priced call girl."

I feign shock. "Excuse me, but she was hot, and I wasn't looking for an intellectual discussion that night."

Simone brings us our shots, and we both toss them back and suck on the lime that accompanies our drinks.

Changing the subject off Liv, I ask him, "What are you going to do?"

"I don't know what I can do at this point," he quickly responds. "I can't make her like me. She isn't my girlfriend, and I don't know how I can change her feelings for me."

I pull out my phone and check my messages. "Is she worth it?"

Jameson goes to speak and then stops abruptly. I can see he is trying to choose his words carefully. I put my phone down to give him my full attention.

"I don't know. I'm friends with Eduardo, but I know my limits of trying to cross that guy. When he sets his sights on something, he won't stop until he gets it. If Emma wants him instead, then that is her choice. I can't make her want me."

I know that, without a doubt, Liv is worth it to me and more. She is my everything. There is nothing I wouldn't do to claim her as mine. The thought of anyone else with her makes my blood boil. I don't care if it makes me look like a caveman, but I will gladly throw her over my shoulder and prevent her from talking to anyone else if need be. I hope that guy from today doesn't become a future problem. I saw his chicken-shit face and knew I had stopped that before it started. I will annihilate him if need be.

Jameson and I take another shot and change the subject to lighter things. He asks about how my parents are and about the upcoming visit with Liv in tow. I know that my mom will love her. What's not to love about her? She is the girl next door. She's tall, sexy and does so without trying. There is nothing fake about her.

She's also intelligent and driven. Even with her hair in a messy bun, she's elegant, with her long neck and beautiful features. My mom will be ecstatic to see us together.

Let's be honest. Liv is hot as fuck in my eyes and has rocked my world. She's the entire package and all mine. Jameson isn't wrong about my last date, but my priorities have changed, or it could just be because of my girl. I like the way that sounds—*My girl.*

While I daydream about Liv, Jameson changes the conversation to lighter subjects and seems in better spirits. The alcohol is probably a temporary balm to ease his calloused thoughts.

I'll have to find out more about Liv and her roommate. If she is in danger, I will make sure she's safe.

CHAPTER TWENTY-FIVE

LIV

I replay the conversation with Dax over and over in my head. I still can't believe that he wants me to meet his parents. As I drive toward his place, I do my best to control the butterflies in my stomach.

The week flew by with our busy schedules. He's working late today and wants me to meet him at his house so we can leave from there.

At first, I was reluctant to go over and let myself into his place without him there but he assured me it was fine. When I told Emma about our plans, she...well, she squealed while jumping up and down, clapping her hands. In her mind, this means we've moved from casually dating to a serious relationship. Maybe that's what has butterflies going rampant in my stomach. But at the same time, I know in my gut this is what I want. He is what I want.

When I asked her if she thought things were going too fast, she just gazed at me with a faraway look in her eyes. I called out her name, and she looked at me and smiled. Her smiles hardly reach her eyes these days. Far from the girl I graduated nursing school with—a girl who has become one of my best friends and confidants.

She thinks I don't notice how she always tries to appear so happy and self-assured. However, the smile she gave me was a no-holds back one. A full one with a hidden meaning—a secret she knew that she wasn't sharing.

"Liv, sometimes you just have to take a chance. Especially, if you know he's the one."

I wait for her to elaborate, but no explanation comes.

Then she gets right to business, picking out my outfit. She helps me get dressed and do my makeup while dancing around our apartment. I keep my alcohol intake to only one glass of champagne as we primp in front of the mirror, and I let her help me enjoy getting ready to meet my man and his parents tonight. I would hate to show up at Dax's parents' house to meet them looking anything less than my best. You only have one shot at making a first impression, right?

I decide on a black fitted jumpsuit—classy, comfortable–and the shoes I borrow from Emma pull it all together. At least that's one thing we can share.

I look at myself in the full-length mirror, turning back and forth to get a good look at the whole ensemble. I'm officially almost six feet tall with these stilettos, but Dax is a tall guy, so I can get away with heels like this.

Brodie pops into my mind. He wasn't as tall, so I tended to wear short-heeled shoes. Thinking about him immediately makes me sad. I should really check on him again soon. I have had a lot of clinicals, so I haven't had the energy or time.

Between seeing Dax, hanging out with Emma, studying and running, driving across town to Brodie's house isn't the easiest. I need to make time in my schedule to see how he is holding up.

After getting an Uber over to Dax's place, I make it there in record time. Or, maybe between my rampant thoughts and the chatty Uber driver, I didn't pay attention . Either way, I get out of the car and this time get to walk in through the front entrance.

Having a concierge in Houston is a nice luxury. I'm let in on through to the elevators. I hit the button for the floor of Dax's luxury apartment. I let the ride relax me as I am trying my best to collect my thoughts.

I need to calm down after overthinking about him wanting me to meet his parents. I was excited when he let me know the plans and concerned that maybe things were progressing too fast. I am here now, so I hope everything goes smoothly tonight.

I walk the hall slowly, and when I get to his door, I feel calmer. Or so I thought. I ring the doorbell and am greeted by a very sweaty Dax.

"Hey, babe. I just finished a workout downstairs and need to take a quick shower."

That's it. My pulse has fully spiked. He is clad in only a pair of gym shorts hanging precariously low on his hip. I run my eyes up and down, blatantly drinking in his body. How can all this man be mine?

I see beads of sweat pooling on his chest, and I get the sudden urge to lick them off to see how he tastes. I bet he tastes like the sea—my favorite happy place. I lick my lips at the thought. My thighs clench in reaction, and my gaze darts up to meet his eyes. He must notice my response to him because he ushers me in quickly, closing the door behind me.

"Jesus, Liv."

The hungry look in his eyes makes me flush. It quickly spreads to my face as he continues perusing my body. He lands his final glare on my lips. He moves toward me, his eyes growing dark.

"Keep looking at me like that, Liv, and my parents will be very sad that we won't make an appearance tonight."

I envision following him in the shower and spending the rest of the night worshiping his body. He leans in and places a quick kiss on my lips. The soft, warm sensation of his lips on mine make my heart race even faster.

Control yourself, I chastise in my head.

"We have a whole night ahead of us," he says as he walks away to shower.

A whole night. The reality of the situation comes storming back to my brain. I've thought about this night over and over since he asked me. My nerves are getting more worked up each time. I absentmindedly chew on my bottom lip.

He returns after his shower and notices the change in my behavior immediately. His hands come to my arms, rubbing up and down in a comforting motion. He stoops to look me in the eye.

"Hey, don't worry about it. They are going to love you," he whispers.

He is standing there in his towel with beads of water dripping around his neck from his hair. His hot breath causes an eruption of goose bumps along my arms as he continues to rub them.

He places another kiss on my lips, pulling me in close. His tongue sweeps across the seam of my lips, and I open for him as he deepens our kiss.

I can feel his erection growing against my stomach. Only a towel spread thin against his growing erection separates me from his dick. He steps back, and I immediately feel the loss of his body heat against mine.

He turns around, walking away, but smiling at me over his shoulder. I hear him mumble something about needing another cold shower as he walks off to get ready.

I stand there watching his retreat, and when he gets to his bedroom door, he turns back around and looks me up and down.

"You look beautiful tonight, Liv. I'll be ready in a few minutes. Make yourself at home, okay?"

I look at him like a woman starved for affection. Although, I am only starved for Dax. My Dax.

"Okay," I answer back in a breathy voice, letting him know how much he affects me.

His laugh echoes through the room as he closes the door behind him, leaving me alone in his apartment. True to his word, Dax is ready in less than ten minutes.

"Ready to meet my parents?" He grabs his keys and holds his hand out to me, and I take it eagerly.

"Yes," is the only word I can get out as we make our way out of his apartment and downstairs into the parking garage.

Of course, he drives a Range Rover. It's a Defender, and I can imagine his surfboards on top as he cruises over the sand in such a rugged yet luxurious off-roading vehicle. It fits him perfectly. His scent envelopes me on the drive over.

"Where's your car?" I ask as I close the door. It smells of sandalwood and clean laundry. I wish I could bottle his scent and use it to permeate my pillows. To be able to wake up to the smell of him every day would be heaven.

"Oh, that was my parents' car. Mine was getting detailed that day and I had to leave it overnight. Too much sand to clean." He laughs.

I realize that I don't know much about him now, but I will change that soon.

We roll up the driveway to Dax's parents', and I can't believe what's in front of me. This family is undeniably wealthy. When he told me that his mom headed the hospital's charity events, I thought they might be rich, but I didn't have confirmation until now. Watching their mansion-like home come into view, I am awestruck.

He rounds the car and opens my door, helping me out. "Always a true gentleman." I tease as he takes my hand. Who said chivalry is dead? Not this guy. He has it in spades.

"Always for you, Liv."

Our fingers wind together, and we walk the short distance to his parents' doorstep. With one last look at me, he grabs the doorknob and pushes it open.

"Hello!" Dax calls into the house. "Mom, we're here."

I immediately hear heels clicking toward the entrance. A beautiful tall woman dressed in a simple, stylish dress makes her way down the hallway to us. She's about my height, has shoulder-length hair, and skin so flawless it makes me jealous. She looks much younger than her actual age. As she gets closer, her arms immediately envelop Dax in a hug. Dax drops my hand to lovingly hug his mother back before she turns to me.

"And who is this lovely lady you brought over?"

He laughs and says, "Mom, you know this is Liv. The girl that I have been telling you about."

She has a teasing look on her face, and I know she is giving Dax a hard time. "And also, your date for the gala we have coming up in a few months?"

I notice that she stresses "coming up in a few months," as if Dax isn't accustomed to keeping a girl for long. I try not to read too much into it.

"Yes, Mom. And I know when the gala is." He smirks and then looks toward me.

I reach out my hand and introduce myself to her. "Hi, I'm Liv. Very nice to meet you."

She pulls me in for a hug. "Please, call me Isabella, and I'm so happy to meet you."

A man comes up behind us, ushers us through the front door, and encourages us to follow him to the back of the house. Unsure of what else to say at this point, I place my bag and jacket on the handle of the chair in the living room.

"You have a lovely home." It sounds so cliché, but it is all I can think of to say, and it truly is a lovely place. I'd love to call a place like this home one day.

Dax smiles down at me and takes my hand, leading me along following the couple, which I assume to be both his parents.

"Thank you, Liv. We are very blessed." The man holds his hand out, and I take it.

"Nice to meet you, Dr. Johnson."

"Please, call me Marc. Let's have a seat, and dinner will be ready soon."

I wonder who is making this dinner if she is still sitting here, but I don't think that is an appropriate question. Instead, I just take my seat, folding my legs against each other.

His mom hands me a drink and says, "Wine, okay?"

I nod as she also takes her seat across from us.

"So, tell me the story of how the two of you met."

I immediately freeze and am transported back to that night at the beach. The night that changed my life was seeing my ex-boyfriend and my childhood friend lying lifeless on the wet sand. Dax springing into action, and me? Well, I just watched them, feeling so helpless, despite being trained to save lives. I just couldn't move that time, paralyzed by my fear. The fear of Brodie being dead and, worse yet, feeling as though I am to blame. His life almost ended because of me.

I hear someone call my name. It sounds muffled, like I am underwater. Maybe it's because I feel as though I am drowning in my pain and guilt. That would be a fitting punishment, after all.

I have yet to address these issues, but only because I don't want those feelings to resurface. The riptide of my heart being thrown out further and further, no matter how hard I try to fight the current. I just seem to fall deeper and deeper into the abyss until I am just part of an infinitely lost sea.

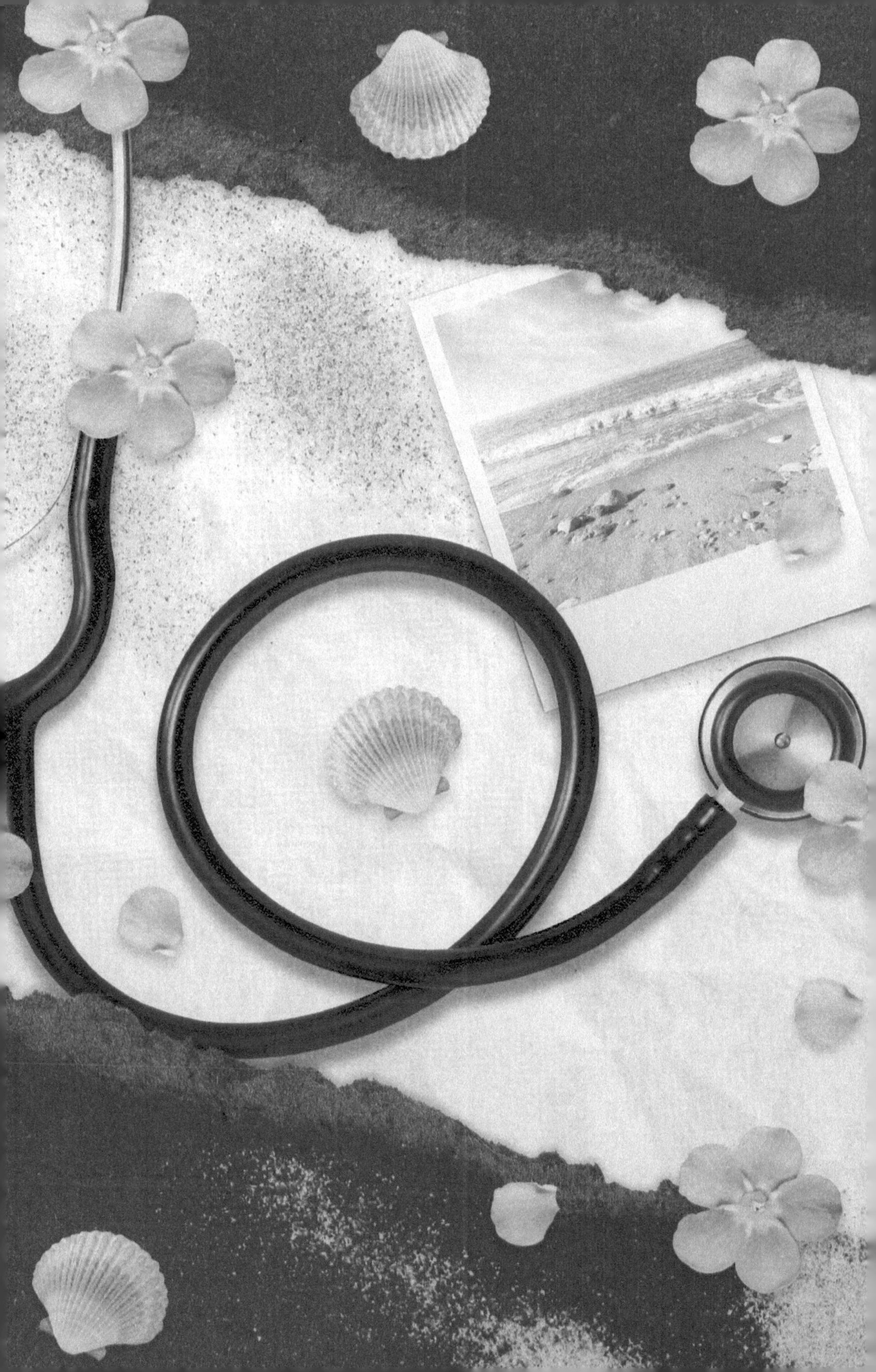

CHAPTER TWENTY-SIX

DAX

I can see Liv drowning in her thoughts. I put my hands on her shoulder and answer my mom's questions. "Liv and I met in the emergency department. Isn't that right, Liv?" I give her a little nudge with my arm.

She seems to return from her thoughts with a shake of her head. I can almost feel the sadness she feels about remembering that night. What should have been the day we met was turned into the day of the accident. I wish we had a chance at a new start. Those were the hands we were dealt; I hope we can overcome that someday.

I smile at her. She returns my smile, and I know my girl is back with me in the here and now, not thinking about the night I almost lost her forever—the night I thought I would never see her again.

My parents are very much in love, and it is still apparent in how they look at one another. I can tell that my mom senses something happened that night because she just looks at my dad, and they seem to be having a private conversation with that one glance.

I want to have that future with Liv, where we can just look at each other and know what each other is thinking. I would like to say that it is that way now because of this intense connection I feel with her. However, this also realistically comes with years of loving the same person. When you are married for that long, you can communicate without words.

Just a single glance says it all between them. I know I will get asked about this later, but my parents are too perceptive to bring it up now.

She continues to hold my hand, and then she proceeds with the story. "Dax hurt his ankle surfing, and I was his nurse. I called his name in the waiting room, and later, he asked me out. Well, he asked me what we did for fun here, and then we made plans to meet up the next day. I didn't know if he would show up, but I am glad he did."

I look at her in disbelief. "You seriously didn't think I would show up?" I laugh and bring her hand to my lips. "Sweetheart, you are stuck with me now."

My mom seems to find this amusing. "Yes, Dax is like his father in many ways. When he sets his mind on something, he gives it all he has got, whether it be with his career or his family. My men love fiercely."

Edith, our housekeeper, comes to the doorway and tells us that dinner is ready. I see Liv look my way and I take her hand, leading us to the formal dining room to take our seats. Even though the table seats about ten people, we sit closer to the end near one another and have a nice family-style meal. The conversation is much more relaxed, and my parents are genuinely nice and caring people.

I see Liv's shoulders relax as my mom turns her attention to Liv. "So, are you in school too, Liv?" Dad has let Mom lead the conversation, but now he joins in on the questions.

"Yes, I am in NP school and am doing my clinicals at Memorial Hospital, too."

Dad looks at both of us. "Well, that explains Dax's chipper mood when he returns to the office."

I shake my head at this comment, but maybe it is true.

Liv interjects, "I don't see him very much. He is very busy, but so am I. I am glad he can make time for us and we have similar schedules, which makes it easier."

This seems to please my father. I know he thought maybe I am focused too much on something other than the endgame that he feels is my career—continuing as a partner with him at his practice. It is, to a certain extent, but Liv is also my endgame.

As if reading my thoughts, he says, "So, are you planning to stay in Houston?"

Liv is quiet for a moment before she speaks, and I swear my heart stops for a minute because we haven't precisely discussed what we will do after she graduates. We have barely had time to rekindle our relationship, never mind planning our future after graduation.

"Well, Dax and I haven't thought that far. I'd like to think we are taking this one day at a time. I guess that is dependent on a few things."

With this, my heart deflates, and I look at her and smile, even though my posture is stiff. She rubs my hand with her thumb, much as I did in the hospital after Brodie's accident.

"I am not opposed to staying, though. My mom lives a few hours south of here, and it is within driving distance. I guess we will see."

I could kiss her, but out of respect for my parents, I just nod in agreement. "Who knows what the future holds, Dad."

He seems to accept this answer, and Mom tells us about her charity event and all that went into preparing such a night.

"So I hear you will be Dax's date for the night?"

Liv laughs at this and says, "Yes, he informed me of this the other day, so I guess I am going. It is for a good cause, so I look forward to being there."

Mom nods in agreement. "It really is, and it is also a good time. It is a black-tie event, and there is also a silent auction. It is held in Galveston, hence the name Ride the Wave Gala."

"Oh, I love the beach! That sounds like so much fun. Are we staying there overnight?"

I look over at her and laugh. "We definitely could."

My thoughts go to staying the night with Liv in the hotel and ravaging her until the early morning. She looks at me, not realizing what she implied, until she sees my eyes smolder. I think of all the places I will fuck her in that suite.

Her pupils dilate, and then my dad brings his hand to his mouth with a pseudo cough. The interruption is just enough to break the lust-filled trance we share.

Liv glances away from me and looks at my father, who now is sporting a smirk, letting us know that he has an idea of where our minds were going.

This causes Liv to straighten her posture and snap her attention to my mother.

"Where is the event taking place in Galveston?" she asks with exaggerated interest.

Mom, less enthused by what transpired, quickly answers with pursed lips. "At a wonderful hotel on the seawall. There will be formal indoor dining and outdoor dancing with a band."

Liv looks pleased. "Oh, that sounds lovely. I am sure that it will be a great event."

Mom can't hide her excitement. "Of course, we are still in the planning phase, but it takes a lot of planning to execute such a huge yearly fundraiser. We have four tickets already for us, so you don't have to worry about the ticket."

Liv looks a little confused. "I can pay you for the ticket cost if you'd like."

I place my hand over Liv's to stop her train of thought. "No. My mom didn't mean it like that. She is just telling you that it is covered, and you will, of course, sit at our family's table."

This eases her thoughts a bit. "Okay, I just didn't want to assume that. Thank you for the ticket."

"Liv, you never have to thank me for anything like that. I want you as my date. By the way, Mom, are Garrett and Hannah going?"

Liv looks at me in question. My mom seems to notice her question also.

"Has Dax not spoken of his brother and his wife to you?"

Liv puts her head down and shakes it no.

Damn it. I don't want her to think that I am hiding secrets or that I don't want her to know about my family. It just hasn't come up yet. I would like this woman to know everything about me. We just haven't had time to do that with each other.

"Sorry, Mom and Liv. I just hadn't mentioned him yet. You will meet him next, trust me."

This seems to appease both women. There just hasn't been time. On one hand, we are both very busy with school and work. On other hand, I'd rather spend my little time with Liv worshiping her body instead of talking about my family, although I do love them dearly. They are just not at the forefront of my mind when I'm with her.

I can officially not spend more time with my parents as my thoughts have become preoccupied with getting Liv back to my apartment. My dick has been at half-mast since that last topic, and I am in a rush to get out of there. We say our good-byes. My mom lets us off the hook when I tell her we must get up early the next day. I help Liv into my Rover and round the other door like a man on a mission.

As we drive away from their property, I replay the night and smile. Liv is perfect, and I'm sure my parents love her as much as I do.

Love her. Do I love Liv? I can't believe I am thinking this, but it feels right.

Instead of trying to fight my feelings for her, I will embrace them and see where it goes. I already know my feelings for her, but I need her to come up with the same certainty as me. There is no one else. She has been my obsession from day one. I knew I felt this pull toward her. I just hope she can accept it too.

I turn on the radio and Imagine Dragons fill my speakers with the song "Follow You." The beats sound fantastic through the speakers, and Liv loves this band. She has no idea how fitting this song is. I do not doubt that I will follow Liv to the ends of the earth, anywhere, as long as it leads me to her.

CHAPTER TWENTY-SEVEN

DAX

My hand rests on her thigh as we get close to her home. I wanted her to spend the night at my house, but it would have been too presumptuous of me to drive straight there. Reluctantly, I take her to her house and hope the night doesn't end too early.

I move my hand a little higher up, wishing she had worn a skirt. I make a mental note to buy her more skirts in the future. I'll buy her a hundred if it allows me more access to that pretty pussy of hers.

We pull up to her place and place the Rover in park. I look over at her and gently bring her head closer to mine. With my fingers splayed in her hair, I gently kiss her.

"I'll walk you up," I say against her lips.

I get out and walk around to her side, helping her out of the SUV. With my hand on the small of her back, I lead her up the walkway.

She puts the key in the lock and turns, the click sounding loud in the quiet night around us. She doesn't move her hand and doesn't look up, but I hear her take a breath.

"Do you want to come in? Emma is working tonight." Her question is like a plea, and I have no desire to turn her down.

She looks up, and I place my hand on hers and turn the knob. Shuffling us through the doorway, I grab her clutch and throw it on the table, the contents clattering to the floor. I turn us around quickly and push her hard against the door.

"Yes, Liv. I want to come in." I manage to get the words out before my mouth finds hers. Even though we have had sex at every opportunity, I can't seem to get my fill.

I pull her hair back and move my mouth to her neck. I pepper her skin with open-mouthed kisses, gently sucking as I go.

"Can you feel what you do to me?" I whisper in her ear as I grind my erection into her.

Her quiet, breathy moan is her only response as she melts further into me.

I can't seem to think about anything else except taking Liv hard at this moment. I want her so bad my cock has been standing at attention since we left my parents' house.

I thought of all the dirty things I wanted to do with her at that gala months from now. I needed desperately to get away from my parents' house, and nothing but wrecking Liv will ease this relief.

Thank God her roommate is gone. As much as I like her, her presence here would be a buzzkill, to say the least.

My fingers loop under the fabric at her shoulders as I start to take her romper off and curse this one-piece outfit. I undress her quickly, careful not to rip her outfit like the Neanderthal in me wants to. It drops to the floor in one fluid motion.

I can't help but stare. Her nearly naked body is exposed just for me. The reflection from the lamp on the table makes her tanned skin glow. She isn't wearing a bra, and she has on nothing but a black lace thong. I hear her whimper, which wakes me up from my lust-filled haze.

"Fuck, you're beautiful."

The next kiss is hard and punishing. I let all my desire for her pour through the kiss, so there's no doubt about how I feel for her. My hands find their way down her sides and across the swell of her hips. In one quick motion, I palm the backs of her thighs and bring her legs up to wrap around my waist.

I hold her up and grind my solid length into her. I can feel her warm center even over my clothes, and I immediately regret not ripping my clothes off before I picked her up.

I put her down quickly, not breaking the connection of our kiss. I fumble with the button and zipper and push my pants and boxers down. Her hands worked with me to get them off.

Picking her up again, I brace her back against the wall and hold her with one arm while one hand wraps around us, moving her thong to the side. I'm lined up perfectly, and the head of my cock finds her soaking wet. With a slight push forward with my hips, I push past her entrance as her pussy sucks me in.

Liv gasps and buries her head in my neck. "Oh god." The words fall from her lips as her head flips back, her mouth open in a silent moan.

I kiss her and plunge my tongue into her mouth. At the same time, I pull out and then begin to move again. She meets my thrusts as I take her forcefully against the door. It is a quick and dirty fuck, but I am too consumed with this woman to take it slow. Next round, we will go much slower, I promise myself. Then, I can worship her body instead of this need I currently have to fill.

The familiar tightening in my balls makes me realize that I will not last much longer. I flick the nipple on her breast with my tongue and bring my finger around to her clit, and flick it hard in a similar fashion. She comes around my cock, squeezing it in a death grip.

I pick up momentum fucking her through her orgasm as I come right after her. I feel her walls continue to spasm around my cock, taking every last drop I have to give. It prolongs my orgasm, and lights flash behind my eyes. I thrust one final time to feel her warm heat again and then drop my head into her chest.

Fine tremors move through me as I kiss upward along her neck to find her lips. I smile against her mouth, almost giddy in my post-orgasmic haze. I look into her eyes and gently place her feet back onto the ground, but her legs are shaky.

"Are you okay to stand for a second?"

"Yeah." She giggles. "I'm fine. Actually..." She pauses to catch her breath. "I'm great." Her eyes widen for a second, and she shifts uncomfortably.

As I take a step back and look down at her, I can see my cum dripping down her legs. I kiss her forehead. "I'll be right back."

I go to her kitchen and grab a towel, wetting it with warm water before I bring it back to clean her up. As I make my way back, I see her stepping out of her outfit instead of putting it back on, and I can't help but grin. I catch sight of the contents of her clutch discarded on the floor. Wow, did I just throw her handbag like that?

I stoop down to retrieve the spilled items and can't help but notice a couple of prescription pill bottles. I know it is an invasion of privacy, but the clinician in me automatically goes to read what the medication in these bottles is and to whom it is prescribed. One is for Topamax, and the other is for Zofran. One pill is an anticonvulsant for seizures, and the other is anti-nausea. I see these medications used frequently for migraines. I shake the bottle at her.

"You okay?"

She walks over to me, and I see my cum still on her thigh. That makes me remember why I came this way–to clean her up. I stand to wipe her legs. Liv picks up the remaining items and discards the clutch on the table.

"Liv, you okay?" I repeat my question as I bend to clean her up more.

"Yeah, I just have been having some migraines from studying and maybe the stress from school. I had to refill my migraine medication, and I have been having slight nausea with headaches and feeling tired in general."

I turn from washing my hands at the sink to look at her. "Are you tired now, baby?"

She goes to grab her outfit, but I take it from her hands and place it over the chair. "We won't be needing that anymore." I grab her and throw her over my shoulder, caveman style. Slapping her on the ass, I say, "Let's make sure you are properly rested then."

Walking down the hall and into her room, I gently place her on the bed. My actions are much softer now than what we just did against the wall. I want to hold my girl all night and not leave her side. Take care of her. Protect her. How great would it be to wake up to this woman every day? To give her morning orgasms or to her waking me up to suck me off.

I pull her into my arms and drag the blanket over us. We settle into a comfortable silence, our breaths the only sound in the room.

I must have fallen asleep because when I wake up and blink my eyes open, the clock reads five a.m. As much as I hate to leave the warmth of her body, I should get going. I have a few things to do this morning, and I want to leave before her roommate gets home from her night shift. I kiss Liv, waking her gently.

"Hey, baby. I have to get going."

She smiles at me with sleepy eyes and starts to get up.

"No, you sleep," I say, kissing her again and gently settling her back into her bed, tucking the covers up around her chin. I watch her for a few minutes before whispering, "I'll let myself out and call you later, okay?"

"Okay, Dax," she mumbles. And then quietly, as if she's half asleep, I hear, "I love you."

I stare down in shock, but she is already snoring lightly. I can't move. What the actual fuck? Did she say that, or was she just half asleep? I don't know how to respond.

I kiss her quickly as I get out of bed as quietly as I can. I tiptoe out of her room and close her bedroom door behind me. Does she love me? I replay her sleepy words as I grab my keys and make my way back to my parked vehicle.

The drive home is a blur. I replay the moment again and again. I was so shocked, it dawns on me that I didn't repeat them back to her. But that doesn't mean that I don't feel it. I wouldn't want to say something like that when she was still half asleep. When I tell her I love her, I want to look into her gorgeous honey-colored eyes so she has no doubt about how I feel toward her.

I can't stop myself from thinking about whether or not she'll even remember. Did she truly mean it? Was she dreaming of someone else? Of Brodie? The thoughts play through my mind as I try to focus on my plan for the day.

My spinning thoughts are brought to a halt when my phone rings. I grab it from the passenger seat and look at the screen, finding Tatiana's name flashing back up at me—a problem I need to address now.

CHAPTER TWENTY-EIGHT

LIV

I roll over, feeling a little sore. I half expect to see Dax there, but it feels cold as I touch his side of the bed. I wonder what time he left last night. I look over to see that it is now eight a.m.

I have a dull throb between my thighs, which reminds me of all the naughty fun we had last night. My skin flushes instantly, and my body tingles with the recollection. I lean over and take a deep breath in. I inhale his scent, which still lingers on the pillow. Wow, I am such a creeper.

Pushing myself up, I rest against the headboard and rub my eyes to wake up fully. As my brain catches up with the light of day, my breath catches in my throat. My eyes pop open, and my hand covers my mouth, stifling a gasp.

Oh. My. God. Did I tell him I loved him? Did I say that? Did he say it back? I rack my brain to remember, but the sleep makes the whole thing fuzzy. Clutching the bed sheets to my chest, I start to panic. *Oh. My. God. Oh. My. God. What did I do?*

Maybe he won't remember, or perhaps he didn't even hear me. Yeah, that's it. Maybe he didn't hear me. If he brings it up, I will pretend I don't remember saying it. I guess that's the only thing I can come up with right now. Deny. Deny. Deny.

I should be more concerned with the fact that he came inside me last night. At least I'm on birth control, but ugh, it just makes me so sick. It's just a multitude of problems for me to deal with.

I try to pull myself together and think about the plan for the day. I need to visit Brodie. It's my usual Sunday Funday at Brodies' house. Except nowadays, it seems to be more sad than fun.

The girls will be here soon for a girl's weekend, and I heard from Val that some of the guys were thinking about coming up to visit Brodie. He told me about it briefly, and I think it would do him some good to see everyone. At least, maybe it will cheer him up.

I quickly shower and get my things ready to head over to Brodie's place. The apartment is eerily quiet. I look over at the desk in the foyer to notice that Emma's keys are not in their usual place, and I realize she didn't come home last night. I wonder what secrets she has been keeping. She has become more secretive since she moved in with me. Hopefully, she will let me know what is going on with her. She is my best friend and I hope she knows she can count on me for anything.

I get ready and head out. As I get closer to my Jeep, I see a note on the windshield. As if reading my thoughts, I see a message from Emma.

Hey, hooker. I saw Dax here. I got out early from work and decided to head out and meet a friend for breakfast. Don't wait up. Xo-Em.

Well, that solves that. A smile forms, and I take off to see Brodie. It is a quick drive at this time of the morning. I park my Jeep in the circular driveway and am greeted by Brodie's nurse, Melissa.

"Hi, Liv. Glad to see you. I was just getting breakfast together. I hope you're hungry." She takes my bag and places it on the hook. "Brodie is just getting ready. I'm giving him his space. Why don't you join me in the kitchen, and I'll make your favorite latte? Do you want it hot or iced today?"

"You're a lifesaver. Hot would be great, thanks." I follow her and place myself on the chair sitting at the kitchen island.

"Coming right up."

I decide to ask her and see if she will divulge information on Brodie's mental health. "How's Brodie these days? I'm so busy with school and work that I haven't been around much."

I don't make eye contact, but I kind of side-eye her so she cannot read my concern. Let's pretend this isn't me being full-on Inspector Clouseau hunting for tidbits of truth.

Melissa hands me my usual angry cat mug that reads—*Woke up, hated it.* I look at it and giggle. So do I, I think to myself.

"He's the same. I heard that some of the guys are thinking about stopping by, and he was looking forward to it."

I perk up. "Yes, Val told me that too. I hope that it happens. He could use the friendship as a distraction."

"Definitely," she agrees. "I'm making Brodie's protein shake. Can I get you a bagel?"

I nod and pick up my mug of coffee. "Sure, that would be great. I'm going up to see him. Can you call me when it is done, and I can grab them?"

"No problem, Liv. Don't worry about coming back down. I'll just bring them up. Please cheer that guy up, will you?" I hear her say as I head up the stairs.

"I plan to," I echo back down the stairs to her. "Brodie?" I call his name as I enter the enormous suite—his room.

"In here," I hear a reply from the side of the room. Brodie is on the terrace overlooking the courtyard.

"Hey, you. I just grabbed my coffee and came up. I hear the guys are coming over to see you, huh?"

He looks over at me with a smile on his face. "Yes, that's what they said. I could use the distraction from my boring life."

I like seeing him like this. The last time he was so depressed. He seems to be in better spirits today.

"The girls are also coming, and I look forward to seeing everyone. I've been so busy with school and work that I couldn't get together with everyone."

He looks at me like he wants to ask me a question. He starts and then stops and looks away.

"What is it, Brodie? Do you want to ask me something?"

He looks up at me. "Liv, are you seeing anyone?"

This is not the question I was expecting, but I feel that honesty is the best policy and that he should know. So, I decide to tell him the truth.

"Yes, I am seeing someone right now."

As if expecting this answer, he asks, "Who? Does it happen to be that surfer guy from the beach when…" He doesn't finish that sentence, but he doesn't have to.

"Yes. It is that same guy. His name is Dax."

He shakes his head at this. "Dax?"

I just look at him. I decide to tell him the whole story. He deserves to know the truth. I leave out the part about him being a patient of mine, and instead, I start with the part that matters.

"After your accident, Dax helped you. He is a physician here in Houston. I didn't think that I would see him again. He tried to contact me a few times, and I didn't answer immediately. I answered one text message. I was out for a run and saw him at this coffee shop. I wasn't ready to talk to him and left. It brought back many memories, and I just wasn't ready. I don't know if fate was intervening, but I saw him while we were at a club with Emma. Then again at the hospital, where I am currently doing my clinicals. We started talking again, and things just got more serious."

He seems to process all this information. "So, are you guys serious then? Like you just said?"

I nod my confirmation. "Yes, I met his parents, and he invited me to a gala where his mom chairs the event. Things are progressing." I look into his eyes and see the sadness there. I don't get a chance to comment.

Melissa walks into the room. "Hey, guys. Here is the smoothie and your bagel you wanted, Liv."

I get up to take the tray from her. "Thank you, Melissa."

She nods and clears off a spot on the table outside. The weather is nice out, and the wind is calm. Even though it is fall, the temperature in Texas still allows for lovely outside dining. This is the best time of year to sit outside.

Melissa places the tray down. The mood has darkened. She looks between us, sensing that something has happened, but doesn't comment. She asks if we need anything else and then exits. We hear a click as the door closes behind her.

Brodie and I go out to the terrasse with the mood now turned somber. I help him navigate the small space and move things around to accommodate his wheelchair. I don't particularly feel hungry anymore, but I decide to attempt eating. We both sit there without saying anything, and I can't take the silence that continues. I put my bagel down and look at Brodie.

"Brodie, say something."

He looks at me. "What do you want me to say, Liv? I can't be the man I was before or be the man you need even if I wasn't…" His voice trails off as he shifts his hand down to his legs and the wheelchair. "I understand that you have moved on, and I can't blame you."

I want him to understand that this—me moving on—isn't because of the accident. This is because of the man he was before the accident. It changed things.

"We had broken up before this happened, Brodie. I considered us not together at that point. I met Dax in the emergency department the night before everything happened. He was a patient there, and I was his nurse. I could tell that he wanted to ask me out. We had made plans to meet up the next day at the beach. I hadn't heard much from you; honestly, things changed for me after I got that video. Well, after that, I considered us not together at that point."

"Liv, I told you how sorry I was."

I go to grab his hand. "And I believe you, Brodie, but this was over for us before that. Now I am with Dax. Things didn't work out for us. We have been friends for many years, and I want to continue being your friend. I want you to know that I will be there for you. Nothing has changed regarding that—our friendship."

He looks resigned but seems to understand, or at least I think so. Honestly, I am glad that we finally had this conversation. It was a long time coming and needed to happen. I want to be honest with him and I owe it to Dax.

I want everyone to know that this thing between Dax and me is serious. I am tired of trying to deny my feelings for him since that day he walked into the emergency department. I called out his name. I knew that there was something there. His tall, lean body and those piercing green eyes did me in. Then that dimple was my undoing. I am smiling at this, and I hear Brodie chuckle.

I look up and see him smiling at me. "You were always so expressive, Liv. You could always tell what you were thinking, no matter what."

I swat at his hand. "Oh?"

"Yep," he says. "And I don't want to repeat what I just witnessed. You can keep all those naughty thoughts about your boyfriend to yourself. I am not there yet to be able to talk to you about Dax."

I smile at him. "That's okay. I always want to be honest with you, Brodie, and I am glad we could discuss this. But now, I am done talking about Dax and wish to enjoy the company of the boy that picked me up from that tire swing all those years ago when I didn't have any other friends. The man who protected me and made me laugh. The man who will always hold my best memories."

CHAPTER TWENTY-NINE

DAX

I look at the name Tatiana displayed on my phone and debate on letting it go to voicemail. I decide to just get it over with and answer. "Hello."

"Hello to you, stranger. I was beginning to think that you were avoiding me."

I stay silent on the line for a minute before I answer this loaded question. It's not that I have avoided Tatiana. It's just that I have been preoccupied with Liv. The girl who I got a second chance with. The girl who just a few hours ago told me she loved me. The girl who I undeniably love back. In her defense, she was half unconscious and had been in a sleep-induced coma precipitated by lots of award-winning orgasms from yours truly.

"Good morning to you. You are calling bright and early. What do I owe to the pleasure of this phone call?"

She immediately gets the wrong idea and purrs into the phone. "Well, I was hoping we could catch up. Get together today?"

It has to happen today. I am now presented with the opportunity to let Tatiana know that I am no longer available for these casual hookups we have been having over the past year. It's time for me to make my intention known about my relationship status with Liv, and I think it best just to let her know. Because I am a gentleman, I don't want to do it over the phone or through text message. I believe this situation necessitates an in-person talk. Of course, I think it best to make it a public venue, if you catch my drift. There will be no yelling or craziness. I also don't want to give her the wrong impression, so I think of the best place I could do it—the gym.

"Well, I was just heading over to the gym. Want to meet there?"

I start getting my gym bag ready and pull out some shorts. I need to do some laundry. I grab a T-shirt lying over a chair in the corner and give it the Dax sniff test. Not too bad, and I can still smell a lingering scent of Liv on it. It smells a little like happiness and sunshine. These are definitely two things I feel when I am with her.

The heat radiated off her while I firmly held on to her this morning while she hung on to me like a spider monkey. I did not complain—only when I had almost woken her just to pry her off me.

"Sure, that sounds good. I am going to hit a pilates class too and we can talk after?"

I hear the sound of her blender going off, probably making her breakfast. The girl is in shape and has one hot body, but it's not the body I want to be wrapped around me every night as I go to sleep or when I wake from said sleep.

"Great, I'll be there. You can find me on the treadmill, I'm sure."

With that, we hang up, and I feel one step closer to seeing this through. I'll stop this before she asks me about being my date for the gala. When I tell her that Liv is my girlfriend or that I am in a relationship right now, that will give her the heads-up that I am not an option for her date that night or any other night. I would have taken her with me to the gala. She was great arm candy. In fact, I enjoyed her company, until I met Liv. My girl is everything I didn't know I was missing.

I decide to press the limits of my endurance. I have a lot on my mind with the upcoming conversation, so I sprint on the treadmill for the last mile of a five-mile run. It is a nice distraction. I feel good, like I could keep on running.

My quick lap or quarter-mile cooldown on the treadmill helps bring my heart rate down. I grab my towel, wipe off my sweat, and clean off the machine I was using.

I see Tatiana walking toward me with a sway in her hips. I see a few guys eye her in appreciation as she walks up to me. She goes to touch my chest and drags a fingernail down my sweaty arm. "Hey, Dax, you ready."

I don't stop her because I don't want to cause a scene. The conversation we need to have requires less of an audience. I grab my water bottle and follow her out the door to where they sell drinks and protein shakes.

"Do you want anything?" I ask as we make our way to a table off to the side.

"Umm, no, I'm good."

I reach for the back of my neck as I begin to form the letdown speech. I notice Tatiana shift uncomfortably in her chair and eye me suspiciously.

"Do you have something on your mind, Dax?" She cocks one perfectly sculpted eyebrow upward, and I grimace.

"I know you think I have been avoiding you these past months, but that isn't true." She seems to visibly relax, until I continue. Before she can say the words, I hold my hand up to stop her. "I know that I told you I didn't want anything serious with anyone or to be in a relationship. That was also true, until now." I see a glimmer of hope in her eyes, so I quickly correct this direction of our conversation. "I met Liv last year on spring break, and well, let's just say we reconnected and decided to pursue an exclusive relationship between us."

She looks at me in shock.

"I met someone, and we are exclusive," I reiterate so that there is no confusion. If a verbal slap existed, then that is what Tatiana's face looks like, and the red that comes up after that verbal slap starts to spread up her face as she looked angry enough to kick my ass, hence meeting in a public place. I am high-fiving myself for being so insightful as to see the crazy in her and realize it straight away.

Just then, I notice a man walking up to us. I look up and see a familiar face. Jameson's friend, Eduardo, is looming over us and taking in the scene in front of him. He looks at Tatiana with amusement and then shifts his face back to me.

"How's it going? Dax, right?"

I nod and shake his extended hand. "Eduardo, good to see you. Thanks again for your generosity at the club the other night. Eduardo, this is Tatiana, one of my work colleagues."

Tatiana turns her gaze to Eduardo and extends her hand for him to shake. *Ah, always the well-mannered professional.*

"Good to make your acquaintance, Tatiana," Eduardo says while calculatingly eyeing her.

There is laughter in his eyes. I wonder how long that bastard has been listening to my conversation with Tatiana.

"So, you don't look like you were exercising here. What brings you over? Looking for a membership?" Eduardo does now laugh at this comment.

"No, I don't need one since I own this gym."

Now it's my turn to look surprised. "I had no idea. The club, too, right?"

He nods and continues. "Yeah, I have my hands in a little bit of everything, I guess you should say. Emma was telling me about the gala. Are you guys going?"

Tatiana must think he means her, not knowing he is leading this into a deeper discussion by his smirk. I scowl, knowing that he is referring to Liv, naturally. It doesn't stop Tatiana from answering, though.

"Well, I thought I was going, but it appears I am without a date."

Eduardo looks over at her, up and down. She seems to perk up at this.

"Well, that's too bad. A beautiful woman like you shouldn't be waiting on anyone that doesn't put you first. Unfortunately, I am already promised to another; otherwise, I would take you." He gives her an academy-award-winning smile and gives her hand another shake. This time as a goodbye.

"It was very nice talking to you. Dax, I thought you should know that the girls will show up at the club for a girls' night. I have everything set up to ensure they are well taken care of, if you understand my meaning. You're working that night, right?"

I run my hand through my hair. "Yep, Liv mentioned it briefly but didn't go into details, but I know that I do work."

I wonder what his relationship with Emma is. She seemed so interested in Jameson, and she just kind of dropped interest in him right after meeting Eduardo. He said he was taken or…what was that strange phrase he used? Oh yeah, *I am promised to another.* What does that even mean?

"I appreciate that, Eduardo." He waves to us and walks off.

I rise from my chair, using this as an opportunity to end this disaster of a conversation that Tatiana and I were having. Even though it was necessary and long overdue, I am glad to have it behind me. I hope there are no problems with her on my end with Liv.

She gets up, sensing that this is it for us too. She pushes her chair in and hesitates, looking up at me before she speaks.

"That night at my townhouse when you got a call from someone…" she trails off.

I look at her, but she can see the answer reflected in my eyes. She opens her mouth and closes it as the realization hits her.

"She is the same girl from the coffee shop too, isn't she?"

I don't bother to deny it. "Yes, the same girl, that's my Liv."

She purses her lips and picks up her bag from the chair. She walks off without another word, and I release a long exhale. Relief floods my mind as I don't have that awkward conversation hanging over my head anymore, and I can just focus on being with Liv.

I head out to my car, throwing my sweaty gym bag on the back seat. I plug my phone into my car connector to play my music, but I decide to call Liv first. After about the third ring, she picks up.

"Hey, Dax."

"Hey, beautiful," I reply. "Where are you?" I can hear that she is on Bluetooth, so she must be in her car as well.

"Just leaving Brodie's house. I had to talk to him. It's also my weekly visit."

I wait for her to elaborate, but nothing comes. I clear my throat. "Ah, that's nice."

"What about you?" she asks in return. "I just left the gym. I had to tie up a loose end with a colleague I met there. Now I am on my way home."

After making plans to meet up later tonight and head to work together in the morning, I end the call, feeling like maybe things will be easier now with Liv. Another loose end tied up.

We had such a rocky start, and I hated how I felt after leaving her on Padre Island. I promise never to leave her side again. I like the new direction my life is taking. It seems to be a bit easier—less stressful. It seems to be the theme for Liv and me. I also wonder what she and Brodie had to talk about. I am just waiting for the floor to drop out. I just hope this time I am wrong.

CHAPTER THIRTY

LIV

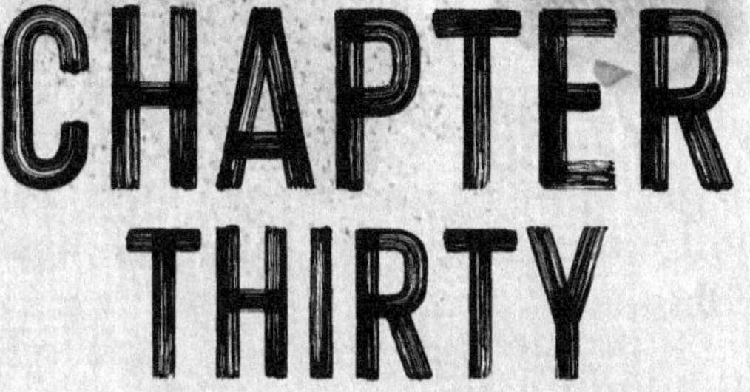

I love waking up to Dax holding me. I feel so safe in his arms. Weeks have gone by with me sleeping over at his place or him at mine. We meet for coffee in the café when we can and are inseparable these days.

The girls have some time off. This is the perfect time to get together before the holidays are around the corner and the gala that Dax's mom is chairing in the spring. I have been waiting for the girls to get here for a visit. Now, it is finally here. I fist pump the air and add a little skip in my step as I try to refrain from giggling like a schoolgirl.

I finish up my group presentation for class and leave for the apartment. I am meeting Emma there, and we are getting ready for the girls to arrive from Corpus at any minute.

Ainsley and Val sure made record speed getting here. They wanted to beat rush hour traffic. I can't say that I blame them. Seeing their text message to Emma and me makes my heart happy.

I didn't realize I needed this outing until now. I have been so tired these past couple of weeks, and I just can't seem to feel rested. I will have to make a note to get some more vitamin D and stay hydrated.

Being in school must be taking its toll on my body. I have felt dizzy from so much reading when studying, and all the hours at the hospital for clinicals to boot. I really need to take better care of myself. I hate to tell Dax about the way that I have been feeling recently—to bother him with something so silly. All it will do is make him worry unnecessarily.

I pull into the parking lot, finish up the rest of my water, and grab my stuff to head on in. I hear a car pull up and turn around to see Ainsley and Val park next to me. I drop my stuff and run over to them, screaming excitedly.

"Oh my god, you're here. I am so happy to spend some time with my homegirls." Val wraps herself around me, shaking me from side to side.

I feel myself becoming dizzy again, and suddenly I feel the need to throw up. I put my hand out on the car to steady myself, and Ainsley comes running up to me.

"Liv, are you okay? Girl, you look green. Are you going to vomit?"

Before I can say anything, I throw up all my water from five minutes ago and some remnants of my salad from three hours ago.

"Whoa, let's get you inside. Come on, Val, help grab her stuff."

The girls help me get into the apartment, where Emma is on her laptop and drinking coffee at the kitchen table. She sees my condition and immediately gets up to come to see what is the matter.

"Liv, what's wrong?" She grabs a rag to wipe my mouth.

"Nothing, guys. I have just been exhausted from school and work. I felt super dizzy today and must be dehydrated because I haven't been drinking enough water. You know how it is?"

The girls look at Emma. I look over to Emma who is tight-lipped.

"Hey, girlies, just make yourself at home. I think you should take something to help with the vomiting. I know you had some dissolvable pills in your bag for that. You and motion sickness. Are you okay with still going out?"

I get up to prove that I am more okay. "Definitely, I wouldn't miss it for the world."

She hugs me and takes my hand, leading me to my bedroom. "Come on.

Let's clean you up, and I'll help you find something to wear."

"Great," I say. "See you guys in a second."

I wave to Val and Ainsley in the living room, who both look at me with concern. It must be short-lived because they are already opening the fridge to see what there is to drink.

When we round the corner that leads to my bedroom, Emma gives me the evil eye. I swear that girl being half Mexican and always talking about old folklore stories can put a hex on you like no other. I used to think it was an urban myth told to scare off people, but that shit is real. I shudder at her attack stance.

"What the fuck, Liv?"

I'm startled and step back from her. "Umm, what is up with you, Emma?" I look at her, confused, as if she has lost her ever-loving mind.

"Are you pregnant?"

I rear back as if slapped with this verbal accusation. Shocked, I attempt to open my mouth and just close it, repeating the first part while looking like a dying fish out of water. I open my mouth again, but she looks at me, lifting one eyebrow upward in question, halting me before I continue to speak.

"No," I comment loudly. "I just had a period last week. It was short, but was still there..." I trail off in more of a whisper to myself.

"A short period? Do your boobs hurt?" she asks as she takes my nipple and twists it. The pain is incredible as I go to smack her across the shoulder.

"What the fuck was that shit, Emma? I mean, seriously, what are we, twelve-year-old boys?" I grab my boob, trying to ease the discomfort.

She looks at me, shaking her head.

"I'll take that as hell yes, they are sore as an affirmation. You need to take a pregnancy test to make sure."

I go to the bathroom to grab an antiemetic pill to stop nausea and turn back to her. "I have an appointment with Planned Parenthood next week to get some more birth control. Dax and I have been mostly cautious too."

She looks at me like I am a total idiot.

"I'm assuming you didn't take Plan B the next day either?"

"I am on birth control, Emma!" I am practically screaming at her because I am feeling so emotional, and she is genuinely pissing me off. I know this is a rhetorical question, but to make sure she knows the answer, I shake my head no. "There's no need for Plan B."

"Well, let's not jump to any conclusions until we know. I think it's best you don't drink tonight, at least until you get a negative test."

I agree with Emma. "I wasn't going to drink tonight anyway, feeling the way I do. I can be the designated driver then."

Emma shakes her head. "No way! We are going to Uber to the club, and you will not babysit the girls."

"Okay, sounds good to me. I definitely want to dance. I am starting to feel better after the medication and am ready to go out with my besties."

Emma goes to hug me. "You know I love you to the moon and back, Liv."

I return the hug. "I know that. I adore you, Emma. I am so lucky to have you in my life. You coming to help me in Houston was the nicest thing you could have done for me."

She looks away when I say this, not meeting my eyes. "Let's get ready, shall we?" With that, she turns around and leaves me to get dressed.

We pull up right in front of the club and get out of the Uber. The club is packed, and the girls are excited. Everyone is dressed up, but my girls are smoking hot. I am so proud that I have badass besties that aren't just knockout gorgeous but so kind and the absolute best friends anyone could ask for. My ride-or-die wrapped up in short dresses and mini skirts on a mission to break hearts.

Emma leads us to the front of the line, and the bouncer doesn't even ask who she is. He just opens the rope, and we stroll inside. Emma waits for us, and we go into the building holding hands in a line to stay together so we don't lose each other.

Most of all, Emma is still hovering like a mother hen over my one episode today. We make our way over to the staircase that leads to the VIP area upstairs. We walk up a single file, and when we reach the top, there is security. They follow Emma, and we sit in a booth. I am the last to reach it, and I thank the guard for showing us the way. He smiles at me but doesn't respond. He doesn't leave either. I think that is very bizarre. Why are they standing there? A waitress comes to take our order and appears a little nervous. She addresses Emma and no one else.

"We'll take a table service of Grey Goose and a water and ginger ale for my friend there." She smiles at me and then looks back at the waitress. "That's all for now." She turns back to us and smiles, looking over at us all together again.

"I missed you guys." She places her head on Val's shoulder.

Val grabs her shoulder and squeezes Emma, who is half her size. Well, maybe that's an exaggeration, but she is petite. I am half a foot taller than her, but I am above average height for a woman at that. The waitress returns quickly with our bottle and drinks. The security guard stops us and takes a shot first with a splash of cranberry in it. We watch him toss it back and then nod his head at Emma.

"I guess he is just making sure it's not diluted."

Eduardo comes over to our table and introduces himself to us. I wave at him and thank him for allowing us to hang out without waiting in line.

"Think nothing of it, Liv." He leans over into Emma's ear and says something. She smiles and then looks at him, and he kisses her on the top of her head. He then goes to the security guard and leans over to talk to him out of earshot. He looks to the other security detail and pats him on the shoulder as he walks off.

"Come on, girls. Let's take some shots and go dance."

The girls take a couple of shots each, and we stand, making our way to the dance floor. Again the security guard stays at our table, but as we make our way down the staircase, another security guard is waiting to watch us.

"I wonder if this is part of the VIP experience?" I mouth into Emma's ear, and she looks at me with a smirk.

"Must be."

She grabs my hand, and we get to the dance floor. We dance to a couple of songs, and then Nelly's "It's Getting Hot In Here" comes on, and Emma gets all excited. The girl can dance, and she draws a little attention to herself.

She pulls me in closer, and we lose ourselves in the song. Some guys head over our way and start to dance with us. I don't care as long as they don't get handsy.

I look up and see a big muscled guy with a tight-fitted Henley shirt that fits his body like a glove. He starts to grind alongside Emma, and I notice that his tattoos creep up from under his chest, extending to his neck.

I look over at a small commotion by the dance floor and catch a security guard that was with us upstairs approaching the dance floor, followed by a very pissed-off Eduardo. He walks over to the dance floor and taps the guys on the shoulder. The guy turns around, and recognition seems to register on his face. He puts his hands up and says something to Eduardo I cannot hear. He backs off and leaves the floor. Emma is now being led off the dance floor by Eduardo. I go to follow, but suddenly a wave of nausea hits me, and I lean over, holding on to a barstool nearby.

I see Emma running over to me, with Eduardo calling one of the security guards to come over to me. I feel the security grab me, lead me off the crowded area, and take me in through a side door. I hear footsteps echo, and Emma is right by me, telling me I will be alright.

I hear Eduardo's voice shout, "Pick her up and take her to my office, now! We need to call Dax to come and get her."

That was the last thing I heard before I passed out. I awake to Emma folding a cool compress onto my forehead.

"There you are, Liv. You made us all so worried."

I look at my surroundings, confused. I'm on a leather sofa.

Emma explains, "You were dizzy, said you felt like passing out, and then did. Eduardo had one of the security guards bring you to his office, and they called Dax. He is on his way."

I smile and think that I can't wait until Dax shows up. Then I will feel better. He makes everything feel better. I lower my head on a very comfortable cushion and close my heavy eyes.

I must have passed out for a while because a few minutes later, another security guard calls to say that Dax is at the door outside asking for entrance into the club.

"Let him in and show him back. I called him, and we are expecting him," Eduardo relays to another person on his phone.

Five minutes later, Dax is rushing through the door to find me. He sees me trying to sit up and runs over. "Liv, are you okay? What happened?"

"I was feeling sick today, and all the business with school and work finally caught up to me."

Emma quickly turns to me and glares. I look at Emma and then at Dax.

"Why do I sense there is more to this story, Liv? We'll talk about it later when I get you to my house. Can you stand? Do you want to go to the ER?"

I shake my head no.

"Okay, let's see if you can stand. Here, let me help you."

I try to stand but feel nausea come at me again. I shake my head and sit back again.

"Okay, to the ER, it is. Eduardo, can you help me get her to my car?"

"Sure, bring your car around back, and I will help her and have my security team escort you to the car. I'll have someone follow you there just in case you need help."

"Thanks." Dax turns around to leave quickly through the door.

I look over and see Emma staring at me. She comes over and moves my hair out of my face.

"You probably are dehydrated and might need some IV fluids. Please keep me posted, Liv, okay? I will get the girls home, and I'll see you tomorrow. I expect complete reports from you then." She winks at me and stands to return to Eduardo's side, where he takes her in a possessive embrace.

Dax comes back through the door with the security guys, and they take me through the back hallways leading to the outside alley. As soon as they open the door, the cooler air hits me, and I feel I can breathe better. The crowds and heat produced by the dancing and all the bodies around me must have been too much and added to my feeling of being unwell today.

Of course, the emergency department is busy tonight, but Dax pulls some strings to get us back sooner, considering I probably look terrible, almost passing out in the chair.

The triage nurse gets me right in, and I am shown to a room off to the side hallways. The nurse comes through, starts an IV, draws some labs from it, and then hangs an IV bag of fluid at a steady pace.

I don't see anyone I know working tonight, and I am immediately thankful for that minor miracle. I don't want to explain to anyone why I am here, especially if what I suspect is my problem is confirmed and also made known to the entire department.

We seem to wait forever, and I must have fallen asleep to the calming sensation of Dax rubbing my forehead. I hear the door open and startle at the physician that comes through.

"Hi, I am Dr. Rose. I think we have worked together before, right, Liv?"

I nod and swallow hard at the anxiety rising in my throat at his mention of him remembering me. Dr. Rose must take notice.

"Don't worry, Liv, anything we discuss here is confidential. You know that little thing called a HIPAA violation and all, right? I had ordered some preliminary labs based on your symptoms before I came in. Is it okay to talk in front of this gentleman here?"

I look over at Dax and smile. "Yes, that's fine."

Dax gives him his hand and introduces himself as my boyfriend, a surgeon here at the hospital. Dr. Rose nods in acknowledgment and continues. "Why don't you tell me when this started and anything else that I should know?"

I tell him about my symptoms, and I feel Dax suddenly tense beside me. I don't want to look at him for fear that I won't see the response I would like on his face.

"Well, Liv, we think we know what may be contributing to this, but we will run a few more tests just to be sure. Either way, I wanted to give you the news that you are pregnant. Early stages, but your HCG levels returned on your blood work, letting us know it is a positive pregnancy result."

Dax squeezes my hand. I feel like the wind has been knocked out of me. Even though I might have expected it, it's another thing entirely having it confirmed.

"I'll be back when everything else comes back from the lab. Do you have an obstetrician, or would you like some recommendations for one?"

I look at Dax.

"We'll take a recommendation if you can provide us with that," replies Dax quickly. "I want to ensure that she is seen immediately, especially if she continues with nausea and dizziness."

"Sure thing, and let me know if you need anything else. The nurse should be back to reassess you after the IV fluids."

I am so desperately trying to contain my last bit of emotions. At that, Dr. Rose leaves the room, and with that departure, I place my head in the trash can and vomit the remainder of my stomach's contents.

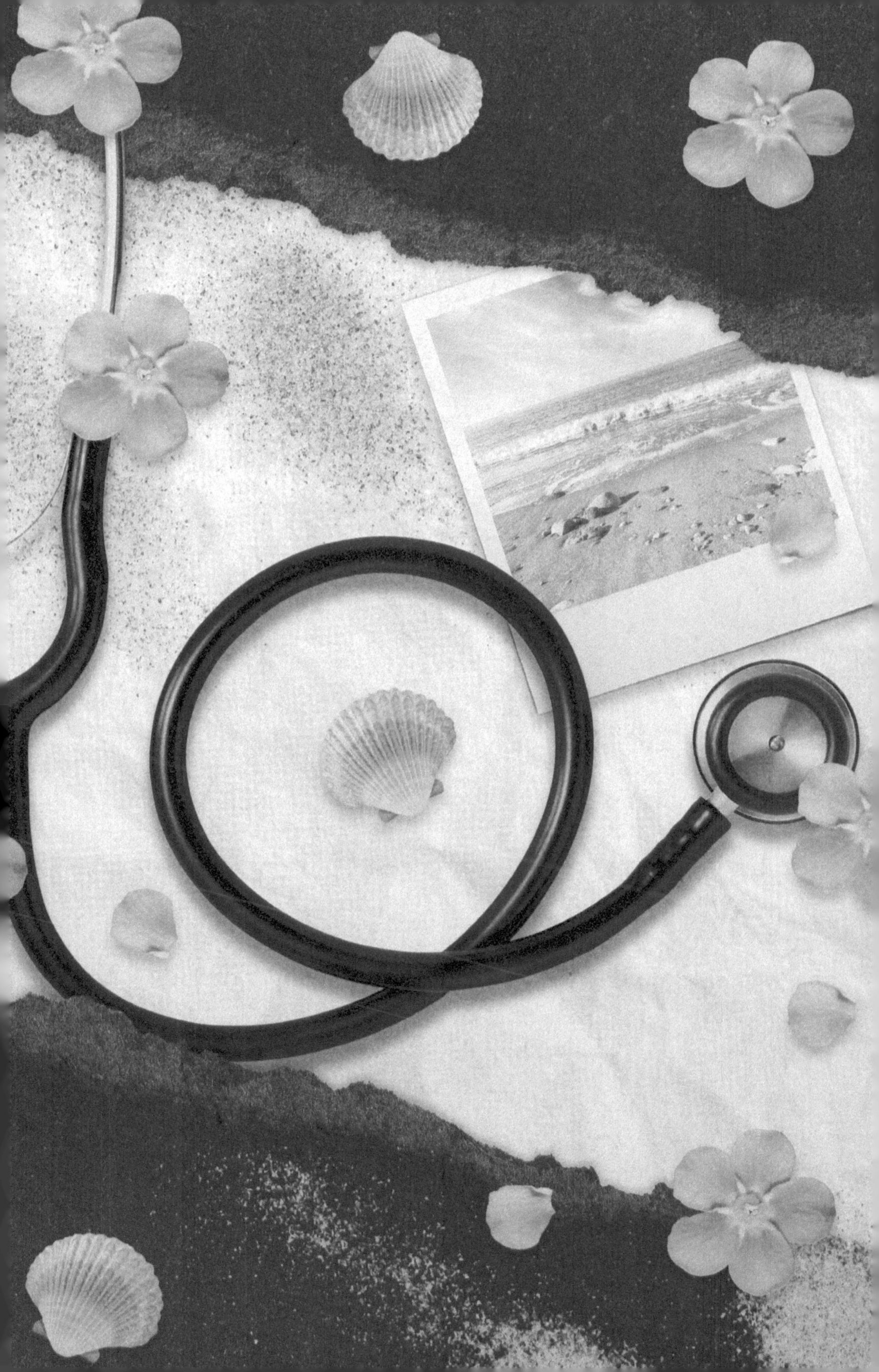

CHAPTER THIRTY-ONE

DAX

As we lie in bed, Liv asleep next to me, I can't help remembering earlier in the evening when I got that call that would change my life entirely.

I finished my case close to midnight and am just writing orders to admit my patient to the floor. I see an unknown number flashing on my screen. I don't know if I should answer it, but it could be important if it's this late at night. I answer the phone to hear a familiar voice. There is music in the background, and then I hear a door close, muffling the sound.

"Hello," I repeat my greeting.

"Dax, it is Eduardo."

I immediately straighten and my back goes ramrod straight. "Is Liv okay?" Eduardo is yelling at someone in the background. He returns to the phone. "Yes, but *she is dizzy, and Emma said she vomited earlier."*

"Where is she?"

"She is here in my office. Emma is with her, and I have security with her in case she needs anything more."

"I'm on my way." I quickly disconnect the call and rush out of the hospital without changing. I need to get Liv.

Seeing her lying on the sofa in Eduardo's office makes me freak out. She looks so pale, and to hear she had been sick without me knowing about it all day makes me furious.

She is such a strong woman, working, going to school, spending time with me, and managing to maintain her friendship with Brodie. It has been too much for her. I think she needs to slow down and take some time for herself. If she moved in with me, it would undoubtedly help with seeing each other, and she wouldn't have to work since I won't let her pay for anything.

The need to take care of her should make me worry because it hasn't even been a year since we have been together, but I can't see a future for myself without her.

I am drawn out of my thoughts when she moves her hand out of mine and rubs her temples. Luckily, I got us into a room in the ER, despite how busy it is. The nurse continues to ask her general questions about the events that led to her coming here.

"When did the symptoms start? When was your last menstrual cycle?"

Liv begins to tell the nurse about her symptoms, and my eyes shoot up at the next question waiting to hear her answer. "Umm, I had a period recently, but it was short and only spotty."

She brings her hands together in a twisting motion, not looking at me. Does she think she's pregnant? So many thoughts go through my mind. We have sex a lot and bareback at that because she is on the pill. I can't even begin to believe she has been feeling this way and still tried going out tonight. What was she thinking? Dr. Rose comes in and asks more leading questions.

I stiffen at her response and look at her. I mean, really look at her. She must notice my tension and rigid posture because she tries to pull her hand away, but I just give her a reassuring squeeze to let her know I support her.

That's when I hear Dr. Rose confirm my suspicions.

"I want to provide you with the news that you are pregnant. Early stages, but your HCG levels returned elevated in your blood work, letting us know it's a positive pregnancy result."

I squeeze her hand again, and she looks at me, judging my response to the news. If she were searching for a displeased look on my face, she would be surprised to see nothing but relief that she is pregnant and nothing serious.

Well, nothing serious as in her health. Getting her pregnant was always going to happen, and envisioning her carrying my child makes me fiercely protective of her. I want nothing more than to throw her over my shoulder, drag her out of there, and show her who she belongs to.

We sit there and wait another couple of hours until the nurse comes in with our discharge paperwork. Liv looks so much better after all of the IV hydration she received here. She looks over the paperwork and nods.

"Are these the names of obstetricians nearby? I guess I should probably call and make an appointment soon. What if I continue with nausea?"

The nurse nods in understanding. "We gave you a prescription to help with that. I know you work and go to school, but you might need to take things a bit slower if you can. I don't need to tell you about the benefits of proper nutrition now that you are pregnant, but if you have any questions, here are some resources for additional information."

Liv and I take the information and thank the nurse.

Liv goes to stand. "Here, babe, let me help to get you to the car in case you start to get dizzy again."

The door closes behind us, and I pull her into my arms. I gently place a hand on her flat stomach.

"Liv, you are pregnant with my child," I say, trying to let that sink in.

God, I love it and how it does weird things to me. I nuzzle into her neck.

"We didn't even get the chance to practice enough in making this baby." I trail soft, wet kisses up her neck and chin. She leans into my embrace, and I grab her by the ass, dragging her in closer to feel the hardness of my cock against her stomach. She moans.

"Yeah, but you made sure to make it count. It must have been one of the earlier times we had sex."

I kiss her. When I think of my baby growing in her, it just makes me harder.

"I think the best part of this is that I get to take you home and fuck you bare as much as I want since you're already pregnant."

She pulls back and looks me in the eye. "Is that all you got from the discharge instructions?" She laughs into my neck, and the breath on my flesh makes my skin burst out in goose bumps. "Take me home now, Dax."

I chuckle and pull away from her to arrange myself. "Let's get out of here, baby." I grab her stuff and hold her pocketbook in front of my junk, along with my coat, so that the waiting room doesn't get a full view of my tented scrub pants.

And that is how we arrived here, on the way home together-the three of us. The drive to my apartment is quiet and consists of Liv looking out the window. Now is the best time, before we get home and become distracted, to spring the question of her moving in with me. I mean, it isn't up to her anymore. This baby just solidifies her becoming mine.

"Penny, for your thoughts, Liv?" I glance at her, but I can't get a read on her or what she thinks.

She turns to look at me. "Are you happy about this pregnancy, Dax?"

I grab her hand and bring it to my lips. "I couldn't be happier. I know it isn't the best time, but I can't wait to see you start to show. Pregnant with my baby. In fact, I'd like you to move in. I don't want you to stress out about working if you don't want to. Let me take care of you both."

She squeezes my hand. "Don't you think that's moving a bit fast, Dax?"

I chuckle at the irony. "Baby, I think we skipped slow and progressed to full throttle. So what do you say?"

She looks me in the eyes to sense my seriousness. I know that she can see how deadly serious I am about this. "Okay, I'll move in with you."

A smile spreads across my face. Honestly, I was expecting more of an argument.

"When do you want me to move in?"

"As soon as possible. I don't want you to have any more problems with feeling ill, especially in the first trimester. It is imperative, Liv, that you slow down a bit. Maybe just concentrate on school for now. You know you don't have to worry about living expenses."

She just nods and looks back out the window.

I pull into my apartment building and park. I help Liv out of the car, and she seems so tired. I can't believe she passed out at that club. I am so thankful to Eduardo for calling me, so I could go and get her. I'll be sure to let her sleep in. I don't have to be anywhere first thing in the morning, so I can make sure to get her a few things from her apartment to wear. We need to plan a lot of things in the next few months in preparation for the baby, our baby.

I pull Liv's clothes off her and lift her arms to place one of my T-shirts on her. Her head hits the pillow, and she is immediately asleep. God, I love to look at her when she sleeps. She is so damn beautiful.

She had her phone illuminated with a text message. I see that she has one text message from Emma and another from Brodie. That's interesting. I wonder what he wanted.

I know that Liv still sees him once a week. She still blames herself for his accident. I wish she could somehow realize that that was nothing more than a terrible accident caused by his poor decision. That's on him, as unfortunate as it is.

I'll let Liv know that they messaged. I bet Emma is worried about her. From what I have witnessed, she has been an excellent friend to Liv. She could have been a good girlfriend for Jameson, but that didn't work out. I know it wasn't because of him. That guy has terrible luck with women. I just don't understand why he can't seem to lock anyone down.

Emma seems to be happy with Eduardo if they are, in fact, a couple. They haven't exactly announced it, and it isn't any of my business either. I'll need Emma's help persuading Liv to give up her job until graduation. I think she needs to take care of herself better for this baby and finish school. I bet she will be stubborn with that, but once she sees it is for the best, I believe she will come around.

I jump in the shower and clean off micro specs of my job. I hate bringing the hospital germy crap home with me. I'm usually at the gym after or at least change into regular clothes before I leave. This time there wasn't a chance for me to do this as I just reacted and left straight from there. I can't fathom the thought of going to bed without a shower after working in the operating room, no matter how tired I am. That's just gross, not to mention unsanitary.

I climb under the cool covers and lay on my side to watch Liv sleep. Her breathing is deep and regular. She is twitching in her sleep, and I wonder what she dreams. Is it us? Does she dream of me or our future together?

The covers are weighted, and I can feel the heat radiating off Liv's body. I can't help but lay here and stare at her, thinking she almost got away. If I hadn't injured myself that day and spent time with her, or if fate hadn't intervened and brought us back into each other's lives, I may not be welcoming a baby into the world soon.

I get her into my arms and nuzzle my face into her neck. Her hair smells like her shampoo. Coconut and vanilla scents permeate my sheets, and I swear I have died and gone to heaven. I inhale, taking a deeper breath. She awakens a little to rest her hand on my chest.

I whisper into her ear, "I love you, baby."

She smiles without opening her eyes. "I love you."

I turn off the light and fall asleep with Liv and my unborn child in my arms.

CHAPTER THIRTY-TWO

LIV

Dax persuaded me to take Monday off, so I am trying to call some obstetrical offices to schedule an appointment. When I finally find one I like or think I might like, I book an appointment for my initial visit.

I must only be a couple of months along in my pregnancy. Dax and I were careful because I had taken my birth control religiously. I know it isn't one hundred percent effective in preventing pregnancy, but pretty damn close. I guess I am the exception.

Geez, I must be a Fertile Myrtle. I thought that was a period I had at that time. It was light only for three days. After reading my old nursing book on maternity, it looks like that must have been the implantation phase. Ugh, I touch my temples and feel a migraine coming on.

I am hit with an unwelcome thought as I stroke my head and rub my forehead. Oh, shit! Was it my migraine medication that caused this? I pull up my friendly Google and type in the desired question. Motherfucker. I can't believe it. That must be it. I have had such intense migraines with the heavy workload and school compounding the stress that I forgot that could be a side effect of decreasing my birth control efficiency. I am such a dope.

Ugh, and I am so screwed. Dax must have some excellent swimmers to match my unparalleled fertility. I throw my head down into my arms, and I laugh to myself. I should find this situation more of an upset that I find myself pregnant and unwed, but I can't help but feel joy at carrying Dax's baby. He seems truly happy about it too.

I must admit that I was apprehensive about his reaction to the news of this pregnancy. We spoke briefly last night and agreed not to tell anyone about it. I will tell the girls that I was, in fact, just sick with a horrendous stomach bug.

I know I won't be able to lie to Emma, so, I will confide in her. I know she will be able to keep a secret, since I suspect she has several secrets of her own with how sketchy her behavior has been. I've been giving her space, hoping that she will let me know what is going on with her, but that has not come yet. I have to have someone in my corner.

I return the text from Brodie telling him about my stomach bug without reading his message. I can always do that later. I should stick to the same lie and bring Emma's number to my contact list. I hit the call button, and she picks up after a couple of rings.

"Hey, girl, how are you feeling?" Emma's bubbly demeanor radiates sparkles and rainbows down the line.

"I am feeling better. I just booked my first obstetrician appointment."

There is a pause before Emma answers. "So it's true then, confirmed?"

I nod, knowing she can't see it "Yes, it is confirmed," I echo back. "I am pregnant with Dax's baby."

She lets that sink in for a minute before replying. "Are you happy, Liv?"

I am stunned by this question, to be honest. I figured she would ask if I plan on keeping the baby. That seems like a more practical question I would expect Emma to ask. She doesn't, so I answer without hesitation.

"Yes, I am excited. I figured this would happen later, but it was always Dax, Emma. I know it's weird to say, but I feel I was destined to be his since the day I met him. The way he makes me feel and the way he touches me. It seems familiar, like I was already his, and he was mine."

She is silent for a moment and then lets out a breath on the phone.

"Yeah, I understand that. Sometimes, you can't fight who you end up with. Sometimes, it is just the way things are meant to be."

I wonder if she is talking about Dax and me at this point, but I know she tends to shy away from questions of a personal nature, so I decided to let it go.

We end the call, and I go to my closet, searching for something to wear. I spot the dress I got for the gala and decide to try it. It fits like a glove when I finally zip it up. Unfortunately, the gala is in a few months. I will probably have a new situation on my hands in search of a looser dress—

A knock sounds at my door. I wander over to the window and look out. Immediately, I see the familiar car and let Dax in.

"Hey, gorgeous." He brings me in and kisses me. I open the door wider to let him in, and he takes a step back. "Are you going somewhere without me?" He cocks an eyebrow upward as he looks me up and down with lustful eyes.

"Umm, no. I was just trying on the dress I bought with Emma for the gala. I wanted to make sure my fat ass still fit into it, but maybe not for long." I shift from foot to foot. I have never really been unsure, but being pregnant has me feeling so many emotions.

Dax grabs me by the waist and pulls me close to him. He puts two hands on my ass and squeezes.

"I can't wait to see you looking pregnant, Liv. The thought of you carrying my baby makes me all kinds of crazy."

He nuzzles his face into my neck, and I squirm from the ticklish feeling of his stubble on my face. His hot breath sends a sense of euphoria straight to my nether regions. I clench at the thought of ripping this dress off and straddling him on the couch.

What the ever-loving fuck is going on? I am so horny, and I hope this is the pregnancy and not the fact that I just can't get enough of this man's dick.

As if reading my thoughts, Dax grabs my ass, pushing my tender boobs up against his chest. He throws his face in my cleavage.

"I could get used to this too, Liv," he says in a low, raspy voice that sends a bolt of electricity to my core.

My nipples pebble underneath his hot breath, and I let out an unexpected moan. Dax takes this as an invitation and walks me back to my bedroom.

He kicks the door closed with his dramatic flair as he deposits me on the bed.

"I must be back at work soon, so I just came in to check on you. This will have to be a quickie."

He starts stripping his clothes. I have never been more turned on than to see Dax strip for me in broad daylight. His tall, lean, and toned body makes its way over to me. He is the perfect male specimen, and he is all mine.

I lick my lips. His blue eyes widen, then close to slits in a lust-filled trance as he saunters over to me. He makes quick work of the dress, peeling it off me and tossing it gracefully onto the chair at my desk.

He hovers over me on the bed, pulls me in close, and in one quick thrust, enters me as if he can't wait a second longer. His blond hair falls over his eye as he throws my legs over his shoulder and drags me in close. He is grabbing me by the hips as he thrusts in over and over. I am so wet from the strip tease that I begin to rock into him, matching his thrusts.

"Harder, Dax, please fuck me harder."

He looks pleased with this and gives me exactly what I want. This act is quick and dirty, and I love every second of it. I come with a series of expletives that sing his praise as his thrusts and our breathing become erratic.

"Fuck, Liv. Fuck!" he shouts.

He spills inside and lowers himself to kiss me so tenderly that I feel my chest squeeze. I am amazed that he can fuck me so thoroughly and then be so sweet. A juxtaposition to the animalistic fucking and then tender caress as he peppers soft kisses along my neck.

He lowers my leg onto the bed as he releases me. His cum drips down my leg, and his nostrils flare in his usual possessive way. He pushes it back inside and then rubs it around my clit.

He takes his finger and says, "Suck, Liv."

I lick and suck his finger, and immediately, he comes in for another kiss.

"God, I love you." He backs away and starts to get dressed.

I sit there, taking in the way Dax is with me, totally grinning at this side of him. I mean, who doesn't love an alpha male, right?

He runs to the bathroom to grab a towel to clean me up. I stare into those penetrating eyes that were my undoing in our first encounter and look away. I try not to sound needy, but I know that is exactly what I sound like when he is standing over me, fully dressed, as I still am naked, exposed, and vulnerable. I grab my blanket and wrap it around me.

"Don't hide from me, Liv."

I meet his stare.

"There is something I need to ask you."

I immediately tense up, thinking the worst. *Is this where he leaves me, or does it change for the worse now that I am knocked up?*

I look down and then around, thinking of what he will say. What if he has changed his mind about the baby? About me? Without beating around the bush, Dax lets it all come out.

"I want you to move in with me now." He lets out a breath as if trying to get the sentence out without pausing for a comment.

"I want to be with you, and I think this is the next step."

I look at him in surprise. "Dax, we already talked about this, and I agreed, remember?"

He looks at me. "Yes, I remember, and you still haven't done it. I also wasn't finished with what I was going to say. You have been so tired, and I think it would be easier on you if I were there to share some of the burdens. You could quit your job and just focus on school. I would love to wake up to you here every day without us going between each other's places."

I look at him, processing both his spoken words and the vulnerability in what he left unsaid. I mull this over for a moment, losing track of time. It must have been longer than I realized because he calls my name, bringing me back to the present.

"Liv, what do you say? Will you move in with me and let me take care of you? Quit your job and just focus on us and finishing up your degree? That's a lot in itself."

I hear the sincerity in his voice and see the love in his eyes. Before I have time to second-guess myself, I answer. "Yes, I will, Dax. I'll fully move in with you."

He gives me this smile that reaches from ear to ear.

"I'll quit my job and focus on school and us, too."

He kisses me and leaves to dispose of the washcloth in the bathroom.

"When do you want me to move in with you?" I ask from the bedroom.

He returns now and envelopes me in a soft embrace. I pull away to witness his facial expression.

"As soon as possible. I want to start my future with you today. I want to start my family with you today."

I am shocked and so delighted to hear him say this. "Okay," is all I say.

"Okay?" he asks as if needing the verification.

I nod and repeat the words to him twice. "Okay, okay. I'll do it whenever you can help me move my things."

He goes to my closet and grabs a duffel bag. No time like the present.

"I get out of work at nine tonight when my last OR case should finish. Pack a few things, and I'll send for the rest. I want you in my bed tonight and every day after that."

I look at him, stunned.

He kisses me deeply and pulls away. "I have to go, Liv, but I'll text you when I am on my way. I guess you are stuck with me now, baby?" He says this as if he posed a question, but I know this is not a question or up for debate.

"I'll be ready," I reply in haste.

This simple reply is all I can manage as I am stunned by his words. He smiles at me before exiting my room. I hear the door close behind him.

"What in the ever-loving fuck am I doing," I say aloud to no one in particular.

I laugh and shake my head, burying my face in my hands. That man is so possessive, and I can't help feeling lucky that he is mine.

I grab the duffel bag and begin loading it with clothes and toiletries. I return my dress to a hanger and throw on some yoga pants and a sweatshirt. My hair is in a messy bun, and I go to make myself some dinner before Dax returns and takes me off to his place.

I look around at my surroundings and think about how I never got settled in this apartment. It's as if I already wanted to move in with Dax. We are one step closer to our life together, our future. Now, I just need to tell Emma about this, and oh god, Brodie.

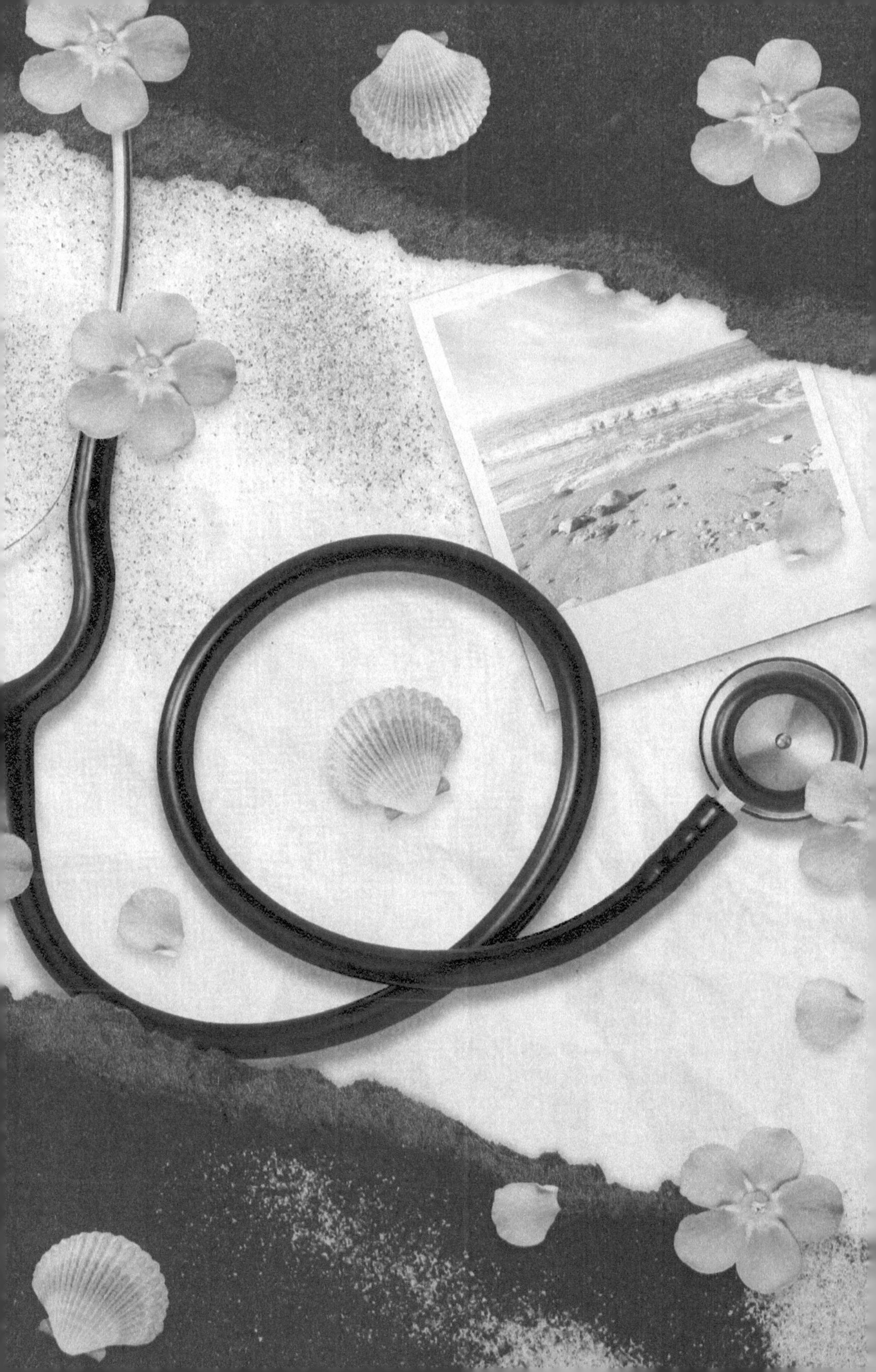

CHAPTER THIRTY-THREE

LIV

I have settled in nicely with Dax, and my life just seems to be so perfect. I gave up my job in the emergency department after much persuasion from Dax. Even Emma, the traitor, agreed that I was burning my candle at both ends for a while.

"Dax, can you come in here?"

He steps out of the closet with his suit on, and I am floored at how delicious he looks in it. His toned, tanned body and his green eyes meet mine.

"Did you have fun golfing today?"

He gives a throaty laugh. "No, I never enjoy these charity events, but it was for a good cause. Now just the dinner and silent auction tonight to end it."

I suck in a breath and bite my lip to stifle a groan as his gaze sweeps over me from head to toe. He sees my reaction to him as he makes his way over. He grabs me by the hips and presses a kiss to my forehead.

He bends to whisper in my ear, "Be careful, Liv. If you keep looking at me like that, I'll ruin that dress and ravage you here for the rest of the night."

His hot breath on my neck as he peppers kisses up and down my pulse point makes me giggle.

"Are you laughing at me, Liv?" he asks in a playful tone.

"No, it just doesn't seem like such a bad idea."

He pulls his head back to look at me with mischief twinkling in his eyes. "My, how insatiable you have become, Liv. I think I can get used to this. I just might have you pregnant again very soon if you keep this up."

Without thinking further, I reply, "I think I might want to be married before I have any more kids, Dax."

I immediately regret that outburst as he pushes back and leaves my embrace. He looks at me, and I don't know how to read what is on his face.

"I agree. That is probably for the best."

He turns around and leaves me alone as he retreats into the closet. I call out to him with indecision. "I was hoping you could zip me up if you get the chance, Dax."

He returns from the walk-in closet looking a little nervous for what seems like forever. "Sure thing, baby." He stands behind me, and I attempt to take back those words that so hastily left my mouth.

"Umm, Dax, I didn't mean we should get married. I just thought, well…I don't know why I said that."

He slowly zips up my dress and places a chaste kiss on the back of my neck behind my ear. I shiver at the unexpected contact, and he slowly pivots me around so I am facing him.

"I couldn't agree more."

I look at him, confused, and as if he senses my confusion, he takes a small black box out of his pocket and drops down to one knee. I gasp and step back. He looks up at me with a knowing smile.

"Now, Liv, you aren't going to make me chase you again, are you?"

I shake my head no.

"Very well then." He takes a moment and then looks at me with adoring eyes. "Liv, The first time I met you, I knew that I felt something different and that you were the one for me. You make me feel things and want things I never thought I would. I thought I almost lost you after that night at the beach. When I found you again, I was given a second chance, and I know I couldn't let you get away from me again. Now that you are pregnant with my child, I didn't think I could be happier. Will you marry me and make me the happiest man alive? Will you be mine forever?"

I look down at him with tears falling from my eyes and trailing down my face. "Yes, Dax, I will marry you. I'll be yours forever."

He quickly gets up from the floor and drags me into a tight hold. "Liv, I love you so much."

He kisses me so passionately that I feel it down to my toes. He takes my hand and places the ring on my finger. I wrap my arms around his neck and bring him closer for another series of kisses. He chuckles, and I feel it vibrate from within his chest.

"Why are you laughing?" I ask.

He pulls back to look at me. "You haven't even looked at your ring."

Realizing he is right, I smile and look down at my finger. "Oh shit." I pull up the huge rock that is my engagement ring. Watching as the light hits the facets just looks so beautiful and I have to admit that it is a gorgeous ring.

"I love it,'" I whisper.

Dax, of course, hears me. "I am so glad you like it."

"It must have set you back a bit, huh?"

He kisses me again. "Not too much, Liv, and you are worth it. I want you to have the best."

Feeling so blissfully happy, I give him one more kiss as I head over to the bathroom. "I better finish getting ready for my future husband then."

This seems to please him. He nods. "You better hurry, future wife, or we will be late for the Greater Houston Drive for a Better Life Invitational Gala at the country club," he says mockingly, taking a sip of his whiskey. He smacks my ass as I retreat to finish getting ready.

I finish touching up my makeup from the tears of happiness that tracked down my face and grabbed my clutch. I shift around in my dress, glad that I was able to use this dress since I won't fit in it for the upcoming gala. I stuff a few items in the clutch—basically just my phone and lipstick. I don't need much, since Dax is driving, and I live with him now so there's that.

I head out, and Dax is waiting in the living room, sipping a whiskey and appraising me up and down. He lets out a low whistle, and I turn around in my best modeling attempt. He puts his glass down and reaches for my coat.

"Liv, you look stunning."

I blush at his words and feel the undertone of desire laced through his sultry voice. "Well, I figured I would wear the dress I had bought for your mom's gala. She's co-chairing since I won't be able to wear it a few months from now," I say, verbalizing my thoughts from earlier. I absent-mindedly placed a hand on my abdomen.

He opens up my coat for me.

I turn around in my coat and fasten the button in front. "It's a bit chilly tonight, and it will do you good to stay warm." He squeezes my shoulders, and I just melt in the warmth his strong hands provide.

"Thank you, baby."

He smiles at this. "You're welcome, baby."

He grabs my arms, and we make our way out of the apartment. He locks the door behind us and hits the button for the elevator to bring us down to the ground floor. He holds the door open for me as we step out into the parking garage.

He opens the door, and I step in. I hear it close and see him make his way over to the driver's seat as he slides in with one graceful, fluid motion. Everything this guy does is so sensual that I feel like straddling him in his seat. As if sensing the change in my breathing. He turns my way, and I bite my lower lip.

"We don't have time, Liv, and I am sure I will wreck all your hard work tonight if you keep giving me that come fuck me look."

I shake my head and laugh, looking out the window as he reverses the car.

We slowly pull up to the gates of the exclusive country club that boasts beautiful stone walls and lush greenery in the heart of Houston. This landmark is the oldest country club with the most lavish ballrooms and outdoor venues. It makes the perfect event for yet another of the many fundraisers to benefit the hospital and community it serves.

As we pull to a stop at the front entrance, Dax opens my door and gives his keys to the valet. Dax and I walk hand-in-hand into the grand foyer and are quickly led into the elegant ballroom, where live music permeates through the doors. We check our coats at the designated station. Dax takes my hand and escorts me to the ballroom.

"Wow, this sure is something, huh? Did your mom assist with this too?"

Dax laughs. "Not sure, but probably."

"I am sure she would love to hear you say that though. I know she works very hard to make these events monetarily beneficial for the hospital, and they equally love her for it. Come on, let's get a drink. I want you to stay hydrated with water this time."

I pull away and lay my arms in my best defensive stance across my chest. "Oh, Dax, aren't you being a bit overprotective? I have been feeling much better. I think a lot of the stress I was carrying is gone with quitting my job and moving in with you."

He looks at me with the utmost adoration, and I think I can melt on the spot. "I am glad that you accepted my help, Liv. Knowing that you will be my wife, I can't wait to tell everyone the good news."

I smile widely at that. "Yes, but do you think it's good to say anything about the pregnancy before the first trimester is over or until we have seen the OB doctor about this?"

He gathers me in his arms and brings me close. "I want to marry you, Liv. You were always my endgame. Now that you are carrying my child, let's just say my life is much better. I cannot wait to welcome our son or daughter into this world with you."

I stroke his cheek. "Thank you, Dax. Hearing that means the world to me."

He takes my hand, tugging me over. "Come on, let's go get that drink. I'll even let it have carbonation."

He guides me to the bar and orders himself a whiskey on the rocks and seltzer water with a lime twist for me. He hands me my drink.

"Wow, guess I better enjoy the sodium now until all I'm allowed is flat water soon, huh."

He doesn't answer, but I see the smirk he tries to hide as he sips his whiskey. I see his mom and dad approaching. His mom reaches us first, hugs Dax, and pulls me in for a hug.

"Liv, so glad you could make it. You look amazing tonight."

I withdraw from her embrace, keeping hold of her at arm's length. "Thank you, Mrs. Johnson. I love how everything turned out, and it looks like a large showing of people, yeah?"

Mrs. Johnson is giddy with excitement as she lets me go to flip her arms around toward the venue. "Yes, we should do very well tonight, Liv. I am delighted with how things have worked themselves out and the amount of money the hospital will receive from the proceeds. The money will help to offset the costs of some much-needed equipment for better patient care and services."

Well, I guess that answers my question about her helping with the event.

I go to drink my seltzer water when Dax's mom suddenly gasps. She grabs my hand, and I almost spill my drink from the sudden movement.

"Oh. My. God." She looks at Dax and then at me. "Is that an engagement ring?"

I look at Dax and he smiles, answering his mom.

"Yeah, Mom, I asked Liv to marry me before we got here. She made me the happiest man on earth by agreeing to be my wife."

He brings me over to his side and kisses my cheek. Dr. Johnson, Dax's father, takes this moment to come over as his mom has my sparkling engagement ring in her hand, twirling my finger in the light to better look at my monster ring.

"Wow! That's some ring you got there, Liv. Are congratulations in order?" He slaps Dax on the shoulder, and it appears we have a small audience attempting to invade our somewhat private moment.

I see more and more people looking over at us and talking to one another, pointing our way. I am sure that this will be all over the hospital this week. One thing is clear: I need to tell Brodie about this before he hears it from anyone else.

A panic sets in, and I can't help but to feel a sense of foreboding. A feeling that something is very wrong.

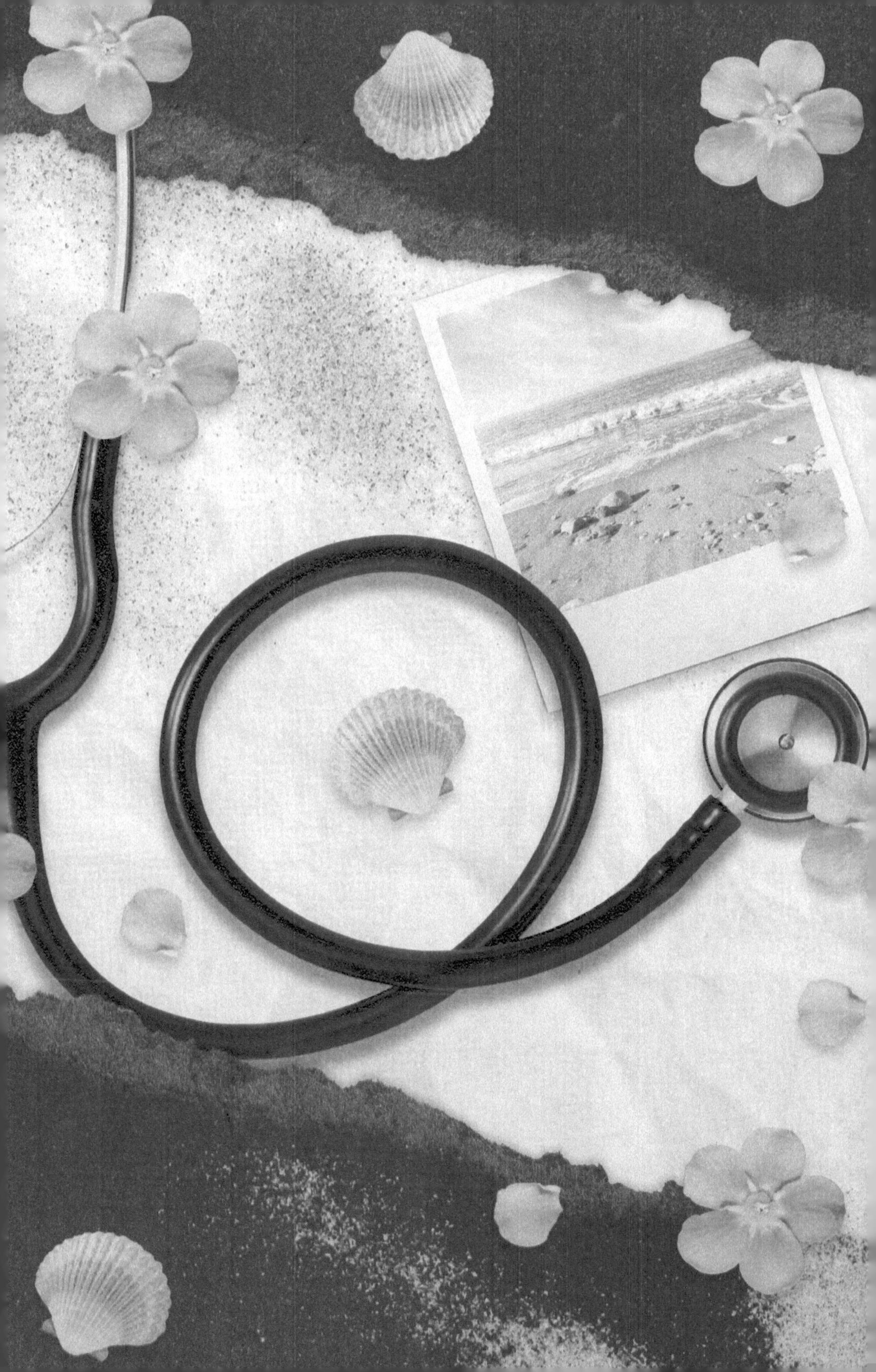

CHAPTER THIRTY-FOUR

LIV

I have gone over in my head multiple times the way this will play out. "Hey, Brodie, you will never believe what happened. I got knocked up, and now I am engaged. Surprise."

No, there has to be a better way to come out and tell my ex-boyfriend, who has suffered a terrible trauma, the news of my engagement and the birth of our baby. I play the scenario over in my head and conclude that there is no easy way to say this.

When I told him that Dax and I were reconnecting and our relationship was progressing, I thought he took it pretty well considering the timing, but this news might be too much for him to handle.

I know that he cheated on me, but our friendship was always the baseline foundation. After his accident, I was always going to remain his faithful friend. All the betrayal became a wash after his accident, and I couldn't be angry at him any longer. As he knew it, his life had ended, and I remained the only constant he had left. I just hope he can be there for me too.

I pull into the circular driveway I know so well. I slow my steps to help with nausea that persists throughout my first trimester. I grab a ginger chew from my bag and discard the wrapper in my messenger bag.

"Well, here goes nothing," I mutter as I ring the doorbell.

Melissa greets me, and her smile turns to one of concern when she sees my face. "Liv, are you okay? You look green."

I nod as I step through the door, swinging my bag around. "Yeah, just a little tired."

She seems to accept this excuse. "You have been burning your candle at both ends, Liv."

I laugh at this. "Yeah, I have recently heard that from a couple of people."

She takes my bag from me as I slip out of my jacket, which she retrieves and places on the coat rack. "You need to slow down. You are a hard worker but trying to do too much. Please try to take care of yourself. Do you want a latte?"

I shake my head. "No, I'll take sparkling water if you have it."

"Sure thing. I'll bring it up to his suite."

I make my way and hear familiar voices. I open the door and see Brodie watching a video on his flatscreen of our group of friends hanging out on spring break from years ago. That was our senior year of high school if I remember the video correctly.

He doesn't turn to look at me or acknowledge me. He just keeps watching the video. I'm laughing, and he is carrying me to the water, and we both are splashing around. Syd is filming it, and I hear her voice above all the others.

"Come on in, you lovebirds. We must get the bonfire started before it's dark."

He puts me down and gives me a quick kiss as we run back to shore. "Brodie?"

I go to place my hand on his shoulder, and he blinks a few times as if slowly waking from a trance. He looks over at me, and I see the pain and heartache in his eyes.

"Brodie," I say in a softer voice. "Are you okay? What's wrong?"

He shakes his head. "Everything is wrong, Liv. My life was not supposed to be this way. Especially me in this wheelchair. You, with another guy instead of me."

I fight back the tears threatening to spill from my eyes. "I'm so sorry,

Brodie. I couldn't visit you last week. I had been feeling sick and rundown."

He immediately look over at me with concern flashing in his eyes.

"Are you sick?"

I swallow hard, not wanting to tell him why I was absent.

He looks back at the TV when he realizes I will not answer that question. "You know, the guys didn't make it over from Corpus to come and see me. I know the girls made it, but no one even came by. I don't know, maybe they were in Houston, just not over at my house."

I proceed with caution in how I am going to answer that.

"Did the girls go over to see you?"

I nod. "Yes, but we didn't see the guys here, so maybe they really couldn't make it. Emma, Ainsley, Val, and I went out. I wasn't feeling well. I went home and then had to go to school and work the next day. They stayed out with Emma, but I didn't see the guys around, like I said. You know they would have found us."

He seems to think about this. "Maybe they were busy after all."

I smile reassuringly. "I am sure they were, Brodie. We all are. I wouldn't take it personally." I am sitting on the side of his bed now and get up quickly to comfort him. As I do this, a wave of nausea hits me, and I run to his bathroom and begin to dry heave.

"Liv, are you okay? Are you still sick?"

Melissa comes into the room with my drink and hears me retching over the toilet. She comes over to gather my hair and hand me a paper towel. "Here you go, sweetie."

I carefully wipe my mouth, avoiding any fast movement that could cause nausea to return to full force. She hands me the seltzer water, and I take it, sipping a minimal amount.

"Thank you."

She nods and immediately looks at my hand, where my large engagement ring catches her eye. Her mouth forms an "O," and then she looks at my flat stomach. Her eyebrow raising in question is the only indicator I receive that she suspects my nausea has something to do with my early pregnancy. She gets up and walks to the doorway.

"I'll let you guys catch up." She turned back to look at me with a sad smile as she shuts the door.

The air in the room has shifted. "Brodie..." I trail off, and he shakes his head.

"Liv, I don't want to hear it."

"Brodie, I need to talk to you." I walk over to him and pull up a chair next to his wheelchair. "Brodie, I am pregnant."

Even though Brodie had his suspicions, I had yet to admit to him that I am, in fact, pregnant.

The sob that he lets out is my undoing. I get up and throw my arms around him. "I am so sorry, Brodie. The pregnancy was an accident, but I love Dax and this baby."

"No, Liv, I'm so sorry." He looks down at my hand on his arm and gasps in shock. "What the fuck?"

He is staring at my engagement ring. "Dax asked me to marry him, and I said yes. I moved in with him recently, once I found out I was pregnant. I've been so sick with the pregnancy that he wanted to ease my burden so I didn't have to worry about paying rent or working. He just wanted me to focus on school at this point. Too much stress isn't good for the baby."

He just keeps shaking his head. "No, Liv, you were supposed to be mine, never his or anyone else's."

All I can do is listen to him. I know he has difficulty accepting this, mainly because he is lonely. "We were over before Dax. Our friendship was never over, though. You will always matter to me."

"I want you to leave, Liv. Please leave."

I stand, feeling like he just verbally slapped me with his words. He always knew how to cut me with his wicked tongue when he didn't want me to witness his hurt.

"You don't mean that. How can you say that?"

I hear him call for Melissa on the intercom. A minute later, Melissa is in the room, and she is cautious as she must have listened to the outburst from the room.

"Melissa, can you please escort Liv out? I am not feeling well and would like to get into bed."

I make a final attempt to reach him. "Come on, Brodie. Please, listen to me. I am so sorry for how this happened."

He moves his chair over to the bed. "I know, Liv, but I can't deal with this right now. I want to be alone."

"Do you want me to come by next week? I know the holidays are coming, but I usually come by."

"No, I don't think we are going to be here. My dad mentioned a cruise or getting away for a bit."

I nod in acceptance. "Oh, well, after the holidays?"

"Sure, after the holidays," he repeats.

Melissa patiently listens to our exchange. She nods and beckons me to follow her. "Come on, Liv. I'll walk you out."

I go to grab my things and head for the door. As I pass the threshold to this suite, I turn around to see wetness pooling in his eyes. "I'll always love you, Brodie. You'll always matter to me."

He turns his face away from me. I walk out, leaving a piece of my past behind as I walk toward my future.

CHAPTER THIRTY-FIVE

DAX

I return from work late. I carefully open the door so as not to make a sound. I place my things down and turn on the light in the living room of our apartment. I love the way that sounds—our apartment. It took minor convincing, but Liv officially moved in with me, and I couldn't be happier.

Eduardo had her things packaged up, and the movers shipped them to our place. I didn't even have to lift a finger. I am sure that had something to do with Eduardo wanting Emma all to himself.

That is a weird series of events, yet no one asks. They seem happy, and that's all that matters to us.

I look up and see Liv sitting on the couch, holding a tissue in her hand. Her face is red and puffy, as if she has been crying for hours. I immediately tense up and run over to her.

"Liv, are you okay? Is the baby okay?"

She nods quickly, setting my nerves at ease. "Yes, we are fine."

I just wait there in silence, hoping that she will confide in me about what happened to her to make her feel this way.

"I went to B-Brodie's house today to visit. I was sick over there vomiting, and after seeing my ring, he kind of pieced things together very quickly. I told him about us being engaged and the baby. He didn't take it too well. He has a lot going on with his depression and loneliness, and I think this just sent him over the edge."

I go to hold her and bring her into my arms. "Liv, it will be okay. He just needs time to process this. He realizes that his life isn't the way it was, and it's gotta be hard to accept. You are still there for him, which says a lot about how much he means to you as a friend and what kind of person you are."

I give her a quick kiss, and she just sobs louder. I also think her emotions are heightened due to the pregnancy, but I don't want her to turn them on me if I mention them. I wish she wouldn't have all this stress on her with the baby, school, and this never-ending drama situation with Brodie.

"He told me he wants to take a break from seeing each other over the holidays to work through his problems. I am just afraid that he will spiral into major depression or worse. He was watching old videos of all of us when I got there. Over the past months, he had been withdrawing from our chats during the times I went over. Every time I leave, I feel something is wrong, and I can't shake it." She begins to hiccup, and I get her a glass of water.

"Here you go, baby. Drink this."

She takes it and gulps it down in between sobs. "Thank you," she says quietly.

"You need to respect his wishes. Give him the time he needs to process this, Liv. I mean, fully process it. It is a lot to take in, and he knows now that you have moved on. Go back and see him after the holidays, but we will go on with our lives, beginning with you taking it easy."

She seems to contemplate this and nods in agreement. "Okay, I'll let him take this at his own pace, and then after the holidays, I will be back in his face to help him and be the friend he needs."

I'll never know what I did to deserve a girl like this.

I stand up and extend my hand to her to help her up. She gently places her hand in mine. I lift her from the couch, leading her into our bedroom. I go to turn the light on and release her hand.

"Wait here. I am going to run you a bath."

She nods, and I make my way into the bathroom. The water begins to fill the sunken tub, and I add in her vanilla honey almond scented bath that became embedded in my senses from day one.

This smell is what I first remembered when I met Liv over a year ago. I whispered in her ear that evening in the ED and inhaled her scent, wishing I could capture her essence in a bottle. I have to admit that I have jerked off a time or two to a similar smell and the memories of being with her before she returned back into my life. I just can't get enough. She is my addiction.

I dim the lights and grab my phone out of my pocket. I hit the mix selection on my Youtube music mix, and Kaleo's "Way Down We Go" intro starts to fill the Bluetooth speakers.

I go to the bedroom and see Liv standing by the bed in her silk robe. She starts to walk toward me, and my cock twitches in my pants at the sight of her. Now, I've never been a religious man, but seeing her like this…fuck, I'd drop down on my knees and worship her in a heartbeat.

Her eyes, which had been crying, are now firmly planted on me, and I stay rooted in place as she saunters into my embrace. I pull her to me, and my cock is firm and hard, pressing into her stomach. I gaze down at her with lust-filled eyes as I scan her face for any hesitation that she may have.

When I don't doubt that she wants this, I lift her, and her legs instantly wrap around me. I undo my scrub pant strings and let them fall to the floor as I quickly step out of them. The music is louder in the bathroom, and the scent combined with the erotic, soulful beats prevent me from placing her in the bubble-filled tub.

Instead, I lift her slightly and place her back against the wall. Using that as leverage, I tuck my underwear waistband down just enough that my dick is entirely at attention. I set my hand around her firm ass as I line myself up and, in one stroke, I am wholly engulfed in her warm heat.

She gasps, and her head falls back momentarily, allowing the silk robe to open, partly exposing her full breasts for easy access. I suck on one nipple, and she lets out a soft moan. Her breasts have become fuller since her early stages of pregnancy, and I am thoroughly enjoying this side of Liv.

My thrusts pick up, and I don't know if I can last any longer. She just feels too good. I swirl my dick around and around as I plunge in over and over to hit that spot, one that I have come to know so well. Her breathing increases, letting me know she is almost there.

I don't want to finish before her, so I lean into the wall for support as my hand goes to pinch her clit as I suck on her other nipple, flicking my tongue simultaneously. She cries out, and my mouth engulfs her cries. Her orgasm clenches my cock as I come in spurts inside her, filling her until I am spent.

We both stay like that against the wall as our breathing slows down. My head is on her neck, and I trail kisses up her jaw. I press a quick kiss to her lips and smile into it.

"God, I love you, Liv."

She smiles back at me and reaches up to touch my cheek. "I think you promised me a bath?" she says as one eyebrow lifts and a smirk plays on her lips.

Still impaled on my cock, I turn around toward the tub and gently release her into the water. I see my cum dripping down her legs, and I'm mesmerized at the sight. What can I say? I am one possessive asshole.

"Come on, let's clean you up and soak for a while, huh?"

"Mmmm, that sounds great."

She gets into the tub, and I get in right behind her. She leans against me. She smells of all my favorite things.

I think about my future with Liv, and nothing feels more right. She is carrying my baby, bringing another little human into this world that we created. This baby growing inside her, which is equal parts of us, reminds me of how perfect my life is.

"Hey, Liv?" I pull her face around to look at me. She twists her body, and I place my hands on either side of her face.

"Let's go away for the holidays. We can spend Thanksgiving with my parents, since your mom is on call this year. After that, we spend Christmas and New Year's somewhere. What do you say? It might get your mind off things, and let's take some time to ourselves before the baby gets here."

I instinctively move my hand and place it on her mostly flat abdomen. There is a small bump that no one else would notice unless they saw her like this. I'd likely have to rip their eyes out if that happened. Hey, no one ever said I wasn't an alphahole.

She bites on her lower lip, and I go to kiss her. She pulls away and looks into my eyes with a smile. "Yeah, let's do it. Let's get away for the holidays."

I smile and kiss her again. "Okay, I'll book a getaway trip for us this week."

"Okay."

She settles back into me, and we stay like that until the water turns cold. I get up and grab our towels. I help her out of the tub and wrap her in a towel. I grab her gown from the hook by the closet and help her dress. I take her hand and lead her right to our bed.

"Let's go to sleep."

She doesn't argue with me, and I get into the bed commando, pulling the covers over us. She rests her head on my shoulder, and I gently stroke her arm as her breathing evens out, and I can tell she is asleep. I kiss the top of her head and follow suit, letting sleep engulf me.

CHAPTER THIRTY-SIX

LIV

We hear the seat belt light ding above us. The flight attendant comes over the speaker announcing we will be making our final descent and landing shortly, arriving at our Caribbean destination.

Yep, Dax convinced me to take a plane for the holidays, so we are spending Christmas here. Spending a winter holiday in places like Aspen for Christmas and New Year's might be more fitting. However, Dax immediately dismissed that idea, and here we are on a populated beach surrounded by crystal-blue water and white sand beaches galore. What can I say? The guy likes the beach and surfing, which is fine by me.

I am finally starting to show during this hush-hush pregnancy. I plan on lying on the beach with my pregnancy bump on full display. I got the perfect white bikini, which Dax about ripped off me when I showed him by modeling it the night before we went away. The guy has a ferocious sexual appetite. Since this pregnancy, I can match him in the bedroom, kitchen, or any surface he decides to take me. I have sex on the brain, and he has to take this girl from behind and make her scream most days.

Speaking of which, I think we should start looking for a house with more privacy than the apartment he currently resides in. I walk to my car and make eye contact with another tenant in the complex. She immediately blushes and puts her face down, briskly walking to her door. Yep, she definitely heard our vocal lovemaking. I'll have to talk to Dax about that soon.

We get our luggage from the back of the taxi and are on our way to the resort. He wants to stay in a more central location with access to restaurants and attractions. I don't care where we are as long as we are together.

We have been in a whirlwind of a relationship. It hasn't even been a year yet, and I feel like I have known this incredible man my entire life.

That thought instantly puts me on edge, considering that the man I have known for most of my life has decided to ghost me. Even though I am happy with Dax and preoccupied with my new life, I still haven't talked to Brodie. He remains at the back of my mind with uncertainty. We left our friendship on bad terms. The last time we left on bad terms, he ended up in a hospital for months, recovering from an almost fatal accident. An accident that changed his life forever.

Thanksgiving came and went. I barely spoke to my mom since she was working that night. She had to satisfy her turkey craving with a hospital-sponsored dinner for all the unfortunate employees that had to work saving and maintaining lives at the hospital. That is our typical mother-daughter relationship. We are both always working. At least now I have been able to focus solely on school–a luxury that Dax affords me.

I didn't try to contact Brodie because I respected his wishes to be left alone so he could work on some issues. Though, he is never far from my mind. This is the longest I have gone from seeing or talking to him. It is nothing but radio silence on his end. My text messages to attempt to check in have also gone unanswered.

I tried to text Melissa, his nurse, but she respects his wishes and champions patient confidentiality. I have two weeks off before my school schedule resumes, and Dax has to return to work.

Dax takes my hand in assisting me to our room, and I am immediately blown away at the opulence of this suite. It appears that Dax spared no expense.

I make a beeline to the bathroom. This little pea has suddenly turned this body into a peeing machine. I intend to make a beeline to the toilet when I notice a present or two lying on the bed.

I halt with my hand still on the doorframe as I slowly turn around and go to the bed. I touch the boxes and turn around as I sense Dax is now in the room. He is standing in the doorway, watching me.

"Umm, what is this, Dax?"

His eyes smolder, and he walks my way. He stops midway, engulfing me in his alpha presence. I feel my core clench in anticipation of him coming over to me. Instead, he stands there without advancing farther.

"Open it, Liv," he commands.

I turn around with a look that must be confusing as he nods his head in encouragement. I pick up the first box, the larger of the two, and slowly open the present. I gasp in surprise as I reach to pull the most elegant white dress from the garment box. I almost can't believe my eyes, except that I am holding the dress as my fingers float over the satin fabric and gorgeous embellishments along the collar.

I go to turn around and see Dax looking intently at me.

"Liv, since that day in the emergency room, I knew that you were the most beautiful woman I had ever seen. I vowed to make you mine then and vow to keep you as mine forever. You already said you would marry me, but will you marry me now?"

Without hesitation, I reply, "Yes, I'll marry you now," as the tears fall freely from my eyes.

I go to Dax, who takes me into his arms and kisses me so passionately that I forget about having to pee. We decide to christen the new bedroom and lie in bed holding each other. I must have dozed off because I wake up to see Dax scrolling through his phone. He looks down at me and kisses my forehead.

"Hey, sleepyhead. I thought you'd never wake up. You must have been exhausted."

I stretch out and kick the blanket off. "I think it was a sex-induced coma." I look over at Dax, slowly admiring his still-naked form. I just can't get enough of this man as I bite my lower lip. I think of his muscular arm, which I once admired for the first time in the ED where he was a patient. If he only knew of all my evil thoughts.

He smirks, watching me, and shakes his head. "Liv, what am I going to do with you." He laughs. "I can think of a couple of things that make the top of my list right about now."

I nuzzle into his neck and lick up the side until I get to his ear, where I whisper as I suck on his earlobe, "But first, I have to pee." I make haste in getting up, throwing a wink over my shoulder to Dax as he throws a pillow at me.

"You, Liv, are a fucking tease."

The pillow misses me, and I notice the tenting in the sheets.

"Aw, baby, I promise to take care of that for you in a bit." I bite my lip while batting my lashes as Dax attempts to stifle a groan.

"Hurry back, you little vixen."

I laugh and go to take care of business.

I return and jump back into bed, nuzzling up to my future husband. I think about the presents and realize I still need to open the other box. I don't know how I forgot to open this one too. Ugh, placental steal syndrome strikes again. The placenta is stealing all the blood meant for my brain. I swear I am in a perpetual brain fog.

"Dax?" I sit up and turn halfway to look at him when a thought comes to mind. "Why did you bring the wedding gown to the resort?" I think I already know the answer to this question, but I need confirmation. "You had this all planned when you asked me to go away with you for the holidays, didn't you?"

His eyes light up as if he was wondering when I would notice and ask him about this.

"Well, Liv, I thought it would be a great idea to get married while we are here. We are getting married on Christmas Eve. I have all the details sorted, and I just need to know if you are okay with this?"

I look at him in shock. "Christmas Eve? Like in a couple of days?"

Dax just nods , waiting for me to respond.

"How did you know about the dress? I don't even know if it will fit."

"It will fit," he replies in earnest. "It is a present from Emma and Eduardo."

Dax must see the moment when I realize it will fit because that little minx sized me, claiming that she wanted to make sure we could get gala dresses in time for me since it would be more than likely tailored to fit due to my advancing pregnancy.

"Oh, I didn't look at the shoes, which I assume is the other box," I cry out as I jump out of bed, searching for the shoe box.

I pull the cardboard box open, gazing at the most beautiful white, iridescent beaded shoes with a touch of blue appliques. I notice that they have red bottom soles and immediately cry at how much these beauties must have cost.

I look up, and Dax answers, "Likewise from Emma and Eduardo. It's your something blue, she said."

I touch the perfect-looking blue stones on the embellishments and feel grateful to have such a good friend. "Beautiful. I just need something borrowed."

Dax goes to get up from the bed and opens his suitcase. He removes a package and hands it to me. I open it up and pull out a felt bag. I pull back the drawstring and pull out something mesh.

"Oh, how lovely, Dax." I am looking at an antique veil that is so simple but elegant in style. "Your mom wanted you to wear that. It was hers from her wedding to your dad."

I immediately think of my day and realize that he will never get the chance to walk me down the aisle. A life that was taken too soon.

Sensing my emotional state, Dax comes up and removes the veil from my hands. He places it on the dresser and pulls me into a solid embrace. I gaze into his eyes and see all the love and compassion pouring out from his piercing stare.

He nuzzles my neck, and I tilt my head to the side, giving him more access. He pulls me into his embrace, and I feel his erection pressing against me.

I kiss him and wedge my thumbs into the waistband of his underwear, pulling them down. His hard, thick cock pops out in a full display. I drop to my knees and look up at him. His eyes narrow into slits as he takes a deep breath in, trying to curb his reaction to seeing me on my knees in front of him.

I place him in my mouth and take him in all at once. He groans and grabs the back of my head to hold me in place. I pull back and look up into his eyes as I slowly lick the underside of his thick cock, rolling my tongue around the head of his penis. His eyes flutter closed.

"Fuuck, Liv."

That is his undoing, as I don't get another breath in until he comes down my throat. I lick my lips as he helps me to my feet.

"My turn," he says in a low, husky voice.

I doubt we will be leaving this room for the rest of the night.

CHAPTER THIRTY-SEVEN

LIV

The wedding ceremony was beautiful. Dax had everything prepared for our special day. He gave me another present that morning: a simple yet elegant earring and necklace set by David Yurman. I have never had such pretty things before. This man is so thoughtful and tries to make everything so easy between us. The resort even provided two witnesses to complete the marriage ceremony, and all the paperwork had been completed, just requiring my signature. How he managed to do all that is beyond me.

The wedding was straightforward, with my favorite sound of the waves in the background reminding me of my first day with Dax. The beautiful memory of our time at the beach has replaced the one where Brodie had his accident and caused us to leave each other. I thought I had lost him, but fate had a way of bringing us back into each other's lives. We are married and plan to spend the rest of our lives creating new memories.

The next best thing is seeing our baby—a life we created together. Dax has been so devoted to me since we reconnected and can't seem to get enough of me. Having more children with him makes my ovaries do a happy dance. We would have had a baby after the wedding if I were not pregnant already. We went straight to the room and got reacquainted with each other as husband and wife on every surface of that room.

He mentioned that Eduardo and Emma had been accommodating throughout the preparation, and he couldn't have done it without their resources. I'll be sure to thank my homegirl as soon as we get back.

We just finished a beautiful dinner and will ring in our first new year together as Dr. and Mrs. Dax Johnson. I still can't believe that I am married. I look down at my hand. My ring finger's enormous diamond and wedding band rest on my slightly rounded belly.

I begin to reminisce about this year's events—a year that had a lot of good and bad times. I hope I can get through the rest of the year without incident, but I feel that would be wishful thinking. This new year is sure to bring a better time for us. I can't wait to see our baby and then finish school. Ideally, it would have been finishing school before our baby's birth, but I don't regret anything or how it happened. The end result is the same.

We watch the fireworks display lighting up the sky as distant music plays the old popular Scottish song we always sing in the new year. The song is meant to be nostalgic in remembering good times spent with friends.

"Happy New Year, Mrs. Johnson," he echoes the lingering remnants of pops in the air.

He brings me out of my thoughts. He looks at me with so much love and adoration, I start to tear up.

"Happy New Year to you, my husband."

His eyes dilate, and he kisses me. "God, I love you, baby," he says as he nuzzles into my neck, as the scratchy sensation of his whiskers tickle my cheek.

"I love you, Mr. Johnson."

"I'll be your Mr. Johnson," he says as he exaggerates his movements by rubbing his face around my neck, peppering me with breathy kisses.

I laugh, trying to pull away with the ease of our playful banter. I haven't felt this happy in a while.

I realized how busy our lives are and that I haven't talked to Brodie. I refuse to let all my troubles bring me down right now. His absence isn't part of them. I know he is trying to cope with his issues.

Instead, I choose to be in the moment with my husband. I must let go of the guilt as we ring in the new year. I know it isn't my fault. Hopefully, Brodie can accept this too.

Besides, all that drama will await me when I return. Tonight I will be enjoying my time with my husband.

The alarm goes off at four thirty a.m., jolting me from my sleep. I look around, hoping we are still on vacation, but sadly we are already home.

"Oh godddd." I place my hand over my eyes to shield myself from the assault of light coming from the bathroom. "Is our vacation already over?"

I hear a chuckle as the closet door opens and closes. "Rise and shine, baby." He comes over to kiss my forehead as I groan.

"It's so early."

I hear laughter as he shuts the bathroom door, and the sound of the shower starts up.

"I can't believe I have to get back to my clinicals for school. I feel like we just got home with no time to spare," I grumble as I throw the covers off my body exaggeratedly.

I hear the shower turn on and decide to check my emails and messages while Dax is there. I'm mostly out of bed anyway. It takes me four times as long to get ready, so I know he will be out soon. Sure enough, the door opens ten minutes later. He has a towel wrapped around his waist and starts to pull on his clothing.

"I'll get you a protein shake for breakfast with your prenatal vitamins."

He leaves the room before I can thank him. He always seems to take care of me. I have to admit that living with him does have its perks.

I sit on the edge of the bed and prepare myself for what lies ahead. My nausea has subsided, and I no longer have that dizzy feeling. I take great care to sit on the edge of the bed before standing too quickly since I passed out before, albeit a while back.

I haven't been to clinicals in two weeks. The semester ended with a holiday break, which seemed to go by in a blur of activity. Between finding out I am pregnant, moving in with Dax, going on vacation for the holidays, and getting married, a lot has happened this semester.

I stretch and get out of bed, lifting my pajama top off and throwing it in the hamper as I make my way to the bathroom. The shower does little to wake me up for work. When I step out, I am greeted by Dax handing me a liquid breakfast and my prenatal vitamins.

"Thanks, husband," I say as I take the beverage from him, giving him a chaste kiss.

He smiles at me and goes back out to the kitchen, and once I finish getting ready, I join him.

"Are you ready to go, babe?" He hands me my water bottle and a packs lunch.

"You made me lunch?" I ask, but it is apparent that he did.

"Yes, I want you to have a nutritious meal for you and Dax Jr."

I lift one eyebrow in question. "Dax Jr., huh?"

He smiles, stopping my heart with how happy he looks. "Yes, I know it's going to be a boy."

I touch my stomach instinctively. I don't know how, but I feel it too. I also thought straight away that it was going to be a boy. I can just sense it.

"We will find out soon enough, won't we?"

"Definitely. I have to know, but I don't care if it is a boy or a girl, as long as our baby is healthy." He grabs my hand. "Now, let's go. We are going to be late."

We get to work in no time and walk inside the hospital for the first time as husband and wife. I still can't get over this realization. The nuptials we shared a couple of weeks ago seems to have become second nature. We are officially Dr. and Mrs. Dax Johnson.

As if sensing my thoughts, he says, "Now everyone will know that you are officially mine forever, Liv."

I smile at his declaration and secretly love that he claims me like a possession so unabashedly. We go up the elevators, and he pulls me to his side. The elevator dings and we head out. Standing in front of the OR doors, I am drawn back to the time I once was waiting at similar doors for Brodie.

I feel the tug of sadness for my longtime friend and former boyfriend. I continue to stare at the doors, and Dax nudges my chin in his direction. "I love you, Liv. Please try to have a good day," he says, frowning, as if sensing my thoughts.

His expression is then hidden as he lifts his coffee cup to his lips, but I can't hide my own feelings. I know he can read it on my face, and I hate that he knows. I don't love Brodie that way, but we had a lot of years together. I look him in the eyes as I stroke his cheek.

"I will be thinking of you today and counting the hours until I can have your cock in me."

He immediately chokes on his coffee.

Once he recovers, he grabs me and kisses me, and then he whispers in my ear, "I'll hold you to that, Liv." With that, Dax winks at me and walks away, swallowed by the operating room doors where some people live, and some die. I hope I don't have to be at the end of these doors awaiting that type of news again.

I'm due to be in class in one of the hospital conference rooms on the fifth floor. Although I am dreading our assignments for the day, I am starting a new rotation in the ICU and am pumped about learning more about critical care medicine. I have a few of them and hope to be in the emergency department as a clinician. The ICU will provide a lot of good experience this rotation.

I've already spoken with the program director and changed my name, updating my new married name, Olivia Johnson, and letting them know that I am expecting but that it shouldn't impact my graduation in May. At least I'll be finished before the baby comes, or as Dax puts it, Dax Jr..I just hope everything goes as planned. I know this will all play out, but I want to be proactive. Just because I will be a mother doesn't mean I don't intend to have a career. I worked too hard for this.

Dax is supportive of my decision, and I have a great support system. Unbeknownst to me, Dax had already informed my mom of our situation when he asked for my hand in marriage, and she has agreed to finally take some much-needed time off to help me take care of the baby, and I will prepare for my NP boards during maternity leave.

Dax and I have had a whirlwind romance, but I know the outcome would have been the same even if we had dated longer. Sometimes, you just know when you meet the right person. The sex is great too. With how busy we both are, I know the months will fly by, and our baby will be here before we know it.

CHAPTER THIRTY-EIGHT

DAX

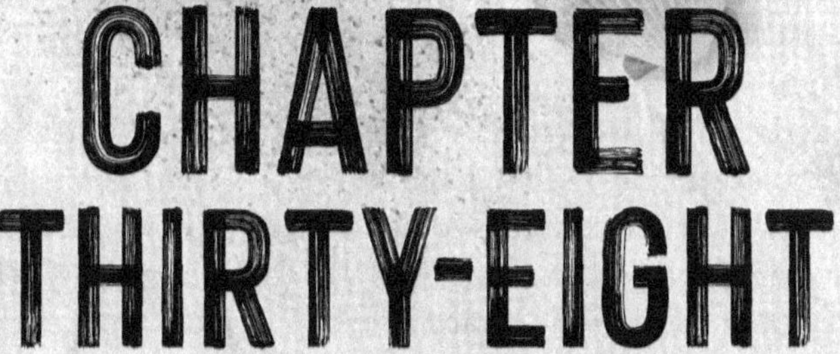

Liv and I fall into a routine of work and school. We'll both be finishing up our respective programs soon. I go do rounds for a bit on some post-operative patients and then take the stairs down to the operating room to dictate my notes after seeing some patients.

Liv seems to have more energy once she hit her second trimester. She also seems to limit her caffeine consumption to one cup of coffee daily. I told her that was fine, even though she continued to worry about the effects on the baby. We discussed it, and she chose to have it mid-day. She can enjoy it and the caffeine boost of energy it provides to seamlessly continue the day. She carefully explained her rationale for picking that particular time of day and as long as she keeps it to a minimum, it should be okay for the baby.

I have a bit more skip in my step because today we will find out the sex of our child. Nothing could bring this day down. I text Liv to let her know I will get my coffee with her and meet her there. We will leave together for her OB appointment right after. She had already cleared this necessary appointment with the clinical professor and agreed to make up the time by staying an hour later today when we return from her doctor visit. I have things to catch up on anyway, so I will return too to stay and wait for her after.

I get in line, order my café Americano, and text her to let her know I am here. I see Tatiana in line talking to someone. I try my best to avoid her, but sometimes it is inevitable when you work with someone.

I never bothered to tell her about getting married. If they cannot see the wedding ring on my finger, that is their problem, not mine. I don't discuss my private life with the staff. They already gossip enough about everything under the sun.

All of a sudden, I hear a familiar voice as I move out of line to see Tatiana looking eye to eye at Liv. I see red and watch as Tatiana spots her wedding ring. Liv's hand instinctively goes to her baby bump as if protecting it.

That's when I hear Tatiana say, "Wow. What did you do? Trap him by getting pregnant?" She steps toward Liv, and I quickly make my way over there. She snorts, "Typical."

Liv looks my way, and Tatiana follows her line of vision.

I look at Liv without regarding or acknowledging Tatiana. "Liv is everything, okay?"

I see her eyes swimming with tears that refuse to fall. I'll be damned if I let this bitch make Liv more emotionally stressed than she is already over someone who was a meaningless fuck to me. I grab her hand and kiss it.

"Why don't you order your coffee and grab my order please? I'll be right there."

She looks at me and then at Tatiana. "Sure."

She turns around and moves toward the other side of the counter. As soon as she is out of earshot, I turn to Tatiana, and she pops her hip out with her hand resting on it.

"What the fuck is that, Dax? I don't even hear from you, and then I find out that you are not only married but that that girl is pregnant. Do you know if it is even yours?"

I fix my stare on her, and the anger I feel is nothing compared to the thought of her sudden start of the rumor mill. I have to set the record straight so that this doesn't become a problem for Liv and me. "I already told you that I met Liv a year ago, and we lost touch until we restarted our relationship."

Her eyes widen.

"I didn't just meet her and then get her pregnant. I've pursued her for over a year and finally got her to commit to a relationship."

"So, while she wasn't answering you back, you fucked me."

I cringe at the words, not wanting to publicize this conversation in case someone overhears. I nudge Tatiana off the side. "Look, I admit it happened quickly after that, but it was always her. I told you this at the gym. I'm sorry, but anything we had, as I said before, is over. She is my wife now, and we are having a baby."

She looks at me as if she hates my guts. I can't say that I blame her.

"Can we at least be civil to each other at work, Tatiana?"

She narrows her eyes at me. "I am a professional, Dax. Of course, I can be civil. Outside of work, you're a complete asshole." With that, she walks off, leaving me there, pinching my eyebrows in frustration.

Liv returns to my side and nudges me. "You okay?" She looks at me with concern as she hands me my coffee.

"Yes, but I should be asking you that," I reply as I take the coffee from her.

She just shrugs while taking a sip of her coffee. I lean down and kiss her very inappropriately for the workplace setting as she lets herself yield to my embrace. I pull away, and she looks up at me, smiling.

"Are you ready to go find out the sex of our baby?"

"You mean for them to confirm that it's a Dax Jr.?"

She hits my arm playfully with her hand, and we walk out of the hospital to our car. The incident with Tatiana is already forgotten. A quick ride later, we pull up to the OB office we selected together, which is close to the hospital. We make our way to the check-in desk and are told to have a seat by a lovely older lady that resembles a super sweet grandma.

"We will be with you in a minute, dear. Such an exciting appointment."

We nod in agreement with huge matching smiles awaiting the news. She closes the window, and I pull Liv into the seat next to me.

Five minutes later, we are called back. She changes into a gown and takes a seat on the table close to an ultrasound machine that will let us know if it is indeed a baby boy we are expecting.

The sonographer comes in, and I sit up a little too eagerly. I swear I am more excited than Liv is to find out what we are having.

"Are you ready to find out the sex of your baby?" the sonographer asks.

"Yes," we say in unison and laugh, looking at each other.

I get up from my chair and move toward her to watch the screen together. Some lukewarm gel is placed on her lower abdomen, and the cold probe moves around Liv's belly. A couple of buttons are tapped on the machine, and I hear the sound of our baby's strong, rapid heartbeat.

"Fetal heart tones are at one hundred forty-five beats per minute. That sounds like one healthy baby to me." She looks our way and smiles. She moves the probe around again and looks at us. "Okay, do you guys want to know the sex of your baby now?"

Without hesitation, we both say, "Yes."

She laughs and prints a couple of pictures out. "Okay, guys, here you go. These are copies of your baby boy's first pictures."

Liv quickly takes them, and we both look in amazement. She is crying as I place my fingers on the pictures as if I can memorize his 3D face with my fingertips.

"We are having a boy, after all. You were right, Dax."

Liv looks up at me with so much love in her eyes that I know without a doubt that I am the luckiest man alive. I grab her hand and kiss it.

The ultrasound tech stands and announces that the doctor will be in in a minute to address any additional questions or concerns about the pregnancy.

I barely hear anything else when I see Liv get a text message and see that it is Brodie. Her finger hovers over the message button. I look at her, wondering what has caused this change in her behavior. She shows me the name displayed in her text message. She looks at me. I'm sure she sees the initial flash of anger and then that of concern flash a second later in my eyes. She had not heard from Brodie in almost four months. Not since that day he found out about us being together and Liv having a baby.

"Boy, he has impeccable timing, doesn't he? What are you going to do, Liv? Are you going to text him back? See him?" I look up at her, and tears begin to form in her eyes. "Don't worry about this anymore, Liv. You don't need to stress yourself out."

Just as I reach to wipe a tear that is slowly rolling down her cheek, the OB doctor walks in. She looks at us, and we both smile at her. She just assumes Liv is crying from happiness, and we don't let her think anything less.

After receiving a clean bill of health, we stroll out of the office holding Dax Jr.'s pictures. I rub Liv's hand possessively with my thumb. She smiles at me, and we make the short drive back to work. We park, and I stop her before she can get out of the car.

"Liv, is it okay if I drive you to Brodie's house after work? I don't want you over there alone getting all worked up about whatever he might say. I won't go in with you if you don't want me to, but I will drive you there and back."

She must see how much I love and care for her because she agrees without hesitation. "Yeah, okay. That would be great." She looks at me as if she thought I would argue with her.

"Yeah? Okay, great. I'll meet you later."

I am relieved at her acceptance of my help. "Just text me when you get out, and I'll meet you. I don't have much left this afternoon."

She just nods, and we part ways at the entrance. I watch her retreat. I won't let her worry about this anymore. I know they are friends and have a history, but she is my wife, and I won't have him continue to upset her. I will do what I need to do to protect my family.

CHAPTER THIRTY-NINE

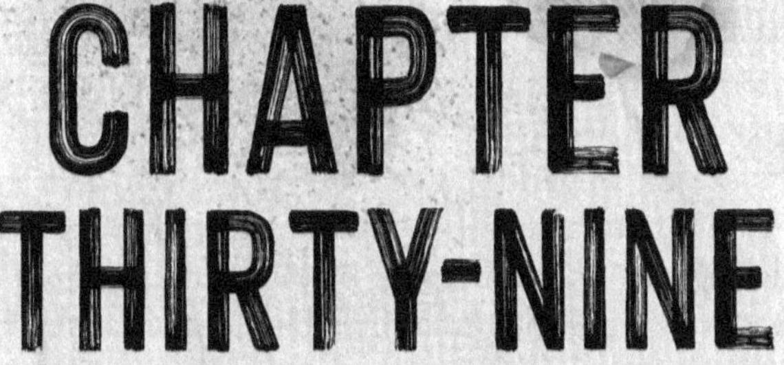

LIV

I text Dax that I am out and will be waiting for him by the hospital entrance so we can walk to our designated staff parking lot. The rest of the day passes so slowly that I can barely concentrate. What should have been a great day turned into a stress filled one as I stare down at the text message sent hours ago.

Liv: I'll be over there soon, so we can talk.

Brodie: I'll be here waiting for you.

I don't know why that response bothers me, but it does. I get the feeling that Brodie has a hidden meaning, but maybe I am just reading too much into it. He was my boyfriend and friend for so long, but he has to realize that I am nothing more than his friend now and I am married to another man—a man I love with all my heart.

I would never give up Dax. I felt this deep connection with him the first day I met him in the emergency department. The way that he touches me and the shivers that run through me when he brushes against me, I don't think I'll ever feel that with another person. I know that I won't.

Deep in thought, I barely register that Dax is calling my name. He touches my shoulder, and that's when I feel it. The goose bumps cause my skin to prickle at just his mere touch.

I look up at him, and he helps me stand, grabbing my bag and slinging it over his shoulders. He brings me into a side hug and kisses the top of my head.

"You ready to go see Brodie?"

I nod. "Yeah, let's go."

I must have been deep in thought because before I know it, we are pulling up to Bodie's father's house again, into the circular driveway I have come to know so well.

Dax places the car in park and gets out of the vehicle. He has my door open and is helping me out before I can even grab my bag.

"I'll wait here, Liv. Let me know if you need me to come up." He gives me a look that conveys all his thoughts. Thoughts that say he isn't happy about this and will gladly pick me up and carry me out of there if necessary.

I knock on the door, and Melissa opens the door. She embraces me.

"Liv! I've missed your face." She grabs my cheeks and places a kiss on each one.

I laugh and pull away. "Good to see you too, Melissa. It's been a few months."

She looks up to see Dax staring at her from the car window. She looks at me and smiles. "Well, that must be the boyfriend, huh?"

"Well…" I lift my ring finger, and she grabs it to examine it further.

"Girl, that is some rock. And is that a wedding band, too? You have a little explaining to do. Come on in." She waves to Dax and ushers me inside. "Usual coffee, Liv?"

"No. No caffeine for me. Maybe a decaf tea?"

"Sure, I have some decaffeinated ones in the kitchen. Follow me."

I place my stuff down on the chair in the foyer and follow her. She throws the kettle on, grabs a couple of bags from the canister, and drops them into a mug.

"So… tell me about this husband of yours?"

"Well, we got married over the holidays and are now expecting our first baby in a few months."

She whips around and looks at my belly at this bit of information. I push the flowing fabric taut over my belly to accentuate the curve of my growing baby bump. The dress helped to cover most of the evidence. I sway back and forth while holding my dress for effect, and she laughs.

"Oh, my goodness. Look at you. You are adorable pregnant, Liv. You know, I had my suspicions last time I saw you and you had all that nausea."

My cheeks blush. "I think that might have been all the vomiting I did over here, but thanks for downplaying it," I comment and let go of my dress. "Thanks, Melissa."

The kettle begins to whistle, and she goes to pour me my tea.

"A little milk?"

"Yes, please."

She nods. I take the mug from her, feeling the rising hot steam and blow across the cup.

"So, tell me. How is Brodie?"

She stays quiet for a moment before answering. "Better, I think? It has taken a while for him to get there, but I think he is finally letting go of the anger and has accepted his situation. I will let him tell you about it."

I nod and follow her up to Brodie's room. She knocks on the door, and I hear him ask us to come in. I walk into the room and see Brodie for the first time in four months. He looks good. There is some color to his cheeks, and he is smiling. A complete smile directed at me. God, how that smile used to knock me off my feet.

I place my tea down and hear the door shut behind me. I stand there looking at him, not knowing what to do.

"Do I at least get a hug?" he says, surprising me.

I run over to bend down and embrace him. He leans his head into me, and I fall into his lap, crying.

Maybe it is the hormones causing me to become more emotional, but I can't stop the tears from flowing.

"Liv, don't cry, please. I have so many things to say, and I don't want to be the cause of your tears anymore."

I stop crying and look up at him. I realize that I am still sitting on his lap, so I get up to take this opportunity to grab a tissue. As I grab the tissue and dab my eyes, he notices the wedding ring on my finger.

"You're married now?" It comes out as a question, but he already knows the answer.

"Yes," I answer without hesitation.

He looks at me with sadness but continues. "I am happy for you, Liv.

Really. I'm sorry that I caused you so much pain. I was depressed after the accident and that never seemed to pass. I went away to get help for my depression by enrolling in an inpatient treatment facility.

"I learned a lot while there. I dealt with my issues of the accident, with you, and my life moving on from here on out. You know, my future. I just needed this time to get better, and I finally felt like this weight was lifted off my shoulders."

"I am happy for you, Brodie. I was apprehensive about you coping with everything. I sensed you were struggling, but I didn't know how to help you. I am glad that you got the help you needed."

He moves closer to me, and I looked down into his clear eyes. I see how much he cares for me, and I am glad I came to see him.

He looks at my ring. "So tell me about this husband of yours."

I start, but then hesitate.

"Liv. I want to know how happy you are."

I nod. "Well, Dax and I reconnected about a year later. He had texted me a few times that year, but I was just not ready to date anyone. Focusing on school and...." I look around before meeting his eyes.

"I know, Liv. Please finish."

"I ran into him once at Starbucks and then again at my clinicals." I touch my ring, remembering when I tried to run from him. "I guess it was meant to be. There's something else, Brodie."

He looks at me, and then, as if realization clicks, he remembers our last conversation and quickly looks at my belly. I see his eyes widen and then meet mine. "Wow. You really are pregnant."

I nod, and I see his eyes glaze over. I go to stand nearer to him and touch his cheek. He looks up at me.

"I am happy for you, Liv. Promise that I will get to meet your..."

"Son," I say, and he smiles. "I am having a boy."

"That's so great, Liv."

I look to see if he is sincere and I know he means it.

We are catching up on a few things when I get a text message. I retrieve my phone and see that Dax is asking how things are going.

"Well, I better get going. Dax brought me after work and is waiting for me outside."

"Of course," he replies, and I see the smile that I used to love. "Please don't stress yourself out by coming over to visit. Just text or call me if you can, and I'll see you soon."

I hug him and kiss him on the cheek and leave the room. I stop at the door once more before leaving to find him turning away toward the balcony. I hesitate before leaving, but I can't go back to him. I feel like my life has been split in two, and I have to take one road while turning my back on the other.

I close the door behind me, and the click makes it feel monumental. I feel a sense of dread wash over me, and I can't shake this feeling. I want to run in and hug him again for some reason, but I talk myself out of this feeling of dread I have. I say goodbye to Melissa, returning her my now cold mug of tea.

"I hope everything went well, Liv."

I hug her and grab my stuff. "It did, but I feel like I won't see him again, and it unsettles me."

"Oh, Liv, you know that isn't true. He is doing much better, and I am glad he got the help he needed."

"I agree. You are right. Well, I better get going."

She walks me out, and I get into the car with Dax. He looks over at me and, without saying a word, returns his gaze forward and starts the car. We drive off, leaving me with a sense of foreboding.

CHAPTER FORTY

LIV

ONE MONTH LATER

Emma, who has been MIA recently, finally shows up at my house to drop off my dress for the gala. It seems like a lifetime since I was at Dax's house meeting his parents, and his mom was talking to me about the gala.

After finding out I was pregnant, I worried about my dress, but Emma had taken my measurements from the wedding dress and guesstimated how far I would be along to ensure I had a proper evening gown for tonight.

"Okay, Liv. Let's see how it looks."

I grab the material and feel the softness of the fabric as it moves freely through my fingers. I do a little squeal, and Emma can't stop herself. "I'm going to pour myself some wine to see this. I know you still have some around, right?"

I laugh because the girl knows me too well. "Yes, in the rack on the dining room table."

She looks into that room and smiles. "Perfect, you go show me how stunning you will look in this dress, and I will get myself a glass of my favorite cabernet."

I run off into the bedroom and strip down into my panties. I obviously can't wear a bra with this top, and my boobs have never looked better. My bra size is larger than it was before, and Dax seems to enjoy the large handfuls he gets these days.

I lift my arms and slide the dress down. The fabric floats down my body, and the coolness feels fantastic against my skin. In the mirror, I see that the dress fits perfectly. It hugs my curves in the right spots and flows out around my midsection. It is a little short for me, but I'm sure Dax won't mind that. I twirl around and see it flare at the sides as I swing back and forth.

I run into the living room as Emma is already refilling her glass. Her lips are pursed, and her hand is shaking. I stop and take in my friend. I wish she would confide in me about what is bothering her. She thinks I can't tell but is always skittish and evasive when I ask her questions.

She turns to look at me, hiding her feelings behind a mask. When she sees me in my dress, that beautiful smile reforms on her face.

"Look at you!" she says as she skips over to me. She grabs my hands in hers, jumping up and down. "Liv, you look ravishing in this dress. Dax is going to rip this off you after the gala."

"Ha, that's where you're wrong, Emma. He'll throw the back over my head and take me from behind up against this wall instead."

Emma almost spits her wine out, but instead, she snorts it out her nose. Choking, she sputters, "Why, Liv, you little minx. Now that is the funniest thing I've heard. Where is my shy friend I once knew?"

We both chuckle at my brazenness and discuss our plans for the evening.

"Where's Dax?" she asks.

"Oh, he went to pick up his altered tux and should be back soon. Nothing like waiting until the last minute." Not wanting to broach the topic because I am sure she will avoid it, I decide to ask anyway. "So, how are things with Eduardo? You seemed to be happy with Jameson, and then you met Eduardo…" I trail off to see if she will willingly fill in the blanks to the mystery of their secretive relationship.

Before she can speak, I add, "I never did thank him for helping that night months ago when I found out I was pregnant. Fainting—passing out at his club was not one of my finer moments."

"Oh, Liv, don't even worry about that. Yeah, I liked Jameson, but it wasn't there. When I met Eduardo… I don't know. He makes me feel…." She grabs her lip, rubbing it back and forth.

"Happy?" I answer for her, but she shakes her head.

"Even better. He makes me feel safe."

I look at her in confusion. "Safe?"

She looks at me as if she wants to say more but thinks better of it. She gets up and drains the remaining wine from the glass in one big gulp before placing it into the sink. She picks up her keys, and I know this is the end of our conversation.

"I better go. I still have to get a quick bite before seeing you guys later at the gala."

"Sure, I'll see you there. We are sitting at the same table, right?"

"Of course. I'll be sure to let Eduardo know." She walks out without another word, and I sit there stewing over what she meant by that.

I go to my phone and call Dax to see where he is. He lets me know he is on his way, and I decide to take a bath before he gets here. I could use a good relaxing soak.

I slide into the tub, let the lavender scents take over, and place a warm rag over my eyes. My phone rings and I answer, thinking it must be Dax forgetting to tell me something. I hear someone on the other line, but I need help to get through.

"Hello?" Maybe it's a bad connection.

"Liv?"

I immediately sit up. "Brodie? Is everything okay?"

He answers more quickly this time. "Yes, Liv, I just wanted to hear your voice. What are you doing?"

I relax a bit and sink back into the tub. "Just relaxing a bit before I have to go to a gala for Dax's work later. Why are you breathing so hard?"

"Huh, I didn't realize I was. I have been under the weather this past week, and I'm going to have Melissa bring me some Tylenol and get to bed."

"Please take care of yourself, Brodie."

There is a pause before he replies. "Don't worry about me, Liv. Have fun at your party."

I hesitate momentarily. "Okay. See you soon, Brodie?" It comes out more of a question.

He hangs up abruptly. I sit there staring at the phone.

I hear the door close in the distance, awakening me from my stupor.

"Liv, I'm home." I hear the sound of keys hitting the table in the foyer.

"I'm in the bathtub," I respond and see Dax as he strolls in and places his tux on the bed. He walks over to me and strips down.

"No, we don't have time to take a bath, Dax. We'll be late since I still have to get ready."

He goes to help me out of the tub and pushes me over the sink. "Who said anything about a bath, wifey?"

I look at him in the mirror as he lines himself up with me and pushes in. He takes me hard and fast while I brace myself against the mirror. My protruding stomach is not letting me extend too far over.

Dax fingers on one hand trace over my clit, moving and pinching, as the other hand rests protectively over my belly. He sucks on my neck, and I am coming all over his cock with his last thrusts as he spills in me with one last groan of pleasure.

He stands there, still, looking at my reflection in the mirror. His cock twitches inside me as he pulls out. The evidence of our lovemaking drips down my thigh.

"Well, that is a visual I can get used to, Liv. You bent over, pregnant, dripping my seed down your leg."

I turn around and place my hands on his chest. Thinking he is joking, I almost snort at this comment, but his expression tells me he is not. "Don't tell me you want to see me pregnant all the time. Dax?"

He comes over with a towel and cleans me up. "Liv, I want as many children as you will give me."

"You're serious, huh?"

"Oh yeah, baby," he murmurs into my neck, kissing his way up to my ear. "Now, let's shower and get dressed before I end up taking you straight to our bed. My parents would be deeply disappointed in us for skipping the whole gala."

Despite Dax's best efforts at getting me to go another round in the sack, we leave on time and are greeted by his parents as we walk into the event.

It is stunning.

The historic hotel on the seawall boasts a beautiful venue, and the cause is even more spectacular. Dax's mother goes to the microphone on stage to welcome everyone and encourage us to take an assigned seat for dinner.

Just as we walk to our table, we see Eduardo and Emma approach from the opposite direction. I hurry over to Emma and hug her.

"Geez, Liv, you'd think I didn't just see you a few hours ago." She laughs, but I am so glad to spend some time with her after I finally quit my job in the ED.

I haven't seen her around as much as I used to, and it makes me sad that we are drifting apart.

Eduardo shakes Dax's hand, and we all get settled in our seats. Dinner is served, and the silent auction follows.

My phone rings, and I see that Melissa is calling. Emma looks at me, and I show her who it is.

"Excuse me. I need to answer this, Dax."

He helps me up from my chair, and Emma excuses herself to follow me, but before she does, she mumbles something into Eduardo's ear. He nods while looking toward Dax, who looks as confused as I feel.

I make my way out of the room housing the gala and pass the bathrooms leading to an outside door. With less noise, I can hear Melissa better. She never calls me. I am curious and worried at the same time as to why she is phoning.

As I push through the door, my phone starts ringing again, and I quickly answer it. "Melissa, just a second."

Emma moves through the door after me and grabs my arm. "Okay, I can hear, Melissa. I am sorry. Go ahead. What is it?"

"Liv." Her shaky voice comes through on the other line. "It's Brodie. He went to the hospital in an ambulance. He had been sick, and tonight he had a fever, and I called the doctor to come over and look at him. Before he could get here, Brodie went unconscious, and I called the ambulance. They took him to the hospital."

I drop the phone and slump to the floor.

"Liv!" I hear Emma say as she picks up the phone, and Melissa tells her the story again.

I see Emma trying to shake me, but I can't listen to her or hear her words. It's as if I am underwater, and everything is muffled. I see Dax and Eduardo come running through the door, and Dax helps me up. I hear Emma giving them the information as I feel Dax moving me through the venue and out the door.

A black SUV comes around the corner, and the door flies open. Dax helps me get into the car, and Eduardo and Emma drive us to the hospital that Brodie was taken to not long ago.

CHAPTER FORTY-ONE

LIV

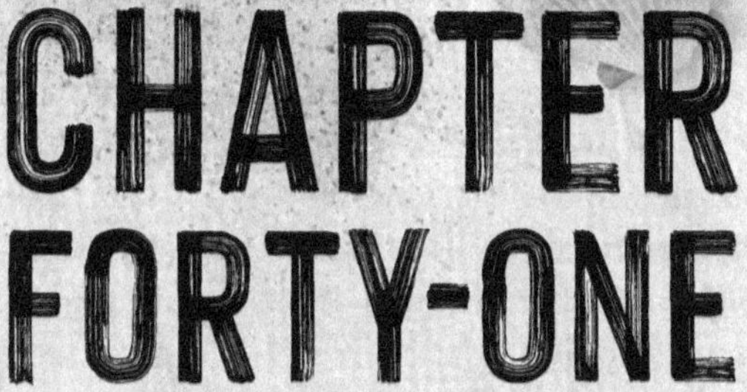

The asphalt streets go by in a blur, and my emotions are laid out with them—flat and run over. We make our way into the emergency department, and Dax immediately goes to the front desk to ask for information.

We are not related to Brodie, and they are not allowed or obligated to tell us anything. I spot Melissa and run over to her, hoping she can get us the information about Brodie. She hugs me and tells me Brodie's parents are on their way over.

It's like déjà vu—feeling helpless, watching and waiting for news. We are again waiting to see if he will live through that accident. I'm not sure what he did after the accident and rehabilitation. He was so upset with his condition. Being paralyzed and dependent on assistance for everyday activities like daily living.

He had always been a carefree soul. I thought I had lost him once, and I saw him dying inside after that each day, his emotional state getting worse. He disappeared from my life after receiving inpatient help for his major depression. I saw the spark of life back in him, if only for a brief moment. He looked finally at peace with himself, but then this happened. What exactly happened? That is the answer I need, and again find myself waiting.

We sit out there for what seems like an eternity. Brodie's parents are here. They are arguing with each other again. I look at them and want to slap them both. *Please give it up already. Can't you get along during this time when your son needs you?*

I never did like his parents. They were always so self-absorbed, his dad with his career and infidelity. His mom was always doting on his father, caring more about him than her son, until he traded her for a younger model. Now she is just angry and drunk most of the time, botoxing her face to try to land herself another husband.

Melissa is walking between us and Brodie's family. She was there more for him than they were, even though she was paid to do that job. I know that she cares about Brodie.

The door finally opens, and time stands still. The voices quiet around us, and the doctor makes his way to us with another man with a security badge on his uniform.

I stand up, as does Dax, watching them make their way over to Brodie's parents. I hear a scream and then sob as Brodie's dad walks off, holding his hand over his face. For once, I see his dad take his mom into an embrace, and they hold on to each other, crying.

I know this isn't good news, and I sink to the floor as Dax catches me. He lifts me, walks to a chair to sit, and places me in his lap.

Emma goes over to Melissa, who is also crying, and I see her talking to them. Emma returns with tears in her eyes and goes over to hug me.

"I am so sorry, Liv. He didn't make it. He had a terrible blood infection, and his heart just gave out from septicemia."

She stands to kiss me on the head as I ugly cry into Dax's chest. Eduardo goes over to hold Emma, and they sit beside us. They are not leaving me this time. He gives me the comfort I need without saying another word.

Brodie's parents make their way over to the doors and disappear for a while. I don't know how long we sat there like that, but Brodie's parents finally return from what I can only assume was saying goodbye to their son.

I look up at them and stand as I talk to them. I hugged them both, and they tell me they will call me with the funeral details. They leave, and I walk over to Dax. He stands to hold me.

"Are you ready to go?"

"Yes, let's go home."

We all walk out, and this time I feel like I am leaving behind a part of my life.

I step out of the SUV to hear thunder cracking across the sky. The wind picks up, and the leaves rustle in the breeze around me. Of course, today it would be raining, and a storm is approaching.

Dax holds my hand as we make our way to the gravesite, where Brodie is finally laid to rest. Eduardo, who offered to drive so Dax can be with me, and Emma are walking behind us.

I look at the man holding my hand beside me, and I am so thankful to have such an understanding and loving person who supports me in all things. He was my rock that day when Brodie was injured, and he is my rock now, two years later, after Brodie's death.

We take our seats. The priest talks about the Kingdom of God, a long speech about his son returning to be reunited with him. I look around at all our friends who made it to the service to say our final goodbyes. Everyone made the trip, and I feel that maybe Brodie is smiling at all of us. He isn't suffering anymore and I hope he finds peace in the afterlife.

Raindrops start to fall. We stand to each drop off our rose on his casket in our final farewell. I hold mine above the coffin and let it hover there. Dax waits patiently as I reluctantly release it. I see it land with a sickening thud as it makes contact with the wood.

I walk away and look at the sky, letting the raindrops land on my face. The heavens release the rain at that moment, and it comes down heavy.

I stand there, letting the water soak me, crying.

"Are you crying too, Brodie?" A whisper that falls into a gust of wind.

Dax looks at me with understanding, grabbing my hands. "Liv, you are getting drenched, baby. Let's go."

I can't make myself move from this spot. He kisses my lips softly and picks me up in his strong arms, carrying me to the car. Ahead, I see Emma tearfully watching me through the passenger window.

Eduardo runs to the other side and opens the door for Dax to get in, soaking himself in the rain. I begin to shake as Dax continues to hold me in his arms. He rubs his thumb around my hand in a circular pattern, reminding me of when I was waiting to hear news about Brodie's surgery. The comfort I felt then continues to bring me comfort now, even though circumstances are very different.

I don't remember the drive home. I'm in our bedroom, and Dax is helping me out of my wet clothes. The last thing I remember is falling asleep, surrounded by warmth from Dax's body as he engulfs me in a solid and secure embrace. I go to sleep warm and feeling loved, despite the hole left in my chest at the loss of a life taken from us too soon.

I lay like that for almost a week, barely getting out of bed, as Dax continues to take care of me. He lets me mourn in my own way without letting me neglect my basic needs. He helps me shower, dress, and eat.

One night, I dream of Brodie. We are young in school, sharing snacks, drinking juice boxes, and swinging together. I look over at him, wanting to go higher and higher. He looks over at me with concern and tells me to be careful.

"Brodie, I know what I am doing," I scoff at him, and he draws his brows together.

I reach higher and then jump off the swing in one quick motion. He drops his feet to the ground, running toward me. Dirt kicks up around me in a plume of dust. He makes his way over, and I realize I have this scratch on my knee. He picks me up and asks if I'm okay.

"It's just a scratch, Brodie."

"I know, but I don't like seeing you hurt, Liv. Please tell me that you'll be more careful. I might not be around to catch you if you fall next time."

"I promise, Brodie."

He flashes me a toothy smile, and my heart catches.

"I'll take care of myself, even if you aren't there."

"Great, let's get the nurse to give you a Band-Aid, and make sure you act a little sicker, so maybe we can get a lollipop too."

I wake up in the early morning with the dawn showing its first rays of sunlight through the window's blinds. I get up to go to the bathroom. I wash my hands and look back at my reflection in the mirror. I see my sunken eyes with bags under them and feel my baby kick. I haven't been happy this week—no happiness in me to even enjoy that new moment of movement in my belly.

As I walk out, I remember my dream about Brodie and my promise to him. I'll be okay and care for myself if he isn't there to catch me. I never did get to say goodbye, but I somehow think that was his way of allowing me time to do so.

I go over to my husband, who is still in bed. When I return to bed, the mattress shifts, and he sits up.

"Liv, is everything okay?"

I get into bed and grab his face, giving him a hard kiss. "Yes, and I think it will be okay from now on."

He curls his eyebrow up at me, and I slide into his solid embrace, knowing I can continue living without the hurt, fulfilling my promise to a boy in my dreams.

EPILOGUE

TWO YEARS LATER

I sit on the beach, listening to the waves crashing on the jetties. It is almost morning and the start of another busy weekend. Soon the beach will be crowded, but not now. No one is around to disturb me. My mind starts to go to that Saturday morning so many years ago. I can almost hear the familiar voices and laughter on the light breeze that passes through and blows my hair back, much like a gentle caress.

The song by Bob Marley and the Whalers, "No Woman No Cry," is a faint murmur on the breeze. Seagulls' wings are spread wide, flying high, sweeping low until they land, feet imprinting on the sand. The incoming seawater quickly erases their footprints.

I hear the sound of incoming wet footprints traipsing on the sand, a scrambled run heading in my direction. I turn around to see them walking toward me, hand-in-hand.

I am quickly pulled out of my past and catapulted into the present. I hear the words "Mommy, Mommy," excitement resonating from a little boy's voice.

My meditative trance is replaced with an upturn of my lips as I break into a full smile. My whole world and future now stand right in front of me.

Just then, the sun starts to peek through the clouds in the most magnificent colors of pink, orange, and yellow, with just a trace of blue on the horizon. Its brightness shines down in streaks across the predawn sky.

I can almost feel him with me—my forever light clearing away the darkness.

I get up and walk over to my husband and Kaden Brodie Johnson, our son. "What are you doing up so early, little one?"

Dax is still sporting his bedhead. "Oh, he wanted Mommy, and I knew you'd be out here watching the sunrise, so here we are. Isn't that right, buddy?"

He looks at me with his arms out slightly, asking me to pick him up. I twirl him around, and he squeals into my ear, pressing his head into my neck with a laugh.

"You hungry, my little man?"

He nods his head up and down excitedly.

"All right then, let's get something to eat." I place him on my hip, and Dax takes my hand.

We walk back to our newly renovated condo on the beach farther down the coastal bend on South Padre Island. It is the perfect spot for us. It will hold new memories we can make of us together–doing the things we love, enjoying the beach, surfing, and having family time. A spot for vacation time or even allowing that moment of peace from work.

I look back at the water, the sun reflecting off it. A light breeze blows my hair back and kisses me on the cheek. I smile and remember the promise I made to a friend who will always be with me, riding on the waves of you.

THE END

THANK YOU FOR READING!!!

Did you enjoy reading *Waves of You?* If you did, I would be grateful if you could please consider taking a second to leave a review on one, or all of your choices below. Reviews help to make me a better writer, and I appreciate your words and constructive criticism!
Love you all,
L. Renee Richard

Want to see what secrets Emma is hiding?
Read her story here and enjoy an excerpt from the book:
Emma and Eduardo's story.

"Black Wave" is now available on Amazon
Paperback, E-book, and free on KU.
https://a.co/d/08KXgMB

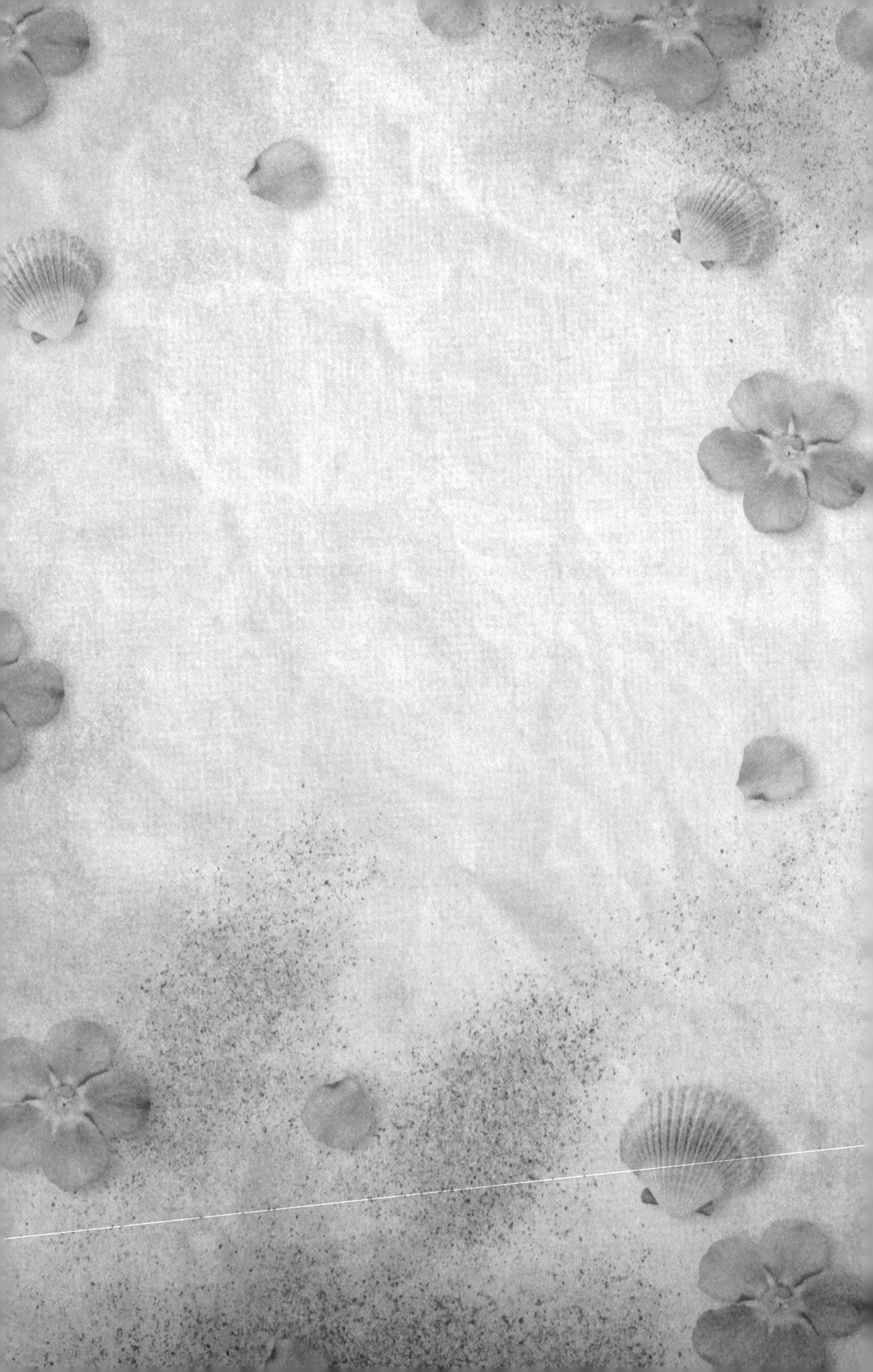

BLACK WAVE

BOOK 1 OF THE
FORGED HEARTS NOVEL

He saw me. He had me. But he won't break me.
What should have been the beginning of my life felt more like a death
sentence–an all-encompassing blackness.
Evie, my twin sister and best friend, is no longer here. Now alone, I've
become as dark as the man who tries to imprison me. Julian.
He thinks he is all I have left in this world.
His to toy with.
To manipulate.
To fear.
But that woman died along with her family that night, and a stronger
woman rose from those battered waves, breathing in a newfound
purpose–to take revenge and reclaim my life.
I am waiting on a black wave, biding my time, until a powerful wave rises
in the aftermath of a storm, unexpectedly leaving casualties in its wake,
ensuring I will once again be free

PROLOGUE

Sitting in my designated alphabetized seating, I barely pay attention to the valedictorian's speech. I hear words carried away in the stifling breeze, along with my hopes and dreams. At this point, that's precisely what they are. I vaguely hear about the promise of a brighter future because I now live in an all-encompassing eternal darkness.

That's right. I was once a cheerleader, a daughter, and a sister. I look to my side, expecting to see anything but an empty seat. The chair should have been occupied by Evie, my twin sister. I touch the tattoo we had inked on our birthday. Something special for us both, a reminder that we would forever be tied together in this life.

What once was a bright future was taken from us in what the police are calling a horrific, unfortunate accident. Now left alone, I am as dark as the man who tries to imprison me. He thinks he is all I have left in this world. Only his to toy with, to manipulate, to fear.

He may have taken everything from me, but he will regret the day he tried to kill my spirit. I will see him dead, if it's the last thing I do. It will mimic the already dead look in my eyes. I have to play the part, play along with the ruse.

The commencement speeches come to a close. We toss our caps in the air in a final good-bye to our last year of high school. I walk away, not bothering to retrieve my cap from the ground.

A hand reaches for me and tugs me backward. Goose bumps on my arms rise in recognition of *his* touch—every nerve-ending screams in protest. I fight the urge to recoil or pull away. I instantly calm my features in a well-practiced act, until I turn around to meet his dark-colored eyes. Julian.

He looks down at me with a wicked grin. I can't believe I never saw it before.

"Emma. How are you holding up?"

The false concern in his voice unsettles me. An average person wouldn't detect this, but I know Julian.

I give him my best attempt at a smile. "Better than I thought on a day like this." I shrug, trying to downplay my tempestuous feelings.

He pulls me into a hug.

I feel the bile rise in my throat as I fight the revulsion his mere presence brings about. I lift my hands mechanically and return his embrace.

He kisses my forehead as any dotting boyfriend would in the public eye.

I sigh. "At least I have you." I get these words out in one forced breath, disguising each spoken word's bite.

My words appear to please him.

He stares down at me and grabs my chin more roughly than I anticipated, lifting it so I am forced to look straight up at his tall stature.

"You will always have me, Emma."

I swallow hard as I verbalize this known truth from my lips. "I know, Julian."

He grabs my arm and drags me to a black SUV with equally dark tinted windows. A man exits the driver's seat to open the back door for us. I get in without hesitation.

What can I do at this point? Not a damn thing.

He gets in after me, and we drive off. There is no one waiting for me. No one I'm leaving behind. I look out the window, seeing the greenery and scattering of bluebonnets along the roadside. I say a silent good-bye to my previous life.

I won't be coming back. Not now. That girl died along with her family that night. Yet, a stronger woman rose from those battered waves, breathing in a new life. The gale force winds gathered all my broken pieces and rearranged them into a stronger and more punishing life-force.

I am waiting on a black wave, biding my time. Until a powerful wave rises in the aftermath of a storm, unexpectedly leaving casualties in its wake, ensuring I will once again be free.

CHAPTER ONE

EMMA

ONE MONTH BEFORE GRADUATION...

I glance at the clock for the third time this hour in anticipation of hanging out with Evie. I never get a chance to see her anymore. In thirty minutes, I am officially off the clock for the rest of the day. She made us a special appointment for our birthday. She thinks I don't know what it is, but I have my suspicions. She's always been terrible at keeping secrets, while I am the master of secrecy. I've been racking them up like crippling debt over the past few months.

I have her present in my bag, and I can't wait to give it to her. Thinking about it makes me smile. I can't wait to see her face when she opens the gift. Another trip around the sun with my sister always by my side. Nineteen, to be exact, and I wouldn't have it any other way.

I am all grins when the door chimes alert me to the arrival of a customer.

I turn around. "Hi, what can I…" I trail off mid-sentence as I stare into the blackest eyes. I try to keep the smile from leaving my face as I hide the disappointment at what his visit could only mean.

"Julian." I grab the cleaning rag to wipe the already sparkling counters. "I didn't expect to see you today." *He can't see the truth if he doesn't look into my eyes.*

Fear.

Shame.

Regret.

"Emma." He pauses just enough to make me hate the sound of my name. "Do I need a reason to see my girlfriend? I just thought I could show you how much you mean to me."

He moves closer to me, and I step back involuntarily. I look around, but there isn't anyone around. My shift is almost over, and then we are closed.

"I miss you, Emma. I won't see you for the rest of the day and I can't get my fill of you."

I move back out of sight from the people passing along the sidewalk, peering in through the windows. I turn to walk away, headed for the back hallway, but he moves quicker and always seems one step ahead. I feel a push at my back as he directs me to the supply room. I enter through the doorway and hear the click of the door closing behind me, but I don't turn around. I stand there frozen. He steps closer to me, and I feel the hard outline of his erection pressing into my back.

"Emma, you didn't think I would forget your birthday, did you?" His words are whispered in my ear, and then I feel his tongue lick from my ear down to my mouth.

I attempt a weak reply. "Julian, you don't have to plan anything. I know you are swamped today and have a business meeting later."

I would try anything to stop his attempt at whatever he wants to do to me now. I only hear his zipper being pulled down as a reply. He turns my head around midway to gain access to my mouth. He kisses me forcefully, biting my lip when I deny him entry into my mouth, drawing blood. He sucks my bottom lip and drives his tongue in. I hear him growl in frustration at the complexity of my multi-buttoned pants. Finally, he unbuttons them and forces them down my legs along with my panties. They pool at my ankles, restricting my movement.

He moves us forward by the shelves and pushes my head down to rest on one as he pushes himself inside me. He sets a punishing pace. He palms my breast greedily as I try to move slightly to steady myself.

"Guess what, Emma?" He slows his pace as he speaks softly into my ear.

I don't bother answering because he doesn't actually want me to. This is just a powerplay for him, allowing me to think I have any say in this.

"I'm going to let you come today because it's your birthday. How does that sound, love?"

"Oh god," is all I get out because, even though I don't love him, my traitorous body reacts to his commands, even the ones I want to control the most.

He reaches his hand around and rubs my clit in circles, gathering the moisture that is instinctually collecting from his languid assault on my body. *I can't believe I used to enjoy this with him. When did he change?* He pulls out almost all the way and slams back in, causing a wave of pleasure that shoots through my abdomen.

"No, no, no," I chant, and I can't help the orgasm that is starting to build from his ministrations.

He pinches my clit and thrusts in over and over until I am a quivering mess. As quickly as the orgasm comes, I am jerked around and simultaneously pushed onto the tiled floor.

"Open," is the only thing Julian says as he forces his cock down my throat. He fists my hair and fucks my mouth until I gag. I can tell when he is close to coming because his breathing has picked up. He forces his cock so far down my throat that I think I will puke. I don't have to endure this much longer as he comes shortly after, holding me to him. I feel it, but I don't taste his release until he pulls it out, along with the saliva dripping down my chin. I gasp for air and look up at him through blurry eyes.

He grabs my chin and holds my stare. "Happy Birthday, Emma. I'll be back tomorrow."

With that, he walks away, and I hear the door chiming, letting me know he has left. I pick myself up like always, vowing that tomorrow will be different. Maybe one day, I'll get away from him. I can't let this continue. I make my way to the employee bathroom and clean up. When I look more presentable, I return to the cafe entrance and see my sister sitting on one of the chairs, waiting for me. I stop in my tracks, immediately self-conscious of my appearance.

"Hey, Evie. I'm just finishing up here. We can leave in a minute." I flip the open sign on the door to closed, and as I walk back, I grab my stuff from the back.

Evie stops me and pulls me into a hug. "I saw Julian leave as I was coming in. He had a smug look, and I knew he had won something. Are you okay?"

I return the hug, trying to convey to her all the emotions I am feeling with just my body language. "I love you, Evie. I'll be okay." *Lie.* It isn't the truth, but what else can I say?

She pulls back from our embrace and holds me at arm's length, looking into my eyes. "You know that you can tell me anything, Emma, right? I'll be here to listen and help you with whatever you need. We can figure it out together. You are not alone."

I nod in acknowledgment and release her. "Let me grab my purse, and let's get out of here, shall we?"

Moments later, Evie and I walk arm-in-arm down the sidewalk. "So, you aren't going to give me a hint about the appointment you booked for us today?" I say jokingly because I am almost sure that we are having matching tattoos inked today. We have discussed doing this for years now. Since we got into high school, we thought this was a great way to show our twin bond on the outside too. Even though we have been adults for almost a year now, this is where the real road to adulthood starts: after graduation.

Sure enough, we stop outside of Dark Tide Tattoo Studio. "I knew it!" I shout while jumping up and down, holding onto Evie's arm. "I knew we were getting tattoos today."

Evie chuckles. "Yeah, you guessed it. Was I that obvious?"

"Well, we have only talked about this day for about four years now. It wasn't hard to guess. Are you ready to get this done?"

"Definitely."

I gather my sister's hand in mine, and we walk into the tattoo studio, ready to ink our souls together.

"Hi, ladies. Just fill out this form on the screen and let me know if you have any questions. I'll need your driver's license too." Lalo, the big biker who will tattoo us, disappears down the hall.

We are just about done signing the required documentation about informed consent that tells you what to expect afterward and the obvious that this is permanent, when Lalo returns, holding a sketch out to Evie.

"I know you showed me the Pinterest picture of the heart for you and your sister, but I modified it and made you something more original if you don't mind looking at it." Lalo hands Evie the sketch, and I move toward her to look at the results.

"Wow, this is beautiful," we chime in unison. I grab the sketch from Evie's grasp to study it further. The original twisted hearts theme is there, but it is in more detail, with our initials in the entwined hearts and our date of birth underneath. To say we like the sketch is an understatement.

Lalo claps his hands together. "Okay, ladies, who is going first? Follow me."

Knowing I might chicken out, I volunteer to get mine first.

"Let's print your aftercare instructions so you can take them home if you need to refer to proper hygiene." Lalo places the clear bandage over Evie's wrist and then leads us to the front of the studio to collect our paperwork. After settling our bill, we leave the studio feeling carefree, as all nineteen-year-old girls should.

We continue our walk downtown and I ask, "Evie, do you want to get any ice cream? I thought we could get some and exchange gifts at the park across the street?"

"I think that is a great idea. I want the usual mint chocolate chunk, please." She walks off to secure a table for two as I am left to order our ice cream. I get my usual bubble gum flavor and place them on the table with napkins and spoons.

Evie takes a massive scoop of hers and groans. "This is orgasmic."

I frown as this reminds me of Julian's gift a while ago. Evie stops midway to her mouth, withholding the next ice cream orgasm, and looks at me before placing the scoop down. "What's wrong, Emma? Is it the ice cream? I'd have that face, too, if I got *that* ice cream." She points at it as if its mere presence offends her. "The bubble gum in there is rock hard. You're going to crack a tooth, babe."

I look at her and attempt a weak laugh. Trying to change the subject, I reach into my bag and pull out her birthday present. I place it in front of her, and this time, my smile reaches my eyes. Seeing Evie happy, in turn, makes me happy. It heals my soul and rights everything wrong in my life right now. She picks up the gift and tugs at the strings holding the box. She removes the top and picks up another box in there.

"You are such a joker, Emma." She undoes the other box and stops when she sees what's inside. She looks at me, smiling with tears in her eyes. "I love it," she says in a hushed voice. She picks up the ring and slides it on her finger. "It's a perfect fit too."

I had it made at a local jeweler. Dave's castings provide quality work and create unique pieces for clients. He starts with the design, beginning with a wax mold. If you like it, then he will proceed with making the jewelry. Like our newly-inked tattoos, I had a twisted heart entwined together to remind us of our sisterly bond–and because she likes them so much.

Evie reaches into her bag, pulls out an envelope for me, and hands it over. "This is your gift, Emma." She clasps her hands together on the table, waiting for my reaction.

I look at it quizzically and then at her. "What is it?"

"Just open it, Emma." Evie shifts uncomfortably in her chair as she resumes eating her now liquid ice cream.

I pick up the envelope and pull out the sheet of paper. I read it aloud, "One month of Krav Maga classes?" This comes out as a question, and I stare at her for clarification.

Evie puts her ice cream aside and moves her hands up and down her pant legs, then places them in a contemplative gesture in front of her mouth.

"Emma, I am just going to come out and say it. I know that you are in an abusive relationship with Julian. I want you to be able to protect yourself. Remember, I know what it is like not to have control over oneself and feel vulnerable."

I wince at the recollection of Evie's trauma. It's hard for my sister to remember when she was almost assaulted in an alleyway. If not for the help of a Good Samaritan, the outcome could have been a lot different.

"I was only able to move on from that with the help of my therapist and the power I took back when I was able to defend myself."

I look at Evie, and I know this is our turning point. I have to tell her what has been happening with Julian and find a way to rid myself of his restraining persona. I *need* to break up with him once and for all.

Evie looks at me, hoping that this will be the day I confide in her and tell her what she already knows. The problem is that she has no idea what I have been through. I shift uncomfortably in my seat and look away. I hear Evie sigh.

I straighten my back. When I look back at her, it is with a new determination. "Evie, I need to tell you something, and need help."

ABOUT THE AUTHOR

L. Renee Richard is a native Texan gone north. She lives in New England with her husband and two teenagers. The other piece of her heart, her oldest son, lives in the south, where she visits him at every opportunity.

She enjoys the beach life, whether warm Gulf coastal waters or the more frigid Atlantic Ocean. She loves her small-town atmosphere, where she can walk down the dirt road to the lake and enjoy their quintessential small town's gorgeous scenic views and earthy smells.

L. Renee is an avid reader with a never-ending TBR. She wholeheartedly prefers the quietness of nature, where she is frequently curled up in a fluffy blanket, either reading a book or writing an angsty romance novel where the journey to a HEA isn't always easy but worth the trip.

KEEP IN TOUCH WITH L. RENEE RICHARD

Follow me on my socials
Author page:
www.authorlreneerichard.com
Amazon:
http://www.amazon.com/author/lreneerichard
Facebook page:
https://www.facebook.com/Author-L-Renee-Richard-105887815914160
Instagram:
https://instagram.com/l.renee.richard?igshid=OGQ5ZDc2ODk2ZA==
TikTok:
TikTok @l.renee.richard
Join my street team:
https://forms.gle/9cnsA4gSfbezY7a17
Sign up for my newsletter:
https://mailchi.mp/authorlreneerichard/signup

Sign up for my masterlist:

https://forms.gle/9QK6wm1ViwFuP6tS6

www.ingramcontent.com/pod-product-compliance
Lightning Source LLC
Chambersburg PA
CBHW021404110726
47901CB00008B/2058